ZERO-G

A NOVEL

BOOK ONE

WILLIAM SHATNER
AND JEFF ROVIN

SIMON & SCHUSTER
New York London Toronto Sydney New Delhi

Simon & Schuster
1230 Avenue of the Americas
New York, NY 10020

First Simon & Schuster hardcover edition September 2016

SIMON & SCHUSTER and colophon are registered trademarks
of Simon & Schuster, Inc.

For information about special discounts for bulk purchases,
please contact Simon & Schuster Special Sales at 1-866-506-1949
or business@simonandschuster.com.

The Simon & Schuster Speakers Bureau can bring authors to
your live event. For more information or to book an event contact the
Simon & Schuster Speakers Bureau at 1-866-248-3049 or
visit our website at www.simonspeakers.com.

Interior design by Lewelin Polanco

Manufactured in the United States of America

1   3   5   7   9   10   8   6   4   2

Library of Congress Cataloging-in-Publication Data is available.

ISBN 978-1-5011-1155-6
ISBN 978-1-5011-1157-0 (ebook)

Usually dedications are made to people you love, to people peripherally connected with the book, to ideals, dreams, vague motivations. In this case, I would like to dedicate a thank-you to a wonderful creative artist.

This book reflects Jeff Rovin's skill as an artist—events that could happen, might happen, will happen are dramatized. His imagination, his knowledge of arcane facts, his sense of drama are astounding. I have never worked with a more creative and inspiring cowriter. None of us knows the future, but here is an imagining of possibilities. My hat's off to you, Jeff, along with my shirt.

ZERO-G

PROLOGUE

OG: STAR FIRE

YUKI OGAWA KNEW that her husband, Makoto, was dead.

The realization did not come from a news report or a personal message from the Japanese Oceanic Research Organization over her Individual Cloud. It was a sense the woman had, perhaps her artist's empathic nature; it was definitely something spiritual, a quality that even the most sophisticated SimAI programs could not match.

Sitting at her easel, painting a canvas, Yuki hovered in mid-stroke, her shoulders rigid, her emotions on hold, waiting to see if her IC confirmed the feeling. If it *were* true, it was not entirely surprising; Makoto was in a facility constructed by the lowest bidder, in an extremely dangerous location. It would even be fitting, given her husband's parting words as she had helped him pack for his ongoing underwater study for the JORO.

"Neutrinos are all about life *and* death," he had maintained as he slid the seven slim, rectangular pouches of shirts, pants, underwear, and socks into the molecular-defrag messenger bag specially designed to hold them as if they were a single folded towel. "They show us a picture of the universe's birth, yet they reveal themselves in their own annihilation—"

"Armageddon and eternity—again," she said. "Why can't you talk about baseball, like Hayao?"

Makoto smiled self-effacingly. "I read a treatise on how a batter can hit a ball twice in one swing. Does that count?"

The thirty-seven-year-old woman had grabbed his face then, her hands flat on his cheeks, and kissed him before he could go on. It had the desired effect. They were both smiling when she leaned back.

"I will explain your work to your son as tiny, tiny particle research," she said kindly. "He's still too young to understand quantum philosophy."

Makoto's smile became paternal. "Does his youth mean that he should not be exposed to grand ideas?"

"In fact, it does," she replied firmly. "Let his head fill with boyhood."

Yuki activated her IC with a gesture, tracing a finger through the air before her forehead. Some people preferred to use virtual hands guided by eye movements; she liked the tactile interface that involved her real fingers. There was a ballet-like grace to it, as opposed to the optic twitches and jerks that had created a generation of migraine-prone youth.

She moved closer so the outer data rim could touch Makoto's IC, which was always on. She thought about the Lasting Individual Video Experience file the four-year-old had created the night before. It came to life, her eyes full of the child's image. Though it appeared solid and immediate, it was merely a shimmer along her neurons induced by the IC's shifting electric fields.

"He created this LIVE file for you," she said as they shared the 360-degree image. She sent it toward him with a thought, mentally adjusted the hovering volume slider down to zero. The boy began talking, silently, facing his father. "You can listen to it later. Look in his eyes, at his expression. All he knows is that his daddy is gone, again, for many more months."

"I know, I know," Makoto acknowledged, annoyed with himself. "I have to go and he must be made to understand. I will find a way to better explain it."

He backed away, breaking the connection. Yuki shut it down. By focusing on finishing his preparations, Makoto had shut her down. It wasn't rudeness; it was necessary efficiency.

"The death of anything, even radioactive decay, may help us to understand the birth of everything, including the cosmos," he had said as he walked through the bedroom door of their bayside home. The condominium was not far from where he had first met her, painting a sunset. "One day, Hayao will understand the importance of my work."

"You haven't asked if I do," she said.

"I've only been home a week." He smiled. "You and I had more pressing personal matters."

One kiss and three hours later, after a hypersubmarine ride that had him slashing through the North Pacific in an air pocket of the ship's own creation, Dr. Makoto Ogawa was hunched over his IC in the expertly designed research facility. Deep underwater, it faced the Sea of Okhotsk to the north, the Sea of Japan to the west, and the East China Sea to the south.

Electron neutrino, muon neutrino, tau neutrino, he thought as he studied feeds from the facility's instruments. Each particle was now known to be its own antiparticle, destroying each other in a gamma flash whenever they collided, but passing invisibly through other matter. They were indifferent to every force except gravity and the mechanism by which nuclei erode. They were indifferent also to all but the strongest magnetic fields, one hundred million Gauss and higher—which, despite the neutrino's absence of electric charge, can still affect the particles via their transition magnetic moment.

That was what Makoto was here to study. He shook his head, tracing the air with his eyes, opened the still-muted LIVE image his son had recorded.

Yuki is correct, the physicist thought. *Hayao wouldn't understand any of it. Invisible space dust left over from the Big Bang, everywhere, all the time. Dust containing messages in quantum code that are the key to understanding who we are, where we came from, where we're going, and why.*

"If we can only look closely enough," he said in frustration. The

Simulated Artificial Intelligence, a scan of his own brain that anticipated information that would be of interest to his real brain, picked out
nothing unusual. Yuki once told him about Michelangelo stepping back
from one of his sculptures, so lifelike, so hard-won from the marble, and
raging at it, "Why can you not speak?" Makoto felt the same way. The
damn particles were all around him and he cursed his eyes, his IC, his
brain: "Why can you not see them?"

Makoto managed to frown with one side of his mouth and grin with
the other side. Yuki was right about that too. Hayao would not have understood, appreciated, or been excited by any of this. What would the
logic of a little boy have suggested? "Make yourself smaller, Father"?
"Use an electron camera"?

No, Makoto thought, which was the cause of his smile. The boy
would have said, "Father, ask Mother to paint you a picture."

"The clarity of youth," Makoto murmured, then reactivated the
LIVE recording to add comments of his own. "Hayao, the complexities
of science and the universe do not yield to simple solutions," he said.
"To study a particle that has never been seen, we have spent seven billion globals and endured pressure that would crush your great-grand-
aunt's steel skull. You have hit that with a bat, you know how hard it is."
He paused, smiled. "Life costs a great deal. Life creates pressure. You
will learn, in time, to accept that."

He thumbed off the recording. Hayao still wouldn't understand—
not now. But one day he would. It has been said, repeatedly, that no
generation ever appreciates their parents' wisdom until it is too late. All
the stories his father told him about living in a time when there were
only smartphones and computers, no ICs to allow tapping into the net-
works with a thought—all that was just so much noise, as his own stories about medical advances spurred by molecular experiments in zero
gravity and societal advances brought on by cybernetic electronometry
must be for his son. Hayao listened because Hayao was happy to hear
his father's voice. But even that would stop, one teenage day.

Makoto touched Hayao's file and continued making his own LIVE response as data streams scrolled up, down, and sideways around him—patterns without change or revelation.

"My son," he said, "I do not expect you to understand what it was like before you could contact people, watch all manner of entertainment, and control appliances with your mind alone . . . let alone understand the importance of space dust. One day you will learn how studying neutrinos can pave the way for even greater leaps. I am here prying their secrets from them . . . or at least trying. They are stubborn." He stopped short of adding, "Like your mother," because Hayao wouldn't understand the appreciative humor in that. "The truth is, my son, no matter how much our world changes due to the action of one generation—younger or older—the other will never quite understand it. But you must believe this: I have been where you are, young and just scratching at life, still seeing it as a little boy must. When you reach where I am, you will understand the larger family of which we are a part, the family of humankind."

He paused the file but did not mark it for access by the boy. Not yet. Yuki would tell him, "It isn't necessary to explain everything, Dr. Ogawa," but there was so much more *to* say. Makoto was a scientist and science required context. He wanted to explain that their nation, which had thrived by providing high-tech entertainment for so many decades, had turned to the sea to forge their future. Hayao should know—from his father's mouth, not from an interactive technology, that as the rest of the world expanded outward, Japan had looked to the ocean floor for food, electricity, and colonization. The boy *should* care that the same tectonic faults that caused earthquakes were now being used to provide access to the "firepacks" that powered much of the Far East. Those facts were a part of the vital reason that his father wasn't home to play with him.

Makoto breathed out deeply. If, in fact, he were working on the firepacks, Hayao might think that was exciting. But nearly massless, invisible particles from almost fourteen billion years ago? Not much to brag about on his sociodates.

It isn't like it was when I worked on the International Terraforming Project in 2039, he reflected.

Back then, a recent graduate of Tokyo Tech, Makoto had spent nine months huddled near the North Pole for the United Nations Framework Convention on Climate Change, proving that oceanic power stations, vaporizing ammonia in the warming waters of the Arctic to produce electricity, might—in great enough proliferation—begin to help reduce that warming. Makoto and his colleagues oversaw one, then dozens, of those generators, which—alongside the firepacks and the development of commercial fusion—helped end, for all time, the burning of fossil fuels. Concurrently, artificial sea ice crafted by a North American team—aided by the micrometer-thin Sunshade suspended in space, at a gravitationally neutral L-1 point between the Earth and the moon—had halted and begun to reverse global warming, saving the planet from rising sea levels and environmental catastrophe. *That work was easy to explain at cocktail parties and in classrooms,* Makoto mused.

How could Hayao understand, let alone explain, that neutrinos appear to us only in the traces they leave as they pass through water and tritium—glimmers of Cherenkov light and telltale electron spectra—or in the unique gamma ray signature of their self-destruction in deep space?

Makoto resisted the urge to delete his unfinished recording.

"Yuki, I could use your help," he sighed as he redoubled his concentration on the study. "I must think, now, not just as an adult but as a boy."

As an adult, Makoto thought his work was profound. If he and his fellow scientists did it right, they'd see and record an afterimage of the universe in its first second of life, a period after the Big Bang when the temperature went from impossibly hot to semi-impossibly hot, when the first particles managed to form—these particles, the ones he sought. And in that way, perhaps, Makoto and his team could discern why matter is here at all.

Makoto looked past the flashing numbers and letters at the spectacular neutrino telescope he had helped create. Just as the early-twenty-first-century PTOLEMY experiment at Princeton had scrutinized decay products from a tiny sample of tritium for signs of relic-neutrino capture, Makoto's DORARGOS project—named for a mythical Japanese creature that was all eyes—watched for telltale electrons from an enormous tritium disc surrounded by magnets and sensor arrays. Around the disc in a huge, clear, doughnut-shaped sea lab, Makoto and the scientists observed the telescope, the ocean, and their own living quarters.

The information the telescope brought them, like almost all data in 2050, appeared directly before their eyes, either hovering in the air or on the surface of the walls or tabletops where they sat or stood, depending on each individual's choice of IC electronometrics.

The IC, he thought. Another useful spinoff from useless political chaos.

Who would have thought that IC and so much more would be the result of a cynical political-economic sleight-of-hand? When China wanted to distract the world and itself from the dual crushing problems of pollution and unbalanced population, the nation of nearly two billion looked to outer space. Rather than clean their air and water or learn to treasure female babies the way they revered male offspring, the central government tried to colonize the moon in 2026. They failed, spectacularly, losing several crews before settling on the construction of a space station.

America reacted to the Chinese push the way they had in the mid-twentieth century, when the Soviets had first tried to claim space— with an accelerated thrust back into space, building their own station and their own moon base. The Russians settled for just a space station. The reasons were maddening to Makoto but the results were epic.

Just as the original space race had spawned countless advances in all the sciences, this early-twenty-first-century space race, spurred by telecommunication and internet giants, produced so much new technology so fast that the politically or religiously or nationally motivated naysayers were all but swept away in a high-profit frenzy of communication, medicine, reproduction, and entertainment—along with the need to crush new crimes like mindjacking and narcetics. It was difficult to complain about the state of the world when your cancer was healed in an afternoon by MedIC programs, your life expectancy was upward of a century, and climate could be adjusted to increase food production anywhere on Earth.

"And it was all set in irrevocable, some would say predestined motion all those billions of years ago when neutrinos popped into existence or decoupled or whatever in fact they *did* right after the Big Bang," Makoto said to himself. Maybe that's what he should tell Hayao. "I'm here for you, my son, because everything *you* are, everything you have, everything you love started with—"

Makoto didn't look up. He didn't have to. The symphony of data was interrupted by a suddenly sour note. The anomaly came to him like a fat uncle's finger in a wedding cake: multicolored streams were all flowing in one direction when, suddenly, a black point shot in the other direction.

Reactions from his fellow scientists began to burble on the edge of his IC.

"... not a tectonic event ..."

"... *no* known geologic analog ..."

"... unprecedented energy pulse ..."

Makoto's own thoughts locked them out. He was focused on the dark point:

A gamma ray emission line, with the distinctive spectral shape of neutrino annihilation—but not in deep space. Impossibly near—inside the sensor array itself—and of impossibly vast amplitude—

Then another word appeared in his mind. Makoto did not know where it came from: his own mind, a fellow scientist, or even a particle itself ripping through his brain and stimulating, informing neurons.

Over.

As the sea lab ruptured and erupted around him, reality seemed to stretch out around Makoto in all directions, flooding his consciousness with more colors and awareness than he'd ever thought possible. For a flashing instant he felt no sensation, since the experience was processed before the pain.

Was this life or death?

Dr. Makoto Ogawa never found out. He strangely, peacefully, even gratefully accepted the universe on its own still unfathomable terms—

And then he was over.

■■

The IC did not confirm Makoto's death. Yuki Ogawa looked out her window, as the rest of megalopolis looked out their windows, as Tokyo Bay erupted. She moved a finger to search her IC but it shuddered when control shifted from Tokyo to a FALL site, the nearest Functioning Alternate Logistics Link.

The woman immediately knew that *erupted* was not the right word. Where there was once a sky and a horizon, outside the window of the bayside apartment was a towering wall of water. Something had thrust it toward the heavens.

"Hayao," she said, holding her hand to him as he looked curiously at the way the walls, floor, and ceiling were shuddering.

"Is this a new game?" he asked.

"No, come with me," she replied.

Since she was calm, he was calm, and they walked together. Not down the stairs to the street—yelling and crying like all the others, at least those they could hear over the onrushing roar—but up the steps to the roof of the apartment house.

Yuki and Hayao stood there for a moment, hand tightly in hand, looking up at the looming wall of water that had become the sky. There was no crest at the top, only sprays shooting upward as though they had lost all weight. They did not come back down.

She lifted her son into her arms, cradling him, hoping he felt the same waves of love that she felt washing over her. Love that was unmistakably coming from her husband—from somewhere beyond *seikatsu* and *shi*, life and death.

As Yuki looked into her son's peaceful eyes, she knew he felt safe and unafraid, even humbled, as his father must have been as the water came forward, rumbling now, smashing them, the building, and the city like an ancient god striding from the sea.

"Come, dear," was the last thing she whispered to him. "Let's go join your father."

ONE

FBI ASSOCIATE DEPUTY Director Adsila Waters sat at his desk in the cramped, windowless command center on board the Space Station *Empyrean*. The comm was the headquarters of what was officially designated as the FBI Off-Earth Investigative and Intelligence Unit. The newly formed division was familiarly known as Zero-G.

Just a year out of Quantico—where he graduated at the top of the FBI academy—Adsila still had that head-of-the-class bearing. His certainty did not come just from learning and following the book but from adding a few footnotes during the eleven months he worked at the Data Intercept Technology Unit at Hoover Command in Washington. He'd had his eye on this job, a space job, since Zero-G was first announced in 2049. To put himself at the front of the line of applicants, he had learned everything he could about FBI operations involving space, especially regarding the hyperplanes that ferried passengers on suborbital flights— what they smuggled and how, sometimes *whom* they smuggled and how. Adsila had used his vacation and weekends to take flights himself. He had staked out airports and their personnel, learned firsthand about the many ways they communicated information. As a full-blooded Cherokee, raised to respond to human and animal nuance in a world otherwise full of noise, he also saw low-tech things that even seasoned agents missed, from hand signals to fingers drumming code on luggage.

At the moment, Adsila was monitoring reports from Earth, scanning intel from Earth-based operatives watching space-bound departures. He was also overseeing the desk staff of three.

Several floors below, the official opening of the most ambitious construction project in human history was about to get under way. Though the National Aeronautics and Space Administration's *Empyrean* space station had been in operation for two months, the shakedown period was officially ended and the first guests were about to be welcomed. There were going to be speeches, a party, and networking—none of which interested Adsila. The twenty-eight-year-old was happier doing a job that had made his family proud of him, a job that he hoped would matter. As his great-grandfather, a powerful shaman, used to say, "When you were born, you cried and the world rejoiced. Live your life so that when you die, the world cries and you rejoice."

••■

Adsila's IC continued to be filled and refreshed with the usual torrent of information, card-size virtual screens accompanied by customized sounds—in this case desert winds and animal life that reminded him of home.

Suddenly, the cry of an osprey shocked him to full alert.

Adsila watched the public advisory that came with it and immediately activated a channel to his superior.

"Director Lord!" Adsila said. "Sir?"

There was no response. Adsila tried again, this time using his full title—a mouthful that Lord disliked and disavowed in the same way that he disliked and disregarded the bureaucracy that had coined it.

"Deputy Director of Earth Orbit Operations Samuel Lord," he said. "Please *respond*."

The tweak did not get a reaction either. Lord's IC was truly off. Again.

Janet Grainger looked over from the desk to Adsila's left. In the two weeks since they'd arrived, the communications director and *Empyrean* liaison—technically, the Associate Executive Assistant Director—had frequently heard her superior use that tone of voice when communicating with Lord.

"Why won't Director Lord keep his IC on?" Adsila complained. It wasn't so much a question as a lament. He didn't expect everyone to live in the Cloud the way he did, but he expected to be able to contact his superior anytime, anywhere.

"Agent Waters, what is it?" Grainger called over.

Adsila flicked a finger, passing the alert to Janet's IC. He could have used his eyes to transfer the data; that angry snap was yet another outward show of the impatience he was feeling.

"Dear God," Janet said as she forwarded the news alert to the other agents.

This is not acceptable, Adsila thought as he rose. Lord was old enough to have amassed a long list of achievements, and that deserved respect. But seniority did not entitle him to rogue behavior. *Cherokee elders honor tribal tradition and instill devotion among the young; why can't he?*

"I'm unplugging," Adsila said, using a snap of his eyes to clear his IC field of vision so he didn't run into anything. "Keep on top of this and contact me if there's an update."

"Will do, sir," Janet replied.

As Adsila strode toward the door his focus was already turned inward. Neuronic bursts blazed in the paraventricular nucleus of the hypothalamus.

And then he did something that Janet had not yet gotten used to.

As Adsila moved, the nearly six-foot-tall pan-gender shifted into his dominant female gender. Adsila had found it useful—at times necessary—to make her way through Quantico and HooverComm primarily as a man. It was less of a distraction than being stared at. But her hourglass figure, strong cheekbones, and frank sexual allure made it easier to maneuver quickly through a group comprised predominantly of men. They seemed to back away like desert dust devils, no less silent and full of wind.

The transition happened swiftly. The visual aspect of the change was controlled primarily by fluid redistribution—quick, sure, and delicate. Breasts and hips formed like blown glass. Adsila's biological sexual flip was achieved with a migration of reproductive organs that had been genetically engineered in the womb. The smart fabric of the FBI tunic adjusted. The switch was accomplished without Adsila breaking stride, though the dynamics of her walk shifted noticeably.

None of the other three team members acted as if they'd witnessed anything.

And why should they? Janet thought as she turned back to her feeds. Space, after all, was the abode of miracles.

■ ■

Kristine Cavanaugh never imagined she'd be disappointed by space.

Since receiving the invitation to the ribbon-cutting on the *Empyrean*, she had tried to imagine the journey, had watched the live shuttle casts on her IC: the Earth falling away, slowly revealing its rounded edge; her youthful ego shrinking as the cosmos loomed; the moon and stars sharp-edged and brilliant; spiritual revelations bursting in her terrestrial brain like World Unity Day fireworks. During that month of high anticipation, Kristine hadn't read science treatises but listened to her SimAI read poetry. William Cullen Bryant seemed to capture her euphoria best in a paean to the planets when he wrote, "Happy they born at this hour, for they shall see an age whiter and holier than the past. . . ."

But the trip had not been what she'd seen or pictured. It had been a crush of noise, stale air, delays, and human proximity that bordered on cow-herding. And then, with other attendees, she was hustled from the ferry to the observation bubble in which the ceremony was to take place.

"Are you ready to hear a few dozen words in a dozen languages by a dozen speakers?" asked the American colonel standing beside her.

She nodded carefully, still unaccustomed to the lack of gravity.

"It will be gross upon gross," the man joked.

The twenty-one-year-old chuckled even though it wasn't funny. After working for two years as a professional companion in Washington, D.C., that reflex came naturally.

Now, a little over an hour after landing and tidying up in a small guest room, she was at the cocktail party in a comparatively spacious salon. It could have been any hotel ballroom in any venue in the American capital on a starlit night, and Kristine Cavanaugh was not only disappointed, she was bored. The speeches were over and the mingling marked the end of the ceremonial phase and the beginning of the careful maneuvering and in-fighting. That game was bad enough in federal buildings on Earth, worse in the close quarters of a space station.

After the speeches, Kristine's frequent employer, Colonel Jack Franco of the Defense Intelligence Agency, had essentially forgotten that she existed. Given her assignment, she was in no position to insert herself at his side. Her job was to help the officer impress others. Judging from the occasional looks from men and women, all of which she discreetly avoided, she was succeeding.

Knowing no one else, the petite, shapely blonde took her white wine and drifted toward the reception area. The server, smiling a little patronizingly, had guided her hand away from the mouth of the wine bottle, down to its heel, and poured in a startling arc that swept backward into her glass as if bent by a gale. Now she looked mistrustfully into the goblet, where the wine torqued and roiled weirdly whenever she turned. She wondered if the same thing might be going on in her inner ear too, as the floor—though unmistakably flat—challenged her high heels like a steep hill, and every movement of her head brought a little swirl of vertigo.

Well, that's an interesting discovery, at least, she thought.

She wondered if her blood was doing the same dance, making her sour, or if space really was a disappointment.

Except for the few bright, hardy stars visible through a surprisingly narrow stretch of glare-washed windows, there was nothing to see outside. So her blue eyes moved impatiently from one guest to another, like a bee zigzagging through a garden that had already been sucked dry of pollen. She recognized a few from the trip up, two from past liaisons, though as far as she could tell, none of the plus-ones had been introduced to the actual guests.

The guests. A human stew of meat and spice but very little nutrition. Bodies low on charisma, charm, and energy.

There was a florid oak of a man with black eyes on a chipped marble face beneath a reddish crew cut. He was wearing a severe dark red uniform with dark purple accents. He was talking to a dark brown man in a Nehru jacket and a tawny-skinned gentleman with a full beard and sheik robes. They were clustered in a cabal-like circle that did not invite outsiders.

Her gaze flitted to a bald man in monk robes, who had a calculating look on his face. Opposite him, apparently watching him closely, was a blank-faced woman wearing a severely tailored olive uniform. Watching her in turn was a tall man wearing a white uniform with black accents. A Mexican general, he was the only one who seemed happy to be here.

Why? she wondered.

The inexpressive woman moved away. A moment later, the Mexican officer left too.

Ah, she realized. *A space liaison.* Romance under the stars, minus the stars.

There were other faces, a few loud voices, and an occasional nod and smile from a passerby. Precipitously close to forcing herself to mingle, Kristine suddenly shifted her attention to a man whom the general's departure had revealed. He was attentively listening to two American military men in the far corner of the room. He looked and acted different from the others. Kristine maneuvered toward him.

Most of the men in the room were statue-perfect and vulpine-eyed. They were all jockeying for the attention of those who could help them, ignoring those who could not, and avoiding those who could do them harm. This new man was considerably older, a little squatter, and a little thicker than the rest. Thicker, but clearly fit and muscular. He was wearing a collarless blue suit over a dark red tunic and a healthy suntan; he had not been up here long. The man held what looked like a vodka on the rocks in one brawny hand while the other hand was tucked in the small of his back. She stared openly at it. There was something about that hand . . .

No, she corrected herself and adjusted her gaze. *It's not the hand, it's the eyes.* There was a gleam in them that seemed to say, "I could be holding a bouquet of roses . . . or an ultrasonic Pulsor pistol. It's up to you."

Before she was completely aware of it, the man had excused himself from the others and stepped toward her, fixing her with those lively gray eyes, which were set under a swath of steel-wool hair.

"First-time spacer," he said. It wasn't a question.

"That's right," she replied. "How can you tell?"

"I saw you watching your wine before," he said.

"You did?" She felt stupid. Of course he had.

"I wasn't spying," he was quick to assure her. "I was an air force fighter pilot for many years—Afghanistan, Nigeria, Mexico. I tend to notice little things. It's a compulsion, actually."

"Not the worst you could have," she said.

"Oh, I've got some of those too." He chuckled.

Kristine's eyes fell back to her glass. She wondered if he knew that she was avoiding his gaze. She looked into so many dead or hungry eyes on the job. These were like a beacon of humanity in the cold of space, an antidote for the impersonal hustle of this room. If she looked too long she might not want to leave. That could be bad for business. Besides, she didn't even know who he was.

"I'm Sam Lord," the man said as if reading her mind—or more likely sensing that she was adrift. He extended the hand that had been behind him.

"Kristine Cavanaugh," she replied, shaking it.

"Not that I blame you," he went on.

"Sorry?"

"The misbehaving wine." He made a faintly dismissive sound and waved a hand toward the window. "The moon? The stars? We see them from Earth all the time. But wine that turns into a gyroscope? That's new. I'm told it's called 'Coriolis cross-coupling.'"

"Sounds dirty," she laughed.

He winked. "It can be."

Kristine started to laugh then quickly stopped herself, looking back furtively to make sure Colonel Franco hadn't heard or noticed her. He was still too busy to care.

"Your date?" Lord asked, following her gaze.

Kristine nodded but did not elaborate.

"Don't worry about him," the man went on. "He's too busy reading IC overlays of everyone in the room. Most of them are. You can tell by the slightly crossed eyes. I think the affliction is becoming permanent, like carpal tunnel and texter's thumb used to be when I was a young man."

Kristine chuckled—the laugh was in earnest with him—as she looked out at the sixty-odd people. It was a strange modern dance they were all doing. Each person stood as if they occupied some other distant room and feigned their presence in this one. Virtual gestures caused real hands and fingers to go slack, as people engaged in IC conversations with invisible correspondents. She noticed one man having two concurrent tête-à-têtes, one conducted with moving eyes and the other using subvocal cues, relayed to ICs that could be anywhere on the space station, Earth, or the moon.

"They're all busy forming Cloud alliances while they talk to the warm bodies in the room," she said.

"That's why they're here." He shrugged. "It's the way of things."

"But not us," she said.

"No. What are your interests? What are you obsessed about?" The man raised a finger to hold off her answer, then turned to a waiter and selected a cracker with a pasty-looking coating. "Thanks, Steph," Lord said to the man. "Doing double duty?"

"Sure. No one's at the bar anyway," he said. "And when Commander Stanton asks—"

"Say no more," Lord said, smiling and turning back to the woman. "Puréed caviar."

"Is that a specialty of the house?" she asked.

"No, it's a necessity of the house," he told her. "Otherwise, those little beggars don't stay put."

She shook her head politely. Before the waiter moved on Lord took a second cracker.

"Even pulped, these are a rarity up here," he explained.

The woman looked down as if overcoming shyness. That wasn't it, given her profession; she was giving herself permission to engage with someone other than the man paying her. "You know what my greatest fascination is?" she finally asked.

"I was hoping you'd tell me."

"Stables," she said. "Our pastor back in Billings, Montana, once said that a church is a place you can visit anywhere in the world and feel at home. That's how I feel about stables. The smell and lighting and sound always make me feel like I'm home."

"Safe," he said. He cocked his head back. "Not like all those piranhas out there snapping here and there for pieces of information."

Kristine nodded. She felt safe here with Lord too . . . *dammit*. She looked away again.

"Speaking of which, I've got to go back and mingle," Lord said. "Come on. Let's dazzle them with our nonconformity."

"You should probably go alone."

"Why? The colonel?"

She nodded.

"We can tell him I bored you, that you couldn't wait to get back," Lord said impishly.

Kristine stopped avoiding his eyes and smiled at him. The man's hand moved to her back now, a warm, comforting touch as he drew her toward the salon's low, parabolic doorway. They drifted through the crowd, through the bazaar of buyers and sellers of power. Kristine had enough of that on Earth, and was glad when Lord didn't linger but headed back into the observation bubble, now occupied by only maintenance and cleaning staffers. She breathed easily for the first time since arriving.

"What are you doing up here?" Kristine asked. "If you don't enjoy being with these people—"

"Actually, I live here," he said.

"Oh? You didn't come up just for the party?"

"No, ma'am," he said, suddenly assuming his formal identity. "I'm the FBI Associate Deputy Director of Earth Orbit Operations. Which is a long-winded way of saying that outside the atmosphere, I'm the director of the FBI."

"Impressive," she said in earnest.

"Not according to my children, grandchildren, great-grandchildren, and a garrulous former wife. They all think I belong safe—there's that word again—in a quiet pasture somewhere, not stationed in a rugged frontier."

"You do not seem like a man who can be outvoted," she said.

"I am not a democracy," he agreed. "For the next two years at least, this is home. And—oh yeah"—he cocked a thumb over his shoulder at the fuzzy image of the moon through the light-opaqued window—"that's my jurisdiction too. Not bad for a kid from Hell's Kitchen. Most of the time I couldn't even *see* the moon from the New York streets. And the stars? Only on Broadway."

"That's where the casinos are?" Kristine said, pleased that she didn't have to check her IC for that.

"Where the casinos are, yes," Lord repeated, a little sadly. The last of the legitimate Broadway theaters had closed in 2040, replaced by smaller off-Broadway places.

"I have to confess," she said, "I didn't even realize the FBI was in space."

"Most people don't," he said. "It's a new branch. A twig, really, just one month old. Our motto is *Ius altus, humile catagraphum.* High jurisdiction, low profile."

Kristine brushed away the Glossator function that had automatically translated the Latin. She studied Lord for a long moment.

"What's wrong?" he asked.

"Just thinking," she said. "I know a lot of federal officials and—let's wait before we go back. I'm not in the mood for my employer just yet."

"I think I can spare a few more minutes," Lord said, looking back at the crowd that was now fully involved with itself. Even the usually standoffish Stanton was socializing.

"Frankly, I would never have guessed you're Bureau," Kristine said. "You're so—not formal."

"That's probably why they offered to put me up here, out of the way," he said, winking. "But, yes"—he raised his right hand—"it's all true."

He tapped a small pin on his jacket. Kristine looked at it closer. It was a small *G* on a blue background encircled with a white ring.

" 'Og'? Or is that 'Go'?"

Lord sighed. "They warned me no one would get it."

"I'm sorry—"

"No, no, the design—that's my fault. It's Zero-G. FBI agents on Earth used to be called 'G-men,' 'government men.' Now we're G-men—in zero gravity."

"I see. The *G* has a double meaning."

"That's right. I should probably put a chip in this thing that feeds the explanation to proximity ICs."

She looked back at the salon. "Where's the rest of your command?"

"They weren't invited," he said. "It costs a lot to bring alcohol to space." He smiled. "I've talked enough. It's your turn. Why are you here?"

She smiled evasively. "Not yet. Maybe when I've had a little more to drink," she said, holding up her nearly empty glass.

"Then let me get you a refill," he said. Once again, the gray eyes glinted invitingly. "Immediately."

TWO

KRISTINE RELEASED THE stem and watched Lord go.

Finally, something good. Kristine breathed deeply. Unlike the recirculated air on the trip up, the air here had a fresh if metallic taste. She knew, from Colonel Franco's urgent need to impress her with his knowledge on the flight, that the station didn't recycle breathable air but made it from people's exhalations using backward-running fuel cells, or gathered sparse particles of oxygen from outside the station with experimental electric scoops.

"The engineers call it 'air apparent,'" he had said. "There's something 'off' about it. They say there could be long-term effects . . . no one knows."

Looking now at the bleary heavens outside the thick glass, she said under her own breath, "I don't care. Right now I like it very much."

Striding slowly, absently, through the dome, smiling at the workers, she thought that maybe it would be possible to start the trip over. From here, from now. It wasn't Sam Lord himself but what Sam Lord had done: he made her feel human.

She thought back to the claustrophobic, windowless NASA Skyshot Spacejet ride just two hours ago. It took off from the National Spaceport like a lightning bolt, pulled a hard left to avoid prohibited airspace near the White House, the National Mall, and the Naval Observatory, then accelerated to Mach 6 before the air inlets shut with an audible snap.

Kristine hadn't required Colonel Franco to tell her that the ship had reached the prerequisite eighteen-mile altitude. She was already holding her breath as the Spacejet—a smooth, slightly flattened cone with jet wings wedged onto its middle—jumped from Mach 6 to 25 in the time it took her to grip the armrests of the form-fitting vegan-leather seat.

Except for the smell of gunpowder on ships that had just come from the cold of space—the result of metal interacting with polycyclic aromatic hydrocarbons, a flight attendant informed her—no aspect of the journey had taken her by surprise. It had all been detailed in a pre-takeoff instructional, projected before her eyes on the IC. She knew why she had to wear the throat-to-toe jumpsuit made of the relatively new "memory material" that automatically adjusted to the wearer for the most flattering fit and, depending on the setting, could redefine curves or tighten abs like an old-fashioned girdle. It adjusted its grip based on skin temperature and blood flow to diminish the press of gravity during takeoff and landing. Kristine also knew why she had to stow her shoes and purse in the specially designed overhead bin. To keep things steady during the hypersonic trip, small but powerful jets filled the tiny storage space with blasted air when the bin door was closed, whistling shrilly as they kept her belongings in place whenever the craft angled and turned. That near-ultrasonic screech was only part of the noise: the external jets screamed loudly as well, and Colonel Franco talked louder still to be heard above the racket.

But none of that, yet, had dampened the thrill of going to the Space Station *Empyrean* as the hired companion for Colonel Franco. She still didn't understand why all the other young women at the agency—naturals and pan-genders both—had declined. There was travel pay, a guaranteed two-day minimum, and the experience itself.

"Read the reviews," her best friend, Manu Mack, had cautioned her. "Space gets terrible notices."

Kristine couldn't believe it. Even as the shuttleplane raced skyward, she remembered thinking, *If my siblings back on the family ranch in*

Montana could see me now, they would be so jealous. And my folks wouldn't have been so worried about me moving to the big bad American capital. She smiled as she thought about how her sister, younger brother, and she used to lie in the field, under the brilliant Milky Way, watching each shuttle streak across the night sky from Cape Frontier in Alaska. *Now— here I am! On the inner edge of space!*

Her anticipation was suddenly high again, and unblemished. She had experienced that thrill once before, the sense of crossing a threshold into terra incognita; it was back when she got so pretty, shapely, and blond that even her own parents knew they shouldn't keep her down on the farm. She wasn't talented enough to be an actress, was too short to be a model, but a local pageant and a bronze trophy brought her to the attention of their congressional senator, who offered her a part-time position on his staff.

Officially she was a personal aide, but in reality she was what the pages at the Capitol derisively dubbed an "office vase." She was a greeter, someone who looked great and played simple to make the lobbyists or political rivals feel sexy or desirable or smart. She stayed with them from the waiting room to the inner sanctum. The leers and ham-fisted innuendo were bad, but not as bad as the money. So when one of the pages told her about D.C.'s top companion agency, she didn't reject it out of hand.

Companion agencies were different from escort services. All were legal since the Sexual Freedom Bill was passed in '32, but CAs had a strictly "look but no touch" arrangement. Happily for Kristine's bank account, the money was good too. But the experiences were even better. She had been all over the globe, in every upscale and high-security building in the Global Alliance, and even under the sea in Japan.

And now the most extraordinary experience of all. But it had been something of an unexpected ordeal. The hissy, jolting ascent of the shuttleplane into Earth's orbit had seemed like a Caribbean sail when she boarded the SK ferry for the remainder of the journey to the station.

Kristine paused and looked back at Earth through the *Empyrean's* big window. She shivered, thinking back on the second part of the transit.

SK stood for Solar Kite, and the instant she'd seen it on the IC tutorial, she knew why. At first it appeared to be a glistening, shark-tooth-shaped chip in the distance, but as it slowly, elegantly tumbled toward them she could see what appeared to be an olden-days lateen-rigged sail with a snowflake-like pattern on its gold-, silver-, and platinum-colored surface.

The colonel was chatting with a brigadier general across the ribbon-narrow aisle so Kristine turned up her audio.

"We at NASA hope you have been enjoying your flight," she had heard a calm female voice say, while the image of the lazily loping space sail didn't change. "This final-stage ferry to the Space Station *Empyrean* will be as smooth and pleasant as the rest of the trip. The Solar Kite will adjust its position automatically to the spacejet, and upon boarding through the airlock we will fly to the *Empyrean*'s levitated geosynch orbit using sunlight and xenon ions from its own electric thrusters. So please sit back, relax, and enjoy the rest of your journey. Thank you for flying Skyshot."

Kristine tried to do all of that, but anticipation was high as she took her first out-the-window look at the newest completed space station in the sky. It resembled a splayed-out octopus with a smaller illuminated starfish lying on top of the thick, stubby central core—the flattened head of the octopus. A slim tower of strange, iterative fractal trusses projected from the core. It somewhat resembled the high, tapered Tokyo Tower on Earth, but with fewer open spaces. Below the weird radial skyline, facing Earth, was a huge circular sail that reflected the planet's terrain with mirror-like clarity.

That's when she had to look away. Her head, like the station, was spinning. The tutorial had cautioned her that without orientation, without a clear up and down, her "Earth legs" would check out. She looked to Colonel Franco for assistance but the back of his head had none to offer. Unlike the relatively spacious shuttle, the rear of the seat in front of her was right in her face, so she looked down at her socks as the Skyshot drifted toward the edge of the *Empyrean*.

The universe is outside and you're looking at a Christmas gift from Cousin Al, she thought. *How dube is that?*

Of dubious substance or not, the moment was broken when a dry, calm, live voice arrived over the ship's IC channel.

"Passengers, we are on final approach to the SS *Empyrean*. Please do not deseat."

There was no mention of traditional seat belts because there weren't any. The chair formed a tight grip with the jumpsuit and required a substantial push on the armrests to break.

Still looking down, annoyed by the mundane view, Kristine had nudged her head and brought up a detailed explanation of the landing in her IC.

"A runway surrounds the outer edge of the station's central hub, below the solar sail," the voice resumed. "Of course, you will not see the microwave guidance beam emanating from the station, a welcoming hand that will guide us precisely to the centerline. It's an infinite runway, for perfect landings every time."

The ceiling rumbled dully, and Kristine felt the shuttle sink toward the inner surface of the runway, which wheeled beneath the spaceplane's extended landing gear. The touchdown was bump-free, and the Skyshot decelerated gently into the station's whirling reference frame. Soon familiar weight returned as centripetal "gravity" took over: once again, outside her window, there was an up and down. When the ship had stopped after several minutes, it seemed as if the vessel had always been a part of the station.

Kristine saw the SK ferry drifting back into space. Then she felt Colonel Franco turn toward her, preceded by a wafting of his perspiration and cologne.

"Nice, huh?" he said.

"Um-hm," she cooed, because that was what men like him wanted to hear.

Franco, she knew, was not stationed on the *Empyrean*. He was only here for the party. She didn't know any of the other guests but could tell from their uniforms that they represented not just the United States but other governments and interests. Not that it mattered. She wasn't here to socialize. Like Franco, her clientele were mostly regulars. They wanted her to show up, show off, and speak only when spoken to.

"Your stowed items," the flight attendant had said with a smile, handing Kristine her black velvet purse and matching high-heel pumps. She pointed starboard. "Each passenger has their own changing room. Please take your time, leave your jumpsuit anywhere, and thank you for flying Skyshot."

"Thank *you*," Kristine had replied, and was on her feet as if the recliner had given her a head start.

She had gone from the white of the spacecraft compartment to the white of the antechamber, where the seat, hooks, and a mirror looked as if they had all been fashioned from one block of glass and plastic. She touched the top of the neckline and the jumpsuit slipped off as if it were a dropped curtain. It swept sideways through the air a little as it fell, like some enchanted cloth in a story, her first exposure to what Franco had warned her was "non-gravitas gravity"; an illusion, a simulation lacking real substance.

It seemed an ironic thing for that man to say.

Kristine unfragged her clothes from her purse, dressed, then stood in front of the mirror. She stared at herself and the relatively sedate, moderately low-cut, backless, form-fitting little black mini-dress supplied by the agency's wardrobe department, likely chosen by Colonel Franco himself. The automatic garment restoration capacity of the fabric had not quite worked in the artificial gravity, revealing the tops of the circulation-controlling panty hose, which sensed extremes of gravity and helped keep blood flowing along the legs. She wriggled her hips, smoothing down the dress, and touched the exit button. The mirror became a window and Colonel Franco was waiting outside.

The young woman stared. Not at him, though doubtless he assumed so, proud in his ceremonial uniform, complete with medals and deco-rations, craggy face, crew cut, and rapier-like body. What caught and held her eye was the looming expanse of the planet Earth behind him through one of *Empyrean*'s octopus-arm portals. It was the first take-your-breath moment she had experienced so far.

Franco had chivalrously, if somewhat mechanically, extended his arm and chaperoned her through the docking bay spaceport, where they joined a variety of ceremony attendees in an electromagnetic shuttle car. They were inside a tube, once again without windows, once more packed together, substantially similar biota without a shared thought or a familiar, welcoming look—territorial, even here.

"Sorry it took so long," Lord said, walking back into the room, a fresh glass of wine in his hand. "Apparently, people like to take my elbow and talk to me."

Kristine started at Lord's voice. She had been trying to see the stars and had not seen or heard him approach.

"That's a good talent for a . . . a Zero-G-man or woman to have, isn't it? Encouraging confession."

"It is," he agreed, handing Kristine her glass. "More accurately, though, it's that I like to listen, to learn, and most people like to talk. Narcissism is as vast as space."

"You say that but you don't *sound* cynical."

"Oh, I'm not. It takes youth and idealism to be misanthropic," he said. Then he frowned. "Except for my medic. He's . . . grumpy."

"But not you."

"Not me," Lord said. "At my age, you realize there's room for every-one."

"May I ask—how old *are* you?"

"I'm eighty-and-change," he said. Then added, "You remember change, don't you? Before e-money?"

"I do not," she said.

"Then, eighty and a frac," he said, resorting to the current vernac-ular.

"I never would have guessed!"

"And it really shouldn't matter," he said. "Ageism is the final frontier. I never understood why a quality envied in wine is frowned on in humans." He ducked his head toward the other room. "Anyway, now I really should get back."

"Me too," she said with open regret.

He offered his arm again. "This time, while we walk, you can tell me more about you."

She did, briefly and comfortably, as if she were catching up with an old friend. He reacted without reacting—but it was more than just being a good listener. He looked at her, saw her, understood her as if her eyes were an IC giving him all the context and additional color he needed.

"Who are those people anyway?" she asked as she finished her narrative. "I saw some of them on the flight up, but what are they doing here? I mean, about half the men and women are companions—"

"Eleven of them are," he informed her. "Three others are escorts. And one of them is a formie star."

"Is *that* Nicky Bligh?" she asked. "I thought I recognized her."

"It is," Lord said, "though I have to confess I'm not a fan of her or the formies."

"Really? How can you *not* be?"

"I like old-fashioned movies," he said, "not entertainment where you plug ingredients into a computer and the SimAI whips something up."

"I love formies," Kristine said. "I put Nicky and Plug Mitchell in a story about volcano divers trying to stop Vesuvius and its spawn, Vesuvius Jr., from erupting. It was very exciting."

"Did they succeed?"

"Plug always succeeds in my formies." She scrunched her face. "I don't like downers. There's too much of that in life."

"But you're so young. You should be happy."

"One day," she said. "One day I'd like to be as happy as you seem to be."

Lord smiled pleasantly. He had no business judging youth; his parents didn't understand a wide swath of things when he was a kid, from video games to his wanderlust to his loneliness. He turned her attention back to the crowd.

"Do you know that standing here, right here, you can see so much of what's Machiavellian down on Earth," Lord said, sweeping a hand across the room.

Kristine's IC fed her a brief biography of Machiavelli but she pushed it away; she didn't want to miss a word of what Lord had to say.

"How so?" she asked.

"I saw you notice the Mexican general," Lord went on. "He's Arturo Hierra, one of the few frontline survivors of the 2019 WON."

"The War on Narcotics we helped them wage?"

"*Ssh*," Lord jokingly suggested. "It's still a big sore spot among the Americas. Our southern neighbors think we did it just to occupy Mexico and create a buffer between them and the exodus from Central America."

"Didn't we?"

"Oh, in part," he admitted. "But the world is more complex than that, than even the newtiae and news minutiae can convey."

He was referring to the news minutia, the constant updates from multiple official, unofficial, and opinion sources, and to profiled futures, a complex series of algorithms used to predict the flow and interaction of events, which were often conflated with or misrepresented as fact. ICs were constantly filtering for personal preferences, but that selective skewing only added to the confusion as partisanship replaced any semblance of a classic education.

"Thankfully," Lord went on, "Arturo is a big fan of the new Mexican economy it created. He's also a fan of Ambassador Pangari Jones of New Zealand, according to my sources."

"What about him?" she interrupted. "The sheik."

"The Prince of Gambling," Lord immediately identified. "Maalik Kattan. His family owns the Kasbah Casino on Palau."

"The one that's done up like in the *Arabian Nights*?"

"The very one. He used to be in oil, but when demand dried up in the twenties they were ahead of the curve on making the Pacific Rim the new playpen. Reportedly, he wants the *Empyrean* to be a gaming destination as well."

"Will that happen?"

Lord smiled. "Where there's money, there's a way."

"The bald guru?" she asked.

Lord grinned at the description. "He isn't, but I'm sure that was the effect he was going for. That's Birousk Rouhani, the leader of the Julijil movement."

"The unity cult," she said.

"Accent on the 'cult,'" he said. "That fellow has been trying to erase global borders with himself filling the power vacuum. He's been trying to convince our government that Julijil is our best friend in Pan-Persia, the only plausible counterbalance to the region's religious radicals and warlords."

Pan-Persia was the name of the state created by Afghanistan, Iran, and Pakistan when they were excluded from the Middle East Confederacy in 2021. Kristine hadn't been there and didn't know much about the origins, only knew that factional violence still plagued the region and was constantly being hammered down by the Pan-Persian Occupation Forces.

"*Are* they a solution?" she asked.

"Zealots only form alliances when they want to expand, not share, their power," he said. "So I'm wary."

Kristine took a moment to think about that before moving on to a large, powerfully built figure.

"That's Ziv Levy," Lord said, "the most successful and influential CHAI on or off Earth. Has his own private shuttle, no transfer required."

Kristine's eyes widened. "Him?" She almost raised a pointing finger but stopped herself. "He's a cyber-man?"

"Cybernetic Human Abstract Individual," Lord corrected. "Proudly indistinguishable from so-called biologicals. Israeli scientists have made him their poster boy—their most remarkable prosthetic human-computer interface." His voice grew even quieter, and his grin thinned. "There's a rumor the Mossad has also made him their most remarkable agent. But I won't say any more." He tapped his left hip.

"I don't understand," she said, looking at his waist.

"The Israelis manufactured my CHAI leg, hip to knee inclusive. We don't think it's bugged, but one never knows. Jerusalem is very clever about such things."

Kristine wasn't sure whether or not he was joking. That could be why she liked him so much: maybe something so serious should not be taken so seriously.

"Our Indian friend is Dr. Vishnu Chadha," Lord continued, "who is being promoted by everyone including himself as a modern-day Gandhi—the one man of science to lead his broken populace from the shadow of social collapse and military bankruptcy into the new frontier of space."

"Do you think he can?"

"It's possible," Lord said, "as long as he remains true to the vision and not the visionary."

That left only one wolfish shark she was curious about amid the brass and diplomats. Colonel Franco had been talking to him almost since he left her. The black-eyed, marble-faced man. Sam Lord and the shapely young blonde looked at him in concert.

"He is Yegor Golovanov," Lord said, his voice mingling respect and derision. "'Go-Low' for short. He's the best and worst example of the power and peril represented by—"

That was as far as he got. Suddenly another voice—a sharp, urgent one—cut in from behind them.

"Sir," a woman said quietly, "may I see you a moment?"

THREE

K RISTINE LOOKED AROUND for the source of the soft, modulated interruption. She saw no one until Lord turned his head slightly.

Directly behind him, like a shadow, was a woman who looked about her own age. The new arrival had sharp brown eyes set in skin that was a smooth, lustrous sienna—space-prepped, Kristine suspected from the sheen. Her shoulder-length black hair moved as if it were deep in still waters. The young woman was wearing the same kind of tunic as Lord with the same 0G pin.

"What is it?" Lord asked the new arrival.

"A PAd, sir."

Lord's expression lost a little of its pleasant relaxation. "Go ahead."

The woman glanced at Kristine. The look was brief, but long enough to convey disapproval.

"Ms. Cavanaugh was cleared to be up here, Adsila," Lord said. "She can hear a *public* advisory. Go on."

Nonetheless, the new arrival leaned a little closer to Lord, and Kristine had to listen carefully.

"Less than ten minutes ago, two hundred kilometers of Japan's northeastern coast were destroyed by a wall of water," Adsila said. "Point of origin was the north Pacific."

Lord was seemingly impassive when he heard the news, but Kristine noticed his eyes flit briefly, protectively, toward Earth as he switched on his IC. Immediately, the feed from Adsila's IC created a translucent download in Lord's field of vision. From the identifying stamp, Lord saw that it was a SecD view from ten thousand kilometers above Earth. Only intelligence services had authorization to view images from the worldwide cooperative of security drones. Even if Kristine's IC were on, she would not be able to see what Lord was seeing.

What the Zero-G leader saw didn't seem to make geologic sense. The region had a restless suboceanic history, but the sea did not withdraw and surge back like a tsunami. One moment the water was at rest; the next instant it reared up like a roped stallion, remained upright, and moved west, crushing the coast. What struck him, in particular, was that the water didn't rain back down—not even droplets. Rising that high, the natural currents and thermal influences of the air should have impacted it. It was as if the sea had been bonded to itself somehow, molecule to molecule.

"How far inland?" Lord asked.

"An average of six kilometers before it just collapsed and washed back," Adsila went on. "Every town and city from Hachinohe to Kamaishi was obliterated. But that's not the only thing."

The view shifted to a JORO recording from atop one of the great rock projections that dotted the Sanriku Coast. It showed the top of the incoming wall. The crest was more like a mane, strands of water spinning upward and attenuating just below the cloud line.

"Distress calls from shipping?" Lord asked.

"Not a one," Adsila replied. "We're getting reports of dozens of missing vessels from freighters to fishing boats as well as four private and one commercial suborbitals."

"But no mayday reports."

"None, sir."

Lord's eyes found Adsila's through the virtual image. They both knew the same thing: that this was not a natural event, and the "public advisory" would soon have a "private intelligence" component.

"I'll be at the comm in a few minutes," he said. "And yes," he added, answering her insubordinate gaze, "I'll leave the IC on."

The woman turned and left with a parting glare at Kristine. The companion and Lord watched her go.

"Adsila Waters, my number two, and chief data analyst," Lord explained.

"If you have to go, Director Lord—"

"I do, though I'm lucky to have a very able team." He raised and wriggled a finger, indicating the IC area around his head. "That's why I'm able to keep this off. Otherwise, it would be a flood of data—'O, that way madness lies; let me shun that.'"

"*King Lear*," Kristine said.

Lord grinned as he leveled the finger toward her. "You cheated. I saw it in your eyes."

She flushed slightly. "Professional necessity," she said apologetically. "I always have my Party Hat on." Kristine was referring to the IC function that monitored cocktail conversations, annotated them, and floated appropriate bons mots into her field of view.

"Don't be embarrassed," Lord said. "The important thing is you know that line now, and its source."

"True, but—"

"But nothing. My impression of you as bright and engaging has not changed." He leaned forward conspiratorially. "Besides, you and I both know there's no such thing as an honest cocktail reception."

With that, Lord put his hand out. She took it and held on.

"Do you think—would it be possible to see you after your briefing? A tour?"

Lord withdrew the hand reluctantly. "I don't know. Earth may need our eyes and ears just now. Planning even a social meeting presents challenges in my business."

"I understand," she said, smiling sadly.

"I'll give it my best," Lord said.

Though nearly sixty years separated the two, Lord had long ago learned what society was just understanding, what the fetal engineering that created pan-genderism had emphatically expressed: that the body, whatever age, whatever sex, was a tool that served the soul. Therein— not age or gender—lay the true measure of a person.

As Lord turned to go, he saw Kristine tense. The young woman's IC buzzed with a proximity alert. Exogenous technology had been developed by America's Homeland Security in 2030 to warn law en-forcement of anyone manifesting physiological signs of hostile intent. Kristine dimly recalled the uproar, when she was five, about whether children should be given the technology to alert them of bullies or pred-ators or whether it forced them to grow up too fast. Now it was standard IC software.

Lord didn't know Franco well, but he knew him well enough. The man seemed unusually tense. Lord also noticed Kristine's uneasiness and lingered long enough to type the air. He'd never quite gotten the hang of virtual gestures, and had a manual interface that allowed him to operate his IC with real ones if he wished. As he had explained it to his tech agent, Michael Abernathy, he liked people to know when he was talking about them. Besides, he wanted his eyes to remain on Franco.

"I'm giving you run of the public area of the station," Lord told the young woman before he turned to follow Adsila. "Your SimAI will guide you."

"Thank you," Kristine said sadly as he strode away.

Lord's back was already facing Franco as the Defense Intelligence Agency officer sidled up to her.

"Enjoy your time with His Lordship?" he asked as he slugged down the last of his bourbon.

"He was pleasant to me," Kristine answered carefully, not wanting to offend her employer. She didn't know whether Franco was upset about this or something else; ExoTech only presented data, it didn't contextualize.

"Lord is an antique, out of place and out of sync," Franco said as he watched the director go.

"Then why is he up here?"

The colonel looked at her. "Two agencies wanted a piece of this very exclusive real estate and the CIA lost. Or rather, they took a tactical retreat—provided the FBI agreed to send Lord."

"Because they thought he'd fail."

Franco nodded. "Which will make it easy for them to take and hold the high ground when his two-year mission is up in '52, a view that's backed by every profile metric in their arsenal ... and by every bet I took back there at the reception."

Kristine bristled at that but was careful not to show her contempt. "So why did the FBI go along with the appointment?"

Franco shrugged. "To buy time, I suppose."

"For—?"

"Prayer?" he suggested. "They've got two years to hope he doesn't muck it all up." He noticed the time on his IC. "Let's get out of here," he said. "I have better things to do than talk about a has-been."

■ ■

Away from the reception, Lord quickened his pace toward the Zero-G command center.

The comm was located along Radial Arm Two, in a microgravity center that simulated the pull of Earth. The location also afford them privacy, away from the central column of the *Empyrean*. There, several floors above the FBI installation, was the pride of the space station: the *Empyrean* command center. Dubbed the Drum, the NASA-run head-quarters was a squat, wide cylinder located in the center of the space station. Like each of the Zero-G team members, Lord had only been there once, during station orientation; up here, NASA and the FBI were independent and fiercely—at times, combatively—protective of their respective autonomy. The only thing Lord had in common with Station Commander Curtis James Stanton was that they had both departed the reception, quickly, at the same time.

The Drum was larger and better equipped than Lord's command

center. Stanton's base had a permanent staff of nine monitoring ship functions and personnel as well as the external environment, watching everything from sunspots to orbital debris. Because the Drum was located at the zero-gravity center of the space station, everyone free-floated among the hovering displays and the tall, wide, "all-seeing" windows. Made of moving microvoxels, they allowed crewmembers to observe and magnify a wide array of locales. The adjustments were made manually, by pinching different sections of the glass and pulling the view apart, expanding it. External mirrors allowed views of the *Empyrean* that were outside the direct line of sight. These windows provided clarity and size far beyond that afforded by the smaller IC. Every section of the station was visible from here, from the uppermost antennae to the docking ports to the lowest radiation sensors.

One wedge-shaped segment of the Drum was electronically scrambled to the rest of the staff so that information could not be accessed from without. This was earmarked for "special communications." Because personal ICs picked up all crucial data from NASA and received messages from Earth, this section had only two functions, both quite different and distinct. One—the publicly announced function—was to listen for extraterrestrial life. The other—not mentioned in any of the publicity materials—was run by NASA's highly secretive Space Intelligence Corps. The SIC had been established to collect intelligence for any government agencies that were willing to work through NASA and pay for the information. Most were, with the notable exception of the FBI. The agency had historically preferred human interaction, on Earth; now they had their own presence in space, their own secret methods of gathering intel.

The kind of functions performed by the SIC ranged from spying on high-profile guests, of which there were soon to be many, to plugging into the satellites of other nations. Given their orbital proximity to most satellites, and lack of distortive atmosphere, NASA was very effective in this function. The SIC was personally overseen by Stanton, who ran it through his trusted lieutenants, Lajos Beck and Zoey Kane.

As Lord moved quickly toward the FBI's comm, he passed through one of the roomier corridors on the station. In this slightly curved concourse, haptic-feedback touchscreens covered walls, floors, and ceilings. The volumetric, magnetically contoured microvoxels displayed not only the image but the physical texture of Hinoki cypress, rice paper, and bamboo. The whole concourse had the look of a nineteenth-century Japanese village, and Lord wondered if this might be some tribute to the lost coast after the disaster—maybe even an automated gesture of solidarity.

During Lord's transit, his public IC newsfeeds told some of the story but not all of it. He saw the first, shrieking headlines: "HIGH" SEAS HELL! and GLOBAL *WARNING*?

Preliminary estimates were that at least a quarter million souls had been washed out to sea. Lord blocked the torrent of public feeds and followed only the stream coming to him from Adsila. One of the many things he had learned as a fighter pilot—something that was no longer practiced, let alone taught—was the importance of a mission. A bombing run, a strafing pass, a takeoff or landing: if you were distracted by glare, by chatter, by a girl you saw at the airfield or spent time with the night before, by any piece of nonessential heads-up data, you increased the likelihood of being off-target, off-time, off your game. You risked failure.

On Earth, the younger Lords called him everything from a fossil to a Luddite, depending on which thesaurus the IC was running. His own granddaughter Genie Jr. lovingly called him "Big Bang Sam," implying that he was old enough to have witnessed the birth of the universe.

All because I choose to witness the world—the cosmos, he corrected himself—*with my own mind and senses, not the way a SimAI filters and interprets it.*

Luckily, one of the few people who seemed to understand him was FBI Prime Director Peter Al-Kazaz. The sixty-year-old had been a field agent for Homeland Security, stationed in Dasht-e Kavir before the formation of the Middle East Confederacy. Living among nomads in the great Salt Desert of Iran, collecting intelligence, Al-Kazaz had learned the importance of spoken words, of gestures, of hesitation, of laughter, of the innumerable qualities that comprised actionable intelligence. The kinds of data Lord noticed with almost supernatural clarity.

"Everything else is a distraction," Al-Kazaz had said before handing Lord this assignment.

Lord smiled inwardly. Kristine Cavanaugh seemed to understand him, at least a little. Or at least, she *wanted* to. And she was smart enough to know that Franco was a bit of a viper. He hoped he did get to spend some time with her before she left. Earthside, the dating options were mostly female vets from his old Suppression of Enemy Air Defenses squadron The Red Sabers . . . and those gals spent as much time reminiscing about the suppression of enemy air defenses during the War on Narcotics as they did making love.

Off-Earth you don't even get that, he reflected. *Everyone is a specialist, and none of it has to do with my area of expertise.*

The corridor narrowed as Lord hurried along. He passed a series of long, wide planters made of highly porous clay: the sides absorbed the water to keep the distribution and balance of moisture stable. The bulbs had been created in a gravity-free environment, genetically trained to spiral around an imaginary plumb line for stability.

As he moved by, Lord gave a passing pat on the shoulder to a man working with the soil. The lean, rangy man did not pause in his labors. He knew whom the touch belonged to and simply raised a hand in acknowledgment.

The corridor ended in a bank of three cylindrical elevators that would accommodate no more than two people but compensated for any delay with a magnetic drive that sped occupants to their destination. The tight space forced occupants to embrace a central aluminum pole, as the elevator pivoted about its center of mass, aligning with off-plumb Coriolis acceleration in the whirling station.

"MIR wing," Lord said as he entered the waiting lift.

"Directly, sir," the voice-recognition elevator replied.

That told him there would be no intermediate stops.

It shot up and, with a trace of ceremony, Lord gripped the pole in the crook of his arm. As a small child, Lord remembered riding the subways in New York City. He couldn't reach the overhead straps but he used to love the poles. When the cars weren't crowded, he was able to swing around and around as the train moved. He even noticed, though he did not understand, the Doppler effect that made his mother's voice seem to rise and shrink as she said, "Sam, don't!"

The first time he rode the elevators in *Empyrean*, that feeling of euphoria came back so strongly that an ExoTech had declared him unstable and a potential menace. He'd had to explain the reason for the reading to Adsila, who had been touring the station with him before the other agents arrived.

"That sounds wonderfully . . . charming, sir," the young woman had said, trying to be diplomatic.

"You mean old-fashioned," he had replied uncritically.

"No, sir."

He had smiled pleasantly. "I don't need tech to read faces, Adsila."

"Sorry, sir—in fairness, I've never ridden a subway."

"But you've heard of them."

She had answered uncomfortably, "From my grandfather. Once."

"I see. Well, you know, I've upgraded countless things countless times in my life, and there's one thing I've learned from that. There's a big difference between an object that's passé and one's that's an archetype."

"Yes, sir."

Lord wasn't sure she understood, any more than he understood when *his* grandfather talked about a Mustang being a *real* car, not a solar-electric hybrid. But one day she would. Lord had studied the dossiers on all his people and they were smart, quick studies.

That was one reason he'd agreed to take this otherwise thankless political appointment where knives would be out for him from within the agency and without.

Lord emerged from the elevator and moved along the handholds to the Military, Investigations, and Research wing—if a series of small cubicles could accurately be called a wing. Labels took on an extra dimension of importance when they could dress up unpleasant reality. Jokingly dubbed the "military-industrial incomplex," the center was located on the highest two floors so that scientists could use the microgravity at the station's hub in their experiments and forensic work, and Lord could use it to help relieve his all-bone, original-cartilage spine. At present, the only other occupants of the wing were members of the *Empyrean's* own security staff. They openly resented the autonomy of the Zero-G team and had little contact with them. Lord wondered if Colonel Franco would be looking into office space up here during his visit. Lord knew that the CIA wanted in, but had been blocked by Al-Kazaz grabbing the only available space; and he had heard that the DIA, NSA, Homeland Security, and other agencies did as well. But the FBI had persuaded NASA to give them first shot, partly because the other agencies were already spending a lot of money on the station's SIC surveillance. The *Empyrean* was an expensive proposition, and the space agency needed that income to help run the station. The FBI had made a tactical decision to hold back in order to grab this piece of real estate.

In the accessway, the same lithium niobate sensors that relayed thoughts to the IC now captured a biometric encephalogram of Lord, invisibly affirming his identity. A door unbolted itself at the end of the passageway—a real wooden door, emblazoned with the familiar FBI logo. Behind it was a wide, three-storied circle of offices surrounding Lord's central command center.

None of the team members acknowledged Lord's presence with more than a look or a single nod. They were busy gathering data on the Japanese disaster.

Lord sat in the ergonomic, sculpted seat behind his desk. It felt good to sit and he both appreciated and disdained the fact that his artificial leg worked more efficiently than his real one.

He linked his IC into the operations center and looked up. Connecting to the system had given him access to a hovering, 1/100th-size, transparent, 3-D projection of the 1,022-foot space station itself, floating in a geosynchronous orbit, levitated by its solar sail above the West Coast of the United States. The private and public sectors were clearly tagged, as were the three docking bays—one of which was almost always reserved for one of the two shuttles, the *Grissom* and the *John Young*, moving in nearly constant rotation from the US Armstrong Lunar Base. Typically, that traffic consisted of robotic shuttles transporting helium-3 from the moon to power the space station's second-generation aneutronic fusion reactors. Security scanners appeared as red dots; there were more than three hundred of them on the *Empyrean*, all of them feeding into Lord's command. Also within the projection were figures representing each of Lord's agents. The avatars moved as the people moved, colored according to rank.

Lord's icon was purple. Agent Michael Abernathy, the IC tech expert who had assigned the colors, swore he did not know that purple stood for royalty.

"Why did you pick it, then?" Lord had asked him when he first saw the display.

"Newton placed it at the end of his prismatic chart, sir," the thirty-one-year-old had explained. "It is a place of honor—"

"Or the ass end," Lord said.

"That's *purely* a matter of perspective, sir," Abernathy had said defensively. "It is not mine!"

Lord had grinned. Many FBI veterans would have put him on that side of the grid. But some would not.

Lord glanced out at Adsila Waters, who stood at a desk facing his, but slightly below it. As Lord's number two, she was expected to have eyes on him as well as the rest of the team. In a crisis, reading body language and watching for hand signals could save precious moments. Being alert to visual cues for stress, fatigue, and particularly inner-ear imbalance in space were also essential.

Lord saw that there were two ongoing investigations. One was the PAd, the other a new IR. The internal recon—triggered by a wayward profile picked up by the SimAI—would continue automatically and would alert them to any activity that fell squarely within their purview. Lord was always careful not to step on the shadows of Stanton's security force.

"Update on Japan?" he asked Adsila.

"JORO reports that an underwater power facility sent a radiation alert point-four-two seconds before the lab went silent," she replied.

"Likely causality?" Lord asked.

The answer came from boyish, ginger-haired Special Agent Ed Mc-Clure of the Laboratory and Space Science Division.

"We don't know, sir," McClure said. "World oceanic groups are working on it."

"Was JORO responsible?"

"They won't say."

"Why?" Lord pressed. "Did they break the planet?"

"Either they don't know anything," McClure suggested, "or Tokyo wants to make sure they haven't discovered a valuable new power source before they give it away."

"What kind of power source could send the ocean into the atmosphere?" Lord asked.

"Localized null-gravity, antimatter . . . a host of theoretical possibilities," McClure told him.

Lord shook his head. "Let's destroy the world as long as we get the patent. All right. This IR matter?"

"Our chem-scan picked up a young woman trying to smuggle Star Dust in jewelry she was wearing," Adsila told him.

Lord did not react visibly to the news but inside he was angry. Star Dust was developed by the military as a limited-use replacement for special-operations eyewear. A laboratory subcontractor slipped samples to black-market scientists and it became a go-to drug of the space-faring young and wealthy. It allowed users up here, and under the right conditions, a glimpse of the dazzling near-infrared sky, brought out the glow and palette of otherwise unseen stars, born or dying in enormous cosmic clouds. Over a very short time it also destroyed the ability of the brain to perceive the visible world at all. The result was blindness or madness, sometimes both.

"Was there a potential buyer?" Lord asked.

Adsila deferred to Janet Grainger, who sat on her left.

"It appears to have been recreational, not for sale," the thirty-five-year-old African American replied. "I'm in the user's IC now, running down leads, seeing where she's been."

"Thank you," Lord said.

He allowed his thoughts to linger on Grainger a moment longer. He liked and very much admired the former director of the Tampa field office, who had been Lord's first hire two months before. She had regularly consulted on security matters involving Cape Canaveral, was passionate about the US space program, and was newly divorced. She told Lord that twenty-six thousand miles straight up was about how far she wanted to get from her former husband.

"Sir," Adsila interrupted, "I've just received a coded signal alert from HooverComm." She was referring to the J. Edgar Hoover Building in Washington.

"Details?"

She waited a moment more. "Not yet, sir. Just a stand-by from Prime Director Al-Kazaz."

"Thank you."

HooverComm had not sent a representative to the *Empyrean* for the ribbon-cutting. Lord assumed it was political: keeping their distance during the shakedown period, in case he screwed something up. That was one reason, he assumed, why not just the FBI but most of the major government agencies had failed to come up for the ribbon-cutting.

Or maybe Al-Kazaz or one of his deputies were afraid of getting space-sick, he told himself. Views of officials becoming ill during takeoff and reentry were favorite IC shares.

"Incoming," Lord heard his IC announce.

Lord touched the air to receive. At once, Colonel Franco's angry voice stabbed into his ear.

"Lord, you smug son of a bitch! Where is she?"

Lord didn't have to ask who he meant. "Colonel, what are you talking about? Ms. Cavanaugh was at the party."

"Cute."

"You've lost me," Lord said.

"I asked her to wait outside our room as I took an IC call," Franco said. "When I ordered her back in, she didn't respond. Are you two having a laugh at my expense?"

"That's ridiculous. I left her there, you saw. She was walking around when I first saw her, she could have wandered away again. Or—she asked to see the station. I gave her a pass. Maybe she's exploring it on her own."

But suddenly, Samuel Lord didn't think so.

"I don't believe you," Franco shouted. "I'm going to contact station security and have them—"

Lord closed the call, cutting him off. He all but launched from his seat.

"Adsila, stay on that HooverComm signal," he said. "Janet, institute a code red for guest Kristine Cavanaugh."

"Yes, sir," she confirmed. "Full search."

"Sir!" Adsila called after him. "Keep your IC on!"

Like a pilot signaling the deck crew, Lord pushed a thumbs-up as he flew through the door.

FOUR

A TIPSY KRISTINE CAVANAUGH tripped. Somehow, she landed on her face several inches behind where she started to fall.

She'd experienced her stumble at the top of a staircase that, rather than rising in a sensible straight line, curled upward like a butterfly proboscis—or at least she thought it did: it was difficult now to discern whether she was up or down, right or left. She didn't know if that was due to the wine or the whirling of the *Empyrean* or both.

"Goddamn space," she said, pushing up onto her hands and knees. She braced herself, placing one hand against the smooth, white wall, and looked ahead. "Goddamn Franco," she added.

"Wait outside," he had barked moments after they reached their small stateroom. "I have incoming."

"Incommming," she said, slurring. "What you *have* is nooo manners, bungho. You pay me to show off, not to . . . to be tossed aside. Ignored. Okay, then, I'll shove off."

The corridor looked like it was moving. The walls seemed to lean away from her, putting her destination, the elevator, farther away.

"Come the hell on, brain," she said. "It was only two glasses."

But it was more than just the drinks, she realized. What had Lord said?

"Cornwallis . . . canola . . ." Both of those references dropped into her range of vision. Neither was what she wanted. And then, "Coriolis," she said triumphantly. "Coriolis cross-coupling." She slurred again, repeating the term to herself. The IC still managed to conjure an explanatory animation of perilymph swirling around the inside of someone's ear, causing a chaos of space-sickness in the vestibular system. She almost threw up right there, but gathered from the running SimAI tutorial that the contents of her stomach would trace a spectacular ribbon shape in the air, and the thought was helpfully sobering.

She shook her head in emphasis and the momentum nearly twisted her around. Standing, she put her right hand on the wall to steady herself, and continued toward the elevator. She reflected that Coriolis would make a lovely name for a little girl.

Kristine giggled as she walked forward. She was still battling an invisible hill, now absurdly steep despite the floor's perfect flatness. It was the greatest funhouse trick she'd ever seen. She tried not to think about the time she puked on the whirling metal cylinder ride at the state fair in Great Falls.

"You're turning too," she said to the station. "Aren't you?"

Centro . . . no, centri . . . *i* . . . petally. "*Centripetally!*" she enunciated the word with a flourish.

The green light above the door indicated that the elevator was available for a passenger.

"Open, please," she said, still braced on the wall.

She didn't move. She couldn't.

"Welcome," the lift encouraged her in a cool gender-neutral voice.

"Coming," she replied as she peered in. "Just let me . . . let me . . . do this."

Kristine switched her right hand from the wall to the door frame to steady herself, then she swung in. The curved pocket door slid shut behind her.

"Destination?" the elevator queried.

"Home," she replied.

"Your quarters?" the SimAI inquired, interpreting and identifying her voice. "You do not require my—"

"No, Elevator. Home-home," Kristine replied as she gripped the pole with both hands. "I want to get the huke out of here. I don't like the colonel any more. I don't like this party."

"Docking bay?" the SimAI suggested.

Kristine smiled and nodded. "That's a good idea. I can have my bag sent up, right?"

"I will inform Station Services, and I will make a reservation on the next shuttle."

"Thank you."

"There will be a delay in the Fractal Tower for an incoming shuttle."

"Fine. Just get me out of—this *place*." She gestured disdainfully toward the world behind the door.

The elevator began to move. Kristine moved closer to the pole, hugging it. Suddenly, she felt as though she was beneath the pole, as if it were a chin-up bar at the gym.

What the huke is going on? Had that bastard Franco dropped Star Dust in her drinks?

Grasping the pole even tighter, she placed her shoulder against it so she could turn ninety degrees and right herself. Now the pole definitely seemed horizontal. She began to lose her footing. Either she was hallucinating or the carriage kept changing position. Ninety degrees one way, ninety degrees another—*Where is gravity?* she wondered. Maybe *that* was the problem. It was missing. There was something about that in the briefing—

Suddenly the elevator glided to a stop. Kristine slid again and found herself once more hugging the pole to her chest.

"Incoming shuttle," the SimAI informed her. "Estimated wait time is twenty-six minutes to arrival, cargo off-load estimated at one hour, ten minutes—"

"What . . . are you talking about?"

The SimAI repeated the information; Kristine barely heard it. She was marooned in a sickening swirl as the carriage turned around and around the central pole.

"Why is everything spinning?" she asked.

"The elevator module is decoupling, for your comfort, from the rotation of the Fractal Tower. Please try to remain calm."

"Let me off," she said weakly. "I don't care where I am."

"Holding for decompression of Fractal Tower and docking bay."

Trying to stabilize herself, Kristine reached out. Her fingertips stopped against a panel set high in one wall. Looking up, she saw that it was a transparent case with a red lever inside. A moment later she found herself cracking through it with her fist and pulling the lever.

A hatch in the ceiling hummed open, exposing the elevator shaft.

"Emergency close must be initiated or the carriage will—"

"No!" Kristine said. "No. I want to get out."

Above her was an open aperture to one of the docking chambers at the pinnacle of the tower.

With a low giggle that was part manic relief, part desperation, Kristine pulled herself through the roof of the elevator carriage and grabbed at a ladder recessed in one wall of the shaft itself. At once the young woman's body pivoted from the rungs so that the ladder became monkey bars, her body responding to the loss of gravity outside the moving elevator. Surprised by this latest shift in her position, Kristine lost her grip and cartwheeled toward the wall. Her forehead struck one of the pylons that supported the elevator's magnetic track and she vanished into the tangle of cryogen hoses and power conduits that lined the shaft.

Her last thought was that it smelled like gunpowder in here, just like it had on the skin of the shuttle.

Somewhere above her, a series of valves unlocked. As if in response, below her, the elevator's emergency hatch closed and sealed. And with a gentle rushing noise, the air in the shaft slowly bled into the vacuum of space.

■ ■

Sam Lord quickly retraced his steps toward the reception, once again thanking the Israeli scientists that he didn't have to do this with just his old bones. The new metal leg was so liberating he had to make sure he didn't push his flesh-and-blood leg to keep up.

"Who has anything on Ms. Cavanaugh?" he coaxed his agents.

"Pulling images off the deck scans," Janet Grainger replied. "I have target leaving the reception, heading into the hall. She was weaving. Looks like the effects of alcohol combined with Earth legs."

Lord quickened his pace. The combination of inebriation and the body's inability to adjust to variable gravity could be dangerous even for veteran spacefarers, and Kristine was not that.

Grainger's eyes danced across volumetric security scans of Kristine's movements. "She entered Elevator C," she said, and immediately brought up the woman's SimAI records. "Records locked, sir."

"DW override," Lord said. "Cavanaugh personal data *now*."

There was no need for Lord to identify himself. The ship's SimAI heard him through the IC, identified Lord's voice, and allowed a danger warrant—which trumped the privacy laws—to give him access to the elevator's audiovisual records.

"G206, last activities," Adsila put in quickly. She was asking for the records of Guest 206—Kristine, and her last communication with the SimAI.

"Let me off. I don't care where I am," they all heard. That was followed by the elevator's admonition: "Holding for decompression of Fractal Tower and docking bay."

Lord simultaneously watched a drop-down, two-dimensional video image, pulled from the volumetric scans. It showed Kristine heading toward the elevator hatch. But none of the sensor positions, none of the backscatter modes or deconvolution algorithms permitted him to see what happened next.

"Hatch status," Adsila asked without having to be prompted by Lord.

"Emergency exit protocol initiated," the SimAI replied flatly.

Lord was swinging around a long, curved section of the corridor that seemed to go on forever. He was just coming to the elevator that had brought him to this level.

"Cancel decompression in shaft!" Lord ordered.

"Decompression of entire sector in progress," the SimAI replied. "Incoming vessel requires cargo access." That meant "no."

"Get me a schematic of that shaft," Lord demanded. "Thermal reading. Any station personnel near the lift?"

"All are assigned to reception and guest quarters, sir," Grainger replied.

"They've been alerted by Colonel Franco, are starting to head over," Adsila said.

"Give them her location," Lord ordered.

"Already done, sir," she said. "But if she's in that shaft they've got to have space suits to get to her."

As Adsila was saying that, Lord saw why. The elevator was connected to the landing bay but without a cupola or doorway. That was about eighteen square feet, times three elevators made of heavy, precision materials that did not have to be manufactured or hauled into space.

Damn PEA-brains, Lord thought.

The Project *Empyrean* Association spent nearly a trillion Globals on this space station and skimped on what they called "structural luxuries." Lord had warned them about that when he did his walk-through up here, but Al-Kazaz had ordered him to back off. Lord was informed that investors wanted the base to start paying for itself—and also to pay dividends. One of the only reasons they even let the FBI up here was that juicy government contract.

"Automated maintenance report showing a heat spike in that elevator's maglev," McClure informed him. "Throbbing like a pulsar on the cryo-cooled rails; the indicated track segment is just below the bay door."

"Dimensions?" Lord asked.

"Looking at her height in the scans," Adsila said. "Matches the hotspot," she added gravely.

"How far down?"

"Eighty-eight inches from the open door on top."

Lord neared the elevators. Beyond them was a narrow spiral

stairwell, cunningly designed to translate, as one ascended, out of the whirling reference frame of the Fractal Tower, into the static frame of the docking bays above. The stairs also became a ladder as gravity dwindled on the way up. There was no door down here, but there was one at the top. That door was airtight and opened into the landing bay.

"Slammer six, *seal*," Lord said as his fingers began playing through the IC images. He saw the bay and its contents, studied them briefly.

"Sir," Adsila said warily. "What are you—"

"Drop the airtight wall *now!*" Lord ordered.

"Stanton wants to know what we're doing," Grainger said.

"Tell him we're trying to save a life," Lord replied. "Adsila?"

"Dropping Slammer," she replied.

At once, a solid barrier fell from the ceiling behind him. There were forty such panels throughout the station in case of decompression. That was one area where PEA couldn't skimp. Lord hesitated long enough to pop a small compartment and pull a palm-size packet from inside. He slapped it on his chest then charged up the stairwell.

"I've got to go through the bay," Lord explained, though he was sure the team had already figured that out. "It's the only way to get to her."

"That door is double-locked during decom," Adsila pointed out.

"My IC signature, shoulder, and body weight versus a low-pressure situation on the other side," Lord replied. "Which way do you think the door goes?"

"You may be correct, sir, but *at* the current rate of decompression you'll be entering a roughly eighty-nine-percent airless environment and lose consciousness in ten seconds."

"I made it to twenty at ninety percent in hypoxia training—"

"This will surpass that level very quickly," Adsila went on. "Do you have a *plan*, sir?"

"Working on one," he assured her.

Adsila was silent for a moment. "We just picked you up on sensor Fifteen C," she said with tense, resigned efficiency. "We will lose you in the stairwell."

"Understood."

"And *you* will lose body heat rapidly," she added. "We're already losing Ms. Cavanaugh's thermal."

Adsila sounded angry and Lord didn't blame her. This *was* reckless. But then, so were at least half of the sorties he had flown back home. His life, his work, had never been about playing safe. It was about doing the job he'd agreed to do. He had always taken very much to heart what his pioneer ancestor Isaiah Lord had written in a diary that had been passed from generation to generation like a family Bible: "You're either in a river, cold and wet and building dams, or you're a beaver hat."

Of course, he had done all those practice drills back on Earth when he was still all flesh and bone. He thought about his metal femur, and his nonmetal epidermis swelling agonizingly away from it, in the near-vacuum of the bay.

"Did you at least take the—" Adsila began.

"Got it," Lord assured her.

She was referring to the BB packet he'd pulled from the door. The "bends bubble" was a single decompression membrane that inflated like a bubble around a person trapped in a vacuum. There was only one in the kit and Kristine would probably need it more than he.

"Have station medics *and* Dr. Carter get ERT for two to the bay access," Lord heard Adsila tell McClure.

"Done . . . Dr. Carter was told to stand down by Stanton's team," Adsila informed him. "They said he'd be in the way of their own medic."

"Did he obey?"

"No, sir."

Lord smirked. He took great comfort in having Adsila and Dr. Carlton Carter at his back. Adsila might not have much field experience but she was already thinking of everything that needed to be thought about. As for Carter, he was seasoned and scary, a longtime colleague of Al-Kazaz. The medic was developing things even Lord wasn't privy to.

"Kristine's vitals dropping below survival viability," Grainger said.

"Threshold?" Lord demanded.

"Rough calculations suggest about a minute," Grainger told him. "She will be comatose by now."

That's a good thing, Lord thought. Otherwise, she might be tempted to hold her breath and her lungs would already have ruptured. If he didn't get her repressurized within two minutes, there'd be no chance of reviving her—and she might be gone already.

He had seen death before, a lot of it, but—and he had to acknowledge that this was driving more than a little of his haste—he had connected with that girl and whether or not a friendship came of that, he'd hoped to see her again.

Alive.

Lord reached the door and slapped one hand on the entry button. The light turned from red to green; that popped the regular lock. Now there was just the emergency lock—which, Lord knew, was designed to be a backup, not a primary lock, so that someone wandering the stairwell didn't stumble in here by accident. Leaning back, he put his entire right side into the door.

It flew in, barely hanging onto its hinges. He felt himself pushed forward by the air in the stairwell, wincing as he was slapped hard by the eardrum-sucking sound of the bay ferociously exhaling into the cold, airless expanse.

The altitude-chamber simulations were remarkably accurate, Lord realized as he hurled himself into the decompressing bay toward something he'd seen in the drop-down: the zero-g-ready freight vehicle to the left of the stairwell. It looked comfortingly like a terrestrial golf cart, with old-style McCandless thrusters instead of wheels, and it was stowed there because the workers were expected to take the stairs, not the elevators. The lifts were for dignitaries and paying customers.

About six feet long, Lord thought, eyeballing the cart. *Perfect.*

Lord grabbed one of the yellow bars of the metal frame to support and steady himself as his head began to swim. He found the bucket seat, nearly overshot it in the microgravity up here. Settling in, his hand hit the start button and his foot slammed the accelerator at the same time, as his other hand aimed the cart directly at the door-free top of the elevator shaft.

As the cart leapt forward, Lord felt his fingers and toes swelling as if they were being inflated. He couldn't speak to his team: he had to keep his lungs empty or they would rupture. As it was, he felt every drop of moisture boiling from his tongue. He closed his mouth. His vision was less a bodily sense than an entertainment center: objects shrank as his eyeballs swelled, a growing, glimmering blind spot caused solid objects to look like tidal eddies. He squinted ahead at the shaft. He could get past all of that, presuming he didn't suffer cardiac arrest as his heart seemed to race.

At least his metal leg bone stayed in place, though it was beginning to get cold, bordering on icy.

Normally quiet, the cart complained in a squeaky little voice as its liquid components began to thicken. Those pistons and gears pushed against cylinders and rods that should have remained inactive in decompression; pushed hard, causing plastic to scream. Lord ignored the noise as he shot the cart toward a dark, open maw.

In Lord's head, his ancestor Isaiah and Adsila were fighting a proxy battle. It was good to be a beaver but, dammit, there was some appeal to abrogating responsibility and just perching on the head of some other adventurer. Every part of him quickly started hurting. Lord felt the gas from his digestive tract already erupting from his orifices. Ignoring the primal fear and incongruous eruptions, Lord kept his foot tromped on the accelerator—one hand directing the thrusters like a runaway train, the other making sure the van der Waals adhesive on the bends bubble was secure. He couldn't afford to lose it here. If he had to, he'd use it himself; it wouldn't help him or Kristine if he perished en route.

Thinking of the woman punched up his courage again. He *had* to get there.

"Sir, we can see you on the volumetrics," Adsila said. "There's a survival kit in your cart—under the seat to your right. There are two oxygen containers and masks there."

Lord was glad for the message: it was something to focus on. He flashed her a wobbly thumbs-up.

The elevator doors yawned in Lord's distorted vision, leading into the darkness of the elevator shaft. His arms felt like they belonged to an ape, long and gangling. He'd felt like that before, when he'd pushed his F26 Vampire into a vertical ascent to a service ceiling that the sims said was impossible. It certainly wasn't feasible for the Shenyang J-11 the Chinese had sold to the cartel force he was fighting.

Do what you did then, Lord reminded himself as he forced his elbows to turn in to the core of his chi, his energy. He had spent his senior year of high school in Hong Kong, before it was turned over to the Chinese; the physical and psychological skills he had acquired there had saved his life more than once.

In the scans, Lord looked like he was panicking—his body contorting, his lips pursed hard, his eyes bulging, his arms akimbo, his fingers clutching.

Then his body seemed to tilt forward and the cart sped up.

■■

"He's pulled out the football bat," McClure murmured off-line, using his father's air force lingo to describe the seemingly desperate illogic of Lord's action.

"What are you talking about?" Grainger asked.

"Even if he gets to the shaft he'll be dead before he can turn it around," McClure replied. "His brain's swelling up and drying out."

"No!" Grainger instantly countered, turning on her colleague. "There has to be a reason he's doing this—"

"Reason *and* intent," Adsila stated calmly. She was reading her own visual displays. "His piloting skills are clearly present. There's no course deviation, not even a millimeter. He's not losing control of anything. He knows exactly what he's doing."

"For a man with a desiccating brain," McClure muttered.

Adsila turned on him. "Watch your mouth. That's your superior."

"Yes, sir, ma'am," he replied smartly but contritely . . . and with a cover-your-ass reference to both genders.

"Another disrespectful crack and I'll unplug you for the entirety of your next off-day."

McClure's mouth clamped shut. The features of the twenty-three-year-old techie—a vintage term he preferred to the more widespread "techer"—tensed visibly at the thought of having no electronometrics in his life for twenty-four hours. He gave the IC drop-down a mental hug.

"Ma'am, is there a way we can brake him remotely?" Grainger asked as she studied her own figures. "He's not going to be able to stop in time."

"I do not think he ever intended to," Adsila replied with an admiring nod.

As the team watched, the head of the luggage cart speared into the open elevator shaft. There was too little air for sound to carry and it was a strangely silent crash as the vehicle's metal framework cracked into the opening and nosed down into the elevator shaft, not quite fitting.

The cart was now outside their field of vision. But the shuttle drifting into the big, wide bay opening was not.

"Tower Command?" Adsila said.

"We're here," a thickly accented Swedish voice replied. "Automated shuttle capture in twenty seconds, bay door on emergency shut as soon as the tail clears—re-ox commencing in eighteen, seventeen, sixteen . . ."

Adsila heard the man but it was a big bay and it would repressurize evenly, which meant it would take much longer than sixteen seconds for Lord to be saved from the punishing pressure. Her display put the process at completion in just under three minutes. She performed two functions at once: she assumed command by Rule 8.25a—the evidentiary incapacitation of the office chief—and then used her new authority to access Lord's real-time medical condition. A brainstem encephalogram caused a body chart to light up: he was alive but every vital sign was in crisis.

Except for his metal leg. That was normal.

The woman fought the urge to switch to her male identity. Adsila had found that "he" was always less emotionally invested in any problem. Just making the decision whether or not to shift was always influenced by whether she was thinking as a man or as a woman.

She stayed put. Emotions were tough, but having two male brains on this problem was probably not the way to go. Especially when one of them was the go-get-'em mind of Samuel Lord.

■ ■

The cart stopped hard, vertically, its rear thrusters stuck just outside the open frame of the shaft. By this time Lord's entire body was numb, so he didn't feel, or even care, as his torso slammed forward. He turned to his right, retrieved what he needed. They were two high-pressure, ultra-condensed oxygen tanks, which, although they looked no bigger than a household fire extinguisher, were designed to keep anyone alive for two hours—assuming local pressure was above the Armstrong limit, which wasn't the case here.

Lord's side of the cart was wedged too closely to the wall of the shaft, so he slid out the other side—which, as it happened, was where Kristine was trapped. He could see her just ahead and below the vehicle. He swung one of the oxygen tanks so it was in front of him and turned it on. He could feel it hissing like a demon and he swore he could see the swell of oxygen as it poured into the shaft. His purpose was not to help her breathe but to try to add at least a little pressure to the area between his position and the top of the elevator.

He shoved the empty container back into the cart and slung the other around his neck. He clung to the cart as he made his way along the shaft wall, not sure he should be touching any of the cryogenic rails. He'd seen an MRI quench once, as he was landing his Vampire—a mushroom cloud of boiling helium let loose over his airbase hospital. He couldn't even imagine how much explosive force lurked in the elevator shaft's vastly greater miles of maglev plumbing, nor did he wish to find out by dislodging a rail and exposing the underlying pipes.

Lord was dizzy but not the way he was as he fought the microgravity and his own rebellious senses. Now he really was a chimpanzee, pushing off from the front frame of the cart, floating over the stubby hood, then grabbing the front bumper. He'd stayed just conscious enough to slap the bends bubble bag onto the girl's stomach and activate it.

In 1.5 seconds, the bends bubble erupted from, and became part of, the bag in which it was stored. It enveloped the girl in a pale cocoon and instantly started the repressurizing process with a micro O_2-generator stowed in the bag itself. Then he moved toward the top of the elevator car, just above the closed hatch, and wedged himself on the struts of the shaft to wait—not for rescue, because he was a pragmatist and the station was a bureaucracy with a sluggish chain of command. His mind on his last, very happy night on Earth—was it just two weeks ago?—he waited for the inevitable chaos in his heartbeat, and tried to work up some curiosity about whether the last moments of hypoxia were really as euphoric as the doctors said.

And then his mind went blank.

■■

"Elevator," Adsila instructed *as the bay* began to repressurize. "Open escape hatch."

"Emergency protocol still in effect," the elevator replied with disinterest.

"Override!" she snapped.

"Emergency protocol—"

"Stop talking," she said.

The elevator obeyed that command.

"Team Leader Lawrence?" Adsila said, checking the station's duty roster. "Where are you?"

"Just entering the bay," the commander of the rescue party replied.

She turned to the drop-down. "Yes, I see you now."

"Dammit, there's a luggage cart in the—"

"Yes, I *know,*" Adsila said. "Director Lord and Kristine Cavanaugh are below it. Enter—*request* you enter," she corrected herself, remembering who was in charge, "through C Elevator."

"My team is there and waiting for the huking Slammer to open."

Adsila searched for a manual override, found none. "Mr. Lawrence, there's no time. Go *back* down the stairwell, pry open C Elevator ASAP, and *crack* the damn hatch." Realizing that she did not have the authority to give station personnel an order, she added diplomatically, "Can you do that?"

"On the way," Lawrence replied.

Adsila stood stiffly as she watched the three-person team double back. Lord was right: *Empyrean's* security was like a well-oiled machine, as he quaintly put it, if all you wanted was an unthinking rapid-response team. They dealt with crises by the gut.

"I've been breached," the elevator interrupted her thoughts.

"Good." Adsila smiled. How appropriate. From everything she'd heard in bars and locker rooms, that was something for which Lord had a certain skill. . . .

FIVE

T HE RECYCLED, REFURBISHED *Empyrean* air had what Lord once described as "an empty quality, like a cave at the top of a mountain." But when he felt it on his face, it had the gentle kiss and smell and taste of a favorite lover.

That was the first thing Lord experienced as he emerged from the bends bubble in the medbay, and the first thing Lord saw once he had emerged was Dr. Carlton "Chuck" Carter looking down at him with a half-smile—at once welcoming and critical.

"Welcome back," the forty-six-year-old Carter said. He flicked Lord's medical history from his IC and looked down.

Lord twisted his head over as the membrane finished deflating and withdrawing like a self-peeling orange. Medical science had come a long way since the days when a patient had to spend weeks in a hyperbaric chamber. Living in outer space had demanded it.

"How long?" Lord asked.

"You've been out for about twenty minutes."

Lord tried moving his head a little from side to side. "I feel a little— *flattened*, like when I used to do those high-g sustained hard turns."

"At a much younger age," Carter said.

"Define 'much,' " Lord replied.

"Under fifty, before you became a trainer."

Lord would have grinned but his cheeks hurt from having hit something. "I stole a few rides after that," he admitted.

The doctor's narrow face grew even narrower. "Regardless, you achieved *those* maneuvers with a jet aircraft, I presume? Instead of trying to become one?"

Lord smiled weakly. He didn't know the doctor well, certainly not well enough to explain what he had just said. Back at Holloman Air Force Base in New Mexico, the 49th Operations Group used to discuss all of their sexual activities in aeronautic terms. What Lord had just described was a hell of a night. When he was transferred to the 4th Space Control Squadron in Colorado, Lord was able to show a whole new generation of recruits how to get around the repressive, politically maddening restrictions against public sexual dialogue.

Lord was pleased that he could twist his head without pain. "What did you do, give me new vertebrae?" he asked.

"You weren't out long enough and, anyway, the Israelis won't sell anyone spare parts," Carter told him. "No," he went on, "you're just built like a Russian battleship."

That was both a compliment and a dig. Those vessels weren't very sophisticated, but in terms of brute force and stability, that was where you wanted to be in a typhoon.

Then, suddenly, Lord remembered why he was here. He rose with a start that reminded him he was, in fact, more human than cyborg, when all the cartilage in his body compressed with an indignant shout of pain.

"Steady, dammit," Carter said, gently pressing him back onto the cot.

Lord yielded willingly. "Kristine," he said. "Ms. Cavanaugh—?"

"The young lady is very lucky," was all Carter said, gesturing behind him with his sharp chin. "*She's* only a Corvette."

Lord turned to glance at a figure on the next thickly padded cot, a figure still swaddled in the translucent variable-pressure cocoon. She was delicate and peaceful, like one of the ladies in Seurat's *Sunday Afternoon*. In repose she looked so innocent, despite her profession. In many ways she *was* innocent. Lord had tested her, earlier, at the reception.

She hadn't reacted to him mentioning that Ziv Levy might be a Mossad agent . . . except for a slight crossing of the eyes, indicating that she was looking up the definition of the word on her IC. She did her job, which meant keeping her nose out of an employer's business.

"Will she be all right?" Lord asked.

"The data says yes," Carter assured him. "It'll just take a while longer."

Lord glanced up at the medic. "Any news from Earth?"

"Nothing new," Carter said. "Nothing good."

Lord lay back. "Your file says you were red-blooded navy, Dr. Carter."

"Twenty-three years, till I came here," he replied.

"You have anything to do with the Redox Offensive?"

Lord was referring to an American operation during the War on Narcotics: an engineered strain of microbial corrosion that devoured white oak or carbon steel with the same ferocity. They sank cartel patrol boats, then underwent suicidal apoptosis to prevent damage to other vessels.

"I did whatever my commanding officer told me," he answered evasively.

Lord looked up at the man's rigid expression. "That's always tricky, isn't it?" Lord asked.

Carter gave him a mildly quizzical look.

"Sometimes it's a game of leapfrog," Lord said, elaborating. "You report to me, yet PD Al-Kazaz has told me to turn a blind IC to your bio-nanite work up here." Lord gestured weakly toward a small adjoining room. "How do you reconcile that?"

"Is this genuine curiosity or a turf war?" Carter asked.

"Doctor, we're here to gather information to avoid wars, you know that."

"And you're here to recover," Carter said. "As for Ms. Cavanaugh," Carter said, ignoring the question again, "her condition means she will have to stay on board awhile longer." He allowed himself a brief, disapproving glance at the shape within the bubble that slowly deflated and inflated like a lung. "Stupid, what they let up here."

Lord frowned. "Bedside manner could use a little work, Doctor."

"Spoken by a man to whom regulations are historically just sugges-tions," Carter replied. "The station chief says you exceeded your juris-diction—his words—'by a parsec.' He also says that the Bureau owes them a freight cart."

"Stanton rubs me raw," Lord said frankly.

"I'll give you something for that," Carter replied.

"Won't help," Lord told him. "He doesn't want us here in general and me in particular."

There was no reason to hold back. Dr. Carter would have read Lord's physiomental profile, would be aware of the many reprimands for what was politely described as "insubordinate and unsolicited ob-servations," the kind that used to get him bumped from command to command. When Al-Kazaz was still the Air Force Commander, Joint Functional Component Command for Space, he told Lord, "You're too good to court-martial, too outspoken to control." Ironically, that frank-ness helped to endear Al-Kazaz to Lord.

"Some advice," Carter said. "This is Stanton's command, not yours. He leaves me alone because he likes having a medic in reserve. You pro-voke him."

"If we'd followed his playgram, a young woman would be dead," Lord replied.

"Possibly," Carter said. "Or we could have lost both her and you. But it's not just that. You had a tour of the Drum. You demanded to have time at the windows, to see how they work. He declined. You had Agent McClure sneak back in to play with them."

"They are useful observational tools," Lord explained. "Stanton should not withhold access."

"So *you* say," Carter replied. He softened for the first time. "Sam, we're not on different teams, here. I can't discuss the bio-nanite work because, frankly, the prime director doesn't want you trying to use it. It's untested tech."

The conversation had become a sermon and Lord lost interest. He mentally ran diagnostics on his IC. The only thing more fragile than a human body in a vacuum was that body's Cloud.

"Is there anything else while you're here?" Carter asked. "Chest, ears, carboxyhemoglobin all look okay and you're showing no more than the usual neurologic deficits."

"I don't think so," Lord said. His IC scan told him his Cloud was fine. The Zero-G commander wondered if some of his own resiliency had been passed to the device when they were cybernetically linked. It was an interesting idea, the symbiosis between humans and SimAI tech, one that scientists were still pondering. The idea was particularly seductive when people—like Lord—had cybernetic parts that had been integrated into their biological systems.

The director winked, thrusting a mental finger at a green icon hovering in front of him. Adsila appeared, facing him.

"Sir! How are—"

"Fine," he cut her off. "Question."

"Go."

"Where's Colonel Franco?"

The query seemed to surprise Adsila. Lord saw her eyes move. He glanced at the sleeping Kristine again while he waited. It took just a moment for Adsila to find the answer.

"Off-station via PriD2. He left with Ziv Levy seventeen minutes ago."

"From the party?"

"Yes."

The two PriDs were private docking ports. They were a traditional design, the same as the original Russian SSVP system from the old Salyut days. The probe-and-cone mechanism, and the airlock through which passengers squeezed themselves aboard, were as basic as the mooring cleats on a seagoing yacht. Both docks were maintained for private shuttles carrying VIPs who could afford a quarter-million-Global flight, those guests who didn't want to wait for the twice-weekly commercial flights.

"What's the shuttle's flight plan?" Lord asked.

"Orbital run, four hundred thirty-two nautical miles up," she replied. "Nothing filed beyond that."

Lord's IC enabled an FBI program that showed him a schematic of the path, its duration, and all the satellites it would encounter. Lord pushed the diagram away while he processed the news. He had seen Franco chatting with the cybernetic man at the reception. He wondered if they were just splitting a ride or if they had business together.

"This is why we need your bio-nanites, Doctor," Lord said, off-IC. "Pop them in drinks, down the hatch, we hear what they're saying."

Carter made no reply.

"What about that message from HooverComm?" Lord asked, still collecting his thoughts.

"Came in twelve minutes ago," Adsila replied. "Priority One. Prime Director Al-Kazaz asked that you contact him ASAP."

Priority One meant that only Lord could take the message.

"Thank you," Lord replied. "I'll be there shortly."

"Sir, Dr. Carter has to—"

"Declare me fit, yes," Lord said. He looked up at Carter. "I'll have his okay. He wouldn't want me returning that pri-one trimmed in red."

The expression was one the FBI had adopted in 2033 when a field agent was shot on Christmas Eve and a country medic anesthetized him until December 26. Unconscious, he wasn't able to share vital information about a bioengineered virus until after the disease was already released, which killed more than one hundred churchgoers. Christmas trees nationwide were trimmed with red tinsel in honor of the victims.

Lord cut the communication. Then, with effort, he sat and waited for his flesh leg to show the same eager willingness of his cyber-leg to leave the cot. Dr. Carter loaned him a steadying pair of hands.

Lord's entire body was a little behind the biomechanical curve, but that was all right. Gathering his strength, he considered what the doctor had told him. Commander Stanton was a fifty-three-year-old hero of the WON. At forty-nine, he became one of the youngest generals in US military history and was put in charge of the Pan-Persian Occupation Forces. Lord suspected that Stanton was given this command out of political expediency. Stanton had been unable to crush the regional opposition there; resigning his commission and moving here was a way to save the reputation of the Pentagon's wunderkind poster child. That left him with some ego-bruising and overcompensating. Lord understood both.

Well, your being here is a compromise too, Lord reminded himself. Each man had something to prove and it was inevitable that they'd end up doing that like elks butting horns.

Lord sought Carter's eyes. "So. Am I fit?"

"If you can stand on your own, I'll sign you out."

Lord smiled, even though it hurt. "Thanks. I appreciate that. And also, the advice. Truly."

Carter smiled back. "You're welcome."

Lord took a long breath then slid from the low cot with an audible *oof*. He swayed slightly as he reacquired his space legs. Fortunately, the sturdiness of the cyber-limb allowed the rest of his body to rally around its stability.

He took a step then braced himself on the small waist-high cabinet before proceeding.

"On my own, you said?" Lord asked.

Carter didn't have to answer.

Lord pushed off the cabinet and stood willfully, legs slightly apart.

"The Colossus of Rhodes astride the harbor," Carter said. He winked hard and a release appeared in Lord's IC—along with the classic Larrinaga painting of the ancient Titan.

With a quick shake of the medic's hand, Lord left the medbay.

The Zero-G facility was the smaller of the two sick bays, located forty floors below the FBI office. The other sick bay was near the Drum. Though, ironically, space was at a premium in space, the PEA's insurance carrier had insisted that there be medical facilities on either side of the station in case of an emergency and Slammers that cut personnel off from one or the other.

Lord would be able to make the trek back easily, but he did not want to wobble on his way in. That was not the impression a leader wanted to make up here, especially when many voices at HooverComm had loudly argued against a man of his age being up here at all.

As he made his way, his head clearer now, Lord once again tried to figure out what Colonel Franco could possibly have in common with the "tea bag"—a disparaging epithet that had been coined for CHAIs and had arisen out of the widespread debate over the tipping point between robot and human. Ziv was a superstar, the most sophisticated cyborg on- or off-world. Apart from his likely being an agent of the Israeli intelligence service, he had global access to scientists, politicians, and media topliners. He was up here to make the case for more CHAIs in space. Lord understood what Franco would want with Ziv, but what could the colonel *offer* Ziv?

Maybe there's nothing more to this than a quick exit, Lord decided. He followed that thread. If Kristine had died, and Franco were off-station, he could only be interviewed on Earth, where the matter—clearly an accident—would get little coverage. If she lived, her employer would have been expected to visit the soft-eyed, hospitalized companion. The profession might be legal, but so was polyamorous marriage and public nudity: not everyone approved. And DIA agents were supposed to keep a very low profile.

Either explanation made sense, but Lord didn't feel them in his bones, the real ones. It was something else.

He stopped at the FBI storage locker for a clean tunic and got changed in the impossibly small room. Not for modesty but for decorum and credibility; he felt it would be wrong to enter the command center wearing a uniform that had been knocked around in the cargo bay and elevator shaft.

As Lord walked toward the command center, picking up speed and confidence, he passed a number of guests as well as members of the *Empyrean* crew. Those he knew he acknowledged with a careful nod; his head still wasn't one hundred percent. But whoever they were, whether they were walking in pairs or talking into their ICs, Lord caught the same words over and over:

Japan. Horrible. How?

It was a subtle but pervasive zeitgeist. It revived the feelings he had experienced as a six-year-old when his first-grade teacher tried to explain the explosion of the space shuttle *Challenger*. The entire class was watching as a civilian, a teacher, headed boldly into space—and perished, while expanding the boundaries of knowledge and human enterprise. He recalled the feelings of everyone at the air base when the World Trade Center and the Pentagon were attacked. It wasn't just a communal feeling of helplessness and loss, there was a crushing sense of impotence: every man and woman in the wing wanted to be in the skies *now*—no, an *hour* ago, ready and watching for any other hostiles. He felt anger as his emotions returned to the sickness every human being felt in 2020 when, in a singular act of sadism, videos of five major world dams were posted on a terrorist website two minutes before they were blown up. There was just enough time for concealed cameras to capture workers running, residents beginning to panic, then all of them—hundreds of thousands of souls in all—drowning. Those videos were posted as well.

Humankind was accustomed to barbarism, to accidents, and to staggering natural disaster. But rational beings were far from inured to them. Lord hoped they never were.

Perhaps that's the true tipping point between human and CHAI, he thought. *Not the body parts, but how and why we react to the world around us.* When you stop feeling, you become amotional—a term that had been coined for the way SimAIs mimicked an emotional response.

Hearing the whispered voices in the corridors, seeing eyes seek his for a human connection, Lord was reminded of the importance of his position. On Earth, he was part of a vast machine that served as a buffer between order and chaos. Out here, he *was* the machine. He didn't have the luxury of steeping in an event, of getting into the emotional pool slowly.

Or dealing with ego-bruised bureaucrats like Stanton, he thought.

Feeling fully himself now, Lord punched Grainger's avatar.

"Sir?"

"Has anyone other than Ziv Levy and Colonel Franco left the station?"

"No, sir. Only the one departure."

"Collect the movements of other guests from the security scans, see who else interacted with Franco," Lord said.

"Yes, sir."

He was particularly interested in five people whom he had also seen with Franco and Ziv at the reception: the Indian doctor, the Pan-Persian guru, the Mexican general, the gambling sheik, and especially Yegor Golovanov, whom the FBI believed to be an officer of the *Red Giant*, a collective of black marketers and Russian mobsters who hid behind legitimate businesses. The Bureau was particularly interested in one powerful *Red Giant* faction, *Cnymhuk*, "The Satellite," based on the International Space Station—which Moscow had purchased in 2047. By that time, its orbit had decayed precipitously. But they found a way, using old Vostok rocket upper-stages, to blast the station back into a viable orbit. The aggressive new Russian presence was, in fact, the act that prompted the United States Congress to authorize and fund an FBI outpost in the high frontier.

Just like the dawn of the space age when we raced the Soviets to the moon, Lord mused. As much as things changed, they didn't.

SIX

L ORD REACHED THE command center in full stride. Adsila was at the director's post and Lord motioned for her to stay there as he maneuvered through the workstations to a narrow door in the back. His IC encephalogram opened the pocket door and admitted him to the aptly named LOO—the Lord Only Office—his tiny private space in the rear. It was literally the size of the airliner lavatories he remembered from his youth, with a chair, a low hoverlight that popped on when he entered (he nudged it, in the microgravity, up into a corner, like a disobedient pup), and, most important, full privacy. Not only was there no noise from personnel, air vents, or plumbing: the soundproofed walls were lined with an electronic scrambler—nothing clever, just a primitive thicket of Faraday-cage metal. The LOO was the only spot on the *Empyrean* where communications were not only secure but could survive an electromagnetic pulse or solar flare. Even *Empyrean* command did not have that full capacity.

Lord remembered to switch off his personal IC as an extra precaution, beyond even the Faraday barrier. There was an infamous trial on Earth three years earlier, when an FBI officer at HooverComm conducted a high-security meeting with his IC dormant but not off. It stored every word spoken by his confidential informant and posted the conversation to a hundred correspondents his SimAI thought might find it interesting. The officer's mistake resulted in the CI's death, and the officer got seven years for involuntary manslaughter.

Inhaling slowly—the walk had been more strenuous than he'd anticipated or let on—Lord scrolled through his private channels via an old hardwired touchscreen in this shielded room until he found a bright white dot pulsing insistently. He punched it, hooking into the LOO's communications system. An array of glowing avatars appeared, ranging from senators to experts in various fields of science and history to international ministers. He selected the Al-Kazaz icon and touched it. After a brief pause Lord finally connected to the HooverComm conversation.

"Hello, Pete," Lord began. "Sorry for—"

"Did it have anything to do with Bureau business?" Al-Kazaz asked, his round face pinched with genuine displeasure. "That is, after all, why you are up there."

Lord smiled disarmingly. "It's very good PR when we save lives," he replied, having expected the question and discarded all but two unassailable answers. He decided to add the second one for insurance: "It's also good for the hearts and minds of everyone up here, a good morale booster for my team."

"Thank good God puppies aren't allowed up there or you'd go chasing them!" Al-Kazaz snapped.

"Not cats, though," Lord said. "Maybe kittens."

"Sam, *any* rogue action like that is fuel for the flame simmering under my ass."

"This *was* a human life, sir. We are here to protect those."

"And a good-looking, very young woman, which fuels talk about where your attention is focused."

"It seems like just yesterday when those same voices were arguing that I was too geriatric for the post. This should balance that."

"It doesn't, Sam. It absolutely does not."

Lord didn't bother to repeat the argument that hadn't worked on Dr. Carter. "How are the condemnations and the commendations tracking?" he asked. "And which of those is leading? I haven't had time to check."

"No, you've been too busy with—what, being smitten again?" Al-Kazaz snapped. "How did you boys used to put it? 'Air picket, target acquired'?"

Lord didn't bother to address that either. He just sat there waiting, as innocent and open-faced as the moon.

Al-Kazaz softened. His eyes flicked to the side to check the GoVerse stats. The Government Universe was a fast, harsh forum for high-level decision makers. It took the place of old-style polling, letting officials know where they stood at any given moment.

"Opinion's at fifty-fifty," the PD said.

Lord nodded approvingly. "Not bad. That's better than the sixty-six percent who didn't want me up here."

"Granted, but it distracts me, distracts us when we have urgent business." Al-Kazaz shook his head. "And Christ, Sam. Think. A dead Zero-G director does no one any good."

"Not true," Lord replied. "It'd make my critics cackle."

"It would make my job hell. It'd be a month, at least, before we could get a replacement approved and qualified for space. Until then it would be Adsila Waters's command. Can she run that office if something happens to you?"

"She seems very capable."

"What she is is 3-D," the PD replied, referring to the unwritten "diversity scale." "Young, an ethnic minority, and pan-gender, my concession to the diversity cops here to get my 1-D old-man choice approved. Do you understand my position here?"

"Fully—"

"Then again, if she were Deputy Director, my Priority One message would already have been delivered! This is a time-sensitive matter."

"Understood," Lord said humbly. "But there's Priority One and there's Priority Zero. I knew we had a little breathing room."

The prime director snickered. "Good sweet god. I am responsible for this, you know."

"Peter?"

"I wanted a veteran and I got him."

Lord knew the storm was at an end. "So what is this about?" he asked. "Japan?"

"Sam, right now everything is about Japan," Al-Kazaz answered. It wasn't a complaint, it was a fact with a fist behind it. "You've got major ports devastated and air control that can't handle outgoing citizens and incoming relief. They're scooping up bodies with tuna nets, for Christ's sake. The stock markets are going to hell on top of politics as usual: the Chinese are trying to play a major hand in clearing the waterways. They're massing a flotilla powerful enough to punch through twenty nautical miles of debris—including airstrikes on flotsam and jetsam. The president is worried they'll invade."

"Will they?" Lord asked.

The rivalry between the nations was ancient, with swaths of territory like the Senkaku Islands eternally in dispute. In Tokyo, the House of Representatives and the House of Councillors were still locked in bitter debate over the fact that Japan lacked a presence in space while Beijing had a fast-growing space station.

"I don't know what China will do," Al-Kazaz admitted. "No one here is sure. And when people are starving or cold or dying, they don't care who brings help." Al-Kazaz glanced at an update. "Look, Sam. Everyone down here is scrambling for explanations. I just got a notice that Mexico plans to oil-and-burn the bodies headed in their direction. Here's another," he said, his eyes moving toward a new update. "People are afraid because there isn't radiation on the bodies, meaning there wasn't some kind of nuclear accident. That means this is something new." The PD took a moment to compose himself. "Sam, listen. The event was awful enough but people are terrified that it might be a new kind of weapon. It wasn't natural. That much we know. An ocean doesn't do things like that on its own."

"What can I do?" Lord asked.

Al-Kazaz regarded his old friend for a moment, then drew a long breath. "Thanks for that."

"For what?"

"Calm," Al-Kazaz replied. "It's a madhouse on top of business as usual. There isn't an agency on the planet that doesn't want to be the one to pin this down."

Lord nodded knowingly.

"Why I called," Al-Kazaz went on, "an astrophysicist is on her way up. Dr. Saranya May. She's five months into a yearlong hitch on the moon."

"What did she do there, experiment with the tides?"

"That was my first question to Director Warren at NASA, and the answer is no," Al-Kazaz said. "She contacted us, in person, for protection. Came in on a supply run."

"Protection relating to this?"

"So she says."

"NASA has its own security personnel," Lord said. "So does Armstrong Base. Did she go to them?"

"That's a big, ugly no," Al-Kazaz replied. "I had Warren and his DC SecDirec Mohalley gnawing on my ankles, wanting to know why she came to us. All they know is that she took personal leave for an Earth visit."

"But she's going back up to Armstrong?"

Al-Kazaz nodded. "Says she has to."

Lord's brow scrunched. "Math isn't my thing, Pete, but the numbers on the clock say this Dr. May would have left the moon before this happened."

"Exactly," Al-Kazaz said.

"Seriously, what was she doing up there?"

"Seriously, Sam, I don't know. Not a clue. Mohalley wouldn't say and I checked with JHAGS. They don't know, though I was told that we are to listen very carefully to what she says and answer yes to whatever she asks."

"So she's been on the drop-down of Joint Homeland and Global Security," Lord said.

"Her name shows up as 'eyes on' but the rest is 'eyes only,'" Al-Kazaz said.

He was referring to the tip sheet JHAGS shared with other intelligence services around the world. In theory, if anyone knew anything about a person on the list they were supposed to add it. That was "eyes on." Privacy groups hated the practice—they described it as social media meets the old Gestapo—so only high-ranking JHAGS personnel were allowed to view it. Now and then, actionable intelligence did show up. Then it became "eyes only."

"Which brings me to you," Al-Kazaz continued. "Dr. May will be arriving in forty-seven minutes. Help her, but work her, Sam."

The irony of that request—after the way he was reamed over Kristine Cavanaugh—was not lost on either man.

"Is that all you've got?" Lord asked. "Those are my instructions?"

"Yeah, that's all," Al-Kazaz said. "We've been crunching this ever since she dropped in. The timing is scary, her fear was scary, but her reluctance to talk was scarier still. She asked for protection and I told her to see you."

"Pete, you know the *Empyrean* isn't a safe house—"

"Wasn't," Al-Kazaz replied bluntly.

Lord understood: it was now. This would be an opportunity to justify Al-Kazaz's faith in him and to have his old friend's back. It also gave him another clue as to what Ziv Levy and Colonel Franco might have been discussing. One or the other of them could have heard of the scientist's request.

"Also, I want you to go see the Gardener," the PD went on. "He sent up a flash twenty-one minutes ago. See what he's heard and have him available for additional work. And, Sam?"

"Yes, Pete?"

"If you're going to die on me, be considerate enough to get murdered in the line of duty on an open investigation."

"With both boots firmly on, sir," Lord assured him.

"Good luck," Al-Kazaz said and signed off—with a virtual slap that landed, symbolically, on the side of Lord's head. Lord hadn't gotten used to those either, the "fingles," virtual IC digits for high-fives, back pats, salutes, and other gestures.

Lord took a moment to savor the silence and solitude, qualities that, up here, were scarce, bordering on nonexistent. Then, slapping still-swollen hands on his knees to push himself from the saddle-like seat—straddling it helped keep the occupant stabilized—Lord went back to the command center. He motioned to Adsila that she was still in charge but did not tell her where he was going.

"You'll keep—"

"It's on," he assured the EAD, pointing to his head as he eased into the corridor.

Lord took the elevator to the bottom level of the *Empyrean* and followed the green line to the Agro center. This was quite literally the lifeblood of the station, where food was grown and water vapor and wastewater recycled. The *Empyrean* was not quite self-sufficient, but at seventy-six percent, that beat projections by over a year. Much of that progress was due to Dr. Lancaster Liba, whom the Bureau had code-named the Gardener. The short, stooped, pockmarked man wore the standard tan one-piece outfit of the agriculture department. He was ten years younger than Lord but looked ten years older. He had made Death Valley flower, ending the Southwest Water Rebellion of 2024. Before heading into space, Liba had turned portions of the Gobi Desert in China into fertile farmland, earning him a National Friendship Award in a ceremony in Beijing—along with friends in the Politburo. He was a longtime friend and confidant of Al-Kazaz, a red-blooded Tennessee-born patriot who had been recruited as an antirebellion spy during that war. He continued to conduct recon for Al-Kazaz. Since he didn't have access to the LOO, whenever he had something to say he notified the prime director with a flame that burned briefly in the PD's IC then immolated any trace of itself.

As soon as he saw Lord enter, Liba straightened slightly from a clutch of cantaloupes—among the least cost-efficient fruits to import—then nodded and turned away. The director followed him toward the green-house nearest them. The greenhouses came in two varieties, each in-terspersed across the one-hundred-by-thirty-yard space—their own windows transparent solar panels that filled with the vastness of space and the sun. The first greenhouse design was large and rectangular, with a slightly curved roof and bulging, rounded sides. The second—and third and fourth, technically—were a trio of interconnected clear domes crammed with foliage. Both positioned their crops to take ad-vantage of sunlight from two directions: from the sun itself, and from its reflection in the station's giant solar sail.

The door, made of shatterproof glass, recognized Liba's encephalo-gram and cracked open. He pulled it wider and quickly followed Lord inside. The windows began to drip, clearing from the rush of cool air; as soon as Liba sealed the dome the warm, soggy vapor allowed them to resume their natural opacity. That made it perfect for clandestine meetings. It was, in fact, an adequate bio-version of the electronics in the LOO: the foggy windows obscured the occupants, in case anyone outside could read lips, with or without an assist from their IC; and the thrum of the reclamation machinery stymied vibrational sensors. The technical ability to turn the vibrations of glass into recognizable speech had long ago forced embassies and corporate headquarters around the world to replace their windows with brick, though it was two years before scientists linked an inexplicable spike in rickets to the ensuing vitamin D deficiency. As a final protection, Lord and Liba sat with IC-scrambling closeness to an electric-field water nanofiltration system.

The Gardener's eager eyes sought those of his companion. Lord's gray eyes smiled.

"What've you got in the vault, Lancaster?" the newcomer asked.

"Not gonna say," Liba replied. "*Station* business."

It sounded like passwords spoken by two old spies. In fact, it was a question Lord asked each of the few times he had talked to the man, a question Liba always answered the same way. There was a secret in the agricultural section, one that Liba would not discuss because it was the project of his employer of record—NASA—and not the FBI. The information was for Stanton only.

"Speaking of things that are station business, I heard about your little adventure," Liba remarked.

"I told you last time, I hate parties," Lord quipped.

Liba chuckled. "I also heard we have a VIP en route to PriD1."

Lord gave him an impressed but questioning look. "The prime director didn't tell you that."

"Nope. Colonel Franco did."

Lord stiffened. "Go on."

"Well, not in so many words, y'understand," Liba said. "Y'know, gardeners, custodians, nurses—people don't see us."

That was why the PD had hired the man for a handsome retainer: he was invisible. Unfortunately, the Gardener resolutely talked to people just as he did to plants, slow and meandering.

"And you know me, naturally nosy," Liba said.

Then the man fell silent, as if he were whittling a stick. Perhaps he was, in his IC.

"Liba," Lord said, coaxing him along. "The VIP?"

The Gardener nodded. "Anyway, I'm tending to the planters outside reception and I hear Colonel Franco yelling at you as he's coming down the corridor, something about stealing his date. Did you?"

"No."

"I thought not," Liba said. "He struck me as a hothead. Then he gets a call, but I can't hear that because Ziv walks by, all those thermal actuators and coiled polymer muscles hissing low, like I was just outside a snakepit. But I see the colonel end the call suddenly, madder now, and he goes running after the tea bag. Ziv stops and I *do* hear Franco invite him to go for a run—on Ziv's own spacewings. So while you were busy hot-rocketing through the landing bay, I poked after them, watering this, watering that. I saw them board Ziv's shuttle, just them and the pilot."

"They filed a single-orbit flight plan," Lord confided. "Do you know why?"

The younger old man nodded. "I heard Franco say it was pretty damn imperative they meet a shuttleplane from Earth," he replied. "He said there was someone on board they had to talk to."

"Did he say anything, *hint* anything, about diverting the occupant?"

"No, sir."

"Did you note the time?" Lord asked.

"I did not," Liba replied. "Damn IC interferes with my concentration and I wanted to be able to report what was important."

Lord put a hand on Liba's arm. "Thank you. This is very useful."

"What's it mean?" Liba asked.

Lord grinned. "Sorry, Lancaster. *FBI* business."

SEVEN

I T WAS A moment Sam Lord had hoped would not happen: when he was traversing these halls to deal with something old rather than something new; when it was about a potential conspiracy hatched on Earth rather than a unique challenge rooted in the unfamiliar expanse of outer space.

Somehow, Franco or his DIA bosses had found out about Dr. May. Perhaps from someone on the moon when she departed suddenly. Perhaps she was recognized coming through the lunar decontamination walkway at the airport on Earth. And now Ziv knew, which meant the Mossad knew, which meant that whomever May had feared when she left Armstrong Air Force Base had grown exponentially.

Space is clean and new, he thought again. *It shouldn't be contaminated by old rivalries.*

But the world didn't work the way he wanted; why should the universe? He gave the cosmos a quick, challenging look through one of the windows as he left the Agro center. He shook an IC fist at the skies, like he used to do at what was supposed to be his flight ceiling.

The devil will not drag you under! he promised the cosmos.

Lord used his security clearance to do a quick check of flight manifests at National Air and Spaceport in D.C. He learned that rather than wait four hours for the lunar shuttle to return to Armstrong, May had

booked a scheduled outgoing flight to meet the *Empyrean* solar kite—
then accepted a ride to the *Empyrean* from Ziv Levy. She must have felt
that a publicity seeker like the tea bag was too well known to do her
harm.

She was probably right. But Ziv wasn't alone.

*Hopefully, she'll be too careful to respond to Franco's ham-fisted meth-
ods of questioning,* Lord thought. The man did not have a reputation for
subtlety.

Lord also wondered how Ziv would get the commercial flight to
stop for him. As he walked, Lord sent a brief message to Adsila.

Chk E-shut recs, he typed in the air, opting to use his fingers rather
than his eyes. Unless the CHAI had managed to scrub the Earth shuttle
records, there might be useful data there.

OK, she sent back.

The *Empyrean* looked—and in many ways behaved—like a child's
toy top.

The Agro center was located on the lowest floor of the massive
tower that formed the pivotal center of the space station. This location
enabled the plants to grow in gravity that most resembled Earth-normal.
Above the tower—direction being relative to Earth—was a rotating, circular hub that was four levels deep and supported the station's eight radial arms. Jutting from the hub, these single-story radial arms resembled
some ancient hieroglyphic representation of the sun. Each outwardly
tapering "ray" was configured for living quarters, recreation, science, recycling, the Zero-G comm, and other essential station functions.

Atop the doughnut-like hub was the ring-like circular runway used
for commercial flights. A circular platform was located at its center, anchored to the hub but not to the surrounding runway. Rising from this
disc was an enclosed, Eiffel Tower–like construct that was effectively
a continuation of the spire below. This was the "mast" for the station's
solar sail, more than 820,000 square meters of Mylar that spread from
the base of the tower like the petals of a sunflower. It collected energy
from the sun that not only helped to power the station but kept it aloft

in its levitated orbit—above and beyond the deadly Van Allen radiation belts—and simultaneously spun the station to generate centripetal gravity. A meshwork of wires also enabled the array to serve as a high-gain antenna for all communications with Earth. No proud, full, forward-topgallant canvas, this: the gigantic sail was silent and eerily motionless.

A series of elevator trips at vertical and horizontal right angles to one another brought Lord to the first of the station's two private docking areas. These ports were located directly adjacent to but separate from the terminal at the spaceward side of the hub. They allowed individuals on sensitive government or industrial business to come and go without standard processing. Both the public and private terminals were athwart the station's zero-g center, where gravity was effectively nonexistent. A series of waist-high rails, pylon-mounted handholds, and carefully spaced sandal-like foot restraints were available for newcomers who had not yet acclimated to the sustained leap and potential weightless tumble produced by every step.

The contrast of the sunlit radial arms and fractal skyscraper with the deep-space side of the station was dramatic. Here, beneath the solar sail, it was not just a dark place; it was kaleidoscopic. Outside the large windows the golden Mylar of the sail reflected the stars back to the stars. The shroud of darkness caused inside by the sail required lighting arrays made of narrow phosphorescent glowstrips laid along the floor and ceiling—though these were muted so that they too would not bounce back off the sails and create a confusion of false paths. Along with dull red spacecraft-warning flashers, they gave the whole place what Lord had always felt was a spooky waterfront feeling, like he used to experience walking along the Hudson River.

Another quality that made the bays a special challenge was that they were decoupled from the station's spin to make the docking maneuver less complicated for incoming pilots. They only had to find and contact the classic docking cone, not match it in a longitudinal roll. For occupants, these bays hovered at the fringe of the station like a hoop skirt, and elevators arriving there corkscrewed lazily from the station's constantly turning central structure into the static frame of the bays. In an emergency—such as depressurization—a helical staircase provided quick egress as long as a veteran spacefarer was handy to pull new arrivals toward it, their weightlessness diminishing the farther they traveled along the stairs.

Ordinarily, Lord enjoyed that transfer process. Many people found it a challenge, but they were not retired fighter pilots. The gradual freedom from gravity, the upward then sideward trip in the elevators—it all reminded Lord of the mildly disorienting, belly-tickling theme park rides he'd enjoyed as a kid and the test planes he'd pushed beyond their rated limits.

But not now.

Holding one of the matte-black aluminum handrails, Lord looked out the viewport some twenty feet away. He began humming the old tune "Sitting on the Dock of the Bay"; it was unavoidable, a programmed response to being in the docking bay, a response he had given up trying to resist. To the left of the viewport was the docking ring, five feet in diameter, which formed an airtight short-sleeve seal with the matching port on the top of the shuttle. Once the "all-secure" notice was given, the hatches opened automatically and, with the help of handholds, passengers could literally float in or out.

They could, that is, if the sophisticated security systems let them, Lord thought.

The first line of defense was the volumetric security scans—algorithms searching for the lines of a concealed sidearm or drug canister. Then there were the mass spectrometers secreted inside the air filtration vents, and the barely perceptible pulse from the non-contact ultrasonogram: both were looking for finer contraband like disease germs, both innocent and weaponized; fleas and other unwelcome insects; and—with the IC's lithium niobate sensors—even EEG traces that might betray antipsychotic medication at work in the bloodstream. There had never been a homicide in space, and no one wanted to host the first.

"Director Lord," a voice broke the eerie calm.

"Go ahead, Janet."

"Colonel Franco spoke with fifteen people at the reception, listened to at least seven others directly, and was within IC range of five more."

"Who did it look like he was eavesdropping on?" Lord asked. Franco was too skilled an intelligence officer to bring up anything sensitive there. But that didn't mean others were as smart.

"Definitely Commander Stanton," she informed him.

"That's nothing," Lord said. Stanton was only interested in station operations, not off-Earth intrigue. The commander might have discussed the new, mysterious Chinese *Jade Star* satellite or the Russian space station, but not much more that would interest Franco. "Go on."

"Another definite was Hiromi Tsuburaya of CBA."

"Was that after I left?" Lord asked.

"About a minute, yes," Grainger replied.

Tsuburaya was the Japanese chief operating officer of Consolidated Bandwidth of Asia, one of the largest news organizations in the world. Lord had noticed her, but that was before the news from Japan broke and she had seemed her usual, austere self. After that, he lost sight of her.

"Next," he said.

"The other three were Sheik Maalik Kattan, Fraas Dircks, and Wallace Brown-Card, all very briefly."

Grainger sent their profiles but Lord knew them all. Franco did not like to gamble—being in debt was not a good idea for intelligence officers—so he was probably asking Kattan which potential foreign sources *were* in debt; Dircks was the pornography billionaire from Holland, whom every operative wanted to know for the same reason; Brown-Card was the CFO of Orbital Banking, which had a branch on the station that was used—HooverComm suspected—for money sterilization, electronic laundering via systems that were not just dedicated but were hidden in an office the size of the LOO. Only the CFO's DNA plus a mystery odor that changed daily could open the door. Lord would have to wait for Dr. Carter's nanites to be field-ready in order to get inside.

"Thank you, Agent," Lord said.

"Action order?"

"Has Tsuburaya filed a departure plan?"

"No, sir," Grainger replied. "In fact, she went to see Commander Stanton's medic for a sedative then went to her cabin."

"Understandable," Lord said. "Okay, watch her. She may come up with something."

Hiromi Tsuburaya had come up through the ranks as a war correspondent; she knew how to dig for news. More important, she knew how to swap influence for news. The fifty-two-year-old could turn an unknown into a celebrity in an hour or less, and that kind of power loosened lips. Even Franco might open up to her, swap information, to learn whatever she might know about the other two space stations.

Lord watched the countdown clock in his IC, which had automatically plugged into the PriD database upon his arrival. Then, as the timer announced two minutes, he saw it.

The arrival of a shuttle, public or private, never failed to impress. Gleaming white or silver—this one was silver—the ships rose into the viewport from below, like old cruise ships appearing through a morning mist or around a waterfront tower in New York harbor. It was a seamless, sunlit pyramid growing until it filled the window—now the nose, then the cockpit window, and finally the delta wing, seen from above. It was following an invisible guidance beam, fully autonomous, once it came to within a thousand meters of the *Empyrean*. Lord saw the probe on the top of the fuselage find the drogue on the PriD, heard the reassuring ripple-bang of the latches, and then the ship was still.

The whir of gears, the rush of air, and then the seals were secure. The hatches pulled back with a faint, mechanical whisper and then Lord was looking down into the shuttle. A moment later a figure appeared, the top of her head toward him. A thin white pole extended up and down from the side of the docking sleeve—at least, relative to the passengers.

The pole was pointing directly at Lord. Grips dropped down on both sides and the occupant partly pulled, partly floated through the hatch. She tucked her knees to her chest, emerged through the *Empyrean* ring, and with the grace of a seasoned space veteran, Dr. Saranya May completed the transfer.

Holding one of the rails while her vision adjusted to the relative darkness, she spotted Lord at once. She met his eyes with recognition and relief and started toward him, eschewing the foot restraints and pulling herself along using the grips atop the pylons. Lord noticed that she was unable to avoid glancing behind her. From where he stood, Lord could not see either Franco or Ziv Levy in the hatchway. They must still be strapped into their seats, either conferring, avoiding him, or more likely both.

Dr. Saranya May was a strikingly handsome Indian-Malaysian woman with silky, raven-black hair pulled into two tight braids that were clipped to a necklace designed to hold them in zero gravity. Her rose lips curved upward and her nose was long and straight. But her most striking feature were her eyes. They didn't glitter like Lord's gray ones. They glowed, like onyx.

Standing five foot four—physical stature mattered on the lunar base, where resources were highly prized and the average height was five foot eight—she wore a simple Armstrong Lunar Base Lab overall that covered everything from her chin down, though Lord picked out her pleasing contours with an experienced eye. She carried only a small waistpac with saddlebag-like extensions designed to carry personal essentials.

Lord's SimAI recognized her and offered a drop-down of Dr. May's official biography. He waved it away. He wanted to hear it from her. You could learn a lot about a person by what they chose to tell—or withhold.

"Director Lord," she said, offering her hand as she reached his side. Her voice was warm, low, and lightly accented.

"Sam," he suggested, smiling as he took her hand.

"Saranya," she replied. The way she pronounced her name was like swallowing smooth chocolate. He could not help but think, *If all work were like this, we'd have a world of laborers.*

"Were you expecting a private escort?" he asked, indicating Ziv's shuttle.

"Yes," she answered thickly.

"I assume they—"

"Asked questions and were disappointed in the answers, yes," she said.

Lord smiled appreciatively. He gestured toward the exit and they moved forward, she in front, using the pylons, he behind, using the rails. Though it was quiet in here, save for the almost imperceptible buzz of the IC's electric field generators, they did not talk—not for security reasons, but because space etiquette had decided that it was bad manners to talk to the back of someone's head. Lord waited.

A moment later they were side by side in the wider corridor beyond the PriD area. The woman's shoulders were set, her back straight, her shoulders locked. This was not a woman who seemed willing to back down from a scrap.

"You spent time in Malaysia," he said.

She looked at him with surprise. "Is that in my biography?"

"Haven't read it," he admitted. "You drew out your tones and there was just a hint of a *mah* at the end of your sentences. I spent time in Hong Kong. That's a classic discourse particle in Chinese, Malaysian, and other Eastern dialects."

She gave him a respectful look and then her onyx eyes narrowed. "I wonder," she said thoughtfully.

"What?"

"If you're naturally curious or naturally an investigator," she said.

Lord was caught off-guard. He was so used to being himself that he didn't think of himself *as* FBI.

"You can decide that for yourself," Lord answered as they approached the first of the elevators. "But I promise you that where we are going will certainly make others curious."

"Where is that?" she asked.

He replied, "My quarters."

■■

Tucked in a deeply cushioned seat of Ziv Levy's private shuttle, Colonel Jack Franco stared out the window at the reflected stars on the Mylar sail of the *Empyrean*. He was still belted in with a shoulder harness, his arms floating idly over the open straps of the armrest.

Ziv sipped a vegetable drink from a squeeze bottle. "I'm the CHAI, but *your* eyes are the ones that look like little machines," he said.

"She was lying," Franco groused.

"And after all you did to get out there and meet her," the cybernetic human responded with his customary diffidence.

Franco peered directly into the Israeli's face. He didn't like the tea bag. He wanted to accuse him of using the media to play on the rest of the world's "new progressivism" toward SimAI and androids, but there wasn't time.

"Don't act like you wouldn't have benefited," Franco said.

"*If* your intel was correct," Ziv pointed out.

"It fits," he said angrily. "It all goddamn *fits*."

Franco looked back out the small window, continued to stare at the heavens without seeing them. He was picturing the woman's soft features, remembering her hard parting words.

"Thank you for the ride," she had said. "I wish I could have been more helpful to you."

"Maybe she'll soften a little while she's here," Ziv remarked. "Or maybe she'll respond better to a less heavy hand."

"Sam huking Lord?"

"Sam Lord, yes," Ziv replied with more respect than Franco was inclined to show him.

The CHAI flexed his fingers, which weighed more than twice that of the colonel's hands combined.

Franco wasn't listening. He was picturing the images he had seen from Japan—destruction so thick that it had created an offshore reef that had impacted the entire flow of the Kuroshio Current—appropriately, the Black Current—so that it diverted the southern-flowing Kamchatka Current toward the east. The models were already predicting gross upticks in the ferocious Santa Ana winds along the coast of California.

That pompous flyboy Lord doesn't have to worry about any of those bigger problems, Franco thought. *Zero-G only has to put out little fires. They deal with crimes not disasters.*

"Where are you, Colonel?" Ziv asked.

"Why did she want to talk to *him*?" Franco wondered aloud.

"Ah, obsessing."

"There has to be something I'm missing."

"Charm?" Ziv suggested. "I mean, she talked to him because Lord has bagfuls of that? Because he doesn't buy his dates from a holopop?"

"Some of us are busy working for a living," Franco replied. "Not posturing like our own self-made constellation the way Lord does."

"Some of you are impatient and chauvinistic," Ziv replied.

Franco didn't even hear the man. His mind was torn between the smug, interference-running Lord and the hated *Jade Star* and *Red Giant*. Under the best of circumstances, those shadowy enemy outposts loomed like intelligence black holes, information going in, nothing coming out. He had been working on Earth to change that. Up here, the threat from enemies that had more or less equal tactical footing seemed even more acute—and more frustrating. The Chinese station was big and serpentine and visible from the *Empyrean*. Franco wanted it.

"Still, it was worth a shot, talking to her," Ziv admitted, quietly sucking the last of his beverage.

This time Franco heard the man and nodded. It had been a calculated risk; asking the Israeli for a ride meant taking him along. But the DIA had been tracking Armstrong Base since it was constructed, and this unplanned trip by Dr. May, its *timing*, was extraordinary. Ziv knew that too and Franco was sure the tea bag was already formulating *his* next step—a step that would not involve Colonel Jack Franco.

I can live with that, Franco thought. *If the Mossad gets answers, we can do business.*

"Mr. Levy?"

It was the voice of the pilot. Amit Stein, "Frankenstein," was a fighter pilot with the Israeli Zroa HaAvir VeHahalal, the Air and Space Arm. He went down in a memorable test of the space plane *Kokhav yam—Starfish*—and rather than accept CHAI implants he wore his scars proudly.

"Yes, Amit," Ziv replied. "Tell the Drum that we are ready to depart the station. After Colonel Franco disembarks, which he is about to."

Franco wasn't insulted by the dismissal. It was Ziv's way. The man wanted to be in a relatively secure environment to contact Jerusalem, and a shuttle in Earth orbit was about as private as anyone could ask for these days.

Franco threw off his shoulder harness, pushed gently off the armrest, and floated up to the hatch.

"Thank you for this little adventure," Ziv said. "If nothing else, Dr. May is the loveliest scientist I've seen since Dr. Aharonovich replaced my eyes."

Once again, Franco did not reply. If the intelligence from the moon was correct, Dr. Saranya May represented just one thing: the key to the most powerful science ever devised.

Science that the Department of Defense should be running, not NASA.

EIGHT

D R. MAY SEEMED uncomfortable as they entered the elevator.
It was a tight fit, as ever, and not unpleasant to Lord. Dr. May
was too seasoned a spacefarer, too accustomed to small places to
be bothered by that. It was something else.

"Why your quarters?" she asked.

"They're relatively secure," Lord replied.

"Define 'relatively,'" the woman said.

"Easier if I show you," Lord replied.

"Let me ask that another way," Saranya said. "Why not the FBI
command center? I assume official business is conducted there?"

"There, or in one of the station bars," Lord said. "I wasn't authorized to share your debriefing with the staff."

"Don't you trust your own people?"

"Completely," Lord replied. "Why would you ask that?"

Saranya realized, too late, her error. This man *was* an investigator.
His little half-smile told her she'd just let slip the fact that she had reason
not to trust her *own* staff. Saranya closed her lips and said nothing more.

During the twenty-six-second ride, Adsila informed Lord that in
order to get access to Dr. May, Ziv's private craft had identified itself
to her shuttle using an *Empyrean* ID. That made it imperative for the
shuttle to meet Ziv's ship, which also happened to be before it met the

solar kite. That would have sliced twenty-nine minutes from Dr. May's travel time, in addition to the sixteen-minutes-faster flight time of Ziv's ship versus the solar kite.

Lord thanked Adsila with a text.

There were rules about impersonating an official vessel, and Israel was a signatory to the American Space Station Regulations—the unfortunately acronymed ASS-Regs, which invited derision and noncompliance. Lord's group was supposed to enforce them with heavy fines and possible imprisonment, but Adsila also found out that Ziv's privately built shuttle was registered in Switzerland, which did not have a space program and had not signed the document.

With the few seconds that remained in the ride, Lord took an opportunity to study his companion. Being up here, with him, had obviously not made her feel noticeably more secure. The lines of her lovely face were tense, her fingers were restless, and her breathing was rapid . . . though the latter could be the result of having to adjust to yet another variation in atmospheric pressure—Earth to hyperplane, hyperplane to Ziv's shuttle, Ziv's shuttle to the *Empyrean*—and her third form of gravity—Earth-normal, zero, now increasing centripetal—in under an hour. Biologists said it would take generations to find a balance and possible remedy for those changes, and even then they didn't know if it would come from Earth-born or space-born children. So far, the nineteen children born in American space—including two at Armstrong Base—had adjusted worse to gravity than Earth children to low and zero-gravity. After brief visits to Earth, none of them had gone back—except, reportedly, three Russian children who had suffered muscular degeneration after prolonged visits to Earth. Lord was awed and a little frightened to see the birth of the newest human species since the Cro-Magnon, what scientists were already referring to as *Homo galaxicus*.

Lord and Saranya changed elevators, moving horizontally along Radial Arm Six. This was one of two wings for permanent residents. The FBI had their quarters near a one-g microgravity center; scientists and engineers occupied similar quarters in Radial Arm Five along with

Stanton's team from the commander to maintenance—including the Gardener. Guests occupied Radial Arm Four along with the laundry, recycling, and recreational areas. A robot cart came by to collect clothes and trash each morning and returned the former at night.

Emerging, Saranya appreciated the ease of their strides here and she enjoyed the abundant installations of real flowers, as well as the haptic-voxel gardens and parklands spread across the floor and walls. Mt. Fuji was depicted in one of them, another tribute to the stricken nation. Lord watched as her eyes turned down. This was becoming more intriguing by the minute.

Her avoidance of the image was not the only sign that Dr. Saranya May had a dark, probably dangerous secret. The flowers had more vibrant energy than she did. Something was haunting her, something fresh that she had not yet been able to process. Being here, maybe feeling safe, she was beginning to lower her guard—the fear of being watched, overheard, followed—but also her façade as well. The woman walking beside Lord suddenly, unexpectedly seemed to have more life in her, from her eyes to her light step.

The unique IC/encephalogram link popped the door to Lord's quarters. The light came on automatically and he gestured for Dr. May to enter first. Although the studio unit was small, only 290 square feet—which was fifty more than most cabins—it seemed almost luxurious to her. He had decorated it like a handmade log cabin, and even though the wall was comprised of haptic-display surfaces it was quite convincing . . . even the view of the patio and changing sunlight on the far wall.

Beside it, on a real saddle rack, was a volumetric-display saddle.

"That's . . . interesting," she remarked.

"It's the saddle my pioneer ancestor Isaiah owned," he said. "It would have eaten up my entire clothing and toiletry allotment to bring up the real one, so"—he shrugged—"it's that, for now. The original is at my cabin in the Sierra Nevadas."

She seemed intrigued. "Was it difficult to leave that for this?"

"Well, I do a lot less shooting up here," he admitted. "I hope that doesn't offend you—"

"Not a bit," she replied. "Whenever I'm on Earth, I get in some bowhunting in the Garo Hills, along the Simsang River."

He smiled. "Artemis."

She smiled too—for the first time. He didn't have to explain. The Greek goddess of hunting was also the goddess of the moon.

"Something to drink?" Lord asked. "And by that I mean water or fruit juice made right here in our Agro."

"No," she said quickly. It sounded abrupt even to her. "Thank you," she added. "Sorry, Mr. Levy and Colonel Franco were overly insistent that I try some fruit drink on the shuttle."

"You refused, obviously."

"Why obviously?"

"Because those Haifa Cocktails are enhanced for CHAIs," he said. "Or, put another way, they're spiked. They pack more energy in there for their mechanisms in an arrangement that looks a lot like ethanol—about a hundred proof. But, clearly, you are not wasted."

"Wasted?"

"Drunk," Lord said. "An old term. That stuff's like kerosene rocket fuel."

"Ah."

Lord offered her the one spartan chair with its padded cushion. She accepted it with a gracious nod and sat with an elegance that he had not seen enough of up here. Still achy from his adventure in the elevator shaft, he gratefully if not gracefully flopped on a corner of the small bed. Before Dr. May could say anything, Lord held up a finger. She hesitated and shot him a quizzical look.

He pointed to a wind chime that hung in the center of the room. He touched a button in his IC drop-down and a vent in the ceiling started to whisper. The chime began to sing.

"That does *not* look like it's from your mountain cabin," she said, admiring the design.

"It was made for me in Hong Kong," he told her. "Hand-carved wood top with chimes made from ancient Chinese coins and little bronze bells, hand-selected for the most pleasing tones. Chimes are actually big among my team."

"Earth-feel?" she asked, using a term common to spacers. It meant that something up here reminded them fondly of something down there.

"That's what outsiders think," Lord said. "The truth is, if anyone tries to listen in, to electronically enhance our conversation, they'll get *1812 Overture*–level cannons ringing in their ears, drowning us out."

Saranya seemed almost wistful now. Her expression seemed to say, *If only all solutions were so simple.*

Lord settled back against the wall and waited.

"I want to trust you," she said at last. "I very much do."

"Thank you," Lord said. "I prefer that to 'I trust you because I have no choice, I'm stuck.'"

"I am that too," she said.

"Say what you want, if you want, when you want," Lord told her.

Saranya smiled again, relaxed a little more. She was silent after that, as though uncertain where to begin.

"Can I take your waistpac?" Lord offered, extending a hand.

"I'm all right," she said. "Thanks."

The woman wasn't going to hand anything to anyone, not an accessory *or* information. Despite his calming words, Lord decided to give her a gentle push—for her own sake as much as his.

"So," he said invitingly, his hands open wide, "what can I do to help you? Beyond making sure you are safe?"

Saranya hesitated. "What have you been told?" she asked.

He repeated everything Al-Kazaz had said, which was very little. When he was finished, the scientist's eyes continued to show hesitation. Her lips were still emphatically shut.

"Dr. May, Saranya, I've promised not to probe, to interrogate," Lord went on. "But you came here for protection—so anything you can share will help me do that."

"I'm not sure," she said.

"Sorry?"

"Why I came here, to *Empyrean*. It all seems so hopeless now."

"What does?"

She regarded him, her eyes reflecting that hopelessness. "One of the most secure and isolated facilities ever constructed—my laboratory—had apparently been breached. I couldn't trust anything electronic, not even my IC."

"All right," Lord said, carefully coaxing her. "So you went to Earth."

"I went to Earth to—" She stopped herself, like her brain had hit a wall, like the words were too heinous to utter.

"To try to prevent what happened in Japan?" Lord pressed, just a little more.

She turned from him, coiling a little into herself. "I didn't know about that," she said. "I didn't."

"But you feared something like that."

"Not imminently. God, not like this."

"You knew it could happen, though."

She grew even smaller.

"All right," Lord said soothingly, holding up his hands. "Backing off."

The irony of having half wished for a new cosmic challenge was not lost on Lord. Apparently, he had one here—full blown.

The chimes rang out like a symphony of anvils echoing across a plain. "As much as things change form, their nature remains the same."

Lord caught her general meaning. "The new is just the old, repackaged?"

She nodded. "I came to space to escape the limitations of the Earth. Limitations followed, only they took a different form."

"Every frontier has unexpected obstacles. When I built my mountain cabin, I read up on the history. My God, the first time that old fur trapper Jebediah Smith ran up against the Sierra Nevadas in California? He must've fallen to his knees and both praised and cursed the god that made those mountains. But he went ahead just the same. You've seen the wilderness, on Earth *and* up here. You know."

The woman nodded again, slowly.

Lord eased a little closer, spoke a little more softly. "That's why we're here, in a log cabin, with a saddle. Curiosity has to trump fear. Activity over inertia. Progress over entropy."

"Progress," she said, her voice peppered with sudden distaste for the word. "I became a scientist to expand what we know. Instead—"

Another hard stop. Lord regarded her carefully, trying to find a way in. Words? Looks? A touch? A walk?

A sneak attack, he decided.

"What *is* your area?" Lord asked solicitously. "What do you study on the moon?"

The wall fell like it was painted on a scrim. "You really didn't look me up?" she asked with surprise.

"Don't like the IC," he said.

"Why?"

"Same reason I disliked flight simulators," he replied. "They're a useful tool but, in the end, they're a simulacrum of experience—the same way the IC is a façade of actually knowing things. Wall after wall after wall of cold information."

"I understand," she said. "One of my professors would only use a blackboard. He said he didn't feel like a physicist without chalk dust in his beard."

"So . . . you're a physicist."

Her eyes grew guarded. "Do you never stop?"

Part of him wanted to say, *I cannot afford to! Millions of lives have been lost.* Answers were needed and this was the best way he knew to get them, carefully but without retreat. Instead, he said simply, "I guess not."

She remained tight and was once again very guarded. "Director Lord, I do believe you've turned me into that fur trapper you spoke of."

"How so?"

"You've got me half impressed, half worried."

"Why?"

"I would have thought you'd want all the information you could get as soon as you could get it."

"I much prefer this"—he moved a hand back and forth between them—"to a cold tutorial. I thrive on dialogue, nuance. When you're used to hearing people, not seeing them, in a headset, words become an anchor." He smiled. "I was never very good in school. Couldn't study worth a damn. But what I learned on the playground, interacting with people, using my hands to do things—priceless."

The scientist began to relax a little. "Astrophysics," she replied.

Lord knew that *she* knew she had just made his point. Her living, face-to-face answer, the way she caressed the word, had told him that it was not just her profession but her life.

"So you look outward," he said with the amiable charity of a victor. "Cosmology? Relativistic jets? The supervoid?"

"What do you know about those?" she asked, interested and a little impressed.

"Only what I've overheard in the comm," he admitted. "My science agent, McClure, is a major teacher."

She hesitated, considered her previous surrender, then replied, "I went to the moon to do particle research. Neutrinos and dark matter. I really can't say more than that."

"About your research?"

She nodded.

"Even with—" He circled a finger overhead, at the chimes.

"It isn't just a matter of security, though that's essential," she confided. "It's also about . . ." Her voice trailed off and she struggled to restart it; her mouth refused.

"Finding solutions," Lord said, interpreting. "You want to know exactly what happened and how."

She did not respond.

"It's okay to be scared," he assured her. "It's not okay to feel guilty. You didn't do this."

"It's more than that," she replied. "Have you ever been in a situation where you are the only solution to a problem? Where it is all on your shoulders?"

"A couple of times," Lord admitted.

"Then you know what doubt is like, what that pressure does," she said.

"Actually, I don't," he said. "I've experienced fear, concern for my colleagues, respect for an enemy. But I have never doubted that I would do my utmost."

"Did your training give you that?" she asked.

"No," he said with a smile. "It's my nature."

"I see. Very bold. I am not." She studied the serene face before her. "Have you ever been on a trail that you built in a frontier that is utterly black, with no map?"

"Not yet," he said. "But personally, I'd welcome the challenge. Would you? *Do* you?"

Her stoic non-answer was an answer. But she still hadn't told him what he really needed to know: why she needed a bodyguard.

"Let's talk simple logistics then," he went on. "Does your presence here have a shelf life?"

"It does," she answered that one quickly. "The Armstrong resupply shuttle that took me to Earth will pick me up on the way back to the moon. The ship will stop here to pick me up"—she checked her IC— "in just over three hours."

"Do you *want* to go back to the moon?"

"I do. And I must."

"But you won't tell me why."

Once again, she hesitated. Lord waited. He had promised he wouldn't push because he hoped that right now Dr. May was going to push herself. Lord had been on the ground with enough pilots who had dropped their first ordnance for a kill, who had blown up the wrong building, who saw children in the car of the right enemy, to know what the desire to unburden one's soul looked like, felt like. This was a woman who desperately wanted to talk to *someone*.

"It's more than work," she finally confided. "It's what else might happen if I don't get back."

"What else *might* happen?" he asked as calmly as he could. "Are you saying this isn't a onetime event?"

She took a breath and held it before exhaling. "You said before this is about 'finding solutions.' You were correct. But not just about the theft of data. It is about the possibility of disaster on a scale unprecedented in human experience. It is about weaponized science. That's why I went to see your colleagues in Washington. I could not remain on Armstrong Base, knowing what I knew, and I cannot go back there alone. I need eyes and ears I can trust while I make that chart into the darkness, finish the road I started."

And then the proverbial sun burned through the mist for Sam Lord. He suddenly understood what his place was in all of this. She had been feeling him out, seeing if she could trust him, and overcoming her natural reticence to talk about her work; now he was going to *have* to press her for details. All of them.

What she'd just told Lord—why Al-Kazaz had sent her to him—was that she needed a bodyguard.

Sam Lord was going to the moon.

NINE

SINCE ARRIVING AT the *Empyrean*, Adsila Waters had felt detached from her home world. She kept telling herself that it would pass, that she had only been here a few weeks, but it only got worse.

The feeling here was akin to the experience she had every time she crossed the country by jet: those specks crawling on ribbons of roads; those buildings that barely dented the clouds. *They seem insignificant. What impact do they have, could they have, on me?*

Up here, the sensation was exponential and she wondered at the wisdom of having an office that investigated matters that impacted a globe whose sole acknowledgments of human activity were tiny lights at night; grand landmarks like the Great Wall of China; and the persistent industrial haze that hung over India, China, and Pan-Persia like a campfire in a grotto. Indeed, this was the argument psychologists had made about the difficulties faced by babies born in space. She'd had a heavy dose of it in sensitivity training before coming up here: each successive generation had trouble enough connecting with their parents, grandparents, and great-grandparents. It was one thing when music and clothes were outdated. But a planet?

As she sat at her desk watching news feeds from around the globe and reports from field offices, Adsila was grateful for the one great thread that connected her with the past: her spiritual heritage. That was something she found she had in common with Director Lord. Even though their ancestors may well have fought one another, they had a sense of honored continuity—he through his ancestor Isaiah, she through her Cherokee blood.

She had been raised, of course, respecting the structure of the Cherokee Nation—how the principal chief wielded executive power, the tribal council oversaw legislative power, and the Cherokee Nation Judicial Appeals Tribunal was caretaker of judicial power. On Earth, that mattered; up here, it did not seem to.

But the Cherokee belief system? The fact that all things were connected both physically and spiritually; that was vital, proud, relevant.

"Did everyone see that?" Grainger asked everyone in the command center.

The voice of the associate executive assistant director was urgent, surprised.

"Yes, they're using *Fei-Tengs* on the water," McClure said. "What are they, nuts?"

The agent was referring to the *Fei-Teng, Jing-Que, Zhi-Dao, Zha-Dan,* China's guided bombs. They were old-style ballistics, big and brawny and used to create impressive dimensional images when shared over IC. The live feeds—interrupting all the major newscasts—showed the explosives turning the debris that was clogging up the waters off northeastern Japan into a wall of fire.

"That's not just a visual," Adsila remarked. "That's a statement."

"Not following, EAD?" McClure said.

"The yin and yang of Chinese philosophy," she said. "Water in the morning, fire at night. Beijing is breaking up the detritus, they can defend their action that way—but they're also signaling that they can match whatever was done and whoever did it."

"How do we know *they* didn't do it?" McClure asked.

"We don't," Adsila remarked, watching as the flames reached very nearly to the low-hanging clouds. "In which case this is a bookend. China controls the light with water, the night with fire."

"They may have *planned* this?" McClure said.

"We are only speculating here," Adsila cautioned. "You have ideas, you put them out there."

"That is sick and opportunistic, if it's true," Agent Abernathy remarked.

Everyone fell silent as views from the *Empyrean* registered the line of fire burning on the North Pacific. It was massive and had to be terrifying to the survivors who had already seen so much.

Adsila's mind moved back to her own thoughts, which were an anchor in the face of any adversity. Whether she was on Earth or in space, Adsila often thought about the story of Creation. The narrative was home to her. Roots and stability. So was the voice that came with it. She remembered when her great-grandfather had first recited the tale, rocking in a creaky old chair beside her bed. He told it over and over throughout her childhood, continuing the oral tradition of the tribe, until every word was known to her.

"The Great Spirit *Unetlanvhi*, the 'Apportioner,' created Earth," he had said with confidence but also with awe. "During those seven days, only the owl and the cougar managed to keep their eyes open, watching with wonder what was unfolding . . . the formation of the land, of the sky, of the water. That is why these animals are at home in the dark, their eyes keen and far-seeing. They saw, and bowed to, the sacred water spider who brought our people to Earth in a large basket on its great back. You will know them all," he had told her, "know them more deeply than any who have come before."

Adsila was not certain how much her great-grandfather's belief influenced her choices, or whether the spirit of the owl and cougar were indeed guiding her. But she did know this: when she first saw the design for the *Empyrean*, when she noted its profound resemblance to pendants of the legendary water spider with its many arms and legs and towering basket on top, she knew that this was where she belonged.

The EAD refocused on the data but she wasn't responding with her usual efficiency. She glanced at the time; it was nearly 10:00 p.m. This had been a long shift—fourteen hours—and unusually intense. Maybe it was time to flutter—a youth-expression she had resisted, a conflating of "fly under the radar," but which accurately described what she needed to do: fly, get out of the command center, not think about what some scrap of information might have to do with Japan. Besides, who knew what Lord was busy picking up from their new arrival? Whatever it might be, he wasn't sharing it with her. There was no point thinking too hard about situations when she didn't have all available information.

Adsila rose slowly.

"Going off, EAD?" Grainger asked.

Adsila nodded. "I'm two hours over RCS," she said. "Things seem quiet and I want to *not* think for a bit."

Recommended Command Shift was twelve hours, and it could only be extended in the event of an emergency. As long as the ranking officer on-site could be reached, time off was not only recommended, it was mandated.

"Understood. I'll be here awhile longer," the AEAD told her. "Press conference."

"Will the Japanese newswoman be there?" Adsila asked.

Grainger nodded. "She's going to interview the chairman of the *Jade Star*. I want to see that."

"Very good. I'm going to the lounge," Adsila said. "I need a roomer."

"It's pretty crowded in all the locations," Grainger told her, checking. "Oxygen intake is way up. They had to break out the old perchlorate burners to freshen the air a bit."

"Chatty damn tourists," Adsila said over her shoulder.

The ship was designed to recycle exhaled carbon dioxide as oxygen via the regenerative fuel cells, but that couldn't prevent the air from becoming stuffy.

Grainger punched in a code. "Ma'am, roomer supplies in all the bars are out. I reserved you one can at the Scrub. They're almost gone too."

"Thank you," Adsila said, gracious but also grateful.

The EAD preferred the mushroom tablets produced in Agro, but electronic cannabis sticks were more popular and weed took priority over the mild hallucinogens—though both were several rungs lower than the production of food. Neither was permitted outside the lounge for reasons that Kristine Cavanaugh had made plain and no one was allowed to have more in their system than the lounge electroencephalogram decreed—technology that had not been operating in the reception area due to the lofty status of most of the guests. The Cloud's lithium sensors peered into each patron's dose levels, made the bartender privy to the results, and sealed the door against anyone who had overindulged.

As she headed out, the young pan-gender shut down some of the feeds, but not all of them. Adsila still wanted to be plugged in and accessible to the data here, to Lord's IC, and to major event feeds.

No one on the Empyrean *was ever really off-duty,* she thought as she turned down the corridor. But they did try to maintain a semblance of terrestrial structure.

That was challenging in an environment that had to ride daylight to stay above the Earth. Chronometrically, the hours on *Empyrean* were keyed to Central Standard Time on Earth—to Houston, where NASA's Johnson Spacecraft Center *Empyrean* Command was based. And biorhythmic balance was maintained by mandatory time in darkness—something provided in abundance at the biggest and most popular of the lounges among the station's guest residences.

The largest *Empyrean* lounge was the Scrub, a nickname from astronaut slang to describe any program that not only had many failures but particularly annoying ones. People went here to bond, to commiserate, to wash away the old day with chemicals and optimism. It was consciously designed to be the opposite of the blazing gold expanse of the station—dark, mellow, muted with perpetual nighttime.

The place was serve-yourself. It was kept supplied by a young man named Stephen who held an advanced degree in aerospace engineering; but so did many more capable people. Up here he was one of two stockers, employed to run everything from recycled toilet paper to the lavatories to fresh linings for the docking-bay foot restraints. In the Scrub, Stephen's job was to dole out the limited supplies of alcohol, to provide fresh cannabis and mushrooms for the electronic delivery systems, and to call station security in case people tried to get around their EEG-mandated limits.

On the way, in a deserted stretch of corridor, Adsila had shifted to her male nature. She had seen the male eyes, felt the heat when she had gone to the reception. With so many guests onboard, most of them men, she didn't want the attention.

As Adsila stepped into the unusually spacious lounge—the most Earth-like room on the *Empyrean*—his eyes scanned the place. It was something he had seen Lord do when they came here their first day aloft. Lord had taken a moment to look, not at his IC but at his surroundings. He'd let information flood in, stored in his mind and senses. Adsila knew he had done that because, later, he told his number two to get a warrant to search the cabin of one of Stanton's security officers.

"Yes, sir. Why, sir?" Adsila had asked.

"Because he was having trouble moving his eyes through his IC," Lord said.

"And, sir?"

"And he kept moving his head to focus when he *did* get what he wanted," Lord said. "He has an eggbeater. That could be dangerous for us all."

That was FBI slang for an EEG-beater, an illegal device that interfered with the cortical electric field to circumvent alcohol and recreational narcotic limits. Its users also swore that the device enhanced the high it concealed. The warrant was obtained, the search was executed, the eggbeater was discovered in an earring, and the man was sent back to Earth. Adsila vividly recalled the conversation in the command center, where Stanton came in person to give Lord a dressing-down.

He failed.

"You will bring matters involving my staff, my personnel, to me personally," Stanton had said, then reminded him who ran the station and that "senile judgments" would not be tolerated.

Lord had listened politely, respectful of the man's position, standing classically "at ease," hands behind his back, chest out. When Stanton was finished, Lord dropped his arms to his sides, stepped closer to the brawny station commander, and replied, "My squadron fought a war in the skies over Mexico to stop problems like that and see that EEG law was enacted." Then he'd stepped closer still and said sharply, firmly, "This 'senile' old man doesn't make backroom deals for abusers."

Stanton left in silent rage and no one spoke—until Adsila had said, "I see, sir."

And Adsila did. As the Luddite Party on Earth put it, "More eyes, less IC."

Adsila wasn't quite ready to go that far, but the EAD managed to find a balance.

Entering the Scrub, he recognized half the people crowded at the bar and tables. They were regulars who pushed their limitations to the limit. They were the ones who had managed to pass the unforgiving psych tests to get up here but who couldn't escape themselves no matter how far they traveled. In fairness, once the novelty wore off and the adventure wore thin, being up here broke a lot of good people physically, mentally, and emotionally. Without the distractions of terrestrial activity, space left them naked. Unable to look out, unwilling to look in, they came to the Scrub to anesthetize themselves.

In the center of the Scrub was a small area called the Cockpit. It was a private room whose maximum of four occupants could choose to keep their party private by turning the walls opaque. Right now the walls were transparent, to show the room filled with Colonel Jack Franco, Sheik Kattan, Fraas Dircks, and General Arturo Hierra. Only Kattan and Dircks were using. Franco and Hierra were listening, though Franco was either bored or watching for someone since his eyes kept moving to the wall, toward the door, before skipping back to the table.

Never really off-duty, Adsila thought again—not himself, not the crew, not the DIA, not anyone. Space wasn't a harsh mistress; people were.

Adsila caught Stephen motioning to him from a dark corner. The EAD walked over, weaving through the close-packed tables and stools bolted to the floor for stability.

"I saw Grainger's reservation for you, held your spot as soon as it opened," Stephen said, though without his customary wink.

Adsila nodded with appreciation. It was actually not his spot but the FBI's preferred roost, a small table with two chairs in the farthest corner of the space. It allowed for a certain amount of privacy but also allowed Adsila to discreetly observe almost anyone else in the place.

"Awful what happened in Japan," Stephen said as they moved around the bar. "I can't stop thinking about all those people. What the hell is going on?"

"Still investigating," Adsila said.

"They don't think it was natural," he went on. "Most of the newtiaee say it was some kind of weapon."

"Fear triggers IC searches and drops."

"Sir, if that's true, my IC drop-down time is gonna be off the charts," he said. "I can't stop plugging into all the feeds."

It didn't sound like Stephen was fishing for information, though Adsila had been trained to suspect everyone. It seemed as if he just wanted to talk. That was fairly common up here. Psychologists called it "flocking," the need for people in space to find some kind of biological anchor, like birds in flight. The kinds of cliques that were frowned upon Earthside were actually encouraged up here.

"It's weird how I used to think we were so vulnerable up here and so safe down there," he said. "Error! Error!"

"That's true," Adsila said. There were more safeguards here, backups to backups, than there could ever be on Earth. When things failed, as they did with Kristine Cavanaugh or Stanton's eggbeater, it was usually because of people.

The EAD sat, his eyes settling on a small concave cup in the center of the table—the can. In it lay a coiled tube, a nasal prong, and what looked like a brown lozenge. Above it, hovering in his IC, was the EEG notice: two-lozenge limit. Adsila did not intend to go that high. He only wanted one . . . not an escape, just a whisper from the past.

With skilled fingers, he unwound the tube, unwrapped the sanitized plugs, clipped them to both nostrils, and dropped the tablet into a slot in the can. The cannabis, in aerated form, began to flow and he inhaled deeply, holding it in his chest as if it were sweet desert air.

At night, he thought, shutting his eyes for just a moment so he could picture the vista from his childhood. The stars brilliant above, twinkling brightly, winking, beckoning—not fierce and sharp as they were up here. Back then, at home, there was an atmosphere to spread the light, to turn a sterile mass of stars into a mass of wonder. He thought he could hear the sounds of coyotes rustling in the scrub, of an owl, *his* owl, hooting the story of Creation. Now there was a campfire, warm and friendly, crackling . . . or was that a cougar moving through dry underbrush?

It was time to open his eyes.

Adsila came back immediately, feeling refreshed. He realized how stiffly he was sitting in the chair and relaxed. He looked out into the darkness, eyes fully adjusted—*more* than adjusted, thanks to the can— seeking the body language of anyone like him, anyone who wanted to explore rather than to wallow.

His eyes skirted the central private room, though he caught Franco's head turned to the door for a moment, unmoving. Ziv Levy had just strode in, like a titan, though he didn't bother to take in the room. He maneuvered his large frame through the lounge, past the Cockpit, toward the bar and past it.

His straight-ahead shoulders and direct eyes said he was coming to Adsila's table. He stopped briefly to ask, "May I," then swung into the chair anyway.

"It's a free room," Adsila replied flatly. The Cherokee continued to breathe through his nose, working at softening the sudden feeling of being stalked, trapped. He folded his arms on the table and leaned forward, his glossless eyes narrowing.

"Well, but there *are* certain protocols about joining station regulars," Ziv acknowledged. "Especially for us *zareems*."

"Hebrew for 'outsider,'" Adsila said, reading the automatic translation.

"That's right," Ziv said with practiced unconcern.

The CHAI's eyes took a subtle turn through the rest of the club. His enhanced vision picked out the eyes that snuck distrusting or hateful looks at the table. "I wonder who that's for?" he thought aloud.

"Who what's for?" Adsila asked.

Ziv leaned forward too. "The prejudice. Can't you feel it?"

"I've learned to ignore it."

"I wonder if it's for the tea bag or the panny. Probably both."

Adsila sat back slightly. "Don't use those," he said.

"They're stupid labels coined by frightened people," he replied.

"I said don't."

"I'd be willing to bet something," Ziv went on.

Adsila didn't respond.

Undeterred, Ziv leaned even closer. "I'll bet you that the first *Homo sapiens* had a disparaging term for the Neanderthals," he said. "It was probably something like 'browheads' or 'shaggies.' Or whatever the grunting equivalent to that would be, maybe 'oo-oos' or some drooling sound."

Ziv made the sound, drawing on the echo in his artificial larynx. In spite of himself, Adsila laughed.

"There!" Ziv said triumphantly. "Colonel Franco is wrong."

"Often. What about this time?"

"About Samuel Lord's team," he said. "The rest of you *do* have a sense of humor!"

Adsila's laugh became a knowing grin. This man was as transparent as the cockpit glass: he was trying to align himself with Adsila against the FBI's natural rival, the Defense Intelligence Agency. The EAD didn't bite.

"The Cherokee have a word for people like Franco, for everyone like him," he said with a dismissive cock of his head toward the room. "*Ukshana.*"

"Critics?" Ziv wondered, unable to find a translation in his organic or data memory.

"Close," Adsila said. "Assholes."

Ziv tapped a finger on the table. It sounded like he was wearing a thimble. "Is that you talking or the can?"

"Does it matter?"

"Not really," Ziv admitted.

"How did you know about me anyway?" Adsila asked. "That I was here. No, scratch that," he went on quickly. "*Why* did you know about me? Why did you come to this table?"

Ziv continued tapping. "As I said, we're fellow outsiders."

"You think we're the same?" Adsila said, astonished but sounding almost offended.

"No," Ziv answered patiently. "My—*unique situation,* let us call it, was the result of a misfortune. Yours is the result of planning. Yet to the world and those off-world, whether they say it or not, we are freaks."

"Are you one of those? Not a freak, I mean—a self-hating freak?"

"Not at all."

"I'm not sure," Adsila said. "All that bravado."

"I was like that, always," Ziv said quickly and apparently in earnest. "I can show you the recordings."

"No, thank you."

"And you know, my assessment of me wasn't *my* judgment," Ziv went on.

"What are you even *saying*?" Adsila asked.

"That everyone is unique in some way." The tapping stopped and Ziv's unshining, squidlike eyes pinned his companion. "The point I wanted to make was, we are the same in that people treat us differently. That has typically made bedfellows of different people, uniting them."

Adsila recoiled slightly at the word *bedfellows,* the implication, until he read the definition in his IC. It wasn't a proposition, Ziv did not necessarily mean it to be taken literally. Adsila winked the word away.

"That is a fine theory, not always practical," Adsila replied. "I'm Cherokee. If we had united with the Apache, with the Cheyenne, with the Sioux, instead of fighting amongst one another—"

"There would be thirteen or so United States and a mighty Native American confederacy," Ziv replied. "You've made my point exactly. I said 'typically,' not 'always.' And you would agree that the benefits outweigh the negatives."

Adsila slumped a little. He had been manipulated—very, very skillfully. He continued to breathe in the cannabis vapors.

And the eyes of the CHAI continued to stare in their oily way. "Tell me about you," he said. "Your parents."

"You mean, why did they make me pan?" he asked.

"It is not a casual choice," he said.

"No. It was something they considered strongly, in consultation with their own parents, grandparents, and tribal elders."

"And psychologists?" Ziv said. "I had to get their blessing before major body parts were replaced."

"Yes, but for guidance only," Adsila said. "Thanks to the Sex and Gender Act of 2022, the wishes of a birth parent cannot be countermanded. My parents believed it would be a gift, the power of the medicine man to shift his shape expressed in spirit *and* flesh."

"Has it been that?" Ziv asked. "A gift?"

"That's a stupid question *and* a little too familiar," Adsila replied flatly.

"Again, I'm sorry—the truth is, I'm genuinely interested."

"I'm *me*," Adsila said as if he hadn't spoken. "One individual, just like every other holistic being on- or off-planet. You wouldn't ask a person of color or some other kind of gen-en the same question."

"Maybe, maybe not, though genetic engineering to target hereditary diseases isn't quite the same as pan-genderism," Ziv remarked. "You have to admit that."

"I don't." Adsila pulled the clip from his nose. "And I've had enough of you. I'm not a disease—"

"I didn't say that—not at all."

"It sounded very *much* like that."

"It wasn't," Ziv said conclusively. He reached out and took the man's hand. "It wasn't that *at all.*"

Adsila jerked his hand free but he didn't leave. Ziv was no amateur. He had probably been counting on Adsila's female center to respond to his touch, which was truly electric; to like it enough, to be *intrigued* enough to convince the heterosexual male side of him not to go.

Adsila still couldn't tell whether Ziv was being sincere or if he were after something else. But he was right about one thing. This was the first time in a long time he had had the opportunity to talk about gender with a truly interested and engaged party.

He found himself agreeing with Ziv's assessment: *Because the CHAI and I are both outsiders.*

People around the Scrub were no longer just glancing at the pair of them, they were openly watching. Liberated by the can, Adsila's voice had obviously been louder than he had imagined.

"Let's get out of here," he said abruptly.

"Where . . . and why?" Ziv asked. It wasn't a refusal.

Adsila stood and shifted. In just a few moments, an arrestingly attractive woman with owlish eyes and nails like talons was looking down at him.

"Coming?" was all she said.

With that, Adsila Waters left the lounge, followed by Ziv Levy as well as every eye in the Scrub, male and female alike. She did not notice—no one did—the look the CHAI exchanged with Colonel Franco as he departed.

TEN

THE COSMOS COULD *be a kick in the head,* Lord thought.

He was sitting in his cabin with a beautiful scientist and two matters orbited turbulently in his head like binary stars: how elegant and desirable Dr. May was, and the absolutely unrelated matter of all the personal and professional unknowns and wonder represented by a trip to Armstrong Air Force Base.

From the Earth to the moon, from Hell's Kitchen to Heaven's Keyhole, he thought, using the popular nickname for the base. That was more than a kick in the head. It was a miracle.

At the moment, however, the mission was far more elusive than the woman. He reflected on the familiar territory.

Sam Lord had been married, once. What he and Consuela had in common was a love of speed. They had met by chance on line for the Cyclone, the classic roller coaster at Coney Island, when he was eighteen and just about to start flight training and she was seventeen and about to leave the Bronx to attend Princeton, after skipping her junior year of high school.

It was 1988, an innocent time before texting and viral videos, when people still communicated over landlines and drank cow's milk, when smoking cigarettes was permitted in restaurants and bars, when artificial hearts couldn't successfully replace real ones, when cancer still killed millions.

They had loved hard and fast and married three months later, when Lord was briefly back in New York on leave from Randolph AFB, Texas. They spent their honeymoon on a speedboat in Long Island Sound. By the time Lord became an officer, Consuela Baez had become a mother, twice, and a meteorologist. She wrote the models for worldwide glacial retreat that became the basis for the United Nations Framework Convention on Climate Change initiative in the North Pole.

She had also fallen in love with a coworker, an oceanographer from Canada and former Olympic bobsledder. If the Poly Law had been passed then, Lord might have agreed to what became euphemistically known as a "time share" among triads. But it was 1997 and the legislation was still nearly three decades away.

The couple divorced, and Lord tried very hard thereafter not to hate the sight of ice. He was glad that he couldn't hate Consuela, whose love remained the dearest he had ever known and which he still cherished. But it taught him a valuable lesson that had served him well for just over a half century: when it came to women, lovers, and coworkers alike—flyovers only, don't cut the corn, don't buzz the sunbathers.

Don't get in too deep.

But depth came in many forms, wore different faces, and he knew when his safe cruising altitude was in danger of decay. Consuela had never been afraid of anything. His female pilots all had the right stuff—possibly "righter," since they had to be better than their male colleagues. Up here, Janet Grainger was smart and alert and Adsila Waters was tougher as a woman than she was as a man. His last lover, General Erin Astoria—whom he had finally been able to date when he resigned his commission—not only knew it was just a fling, she preferred it. And in Isaiah's saddle, no less.

Lord could lead in war and command in peace. He flew with women who were in separate aircraft. But closely bodyguard a frightened woman and keep that goal and that goal alone front and center? That was terra incognita, undiscovered country.

The universe is not supposed to respect your comfort zone, he reminded himself, rising from the bed as he weighed what to do next. Worse, Lord suspected that the universe, keen and wily, was just getting started.

"I have a suggestion," he said.

Saranya looked over expectantly, though there was still something taut and guarded about her. For the previous minute or so she had been looking down, then around, twice resisting the urge to finger in to her IC. Being cut off from her work, from her colleagues, from anything familiar was obviously making things worse for the scientist.

"Actually, I have a better suggestion," he said.

"I'm sorry?"

"My first suggestion was going to be that I visit the cafeteria and pick up food," he said. "The second suggestion—isn't."

Her expression became wary. "I'm confused."

"It's not what I think you think," he assured her. "We're apparently going to be working together, so unless you're really hungry—"

"No," she said. "I'm not, at all."

"Good." Lord smiled. "Then I want to play a little game, kind of an intellectual exercise."

She crossed her legs—innocently—and gave him her attention. Lord couldn't decide which of those was more attractive.

"I told you about old Isaiah and his spirit of adventure," Lord said. "My entire family has that. Generations. My grandfather was a police officer in New York—Sam Lord, my namesake. My father flew helicopters around the city for tourists. Now . . . as a kid, I had no trouble going up with my dad, soaring over the rivers, circling the *Statue of Liberty* at an angle that made me feel like I was going to fall out. But my grandfather?" He laughed. "Saranya, I couldn't sit in his squad car when he was off-duty, once every Saturday, sharing a pizza down by the Brooklyn Bridge, without feeling like I wanted to die."

"Why?" she asked.

"Why indeed?" he repeated. "I was bored! I loved the old man, but, Jesus, he didn't talk. Except about baseball, and I wasn't a fan. And he turned the squawk box—the police radio—off so I couldn't even hear what crimes were happening. Anyway, after a couple of years of this I finally told my father about it. I must've been—nine, ten, when I fessed up. I actually felt ashamed."

"To admit you had this problem?" she asked.

He shook his head. "To say something that might hurt my grandfather." Lord eased forward a little. "So: here's the game part, where you learn and I learn. I want you to guess what my father said to me."

Saranya's onyx eyes seemed to come alive. She nodded slightly as she considered the matter.

"Uh-uh—don't think too hard," Lord urged. "Just say what comes into your head."

"All right," she said. "He said, 'Don't be ashamed of how you feel.'"

"Good, but that wasn't it."

"'Always tell the truth,'" she guessed. "A good lesson for a nine- or ten-year-old."

"True, but that wasn't it either."

"'Have a hot dog, maybe it's the pizza that's upsetting you.'"

Lord chuckled, shook his head.

"It had a radio, you said? He told you to turn it up, play music."

"Also a good idea but not the one."

Dr. May laughed. "Then I'm out of ideas."

"No you're not."

"I am," she insisted, losing the laugh as well as the moment. "I am. Please, tell me."

The scientist's last statement was so quiet Lord thought the wind chimes might drown them out. Instead, they seemed to blend with the air that made the little bells sing.

"What he told me—and I guess it was pretty sophisticated for a kid to try and process—what he said was, 'Do what helps.'"

The woman's fair brow creased a little. "Do what helps," she repeated.

"That's right. I mean, that didn't seem to solve anything, did it?"

She shook her head.

"But the longer I thought about it," Lord told her, "my father was right. Okay: how do you *not* be bored in a parked car with your grandfather? I suggested that we park where things were going on! Under the highway, in Central Park, at NYU, where I discovered that I really liked coeds . . . that changed my grandfather too. Turns out *he* was bored and didn't want to tell *me*!"

Lord stopped then, because something surprising happened. Tears had begun beading from the sides of Saranya's eyes—like tiny blown bubbles in the lesser gravity. They still fell but they took their time, like a high-diver preparing to jump.

Lord was off his bed when her face fell to her open hands and her shoulders started shaking. He crouched beside her, his left arm across her back.

"What is it?" he asked.

She just shook her head.

"You can talk to me," he assured her. "Whatever it is."

Then her hands were off her face and clinging to him, climbing across his arms and around him, like a drowning woman.

"'Do what helps,'" she repeated through tears. "I have to trust you."

"You can, Saranya."

Her damp eyes turned helplessly toward the chimes as if imploring them to keep her secret *here*.

"Someone stole my work." He heard her gasp, as if it were torn from her. "It was incomplete, but the heart of it . . . the soul of it was there. And they can't control it, Sam. I think . . . I think they used it, caused— what happened."

The woman couldn't go on but he understood what she meant. Lord held her until she stopped trembling. But even then she didn't let go.

"Who did it?" he asked.

"I don't know. I truly do not."

"What do they want now?" Lord asked. "You?"

"I think so. I'm afraid so. I'm the only one who can *fix* what's wrong. That's why I had to get help."

"So you jumped on the nearest shuttle returning to Earth?"

"It was leaving. I knew I needed help that the base commander couldn't provide—she has her hands full just running the place. So I got on."

"Accommodating of them," Lord said.

She looked at him. "What do you mean?"

"They would have had to put a seat back in the cargo bay," Lord said. "Or are there fold-downs?"

"Fold-downs and a pallet for extra cargo. Plus Captain Kodera *is* very considerate," she said defensively.

"I wasn't being sarcastic, trust me," Lord said. "I understand how it is. You look out for each other up there. It was the same way in the air force."

The woman nodded and continued to sob, but it wasn't just fear; Lord could tell the difference. This was deeper, heaving, *guilty*.

You didn't kill those people, he wanted to assure her. *You are trying to stop whoever did*. But he wasn't sure that would help. This was not a problem of the mind, of reason.

And then she was hugging him, tightly, as though he were the only refuge in a sea of pain. He held her as well, comforting her with his strength. One of his hands was pressed gently in the small of her back and she allowed it, urged it to push her nearer. He did so, and the feeling of her warmth was absolute: her tears, her sobbing breaths, her body beneath the lunar jumpsuit.

Her cheek was on his, but Lord did not press further. She was too vulnerable, then, and she needed to be able to trust him—anywhere, anytime. So he lay back with her and just held her.

At that moment, the universe somehow seemed uncommonly fair and balanced.

■■

Further down Radial Arm Six, Adsila Waters closed the door behind Ziv Levy with a kick of her heel. The light came on automatically and she waved it off. The glow of holoreps of the constellations Ursa Major and Ursa Minor illuminated the room, gleaming, ghostly shapes hanging just below the ceiling.

"The Dippers," he said.

"The Bears," she countered.

Stepping over the small wool mat that her grandmother had hand-tufted, Adsila embraced the taller man, while her lips sought to discover what was organic flesh and what skin was manufactured.

"I am *not* a freak," she hissed. "Not the way you meant."

Ziv was too busy to answer. He was busy moving his powerful legs, arching his artificial spine to keep from falling over as he bore her to the center of the small room. But Adsila didn't let him get to the bed, which they probably would have crushed. Raking her fingers in the front of his shirt and planting her feet on the sides of his pants, she tore back with her arms and shoved down with her legs and feet.

Ziv's tunic ripped wide and his pants bunched at his ankles. He was forced to stop.

"Where do you keep it?" she demanded.

"*Avóy,*" he cried, puzzled. "Where every man does—"

"No, you rabbit, you *deceiver,*" she snarled, dragging her fingernails over both sets of ribs, hard. "Not that. I want the hollow. The smuggler's cove. The fake organ where you stow contraband. Is it a kidney?"

"No, they're real."

"I've heard otherwise."

"From who?"

"We have sources." Her right hand moved down along his side to his back.

"We? You're *on the job?*" he said, reaching behind him with one hand to curl his fingers in her hair.

"You're a spy, I'm the law," she said.

"I've played that game," he replied. "It requires handcuffs and a taser."

"This is not a game," she said.

"*Everything* is a game," he assured her, "and we're both playing. That's why I knew it."

"Knew what?" she challenged breathlessly as her hands ranged along his chest to see how magnificent his Israeli sculptors had made him.

"I knew that we were only for each other!" he said. "Even in passion, you *work*."

She bit his shoulder, hard. "Don't you?"

"Always," he admitted.

Adsila laughed loudly, almost maniacally into the synthetic flesh, her voice deadened by a clavicle made from polymers Ziv used to wear as armor. But where they coupled to human bone, vibrations caused his back to tingle, all the way to his coccyx. He gripped her tightly.

"Tell me about the scientist from the moon," he panted into her ear.

"Sure," Adsila replied hotly. "She rode up here with a disreputable escort, one who sent the shuttle from Earth a false code identifying them as the *Empyrean* ferry." She bit a lobe to hold his ear in place. "Don't bother lying. I checked."

"Why would I lie?" he asked, wincing. He pinched her chin to loosen her teeth. "It was legal."

Adsila pulled at the shredded tunic. "This isn't an Edelweiss vest, Mr. Registered-in-Switzerland."

"Also legal," he fired back.

"Yes, but intent to coerce *isn't* legal," she said then sniffed deeply at his open mouth. "That's not *Zürcher Geschnetzeltes* I smell on your breath."

"It's a Haifa—"

"Cocktail, yes, I know," she said. "You use it to try and get people high."

"You get *me* high," he cooed.

"No detours," Adsila shot back. "Or would you rather explain to the good cop? The one with hair on his chest?"

It took a moment for him to catch up. "Don't!" he protested loudly.

"Give me a reason?" she replied.

Ziv bit at her nose with teeth harder than titanium. Adsila's head darted back at the neck, like an owl, but he was still holding her tightly around the torso. He followed her mouth with his lips and kissed her hard, only partly to shut her up.

The CHAI could feel his polymer muscles come alive, coiling and uncoiling over searing heat actuators. The parts of him that were still human jumped as microelectrodes blazed voltages into remnants of nerve.

He felt more alive than when he had been entirely biological.

Ziv's fingers settled onto her hips, pinching and then slipping beneath the waistband of her stiffly pressed HooverComm issue slacks. She tried to launch herself away, to land on the white blanket of her own bed, but his right forefinger had already found the touchpoint that would part the fabric of her garment, releasing it.

She let him have his way; that was why they were here. She kissed him back, sliding from mouth to cheek to chin and back, savoring the different tastes and textures of the natural and the artificial. Even his saliva was new to her—there was something distinctly biocidal in the taste, and she wondered if it might prove dangerous to her as well.

While he probed with his right hand, his left hand grabbed her braided hair. He pulled hard and they thumped back toward the door, hitting it. Ziv attacked her tunic with his teeth. Pinned between her lover and the door, Adsila undid it—she only had one spare uniform—and then she submitted, her eyes burning only slightly less than the rest of her.

Ziv showed the woman no quarter, nor did she ask for any. She accommodated his movements but nothing anyone had ever said or done could prepare her for this. She cried into his left ear and then, as he entered her, she cried louder into his right. The universe flashed in her brain. Her eyes snapped wide in surprise. The cannabis, the mushrooms—those only gave her foggy visions. This glimpse put her on the edge of eternity.

And it was just beginning.

Whether it was mental, physical, or both, Ziv fine-tuned everything from movement to physical stature as if he were instantly collating and analyzing her smallest reactions, and alternating his movements accordingly. He missed nothing: no twitch was not matched, no retreat was not seized upon, no thrust was not met. She lost sight of everything visual: there were too many other stimuli flooding her. Even his sweat seemed to participate, thrillingly colder than ether against her skin, volatile enough to quell the inhuman heat beneath his skin. He was emanating waves of sexual energy from his body. Adsila wondered, distantly, if something in his cybernetics had scrambled her Cloud interface.

"IC . . . auroric rep," she gasped impulsively.

"You see . . . *what*?" Ziv managed to ask through his grunting.

She didn't answer, except to laugh. There they were, aurora-like representations of the energy waves sloshing before her eyes like an oily rainbow. The laugh became a shriek. Her hands gripped his arms spasmodically. Her thighs tightened against his hips. She didn't know how many times she had climaxed but even they became secondary. Her desire was to hold on to that edge of eternity as though it were the event horizon of a black hole. She came nearer to the infinite now, so near she couldn't howl because she could hardly breathe. She caught a glimpse of his eyes but even the blankness of his stare did not discourage her. For him this wasn't sex—it was running a program, using his skills and tools to achieve a goal, but she didn't care.

And then another level of energy flashed through her, sent by him as though he were overheating. His arms, hands, and fingers were no longer embracing her. They were gripping her chakras, her body's energy centers, in a purposeful and powerful way.

She did not want to resist her own impulses. She felt the supernova coming, and so did he. She realized, too late, that this was a mistake.

How many secrets had he collected this way? She heard herself cry out. How many women had told him everything they knew just to keep him from stopping?

Her fingers gripped his arms again. Her thighs clamped onto his hips again. She gripped him to keep from losing herself, only this time it was completely different.

She knew it . . . and he knew it.

Adsila's female nature fell into itself, collapsed, was lost somewhere inside. Her male side emerged and was greeted by a cry of shock and surprise from Ziv.

He did not stop moving entirely . . . but a part of him did, unwillingly and unexpectedly. His eyes went large with shock as Adsila threw his back against the door and he went with him and Ziv seemed a fraction of the titan he had been just a moment before.

Breathing heavily, cooling rapidly, the pan-gender peered into his face like a cougar eying a hare. A cruel smile twisted his mouth.

"Cat got your tongue?" he asked.

Ziv was a veteran of too many engagements—sexual and otherwise—to panic or even overreact. His breathing, then his muscles, relaxed. The man's characteristic composure quickly overcame his surprise.

"Did you do that on purpose?" he asked.

"What do you think?"

"I think it just—*happened*," he replied. "You're not . . . man enough to try and bargain with me."

"Am I not?" The owlish eyes narrowed. Adsila wasn't insulted. Life was a constant process of learning and he had known many mentors. What he felt was something else. Adsila's breathing picked up again—there was a new high now.

The danger rising in the other man was immediate and radiant. "You are not," he assured him.

"Fine. I'm an eternal student," Adsila said. "What kind of teacher are you?"

In response, Ziv grinned. He reached between them and grabbed himself tightly with his fist. "I can just buy myself another one of *these* if I have to. And by the way—my perfluorocarbon blood will *not* wash out of your Cherokee rug."

The tension passed, the threat evaporated, and Adsila shifted. The flesh against Ziv became softer, rounder. But the Israeli did not back away. He pushed his hips forward, pinning Adsila hard against the door with groin and chest.

"Learn this, 'eternal student,'" he said contemptuously. "You see these eyes?" He leaned closer, opening those dark, cephalopod orbs. "They're an improvement over human eyes. No blood vessels in the way of the retina, no imperfections in the optics, no blind spot." He backed away very slightly, the eyes steady in flat, dull conquest. "Ziv Levy is neither a fool *nor* a one-night stand. I have relationships, if you take my meaning."

She did. Sobriety returned swiftly.

"I will be contacting you, EAD Adsila Waters." Ziv snickered again, and leaned very close. "That could just as easily have been you I grabbed. I wonder—would it have grown back?"

With that, the CHAI took a powerful step back, drew up his pants, and snatched the rug from the floor to cover his chest . . . and to announce his conquest to anyone who saw him. Adsila moved aside and he was gone, his footsteps thumping on the rubber-coated flooring.

Adsila stood there feeling used, though not for sex. She had used him too and she had expected him to try to pull information from her in the midst of passion. But his parting threat—and the rug which she had just *let* him take . . . that fear, that *paralysis* was new, and it was something she began to fear she might not be able to handle alone.

ELEVEN

E VERYONE BUT THE Chinese referred to it as the Icicle.

On the outside, the space station *Ch'ih-zhāng*, the *Jade Star*, was a cold white spear in the darkness, white from the sunlight and frosted by the myriad stars in the distant cosmos. It sat eerily still around its central axis, creating no gravity, while its forward, scalpel-shaped bridge seemed to challenge the heavens like one of the terra-cotta warriors of Emperor Qin Shi Huang.

On the inside, the *Jade Star* was even colder. That was partly due to the design: porcelain-white walls kept uniformly that color by external aerogel shields, gauzy silica that ingested both radiation and micrometerorites. On these walls were intermittent wall hangings made of knotted red cloth—the color of celebration. They floated weightlessly, like seaweed, occasionally stirred by the passage of one of the station's occupants.

Yet most of the impersonal chill was due not to the structure or its trappings but to the personality of its commander, Chairman Sheng Fan.

Small of stature, slight of shoulder, Sheng nonetheless towered like a mountain over the *Jade Star*, its crew . . . and the world below it. He had grown up in the Henan Province, where he had studied Shaolin Kung Fu. He had excelled in Leopard style, and to this day walked with his hands taut, like paws: fingertips pressed to the top of his palm, knuckles forward, thumb clenched. He was like a great cat in the jungle, pushing away branches, vines, roots, his eyes set on prey only he could see.

Seated beside him in his tiny, spartan office was his young personal assistant, Tse Hung, whose quiet expression balanced respect with fear. Tse was not that prey, but he acted like it.

Both men had been aloft since the core of the space station was completed a year before, and both proudly wore the standard dark-olive uniform of the China National Space Administration. Behind Sheng were volumetric images of the flags of China and the *Jade Star*. The former was the traditional red flag with one yellow star with a semicircle of four smaller yellow stars; the latter was a yin-yang symbol composed of the intermingled sun and moon on a starry background.

On Sheng's desk was a plaque that floated on the end of a leather strap, one he had once used to protect his wrists during stick fighting. The characters stood for *fighting achievement*, though he did not mean for them to apply to him as most people thought. They referred to the *Jade Star*.

Sheng raised a finger. Tse activated the IC feed, sitting just out of view of the six faces that appeared before them—heads that hung like little worlds, complete with moonlike logos that indicated the many news services for which each reporter worked.

The forty-two-year-old Sheng looked directly and placidly—some would say dead-eyed—at the face of Hiromi Tsuburaya in his IC. She was one of the half dozen Asian correspondents who had been invited to an exclusive press conference organized by Beijing. Their faces showed exhaustion that went deeper than the usual strain of hardworking journalists. They weren't just competing for news: they were serving populations desperate for answers.

"I wish to assure you, our terrestrial neighbors, our *friends*," Sheng began without preamble, "that every mind, every resource of this outpost is committed to understanding the disaster that befell Japan and, if possible, to preventing its recurrence. Our condolences go out to the people of a great and resilient nation and to the bereaved families."

His words are like the artful knots on the walls, Tse thought as he listened to Sheng. Given how expert he had become at diplomatic rhetoric, it was difficult to believe that the commander had been a physics professor just eighteen months before.

Among the correspondents arrayed before him, Hiromi was the only one from Japan. The language program translated his words instantly. She thanked him with a courteous nod.

"Are there questions?" Sheng asked.

"Yes, Chairman," Hiromi said even as her head was still rising. "Is it your view that this disaster was natural?"

"We have no data to indicate otherwise," the chairman replied with aloof certainty. He said, "Have you?"

"Not yet," Hiromi replied.

There was a hint of accusation in her tone. Sheng paid it no attention.

"Of course," Sheng said softly, "the unprecedented nature of this phenomenon requires that we all delve further to ensure that there is no recurrence."

"I am informed," Hiromi pressed, "that Beijing's humanitarian response has been slow and muted compared to that of other nations. Is there a reason for that?"

"You should ask Beijing—"

"I have," she replied. "They say they are moving heaven and Earth. Have they, sir? Have they moved heaven? Have *you*?"

The question was sharp and clearly meant to be taken as more than just a figure of speech.

"I am one man without the power to do very much," he said. "I am certain that our people will do everything they can to assist in any way they can."

Hiromi's expression was unconvinced . . . and unforgiving.

"Where will China be looking to help find answers?" asked Yingluck Chan-ocha of the Thai WorldNet and its Indonesian affiliates.

"In the seas," Sheng replied. "We have very delicate sensors on our oceanic assets that are keenly interfaced with equipment in various locations on Earth and also on the *Jade Star*. We will explore climatic and nonclimatic data and share our findings with Tokyo and other governments."

"What kind of nonclimatic data?" the woman pressed.

"That remains to be determined," Sheng answered in a monotone that was intended to reassure.

Yet Hiromi's pained eyes narrowed slightly. "Do your scientists have any theories to explain this disaster, Chairman Sheng?" the Japanese reporter asked.

Sheng was impassive. "I believe that we will know more when we have completed our analyses. And yet," he added pointedly, "I feel I must address the unspoken question. Was this an act of war or terror by some nation against your own?"

Hiromi did not deny his assessment and waited attentively for his response.

"Despite the unprecedented nature of the disaster, I do not believe that this was the act of *willful* aggression," Sheng said. "Such savagery would stain the soul of a nation, any nation, for untold generations. I assure you, Hiromi, that kind of barbarity does not exist among *our* people or their leaders. To find such, one would have to return to the Middle East of 2015, or Nanking before the Second World War."

His mention of the latter was a rebuke, lost on no one, an allusion to the ancient hostility between their nations.

The remaining questions were about the space station and its work—though, as always, Sheng politely declined to answer with specifics. He was pressed, in particular, about the new science module that was cloaked not just in secrecy but in a blanket of redundant electronic security measures.

"How would our security methods be known . . . unless someone has tried to breach our cosmic research laboratory?" Sheng asked with practiced innocence.

Tse terminated the IC feeds and, once again, *Jade Star* was cut off from the rest of the universe. The space station didn't have the human buzz and animal proximity of other orbiting installations like the American *Empyrean* space station or the Russian *Red Giant*. The *Jade Star* was restrained in its human interaction. The spacious, cylindrical corridors filled with purpose—and that purpose was not to expand human knowledge but to expand China; not to look outward but to look down. Untroubled by the economic setbacks and collapses that plagued other spacefaring nations like Russia and India, Mother China coursed into the mid-twenty-first century on the backs of powerful dragons: rockets spitting fire. Twice a year for the last ten years, new modules had arced skyward from the Gobi Desert. Once aloft, they powered themselves into place, controlled from Earth, by powerful onboard engineering rockets. They were restocked by vessels from Xichang, Guizhou, Wenchang, and Donfeng. Other ships expanded the station's population exponentially. Now, the 122.7-meter-long station had thirty-two permanent residents. That would continue to grow year after year as Beijing was committed to turning its space platform into a space city.

Sheng pulled his feet up and floated from the seat. As he straightened his legs, his soft boots connected to the floor like little cats' feet. As he moved toward the exit, not wasting a motion, it appeared to Tse that Sheng was gliding—a skill the younger man had not been able to master in all his time on board.

Tse's eyes focused on a sudden barrage of inflammatory IC posts.

"Madam Tsuburaya is not allowing the matter to sit," Tse calmly advised his superior. "Her image and your own are coupled on every newsfeed, asking for an investigation into the station and its scientific experiments—"

"Expected and unimportant," Sheng replied as he slid forward. "Instruct Yuen Mui not to share that with us."

Tse nodded and informed the Ministry of Space Security in Beijing of Chairman Sheng's wishes. Tse knew that the ministry would continue to monitor the feeds, as they had done for nearly fifty years.

He also knew that it didn't matter what the rest of the world thought, only that the huge majority of China's billions would never see or hear the shrill, endlessly recycled complaints from Japanese reporters like Hiromi.

"Your next meeting is in an hour," Tse advised, checking the Chairman's IC schedule. "The premier's staff has just confirmed."

"I will be back before then," Sheng said, looking straight ahead. He did not simply nod in the stoic manner of all Chinese law enforcement, military, and political leaders. That was one of the first silent habits to go up here: in the station's weightless environment, such a move might send an occupant tumbling.

Tse acquiesced by saying nothing.

The diminutive chairman drifted along the station's central tubelike corridor, passing without acknowledgment the dozen or so male and female *taikonauts*, "outer space voyagers," who traversed it with Sheng. They embodied a different spirit than Sheng had felt as a teacher at the School of Aeronautics and Astronautics in Zhejiang University. The specially chosen workers here were not subject to the industrial pollution and gender inequities that plagued the population on the world below. They were happy, they were proud, they were productive—a rare combination in modern China. They were a sharp and vital future.

Sheng took a moment to appreciate how the taikonauts drifted, and even flew, in confident harmony with each other. Tse joined them with a polite smile, inwardly delighted to be no longer attempting to walk, and then the commander was alone in a distant corridor, a sector added just four months before, one that required the highest security clearance. Here the red decorations gave way to black and blue gemstones drifting on ribbons—somber colors further signifying this area's exclusivity.

Seemingly without instigating the move, Sheng turned around slowly midway through the module and entered a door whose Chinese characters indicated that it was the Development and Research Center. His IC EEG pattern caused it to slide back.

Sheng felt his muscles tighten. These were the trials that tested a man, the decisions that shaped futures—but also the risks that made life worthwhile. Even before he entered, he had a sense of what the answer to his one question—to the premier's question—would be. He had pushed the team, worked them relentlessly. But Beijing had expended resources, drawn up a timetable, and expected results. His only task was to deliver.

You cannot put this off any longer, he told himself. The team had needed a device and it had been obtained for them. *The premier will want an answer about its operational status.*

But inside—not very deep inside—Sheng had concerns . . . and his own suspicions. He didn't like Hiromi Tsuburaya. She had a right to her grief, of course. But that did not entitle her to express the darkness in her heart, to accuse him of concealing a Chinese hand in the disaster. Sheng had seen the reports about Japan, both public and secure. He had told those reporters the truth. And yet—

It was not Hiromi who troubled him. Nor was it the solid wall of disapproval represented by the other five reporters. They clearly believed her, or at least had reason not to doubt her. And it was more than just the fraternity of their profession. It was also more than fear and jealousy over China's triumphs in space. It was a sense of the inevitable. Sheng had seen that in the beaten expressions, the broken postures of the once-independent people of Taiwan, of Tibet, of Hong Kong. *The world was to be China, by any means necessary.*

No. What unsettled him was just one thing: ignorance. It was a quality he did not tolerate in others, and less so in himself. The press conference merely reinforced how much he didn't know.

Sheng floated through another, smaller empty corridor. The door behind him sealed seamlessly before the one in front of him opened and he stepped into what seemed to him like the engine room of a scuttled freighter he used to play in as a boy: a huge, cavernous area, only this one had a ten-meter-long oblong, baffle-covered object hovering in the center. It looked like a coffin festooned with rose petals.

Dr. Ku Lung was waiting for him, having been advised by Tse that the commander was on the way.

The lithe, muscular astrophysicist had been floating above the device. He dropped down beside the chairman, facing away, his eyes still locked on the two magnetic horns set fifteen feet apart, which were connected by rows of large, kite-like panels. Three young men and one woman continued to hover high around each side of the object.

"Well?" Sheng's soft word managed to sound like a demand.

"It is essentially ready," Lung replied, cautiously certain.

"Essentially?" Sheng echoed with disapproval. "In what way is it incomplete?"

"Chairman, we built a magnetic lens to focus the ambient neutrino flux," he said. "It has been enhanced to focus them further, to the density of deep-space haloes where they self-annihilate with enough power to prolong the lives of stars."

"I know all of that," Sheng said with rising impatience.

"Yes, Chairman," Lung said. He had not been informing but apologizing. "We know it functions as one and believe it will serve as the other, Commander. So . . . it is 'essentially' ready. We will not know for certain until we test it."

Sheng grew visibly impatient. "You told me that would have been done by now, Doctor." Sheng moved closer. Though he was looking up at the taller man he seemed to be looking down.

"What is wrong?" Sheng demanded.

"One cannot control the forces of the universe on a schedule," Lung said. He was uncomfortably aware of the others staring down at him.

Sheng was staring as well. They were waiting, clearly expecting more—

"You *did* test it," Sheng said. Then he said angrily, "You tested it—this morning!"

None of the four scientists spoke. Lung barely breathed.

Sheng felt his heart throbbing hard, his fingers swelling with blood. "Japan was you," was all he said.

Lung's taut expression said *It was* us, *Commander*. When he spoke, he replied, "The—the device, the *American* device, did not function as we expected."

Sheng was staring past the man at the remembered face of Madam Tsuburaya. It wasn't the inadvertent lie he'd told that bothered him. Nor the destruction they had caused to Japan. It was ignorance coupled with the fact that he was wrong and that bitter, bitter woman was right.

"But I am confident that you have fixed the problem," Sheng said coldly.

Lung was silent. Sheng's eyes sought the others in the room.

"*Have* you fixed the problem?" he yelled.

No one replied. Sheng's eyes returned to those of Lung. The scientist stared into the chairman's dark gaze. "We . . . we . . ."

"It is ready, sir," one of the other men shouted down. "I am very certain that the flaw in Dr. May's computations has been fixed."

Sheng looked up at Dr. Bao Hark, then glared at Lung. "Do you concur, Chief Scientist?"

Lung hesitated. "I would like more time, Chairman."

"Very well." Sheng checked the time. "You have it. Thirty-four minutes. That is when I must report to the premier. What I will be reporting to him is that my team—whose members were hand-selected from over twelve thousand applicants to achieve one goal, *one* objective—that my team has managed to complete the project."

Faced with no choice, like a man about to be shot, Lung seemed to grow a little in stature. "Tell his excellency that it . . . it *is* ready, Chairman."

"He will be pleased," Sheng replied. "And after my conference I will return to see it activated."

TWELVE

WAKING, SAM LORD noticed at once that something was different. Several things, in fact.

Lord snapped to on his cot, its autocontoured fibers holding him snugly in place as always. Unlike most days, however, he had the fleeting sense that he was somewhere else: back in his modest suburban home in Alamogordo, New Mexico, off New York Avenue. That was due to the fact that he was warm—not air-blown warm but human-proximity warm—and there was a woman beside him.

His eyes searched the room in front of him. He saw braids and the back of a lunar jumpsuit. The woman wasn't Erin Astoria, his most recent lover. The hair near his face did not smell desert-dry and dusty, it was the cap-gun smell of space—*or moon rocks*. The metallic taste sat on the middle of his tongue. Obviously, he'd been inhaling the odor for hours.

Hours? Dammit.

Reality returned quickly. Lord was in his log cabin on the *Empyrean*, Dr. Saranya May beside him. He hadn't told the staff about his mission to the moon, but the SimAI knew and should have alerted him of the time—

Carefully disentangling himself from the woman, Lord poked his IC. The clock said they had been asleep nearly three hours.

"Your vitals indicated you were in much-needed REM," the SimAI said after announcing the time. "You may take another sixteen minutes based on relative location to the bay and your go-bag needing only dimenhydrinate—"

"Thank you," Lord said, even though he was talking to a machine. He terminated the audio with a blink.

Easing back as far as he could so as not to disturb Saranya as he stood, Lord checked his IC to read up on the status of the lunar shuttle. It was still on Earth, was nearly loaded, and would be at the *Empyrean* in just under an hour. Though countless hyperplanes had been commandeered to rush humanitarian resources to Japan, the payload of NASA's craft was deemed urgent and vital to Armstrong Base. Besides, compared to massive cargo planes, the shuttle bay was too small to be worth crowding into that already overcrowded airspace. Nearly half its mass was occupied by the thrusters needed to raise it to Earth orbit and, thereafter, the moon.

Lord had pills to treat zero-gravity nausea in his small footlocker and they'd have them on the shuttle. He allowed himself a few minutes to gather his thoughts.

He remembered now, and smiled as he looked down at the woman. Saranya had quickly fallen asleep, as had Lord beside her. He was more exhausted than he had thought and certainly more than he was accustomed to. As he drifted away, he attributed that more to the reception than to his adventure in the cargo bay. Like sitting in his grandfather's patrol car, hanging around doing nothing was draining.

It had been a typical sleep—for space.

When he first arrived on *Empyrean*, Lord was concerned about his dreams. The colors were more saturated, the movements swifter, and the blue-to-black tableaux never involved Earth. There was no longing for home, no mashup with events or people or places of the past. They weren't nightmares but they weren't relaxing either.

After the second night, Lord went to see Dr. Carter. It was only the second time they had spoken, beyond the cursory medbay check-in Lord had undergone when he first arrived.

"Some people might say it's REM taking care of you," Carter had said in his unwelcoming monotone. "Rapid-eye movement," he added.

"Yes, I've heard of it," Lord replied tartly.

"You're adjusting to variable gravity and visual cues that are 'normal' one moment, tilting the next, then utterly absent a moment later," Carter went on, oblivious to Lord's sass. "Vivid and busy and disoriented dreams might be helping you consolidate all of that. I'm not so sure. I do know that babies spend a lot of time in REM."

"I see," Lord replied.

"It's in the orientation manual under 'orientation,' appropriately enough," Carter said. "Maybe, when you studied it, you skipped that part, thought they were just repeating themselves."

"That's right."

Carter turned his sullen eyes from his own IC to Lord. "You *did* read the manual?"

"I keep all four thousand–plus pages at the ready." Lord indicated his IC.

"Yet it didn't occur to you to check there first?"

"Naturally, it did," Lord assured him, moving his fingers to bring the document up. "But honestly, Doctor, look—I don't know a synapse from an apoapsis."

Carter's expression didn't change as his own fingers moved. "Director Lord, your reluctance to learn by any way other than *doing* is well documented in your file. I'm prescribing that you at least familiarize yourself with the contents page so that you do not have to divert staff resources, and I'm informing the prime director that you have been so ordered."

Lord thanked him for his trouble and left, noticing on his way out the petri dish, labeled BN17, stuck to a wall. It was the first time he had confirmed—and it was absolutely no surprise—that both the doctor and Al-Kazaz had secrets up here. Fortunately, Lord had friends in the Air Force Intelligence, Surveillance and Reconnaissance Agency. The BN17 bio-nanite program had two components. One was code-named Merlin, after the magician, and was a purely agricultural project that took genetic engineering to a new level; Lord kept meaning to ask Lancaster Liba about it. The other, code-named Rossum, after a fictional robot builder, was a black-ops study in which microscale surgery robots, with lithium niobate IC sensors aboard, took up residence in the brain, through a tear duct or a nostril or even a skin pore. So doing, the tiny robots could not only rebuild or destroy cells, they could plug into the knowledge and memory centers and broadcast that data. Which was illegal, of course. However, so much of what was unlawful on Earth was often just a suggestion or guideline up here.

Who needs to have nightmares when they sleep? he thought as he left the medbay. *They are everywhere on* Empyrean.

Fortunately for his peace of spirit, Lord had long ago learned that he couldn't fix the system any more than the system could change him. So they circled each other, occasionally crossing swords, each in their own way doing what they thought was best. It didn't make Lord bitter or frustrated. Somehow, despite centuries of partisan and bureaucratic conflict and struggle, the nation and corporations—who sometimes surpassed the military for its deep pockets—had still managed to put a station in space, to gain a toehold on the moon, to colonize the high frontier. In spite of themselves, people and progress were still a team.

As were he and Al-Kazaz, even though he had failed to disclose the nature of Dr. Carter's activities, even though he was one of Lord's subordinates.

And so Lord had dreamt of comets, with himself on the tail, now holding it, now riding it with Isaiah's saddle. Twisting and spinning, he had kept his eyes on the stars that were turning around Polaris like a time-lapse view of the nighttime sky from Earth.

Lord continued to sit, comfortably crowded on the bed. Since there was time, he scrolled over to the schematics of the lunar shuttle to answer another question that had been on his mind before he drifted off:

How were they going to fit in a spacecraft that was laden with everything from spare parts to seeds to amenities like clothes and toiletries?

Lord saw that the shuttle had the capacity to take on passengers by
consigning its cargo to a space pallet that could be deployed behind. He
watched the shuttle model rotate before him.

No, I don't want to make it life-size and virtual, he dismissed the
prompt. Lord disliked the all-consuming "immersive" and "experien-
tial" conceit of IC technology. Though the vast number of users didn't
agree, sometimes it was all right to just watch something or even read it
instead of having it read.

*Like driving one of those tandem buses that used to scare me when I was
a kid,* he initially suspected, though that wasn't correct: the main joint
between the shuttle and the pallet was even unsteadier than that. The
pallet would collect, and reimpart to the shuttle, any twists, imbalances,
or changes in direction. The two units had to move together. *So it's more
like pulling a speedboat behind your car,* he realized. As for passengers,
there were fold-down seats as in a military cargo plane.

He sat there trying to decide whether he should see Dr. Carter
before departing. There were conflicting regulations. The FBI rules—
which Lord *had* read—said, "Only persons expressly named in a
mission-order, written or unwritten, are to be briefed or informed in
any capacity, and then at the discretion of the commander on-scene."
Which meant: Lord still wasn't authorized to tell anyone what he was
doing, with whom, or why. Adsila and the others would figure out
where he was going when they saw him board the shuttle.

But there was also the *Empyrean* charter, which mandated that anyone who was going outbound—meaning to a higher orbit or leaving
Earth orbit altogether—had to be approved for flight by a station-based
medical officer.

When orders conflicted, Lord always ignored the one that was least
convenient. In this case, he'd follow FBI protocol. He was going to the
moon on his own authority.

He craned to one side, slapped the panel that opened the footlocker beneath his cot, and the small drawer whooshed open. He grabbed the small vacuum-packed strip of pills and tucked them in a side slot of the go-bag beside them. He had never needed them—parabolic dives in his fighter had given him decades of zero-g training—but, just in case, he also didn't want beads of partially digested crackers and caviar from the reception circulating through the cabin of the shuttle, literally gumming up any exposed works.

Leaning forward, he placed a hand lightly on Dr. May's shoulder and gave it a gentle squeeze. The woman started as though she'd been slapped. She gathered herself to a sitting position, threw her legs over the bed, and looked around.

"We were asleep," Lord said from behind her.

She whipped around, momentarily alarmed, then relaxed. "How long—?"

"Three hours and a frac," he said. "We've got a little time."

Dr. May inhaled then exhaled again more slowly. Lord stood. He shook out his hands, a qigong energy-stirring exercise he'd learned in Hong Kong. Throughout Lord's life, the ancient technique had proven useful for everything from waking up to fending off colds.

"You shouldn't have let me sleep," she said.

"Why? There's nothing we can do and you needed rest."

"Is there any news?" the scientist asked.

"I didn't check," Lord admitted.

"Please do," she said.

Lord looked at his IC. "There's nothing," he said. "Perhaps there won't be."

"I wish I could believe that."

"What kind of news do you expect to hear?" he asked.

"I truly do not know," she told him. "I wish I did."

"Then let me ask it another way," Lord said. "What else is in danger?"

She didn't answer.

"Saranya? We are past the point of withholding information you consider sensitive. If there are alerts I can give to my superior—"

"I gave him the alerts and he told me to say nothing," she replied solemnly. Her eyes went to the chimes and their jingling. "What is in danger? Everything is."

"Out here, that's a big word, Doctor."

She turned toward him. "No one is more aware of that than I am. You'll understand better when we get to the moon."

"A name, then," he said. "Give me that, for now. What do we call your work?"

She hesitated, then replied, "SAMI. Subatomic Magnification Interface. "

"From the sound of that, you—"

"I've come up with the most destructive force humans have ever gotten their hands on," she blurted. "You say you enjoy trailblazing, Director Lord? I truly hope so, because this is unprecedented."

Lord had spent a half century listening to voices from air base towers, from other pilots. He recognized terror when he heard it. He let the matter sit for now.

Lord left her and packed a few sets of clothes in a small grip, stuffed his go-bag inside, then used the lavatory—an area just inside the cabin with a wall but no door. He didn't have a lot of experience washing in zero gravity and decided to stick with what he had mastered. He shaved using the foaming chemical depilatory CiliAx, which came in a hatchet-shaped container. The edge of the packaging could be used to scrape away anything the lather missed.

When Lord emerged from the lavatory, he was surprised to see Dr. May's eyes and fingers flashing as she worked her way through her IC.

"I'm looking through security images of Armstrong Base," she said.

"I didn't realize you had any," Lord said, a trace of annoyance in his voice.

"I didn't until now," she said. "I never needed any. My lab is in a module that will depressurize if the wrong person attempts to enter."

"They would be wearing a space suit—"

"That won't help," she assured him. "A space suit cannot fit through the inner door of the airlock. And the inner door won't close unless an authorized person enters."

Lord moved toward her. "So what footage is this?" he asked.

"Footage?"

"Imagery," he said, forgetting that not everyone was old enough to remember film.

"It was sent over by your superior, PD Al-Kazaz, at my request," she said. "They are images from a lunar topographical orbiter that show the movements of the only individual up there who also has access to that laboratory."

"And that is?" he asked, still annoyed—but at himself. He saw now that Al-Kazaz had sent the imagery to him a little over two hours ago.

"Dr. Ras Diego," Dr. May replied. "His field is dark energy. Specifically, baryon acoustic oscillation clustering—he looks for clues about the invisible in the large-scale structure of visible matter, whereas I just try to look straight at the invisible."

That part didn't interest Lord. What mattered was why she was looking into Diego's movements, and he said so.

"We fight for a share of the same funding pool," Dr. May said. "If something went wrong with my research, Dr. Diego would benefit."

"Would he kill hundreds of thousands of people for a research grant?"

"I do not believe so," she said. Then added, "I would hope not."

"Not a dazzling endorsement."

"Not a very nice man," she replied. "To me, anyway."

"To others?"

"Civil," she said. "He is very absorbed by his work. Little else matters."

"I thought all Armstrong personnel had to go through detailed psych profiling to make sure they were a fit for an extended stay," Lord said. "How did you two end up together?"

"Honestly? I think we *are* part of a psych experiment. To see how angry lab rats fare fighting for cheese in a maze."

That didn't surprise Lord, unfortunately.

"The thing is, he would not have known my research was incomplete," Saranya went on. "I'm looking to see if I can find some record of his reaction when word of the disaster reached Armstrong Base." She flicked it off. "Nothing."

"Except him legitimately entering his own lab."

"Correct."

"But you still suspect him?" Lord pressed.

"None of my research ever leaves the lab," she said. "Nothing. Someone had to get in there to steal it. That means him . . . or me. And I didn't do it."

Lord checked the time. He cocked his head toward the door. Dr. May rose and exited first. Lord took a last look around before shutting the door, a habit he had acquired when he graduated from flight training.

In his line of work, he never knew when his next mission might be his last. It was good to have in mind a recent image of home, wherever that might be.

■ ■

Lord and Dr. May did not speak during the five-minute trip to PriD1. It wasn't an awkward silence; Lord nodded pleasantly at people he knew, Dr. May was quiet with her thoughts. If she were anxious she did not show it; Lord had known enough mechanical and aeronautical engineers at Holloman to recognize when a mind was working on a problem.

In a way, Lord envied the fact that Dr. May's mind *had* a target.

His own response—"I didn't check"—when asked about the news actually upset him. If something big had happened, Adsila Waters would have let him know. Otherwise, unless he overheard conversation in the Scrub or in the command center, he didn't really *know* what was happening on his home world. Over the past few weeks, Lord had found it increasingly difficult to reflect on earthly problems. It was a subtle change, the same way he'd stopped paying attention to New York City news when he'd joined the air force. But it was real and a little disorienting. The military skirmishes and political machinations and social dysfunctions of humankind were not only distant, they were small and temporary compared to what he saw outside the viewports: the glare of the sun on the vast seas and the proud shoulders of brown-green land that dared to come between them. From up here, time could only be measured geologically, by weather and continental drift, not by human endeavor. Looking down from *Empyrean*, the human population of Earth was as invisible as neutrinos.

From the moon? Lord couldn't imagine what impact human needs would have on him when he got there, since even the Earth's expanse would seem smaller than a fingernail. He could actually envision a time when generations of people, spread across the solar system— thousands of humans living on a self-sustaining moon, inhabiting the Mars colony that would soon supplant the Jamestown Base that failed in 2035—when all of those people would feel disconnected. It was both unsettling and thrilling, the idea of Terran cultural and ethnic diversity giving way to true human heterogeneity.

How long, he wondered, *before evolution steps to the plate and starts spacefarers on the path to several truly* different *species?*

Perhaps it had already begun and Lord was just too close to see it.

The shuttle *Grissom* arrived on schedule, and Dr. May entered the hatch first. While Lord stood at the viewport waiting for the hatches to open, it was odd to see the cargo sledge standing upright behind the craft, the cargo tucked beneath a mesh constructed of carbon nanotubes. The nets were first used in 2023 to collect space debris and deorbit, burning up upon reentry. Over a quarter million pieces of space junk were cleared in the two-year Project SOS—Sterilize Orbital Space—without which the *Empyrean* and its solar sail would have been constantly at risk.

The hatches rolled open and Dr. May entered first. As Lord boarded, floating, his old fighter pilot instincts were on high alert. There was nothing specific; just the active sixth sense of a combat veteran who, as he weightlessly took his seat with the assistance of handholds, glanced out the rear viewport, saw the mesh shimmering like a dewy spiderweb in the sun, and felt very much like a fly. . . .

THIRTEEN

ECHNICALLY, IT WAS translunar space.

The course between the Earth and its moon was so well traveled that it was no longer an exceptional run, any more than a flight from New York to Paris was considered challenging. But to a pilot, heading out beyond the *Empyrean* was open space, just as the airspace between New York and Paris was open sea.

As soon as the *Grissom* uncoupled from the *Empyrean* and turned into its lunar trajectory, Sam Lord felt like he was truly "aloft."

Seated in a slightly reclined seat for the three-hour, seventeen-minute, eleven-second trip, his bag secured in a small aft compartment, Lord played a little with weightlessness. He sculpted a small floating lens from the contents of his water bag, used it to magnify the instructions for an emergency pressure suit under his seat, then tossed the cap through the bubble to see if it would pierce the surface tension or stick inside.

"The absence of gravity is charming, isn't it?" Dr. May asked from the fold-down chair across the 9.15-meter-wide fuselage.

"It is, especially if you're a five-year-old boy at heart." Lord smiled disarmingly as the cap dragged the lens to the breaking point then passed through.

"Like the best experiences in life, it has something for every age, for every mind," Dr. May said, managing one of the few smiles he'd seen on her. She gazed out the small window to Lord's left. It faced the dark side, away from the sun. "I experienced that sense of wonder too the first time. But we've each got our own mental gravity. It kills the joy."

"If you let it," Lord said.

"How do you avoid that?"

"By focusing on what matters at any given moment," he said. "For instance, right now, top of my mind, is: I wish I had my saddle up here, the real one. Feet in the stirrups, thighs preventing me from floating off—what a ride that would be."

"You'd be able to filter out everything else?" she asked, somewhat incredulously. "Japan, politics, your responsibilities?"

"Of course not," he replied. "What happened today was monstrous, overwhelming. But you said it yourself—it's about gravity. If you don't insulate yourself somewhat, if you fail to maintain your orbit, you expend a lot of fuel preventing a crash."

"That's nice, in theory," the scientist said.

"Oh no, it's fact," Lord replied, waving a finger and then allowing his arm to hover. "If I had been thinking only about Japan, a woman would have died today in a depressurized elevator shaft. Everyone must stay loose, but alert. Free-floating, like this hand. We *must*."

Dr. May considered that as the main engine ignited, the zeta-pinch fusion jet engine pushing them down into their seats with roughly 1g of acceleration—and spoiling a little of Lord's in-flight entertainment as his hand drooped back down to the armrest. It also put them, formally, under *Grissom* control and no longer under *Empyrean* authority. Lord was now free to use the secure IC link to the command center to notify them that he was officially off-station and that Adsila Waters was in command.

"I'll let the EAD know," Janet Grainger told him. "She's taking some downtime."

"Glad to hear it," Lord replied. "Make sure you stand down soon as well."

"Getting ready to put the comm on autopilot," she replied. There was no need to ask Lord where he was going: there had only been one departure and it was headed for the moon. "Have a safe journey, sir."

He thanked her, signed off, and watched out the window as the *Empyrean* quickly shrank to the size of a snowflake and then, in a moment, was too small to see.

■ ■

"Ziv Levy is neither a fool nor a one-night stand. I have relationships, if you take my meaning."

The words stayed in Adsila's head as if the IC were set on an endless feed. Their meaning was clear. Whether Adsila wanted it or not, Ziv believed they were now connected, somehow. What he did not understand was the means.

How.

He stood unsteadily in the small room, waiting for the sensations Ziv had impressed on him to pass. But he had been forceful and Adsila's body was stubborn. They lingered, like the ache of a long run across the plains.

Adsila moved haltingly to the bed. He tried to walk steadily, strongly, but his legs were not yet having it. And it wasn't the can he had inhaled. He wished it were.

The young man sat on the edge of the white blanket and found himself reaching for the one end table. In it he found a small, light tan, leather medicine bag—a bequest from his grandfather. In it was a feather, a shell from the Isle of Palms beach, and small, clear packets of cedar, sage, and sweet grass. Keepsakes from home and family, a way to cleanse the spirit.

Adsila resumed his female form.

Clean myself of what? she asked. What was this impulse to get him *off* her?

She had been with bad men before, with men who lusted and left. At times, she—as he—had been one of those herself. What had Ziv done, besides rip through her limits like a comet?

She saw the flashing signal that AEAD Grainger was calling her. Adsila could barely find the energy for a virtual gesture in response.

"Yes?" she said. Adsila was startled when Grainger responded with a surprised laugh.

"Wow," Janet reacted, taken aback herself. "I only reserved one can for you. How many did you end up getting?"

Adsila reversed the image, looked at her own face. It reminded her of a totem, all stiff contours and shadows, drained of any human color.

"There was . . . a guest," Adsila admitted. "I guess I . . . I overindulged."

"Well, don't push yourself," Grainger said. "Director Lord is off-site and put you in charge. We were about to shut down human ops—with your approval."

"Who's on call?"

"Agent Abernathy."

"Very well," Adsila said. "SimAIs on, close up."

Grainger might have said something else; she might not have. Adsila's brain still felt electrified and Ziv's words were still in her ears.

"EAD—are you sure you're all right?" Grainger asked.

Adsila didn't immediately answer. She was overcome by the sudden urge to change sexes, as if that would rid her of the remains of Ziv.

"I'm all right," Adsila assured her.

"May I look at your biometrics?" Grainger inquired.

Access to a person's mental and physical state through their IC was allowed only by permission of the individual or by their designated next-in-line. In Adsila's case, her next-in-line was not a colleague but her father.

"Not necessary," Adsila said. "I just need to sleep this off."

"Very well. Good night."

"Good night."

Adsila put her right hand against the IC and swiped the drop-down clean. In her left hand she still clutched the medicine bag. The bag had been with her since her vision quest, the week she had spent in the wild as a rite of passage. The contents had connected her with nature, with the past and future, with the cosmos. It was her touchstone, her material soul, and its energies flowed through her heart-side hand, her intake hand.

Flowed like a creek, not a river.

There is something wrong, she told herself. Something that was a matter of body, not will. Something she might not have noticed if her male component were not suddenly struggling so hard to emerge.

She allowed it to happen. At once, a sharp pain, deep in his gut, dropped him to his knees on the floor. It felt like embers of a campfire sizzling below his navel.

Adsila replaced the bag in the end table and, with both hands, gripped the polyplastic edge to support himself as he rose.

"Dr. Carter," he said, using his eyes to access his IC.

It took a moment for the doctor to respond. In that moment, Adsila felt the pain grow dull but more widespread.

"Yes, EAD Waters?"

"Where are you?"

"MediLab," he replied.

That was the research lab attached to the Zero-G medbay.

"I'm on my way," Adsila said.

"Do you need emergency assistance?" he asked.

"No," Adsila shuffled toward the door. "But if I'm not there in five minutes—yes."

Five minutes had been optimistic.

The trip to the smaller of the two medbays was not far: a walk along the residential radial arm to the elevator, then a short ride to the bottom of the *Empyrean.* But it seemed to Adsila as though he were crossing the Ozark Plateau and back again.

"Is everything all right?" Dr. Carter asked when the deadline had come and gone.

"I'm almost there," Adsila replied.

"No you're not," Carter said. "You're twenty floors away. What's wrong?"

Adsila wasn't sure how to answer that. "I had a sudden flourish of hedonism a little while ago," he replied. "It took a while, but my mind and body are objecting."

"What exactly did you do?"

"I'm not sure," Adsila replied.

"Stay where you are," he ordered and signed off.

Adsila gratefully turned and leaned against a potted ficus. The leaves shook off a musty smell that gave him something to think about other than his condition . . . and the fact that he had agreed to let someone help him. That was new. It was also unwelcome.

Dr. Carter, dressed in a lab coat, was there within two minutes. He moved forward quickly, taking Adsila by the forearm and elbow at the same time. The fingers on his wrist checked Adsila's pulse.

As they entered the small room, Adsila saw a woman asleep on one of the cots; that would be Kristine Cavanaugh. Carter lay him on the other.

Almost at once there was a soft clicking from a petri dish on a table in the laboratory space. Simultaneously, Adsila felt tickling movement low in his belly and a faint sound mimicking the other echoing from under his skin. Carter turned toward the lab slowly, a look of concern on his face.

"Those bastards," he said.

"Who?" Adsila asked. He craned his neck and followed his gaze toward the dark room. "What is it, Doctor? Sounds like you have crickets in there."

"The bio-nanites . . . they've gone into a pattern-seeking mode," Carter said. He looked back at his patient. "They're trying to turn themselves into relay stations for a signal."

"Coming from—?"

Carter said, "Somewhere inside you."

It took Adsila a moment to process the information. "Inside me?" he said. "What kind of signal?"

"They are most likely coming from a separate set of nanites, reading and sending out all your EEG patterns, even when you're not intentionally transmitting via the IC. You had intercourse?"

"Yes, but I don't see how that's—"

"With—?"

"Ziv Levy," Adsila answered.

Carter shook his head slowly, bitterly. "I didn't think Dr. Uriel's team had gotten this far."

"Who's Dr. Uriel?"

"A visionary with money," he said. "He took the 'bio' out of 'bio-nanites' and produced the smallest robots in history."

"Which have what to do with me, exactly?"

"Of course, sorry," he said. "The bugs with the main EEG sensors most likely got into you through Ziv Levy's saliva—I'm betting lingual vein to internal jugular, dural venous sinuses, then up into—appropriately enough—some emissary veins."

"Are those—?"

"Right here." He touched the side of Adsila's head. "Close to the action. The relay nanites rode in on bodily fluids, possibly his lower-body perspiration through your pores."

"Possibly?" he asked. "What other way could they—?"

Dr. Carter cut him off with a look. Adsila decided not to press the matter. There was only one other possibility and it made him shiver.

"The nanites are receiving that data and sending it to an external receiver," Carter went on.

"From the vagina—which I do not at the moment possess?"

"Higher up, now," Carter said. "But that's how those got in."

Adsila stared at the dead-serious doctor. The EAD started to stand up. "I have to contact Director Lord."

"No you don't," Carter replied, putting his hand on Adsila's shoulder and pressing down lightly. "Not until we find out more about them."

Adsila acknowledged the necessity with a nod and Carter retrieved a small hand-held device from the lab table.

"I'll tell you this, though," the doctor said as he thumbed the device on. "Smart as he is, Uriel didn't count on pan-genderism. I believe the vaginally inserted nanites became trapped in your prostate."

"You're kidding. Do they have claws?"

"No reason to," the doctor said. "This won't hurt much," he added, "but it might take a while."

■ ■

It was Chairman Sheng who gave the order to activate the Dragon's Eye.

Hovering midway between floor and ceiling, Dr. Lung listened and watched, his eyes pointedly avoiding those of the other team members—except for Dr. Hark. Lung saw those pale eyes peripherally to his right, saw them because the scientist's head was held back proudly, not looking down like the others. Hark was the Chinese Intelligence Service liaison who had orchestrated the Chinese end of this piracy. It had been a brilliant scheme; he was confident in his work. If there were a problem with the device, it was in the "execution" by the others. Hark had emphasized that word when he exculpated himself of any responsibility. If this failed, again, he did not intend to be held accountable.

Lung stared at the dark, shielded heart of the device as he engaged the programs, turning them on in sequence and then using his personal code to make sure they synchronized. His fingerprints would literally be on this test if it failed.

Lung received the audible "lock" signal. The process was done. There was a hum in his ears, a vibration in his flesh, and then the device was active again—

Dr. Lung's weightless body suddenly felt as if it were undergoing a 10g push in the opposite direction. As he flew from his post, he listened dazedly to the chatter on his IC. It was coming from a debris-tracking office in Xichang. Static caused by Earth's restless atmosphere made the signal rasp and break up, but portions stuck to his preoccupied brain:

. . . a conjunction alert, medium concern . . .

. . . we recommend a debris-avoidance maneuver, point six meters per second . . .

The voices receded into crackling noise again, then returned. When they did, the characteristic air of professional calm had eroded significantly:

... seeing even more returns now ...

Then, with unmistakable alarm:

Has Jade Star *already moved off its orb—?*

With that, the voices dissolved completely and the static ebbed as well. Lung did not yet know it, but his body—having been thrust through the inner and outer wall of the space station—had drifted out of range of the last working IC field generator aboard the *Jade Star.*

He saw the Chinese satellites *Crane* and *Mantis,* and the city lights answering them from Earth far below. And he thought, *What a stupid thing, to operate the device here, in one of the station's sapphire observation modules, in full view of Earth and* Jade Star's *fellow satellites.* Their failure would be known throughout Beijing in an instant.

He wondered where Dr. Hark was, the physicist with the pale eyes and prodigious arrogance.

Thinking of Dr. Hark, the memory of the moment of activation came back to him: the magnet coils buckling under their own Lorentz force, the cryostats erupting, and that hard gamma light of neutrino annihilation finding not the surface of distant Earth, but the bulkhead of the *Jade Star* itself. Then the huge magnet horns had whirled toward the void between station and moon, and the shockwave made the station whip like a dragon's tail, shivering half a dozen modules into plumes of aerogel.

Lung realized suddenly—*he knew that because he saw it.*

For a flashing instant he understood that he was outside the space station, that the science module had been torn open. He was looking back through boiling tears, through the impossible cold of a vacuum. A vacuum that they had subtly altered: the blast that ripped a hole through the module had unleashed the same destructive force that had briefly been sent toward Earth just hours before.

There was at least one mercy: this time, thanks to Lung, the accident would follow an echoing angularity along the opposite end of the base of an isosceles triangle. As a safeguard, Lung had turned the Dragon's Eye away from Earth and in the direction of the moon. According to his calculations, Earth and the American station *Empyrean* would be spared. Beyond that, though—

I did what I could to save countless lives yet I will still be dishonored.

In the next moment, his rage toward Hark and Sheng, and the sudden, searing pain in his flesh, all vanished in the elation of hypoxia.

The moment after that, Dr. Lung joined the shimmering cloud of particulate matter that wreathed the station.

FOURTEEN

"ADSILA IS FINE, Sam."

Sam Lord had settled comfortably into his seat, acclimated easily into the Earth-normal gravity and uncommon downtime. He was just beginning to look over the interior of the *Grissom* and read about the shuttle on his IC when Dr. Carter contacted him. After briefing Lord on what had transpired with Adsila Waters, that was the medic's economical diagnosis.

"Thank you, Doctor."

"You're welcome. By the way, Director Lord: you exceeded your command."

"Doctor?"

"You still have the charter handy?"

"It's exactly where I left it the last time you asked," Lord said.

"Obviously. You see section 32-15? The text that requires you to report to a doctor for clearance before leaving *Empyrean* for any reason?"

With the shuttle nearing the moon, there was already a brief time differential in their communication. That gave Lord an instant to consider his response.

"I see it," Lord replied. He cast a quick look at Saranya May, who was typing into her IC. "And I *am* with a doctor."

Carter took longer than the delay to answer. "Who? The roster for the *Empyrean* says that everyone who is supposed to be on board *is* on board—except *you*."

"The identity of my traveling companion is classified," Lord replied. "You'll have to get that information from Al-Kazaz."

The silence that followed was even longer. "I will."

"But I'm more interested in these nanites than in my housebreaking," Lord went on.

"No doubt," Carter replied, surrendering to the more pressing matter. "As it happens, *they* appear to be something I'm capable of understanding. At least, now that I've had a chance to study them."

"Explain."

"I didn't—the FBI didn't—think that anyone had managed to produce working nanites," Carter said. "Now I realize how the Israelis did it. They cheated. They're not independent SimAI biological units. They're a sensor, transmitter, crawling mechanism, and logic system. Nothing else. No biological content that allows them to camouflage themselves in a body."

Lord appreciated that extra information. Obviously, that was the eyes-only project Carter was working on for Al-Kazaz. This was his oblique way of letting Lord know.

"So they're just internal audio bugs, hearing and broadcasting what someone hears and says," Lord said.

"That's right. And they're also bigger than any other prototypes I've seen or read about. They're so large that I'm worried that they damaged a few smaller blood vessels on the way to Adsila's skull. I don't think they would have caused an embolism, they just hovered on the periphery of the brain itself, grabbing electrical impulses."

"Damned ugly business," Lord said. He meant it.

"Very. But I might run a couple tests in case."

"I understand," Lord said. "You say you got them all?"

"Each one individually extracted using magnetized acupuncture needles to create new pathways and draw them out."

"Ingenious," Lord said admiringly.

"Thank you."

"But won't Ziv be expecting data?"

"Indeed, and he'll get it," Carter assured him. "Now those nanites are all in a petri dish relaying any songs that happen to get stuck in Adsila's head."

"You're kidding."

"No. All Adsila's FBI conversations will go through a separate secure channel in the comm. AEAD Grainger is setting that up."

"Ziv will be expecting some kind of information to pass between us about my current mission," Lord warned.

"Of course," Carter said. "Adsila is aware of that and working on it. As soon as I release him, he'll be in touch."

"Thank you, Doctor."

"It's my job, but you're welcome," Carter replied, a small, fine edge to his voice as he checked an IC ping.

"What's wrong?" asked Lord, who was used to intuiting moods over radios.

"Sam—you *push* me, dammit."

"I already explained about my departure—"

"Not that," Carter snapped. "I just heard from the prime director. That doctor you're with—she's an astrophysicist, not a physician!"

"A good thing too," he replied automatically. "Happens to be just what I need."

The exasperation in Carter's voice was profound. The man had just been caught in a lie and wasn't fazed.

"You know," Carter said, "this department could be exceptionally productive if we worked together . . . or at least communicated without prevarications and half-truths."

"I agree," Lord said affably. "Tell me more about the nanites I saw in the petri dish on your wall."

Carter hesitated.

"Doctor?"

Lord heard Carter exhale. "All right, Sam. All right. I concede, and *touché*. How about this? When all this stuff is done, how about we go to the Scrub, get a table in the corner, and have a nice chat?"

"Agreed, and dinner's on me," Lord said. "Until then—that was nice work with Adsila. How is your other patient, Ms. Cavanaugh?"

"Mild systemic reverberations from decompression and hypothermia, but well recovered. I can release her tomorrow."

Carter signed off and Lord lay back, trying to figure out what Ziv hoped to gain by spying on Adsila—and in *that* way. There was an intimidation angle, of course; that was Ziv's modus operandi. The CHAI famously used his cyborg body to cow men and dominate women. If that failed, he could be charming. If that failed, there was blackmail or bribery. But Ziv had also been very friendly with Colonel Franco on the *Empyrean*. Was this a team effort? Franco was uncommonly skittish at the reception and especially after. All that concern about Kristine Cavanaugh was just acting out. He felt it then, was sure of it now.

And then there was the other reception—the one for Dr. Saranya May. Why did Ziv and Franco do *that*? What did they know, or suspect? Lord glanced over at the woman. More important, what did she know . . . and not tell them?

Or me?

Lord sent Adsila a few details about his mission that might satisfy Ziv: he said he was going to the moon to safeguard Dr. May there and to secure her research, though he insisted he knew nothing more than that. Which was largely true. Then he wrote to Agent Abernathy to request background data, including financial reports, on all the personnel on Armstrong Base, including the *Grissom* crew, Dr. May, and Dr. Diego. That was standard operating procedure. While debt seemed an unlikely reason to compel one of two—or one *and* two—scientists to commit professional suicide and kill hundreds of thousands, it might point them to a theoretical middle person.

That done, Lord took some time to look at the schematics over the Armstrong Base, especially the module where the science labs of Drs. May and Diego were located. According to the original construction specs and security updates, they were as secure as Fort Knox in its hey-day, before Greece's Paracelsus Project made gold and artificial gold indistinguishable and therefore useless.

Dr. May was still typing in the air but noticed his expression. She stopped and managed a look of concern.

"Is everything all right?" she asked.

"No," he answered honestly. "It appears that when Colonel Franco and Ziv Levy failed to get answers from you, they tried to get them from one of my people. They used a rather crude and invasive form of technology."

"Is your agent all right?"

"Fortunately," Lord said. He leaned over the armrest, closer to her. "Dr. May, I must know what they asked you on the shuttle."

She diverted her gaze. Her eyes flitted to the right as she frowned.

"Saranya—"

"I'm not being evasive, Sam, I promise," she said. "This is hardly the time for that."

"I'm glad you agree."

"I'm just trying to remember—the conversation was short and almost entirely predictable. The colonel was clearly anxious, but trying to hide it with big smiles and solen."

"Sorry? That was—what?"

She was confused, then understood. "Solicitous energy—they say it on the moon. Isolation in space makes some people so stressed they work *very* hard to be your friend."

"I see."

"He was asking how I was, what I felt about Japan, how *horrible* it was about Japan, wasn't it too much for me to run from the moon to Earth in a single day, wouldn't I like to stay on the *Empyrean* . . . It was nonstop."

"And Ziv?"

"He stayed back and seemed uninterested, but I could see that he was getting every word."

"Did Franco say anything that was unexpected, even for someone going—'solen'?"

She thought. "He said it was an honor to meet me, complimented me on my work in very general terms, about how everyone knew I was the best in the field of neutrino research, and then Ziv was offering me a drink."

Lord nodded. "What did he ask as you were docking?"

"I'm not sure—"

"You'd remember," he assured her. "That's the Hail Mary, the last shot an interrogator gets as the subject is being hauled away. It's the one thing he really wants to know."

She glanced away. Lord waited until Dr. May finally looked back at him. "He asked if I knew the people who died in the JORO research center where the 'strike' against the Japanese was first recorded."

"Did you?"

"Yes," she said. "Dr. Makoto Ogawa was a colleague—we met at several symposia over the years. As I was leaving my seat, Ziv asked if we ever worked together. I said we had not." She looked cautiously into Lord's eyes. "Why would that matter?"

"For Ziv? I'm sure he wants to know more of what your research is about, and that's another way in, through sources in Tokyo."

"I see." She shook her head slowly. "I'm accustomed to academic politics but nothing like this."

"In that case, *my* next question will probably seem as fresh as paint. What day and time did you notice your findings were compromised?"

She appeared confused—again. "I don't recall. It was . . . two days ago, around lunchtime . . . maybe a little later?"

"Interesting," Lord said.

"How so?"

"If you took a break, you might not have noticed an electronic break-in," he said. "Are your habits in the lab regular?"

"Yes," she said. "I work from the minute I get there to the minute I leave, at my station. Anyway, there is no electronic 'way in.'"

He was about to answer that there'd never been a lock that couldn't be picked when his IC was full of Janet Grainger. "Sir, there's an emergency on board the *Jade Star*."

"Go ahead."

"Feeding images from the Arrius 2."

Lord looked at the visuals recorded by the satellite NASA was using to try to revive research into the feasibility of hydrogen ramjet propulsion. It was also—as most everything in space nowadays—part of the Ring of Security sensors that watched everything the Chinese and Russians did above the atmosphere.

The image was distant but undeniable. He saw a burst near the end of the long, spearlike space station and then watched it snap like a dragon's tail, the shields rolling like breaking waves. He saw what appeared to be glittering gems scatter around the station like exploding perspiration—finally realizing that those gems were bodies, and body parts, shimmering in the vacuum of space.

And then there was a signal from the cockpit of the *Grissom*.

"We are accelerating to maximum thrust," the pilot informed his passengers. "We just received word from Armstrong Base that something is headed toward us, something vast and very, very fast—"

Lord was out of his seat and at the cockpit door. It was not locked.

"What's going on?" he demanded. "I want to know everything."

"Sir!" the pilot shouted. "Please return—"

"What kind of '*something*' is coming our way?" Lord insisted.

Preoccupation quickly trumped the pilot's concern over the collapse of his authority. "*Empyrean* control does not have that information!"

"They'd have said if it were a meteoroid swarm or satellite debris field!" Lord said. "They must have *some* information or they wouldn't have sent an alert!"

"That's just it, sir," the pilot told him. "They only know there's a directional aberration of some kind because everything in its path is disappearing!"

"Look at this." The copilot pointed to a drop-down display.

"Put it on visual," Lord said. Then added, "Please."

The crew complied. There were numbers, with one column rising fast.

"Gamma spike," the pilot said. "And it's not coming from the sun."

Overhearing, Dr. May had also left her seat and was pulling herself forward on the overhead handholds. "Where is it coming from?" she asked.

"Origin unclear, but it's going to sweep right across our trajectory," the pilot said.

"How is that possible?" she inquired.

"Dr. May, what's the black dot on this Residual Map plot here?" Lord asked.

She leaned past him, studied the data flux. "That's the gamma spectrum . . . Majorana annihilation of neutrinos—"

She stopped and stiffened suddenly. Lord noticed it.

"What is it, Doctor?"

"I saw those exact numbers earlier today," she replied.

"Where?"

She answered, with effort, "They were recorded by Dr. Ogawa's team at the JORO station off the coast of Japan."

The quiet in the spacecraft was like the moments after a car crash, an absurd mix of utter stillness and hell.

"How does your research explain the visual anomalies?" Lord asked, turning toward Dr. May, grabbing the cockpit entrance for stability. "The reports from Japan today," he said quickly. "There was something about the sky *above* the water disappearing."

"Must be a scattering or lensing effect—I wish I could tell you: I haven't seen a neutrino stream condensed quite so much before, to get this kind of annihilation rate."

"So the same thing could be happening here, now," Lord went on. He cocked a thumb aft. "Back there. In space."

Dr. May's expression grew dark. "What's back there, Director Lord?"

"The *Jade Star*," he said. "Or at least, it was. The explosion or what- ever it was took a section of the station with it before rolling our way."

"The Chinese have the SAMI?"

"Have it, *had* it—the physical device, anyway, or what's left of it," Lord said. "Control of it is another matter."

"You're saying it's still *on*?" Saranya clarified.

"We don't know," Lord admitted with a short, angry shrug. "You tell me!"

She looked back at the figures in the cockpit. They were continuing to rise. "This confirms it. SAMI is still operative. God, that would be calamitous . . . if the Chinese cannot control it."

"Specifics, Doctor? It's good that it's apparently facing away from Earth now, isn't it?"

"For the moment. We don't know where the device is facing out here—the *Empyrean* could be at risk. The moon. Us. There's no way to be sure."

"What about moving to a more secure location at the station or on Armstrong—"

"There *is* no secure location," she said. "The JORO station was at the bottom of the sea. It was the first location to be hit. Moving any- where might actually put people *in* danger, especially if there is panic."

On his secure drop-down, Lord informed Stanton and Armstrong commander Blake Tengan of Dr. May's HYPA—Hold Your Position Assessment. Both acknowledged.

"That Chinese station is modular, isn't it?" Dr. May asked.

"Yes."

"If an entire section has been separated, it may try to reconnect . . . there are automated systems that do that on the *Jade Star*, if they're functioning. Who knows where SAMI will be facing then."

Lord continued to take it all in. He was trying to keep up: inside, *he* was trying to connect all the moving parts.

"Give me the worst-case scenarios," he went on.

"There's just one, really," Saranya said. "The incident that hit Japan, now this, were most likely accidents because of the faulty data but at least they were choices. Bad ones, but a human made them. If it's still operating, but intermittently and randomly, due to damage —"

"It's essentially got a will of its own now."

Saranya nodded. "Rudimentary SimAI, most likely. I wouldn't be surprised if the Chinese built in some degree of 'dead hand' intelligence. That device will be looking to fulfill its mission."

"Who would give a machine like that control of its own fate?" Lord asked, even though he knew the answer before he finished asking the question. Saranya confirmed it.

"What good is a doomsday device if it shuts down when the crew dies?"

Lord eased a little closer, regarded her pointedly. "How do you know so much about the subject, Saranya?"

"From colleagues," she replied. "From meetings . . . conferences." And then her voice grew quiet. "That's what the United States government wanted *my* work for."

Lord wasn't surprised. "But you refused."

"Repeatedly and stubbornly, though the pressure was growing," she admitted. "Funding cuts were threatened. Dr. Diego said that he was already planning how to use my lab space."

Lord was caught off-guard again. Not by the fact that the government wanted an absurdly overmuscular weapon but that she was only informing him *now* about the extent of their coercion. Lord was angry that she hadn't shared it with him earlier, though he was angrier with himself that he hadn't asked. Now, it had all the earmarks of a deathbed confession. The only positive impact was that it seemed to put Colonel Franco in the clear. He was a thug but a patriotic one; he would never have given SAMI to the Chinese. He must have been desperate to find out who did.

"So, the problem at hand," Lord said, trying to focus. "Can't someone just send this doomsday device corrected data? Order it to stand down?"

"As you can imagine, every new technology we create is typically keyed to operator DNA and other passcodes," Saranya said somberly. "The people in charge of this device? Those individuals probably no longer exist."

"All right. Then if this wave generator can't be shut down, I'm assuming it can be *shot* down."

"I wouldn't assume that at all," Saranya replied. "If it is intact—and we don't know that—but if it is, then the SimAI can command an army of neutrinos. Possibly other matter, as well—ions are larger, would be easier to handle. In theory, any number of particles can be organized to dematerialize whatever comes toward the device. And I mean take them apart on a very basic level, entering the nucleus of every atom and just ripping it apart."

Lord shook his head. *Build a better doomsday device and the world will beat a path to your lab.*

"Doctor, tell me—what *good* was this research supposed to do?" Lord asked.

"I had hoped to use neutrinos to study the core of the sun and other astrophysical phenomena," she said. "The particles are too small to be stopped or distorted. I want to use them to acquire a detailed, accurate picture of the cosmos."

Lord had no response to that. It was the most heartfelt expression he'd heard in the past twelve hours.

Lord became aware of the increasing acceleration as the *Grissom* sped toward the moon. He shifted in the doorway, tightened his grip a little as the moon's gravity failed to give him any noticeable weight. As he moved, he happened to spot the vast gray-and-white expanse as it rolled into view of the shuttle, filling it with brilliant light. It had a quality that transcended the moment, crushed all other concerns with an almost religious authority: like the moment the door of the cave in Jerusalem had rolled back to reveal the light of God.

They could use some of that now.

"Do you have any measurements, any readings at all, about the potential swath of the gamma activity?" Saranya asked the pilot.

"Only what I'm getting from the *Empyrean* and from Armstrong, and they're still scraping for additional details. All we're sure of is that the disturbance is narrow—it seems to have stopped spreading—but that oblique cone includes us and part of the moon."

"The Armstrong Base?" she asked.

"Unless whatever this thing is slices through a piece of lunar radius longer than fifteen kilometers, it should be all right."

Lord fired Dr. May a look: *Can it?*

She shrugged back with a look of *I don't know.*

He turned away thinking, *I was wrong, Carter. I need a geologist.*

The copilot informed the pilot that they had just entered lunar orbit and the pilot ordered an immediate deorbit sequence, also informing Armstrong Base.

"If we can set down, hopefully we can ride out whatever this is," the pilot said. He glanced back with a half-smile that he probably hoped was reassuring. "The shuttle is designed like a tank. It can take some—"

"Will you look at that!" the copilot shouted, pointing toward the port side of the vehicle.

Lord followed his finger. The area where Lord had seen the moon was distorting like a runny watercolor painting before going black, as if it were experiencing a total eclipse—but one of utter blackness, without the reassuring, ruddy glow caused by the filtering and refracting quality of Earth's atmosphere.

"It's still there," the pilot said incredulously, checking his dropdown. "We just can't see it!"

"The image is shrouded . . . like Japan," Saranya said thoughtfully.

"You got a less funereal-sounding explanation?" Lord asked.

"It's got to do with a spontaneous, parity-time symmetry-breaking effect—"

"Doctor—" Lord interrupted.

"It's self-cloaking," she replied.

"Ah," Lord said. "That I understand."

But before either the crew or passengers could consider the matter further, the drop-down data ceased flowing as, with a whisper, the cockpit of the *Grissom,* and then the rest of the interior, went very, very dark, as close and silent as a cave.

"That's not a visual phenomenon," Lord observed.

"No, sir," the pilot said. "Our spacecraft just died."

FIFTEEN

SAM LORD HAD been in dead aircrafts before. Once, thirty thousand feet over New Mexico, Lord was testing one of the next-gen Mist fighters, with active camouflage covering every inch of the fuselage and wings, when the cloaking system failed and took the rest of the plane's avionics with it. The ship didn't just nose down, it rotated around its central axis because the dedicated gyroscopes were still functioning. Lord was able to operate the flaps manually and used the atmosphere to counter the turn. He steadied the ship long enough to bring it down on a ski slope in Mescalero, earning the rare distinction of having landed a windowless plane in a cockpit blackout. The lumpy scar in the mountain was still there, named Lord's Mogul.

But this was unlike any other.

Technically, this situation was probably as elusive as the others. He remembered stepping from the Mist, and Purvis, his Lackland-trained flight engineer, looking more sheepish than excited to see him. Hours before, Lord had refused to set foot in the plane until Purvis agreed to speed-tape a secondary horizon and steam-gauge altimeter to the glareshield. He'd brought paper charts aboard in his flight bag. She muttered something about magic crystals and dreamcatchers, but the ancient instruments had guided him safely to the ground.

Experientially too, the status of the *Grissom* was new to him. In a fighter, there was air outside—noisy and screeching, in the old days punching the nose down just before Mach 1, or buffeting you on approach to stall. You could feel your way out of the crisis sometimes—there was none of this frictionless, Newtonian, helpless coasting.

The *Grissom* was not just dormant, all primary and backup systems were utterly nonresponsive. Even the emergency batteries were gone. The vessel sank in free fall through a void that didn't make a single utterance, didn't offer any kind of physical resistance or support. It was as though they didn't exist. And with the spreading darkness outside, neither did anything else.

Lord hovered at the cockpit door. He remembered the pilot's name—Kodera—from when Saranya had mentioned it back in his quarters. Now he saw the copilot's nameplate: Landry. In times of crisis, it was always good to keep conversation personal, supportive.

"Captain Kodera, you boys need any help?" Lord asked.

"Thanks, we're getting there," Kodera replied.

The pilot exchanged a look with his copilot. The look was one of encouragement, but also one of personal concern. Maybe the copilot had a family on the moon.

Lord felt Saranya touch his arm. She was either getting her bearings in the dark, afraid, or both. "What are they doing in there?" she asked.

"Pressure suits," Lord said. "Tough to put on, sitting."

He hadn't intended to be glib but it came out that way. It offset the pressure he felt coming from the cockpit.

"Your gear is under the seats," the pilot said tensely. "Landry will get them as soon as he's secure."

"Don't worry about us," Lord replied. "I'm one of those guys who actually checks the safety data at takeoff."

"Old flight checklist habit, sir?" the pilot asked.

"You bet, captain," Lord replied. "How'd you know I was a Zoomie?"

"Your Mist recovery was taught at Fourth SC," he replied. He added innocently, just making conversation, "I loved my aviation history class."

Lord grinned. "Captain, forty years from now, when this flight is taught, you're gonna know *exactly* what that feels like."

Lord meant his tone to be casual and reassuring, and he succeeded—even as they both knew how desperate their situation was. The ship was not the Vampire or the Mist. It was a falling anvil, without wings to glide on or use to decelerate—even if the moon, which was still invisible to them, had a buoyant atmosphere worth speaking about.

"Sam?" Saranya asked anxiously.

"It'll be okay," he said, taking her hand. "Follow me."

They traversed the length of the shuttle in seconds. It was eerie, almost like wading in a pool at night: Lord's feet barely touched the floor and he floated back toward their seats. He bent, felt for the latch under Saranya's seat, and popped it. Moments later he had slid out a one-foot-by-two-foot-by-six-inch rectangular pack. He popped the top and handed her the contents.

"You feel the feet?" he asked.

"Yes."

"Insert your toes there, then press the seams together to seal the rest. The helmet and oxygen are overhead."

"I know. I've had the training," she said.

It was not a rebuke. She was trying to be reassuring—to herself.

Lord retrieved his own suit. Silently, they slipped their arms, legs, and heads into the proper openings—soft gloves and foot coverings attached to the ends. The contractile fibers in the fabric—simpler versions of artificial polymer muscles—would aid the wearer in bending and flexing the suit's joints against the stiffness of air pressurization. The fibers, along with the chemical seal for the helmet, did not require any power beyond body warmth. As long as the wearer was alive, the suits would operate.

"In case the communications don't work," Lord said before they secured the collars, "we'll have to work out some rudimentary hand signals."

Saranya nodded.

Happily, that wasn't necessary. Whatever had knocked out the *Grissom* hadn't entirely penetrated the shielding—they were still alive, after all—nor had it depleted the self-contained power in the suits. As soon as the helmets were locked on, the illumination device above them glowed, a kind of opalescent IC, giving each a soft, 360-degree halo.

"Everything looks so ghostly in here," Saranya said.

"Well, it's not and it won't be," Lord assured her. He rapped on his helmet. "It's here, *we're* here, alive and solid as a moon rock."

"Some of them are actually quite porous," Saranya pointed out.

Lord grinned. "That's why you're the scientist and I'm the bodyguard."

He was already on his way back to the cockpit. The glow was not ghostly but angelic, a welcome relief from the pitch of eternity.

Lord arrived in time to hear the copilot, Landry, address the pilot.

"I'm not getting any response from the braking systems," Landry said. "Not a spark."

"Copy."

"Acceleration ditto."

"Copy," Kodera said, adding disconsolately, "and mea culpa."

"No way, Bob," Landry shot back. "I seconded the maneuver."

"What are you talking about?" Lord asked.

Kodera replied, "If the shutdown had happened before the burn, we could've just orbited until rescue, survived on the air we have on board. But I tried to outrun the wave and now we're on a collision course with the moon. Free fall. There won't be enough of us left to collect."

"It was a sensible risk, right option," Lord told him.

"It's my fault," Saranya told them all. "I should have considered the inverse relation between ionization and penetration. Your caution was reasonable."

Kodera replied with a crooked smile, "Phew. And here I thought I just screwed up."

Saranya said, "Do you have Thrombo or APC?"

"Those drugs are not in our first aid locker," Kodera said. "Why?"

"These ships have a shielding layer," Saranya said. "But even with that, and the suits, that's a ticking dosimetry clock."

"You know," Lord said, "I actually almost understood that."

"I'm sorry," Kodera said, "but I meant—why are you even asking? I don't see a way to set this bird down."

"There has to be one," Lord said. "We just haven't thought of it."

"I'm open to suggestions, sir," the pilot said.

"Well, I'm just an old fighter jock but I believe the first thing we should do is assess the condition of our craft."

"To what end?" Kodera asked. There was an edge in his voice. Understandable.

"To land," Lord told him. "Whatever hit us killed the main engine. Okay. But did the concussion destroy it? Or the ion thrusters?"

"We don't know," Kodera admitted.

"Right. We need those to land so we have to find out. What are we like on time?"

"Lunar impact in about twelve minutes," Kodera said, consulting the handheld rangefinder. Because they still couldn't see the physical moon yet, the rangefinder would have to be their eyes.

"So we have a little wiggle room," Lord said. "How would you gentlemen feel about a little extra vehicular activity?"

"Spacewalk?" Landry looked incredulous. "What happens if power comes back while we're on EVA?"

"We'll keep the hatch open, get you back inside," Lord said. "I assume there's an autopilot."

Kodera nodded.

"Director Lord has a point," Saranya said thoughtfully. "The magnetic shield is dead. But the helium coolant around the superconducting coils is well enough insulated from the heat of the cabin to stay in liquid form."

"Got an idea?" Lord asked her.

"I think so," Saranya said. "If we can compromise that insulation, we can warm the helium inside to the point of quenching, and maybe use that as a descent engine."

Kodera flipped through the QRH, showed her the checklist for an emergency magnet-quench. "We can route this through the vents more or less facing the ground right now."

"That'll be good enough," Saranya said.

"How long a burn does that give us?" Lord asked.

She skimmed through the checklist card. "Wild guess: sixty seconds, at . . . I don't know how many newtons yet." She looked at the terrain that was now in view and on its way up to meet the spacecraft. "Can't promise that'll do it."

Lord regarded the woman with a blend of admiration, puzzlement, and a sudden crush. The knowledge, he expected. But given the frightened woman he had met on the *Empyrean*, her cool demeanor was unexpected.

"But even if that works," Kodera countered, "we'll probably end up tumbling. We'll have to stabilize."

"That's why we need to know the degree of damage, if any," she told him. "We may be able to jerry-rig enough power to fire the ion thrusters."

"Jerry-rig . . . with what?" Kodera asked.

"The helmet displays," Lord said, pointing to Saranya's back. "We can use the battery pack under the O_2."

"Sir, I don't know about that," Kodera retorted, sounding both hopeful and doubtful.

"She can do the science, I can handle the rewiring," Lord assured him. Assured them all.

"Sam, no promises," Saranya cautioned.

"Try your best," Lord said. He winked. "We'll get the same result, I'm sure."

"You'll have to breathe cabin air," Landry remarked. "It'll be thin by then."

"I've had practice," Lord replied. "Just today, in fact."

Kodera pulled a stylus from the QRH binding. "For your calculations," the captain said. "One of those redundancies some NASA old-timers insisted on."

"God bless us veterans," Lord said as he backed away to give Kodera room to exit.

Before leaving the cockpit, Landry retrieved a toolkit from a compartment beneath his seat and gave that to Lord as well.

"The panel's down there," Landry pointed to a spot beside the pilot's station. "The big oblong thing that's not working is the battery. MS3509 connector."

"Roger that," Lord said.

Kodera regarded the team. "All right," he announced, already in motion. "As Yuri Gagarin said, 'Let's do it.' "

Saranya backed up to let Landry out.

"You understand what you have to do?" the copilot asked as he passed.

"The two of us have to seal ourselves in the cockpit," she said.

"Correct," Landry said. "It wouldn't do to have us all sucked out."

"Get back safe," Lord added. "You're gonna be heroes when you bring this baby home."

The four switched places and the flight crew headed toward the hatch while Lord and Saranya eased into the seats. Lord naturally selected the pilot's chair. Once seated, he craned around to shut the door. The cockpit door was solid and the visual electronics were dead, so they both had to settle for listening to the men over the helmet comm.

Saranya punched buttons on her wrist to close Landry and Kodera from any distracting conversation. After removing the tools and letting them float around him, Lord did the same. They continued to listen to the men's ragged breathing, their perfunctory comments about egress and procedure. Saranya was staring at the clipboard.

"You okay?" Lord asked.

"Mmm-hmm."

He regarded her knowingly. "You're going to do this in your head."

She nodded.

"I'll shut up when you tell me why," he said, bending and twisting his body, angling himself toward the panel and grunting with the effort.

"When I started out, all things being equal, the best jobs were still going to men, especially in Malaysia, India, everywhere I looked," Saranya said. "So I made sure that things were not equal, that my calculations were faster and I could function in places where the IC wasn't yet hooked to the AllPower."

"Smart," Lord said.

She smiled. "No, smart would have been investing in AP."

Lord chuckled as he continued to close in on the panel. At least the tight confines of the cockpit, the snug seat, and stiff suit helped him stay in any position he placed himself.

To his right, Saranya was aiming the purely mechanical rangefinder out of the window, estimating their descent speed, refining her guess about the volume of helium in the cryomagnet, the force of its explosive expansion from liquid to gas, the geometry of the vent. The numbers didn't have to be exact, only close enough to let them belly-flop on the moon. It would never be a pretty landing; even if everything went as planned, there were still innumerable variables—had a significant fraction of the ship's mass been knocked away, for example, in the blast? Her only hope was that impact on the lunar surface wouldn't be disastrous.

Finally, Saranya looked down, the glow of the helmet moving with her, changing the shadows in the cockpit. It suddenly looked darker, mirroring her expression. She began to write. Lord glanced over.

"Isn't it funny how we take for granted that things will work?" she said.

Lord studied the panel then plucked a screwdriver from the air. "Not at all," he said. "In fact, they usually do, when you consider how many moving parts even a human body has, how many things can go wrong."

"You're quite an optimist," she said.

"Incurable," he admitted. "And I've got to tell you, as emergencies go, this one's a day at the beach."

"You're just saying that," Saranya insisted.

"No, it's true. It's happening in slow-motion. I'm used to disasters hitting me around Mach 5, usually with a contrail and headed in my direction."

She smiled lightly. "That's a little reassuring," she admitted. "Though very soon the moon will be headed at you at Mach 5 if we don't pull this off."

"I wonder if they'll call the impact zone Lord's Crater," he quipped.

Lord looked into the opening below the panel, which was about three feet square. He saw the main electronics bay that connected the flight deck avionics with the various systems of the ship. Lord disconnected the sick battery, opened up the connector, then freed and spread out the wires inside.

"Would you pop my suit battery?" Lord asked.

Saranya turned to him with alarm. "Are you—"

"I'm sure," Lord said. "We need it. I'll be fine."

"You've considered, of course, that the flight crew won't be able to repressurize the cabin and that when they open the cockpit door—"

"I'll breathe cockpit air for now and open the valve on the tank when they return," Lord said. "It won't circulate without the battery, but it will keep the suit full and the air breathable for ten minutes. Trust me, I've done it at high alt."

"You'll lose your comm unit," she said, pointing to her own ears. "Hand signals may not be enough for this—"

"Crack your faceplate a little and turn up the volume," he said. "I'll eavesdrop."

Saranya's expression became resigned. "What do I do?"

He shifted so his back was toward her. "The red squares on the sides? Press simultaneously and hand me the pack."

When she did so, the electromagnet that held it in place died. So did Lord's helmet light. So did his tanks. He could always bleed them manually if he had to.

Lord pressed the sides of his helmet and raised the visor. As he did, a warm, stale wash of air poured in. It was humid and unscrubbed but it was breathable. To save breath, he motioned for Saranya to angle her helmet light toward the open panel. Then he studied the back of the battery pack, squinting at the small writing, broke into the casing, and started to improvise a connector to match that of the shuttle.

"You copy in there?"

It was Kodera. Saranya punched the men back in. Lord listened hard.

"Yes, Captain," Saranya said.

"Doctor, it's truly weird out here," he said. "More still, more silent, much darker than I've ever experienced. It's like someone threw a blanket on space."

"I can't even begin to speculate on that kind of emptiness," Saranya said.

"Well, for you space isn't empty, is it? You're not seeing it with just your eyes."

She didn't answer. Lord made a circling motion with his hand, urging her to continue, to keep him connected to people, to the familiar.

"Maybe if I get these quench numbers crunched ahead of time, I can head out there with you guys and collect some data before we land," she said.

"If we manage to get these engines back, sure—happy to oblige," Kodera told her. "First Officer Landry's looking at the ion thrusters. I'm nearly at the main engine— Oh-ho! There you are, big boy!"

"Say again?" Saranya said, but then she realized what Kodera was referring to. Through the small cockpit side window she could see stars begin to appear—and the looming crescent edge of the moon. It was close—just a few minutes away in free fall.

"Someone turned the cosmic lights back on," Kodera said with relief. "Maybe we'll have the same luck."

"Different situation entirely," Saranya said. "The stars weren't shut down, the photons were just pushed aside."

"I know that, Doctor," Kodera said with an embarrassed chuckle. "I was just wishing on a star."

Lord made a face and motioned for her to dial back the reality check. She twisted her mouth but nodded. She was scared too, and science was her way to deal with it, but Lord understood pilots. There was romance in their souls, and hope. From the very first barnstormers, they were always looking for castles in the air.

"Not much left of the engine, I'm afraid," they heard Kodera announce. "Looks like we'll have to ride home on Dr. May's cryostat rocket."

"Ion thrusters seem intact," Landry added. "They're just not working with the reactor out."

Saranya settled down. Hearing that she would have the tools they required, she exhaled. Lord had situated himself back in the seat to conserve energy. Throughout this present trial he admired her sudden shift from the wistful, frightened woman to cold-eyed scientist. Now that she had jumped into it, nothing else existed.

Lord let her be. With nothing else to do but stay calm and savor every moment of life, he looked around. It was the first chance he'd had to study the cockpit and there was something comfortable about it. It wasn't just the snugness, or what he had always called the Iron Womb— the comfortable proliferation of metals and alloys, of controls that gave a man like him life. No, there was something else . . . .

"Okay, then," Saranya said. "Better get that burn started. On to the cryostat."

"Heading there now," Kodera replied. "How are you doing in there?"

Lord glanced at the battery pack, and at a standby voltage indicator on the flight deck panel. The instrument glowed only feebly; a trickle was coming from the battery. He gave her a thumbs-up, privately hoping that all their efforts weren't wasted.

"We're all set," she assured the flight crew.

After several agonizing minutes, the captain reported that he was at the cryostat with Landry. Saranya finally looked up from the QRH, where Lord saw that she'd scrawled unnervingly few formulae. He hoped it was because she had the rest of the hard data in her head.

"All right," she said conclusively. "While you're getting the flow routed: what's your estimate of the thrust vector we'll have?"

"Near as I can tell, the vent's pointed straight down at the surface of the moon," the captain replied as Landry drilled out a panel to access the cryostat plumbing. They didn't hear it outside, of course, but the vibration made a humming sound in the wall of the spacecraft.

"I'm guessing we have about thirty seconds of this," Landry said.

"That will give you roughly two minutes to get back in your seats," she said.

"Doable," Kodera told her.

Saranya was looking out the window at the rising lunar horizon when a bolt of alarm shot through her belly, sharp and discomforting. It caused her to jump. Lord noticed.

"What is it?" he asked.

She shook her head angrily, as if she were in denial.

"Dr. May?"

She waved him off. "Captain, when you're done, get back in as *quickly* as possible."

"Problem?" Kodera asked.

She scratched out several figures. "I forgot the damn cargo pallet, Captain. Stupid! *Stupid!*"

"What does that mean?" Kodera asked.

"It means we must execute our burn in"—she looked at the quaintly ticking watch—"forty-one seconds. Either we're flying by then, Captain, or we crash."

"Can't do it," Kodera said, a hint of anxiety finally showing in his voice. "It'll take nearly that long to finish here and shut the door!"

"Why don't we just cut it loose?" Landry asked.

"I have to calculate the kickback, the opposite reaction. . . ." Her voice trailed off.

Lord had been listening to the exchange. His eyes wandered out the window, picked out the only artificial light source on the moon. He had spotted it earlier, recognized the landscape around it, knew it was

Armstrong—humankind's first permanent foothold on alien soil. It sent a thrill down his back to actually lay eyes on it, not just for the achievement: it had the strange quality of a homecoming, the same he used to feel when he flew northward from the Atlantic and saw the first familiar contours of Manhattan Island. Lord had never been to the moon, of course, but his imagination had always been rooted in the sky, in pushing the envelope, in a manifest destiny for humankind. Despite the politics, the bureaucrats, the distractions, there was no bolder statement of that than Armstrong.

Lord was surprised to find other glints here and there, which he realized were exposed silicon from local mining expeditions.

He flipped his attention back to the cockpit. That too seemed comfortable. What *was* it that struck him?

"I'll be damned," he said suddenly.

"Sir?" Kodera asked hopefully.

Lord breathed carefully as he answered; now he really had to stay awake and alert. He leaned nearer to Saranya's comm.

"Got some beautiful antiques up here," he said.

"I'm sorry, sir—?"

"The backup sidestick—it's an old RHC: twist to yaw, with a trim-rate switch; Captain, I can fly this!"

"Sir—"

"No time, very little air," he said. He motioned for Saranya to turn on his tanks, looked at her ticking clock. "Just do what Dr. May said: finish with the cryostat and get yourselves inside. In forty-something seconds. Tell me how to light this bird up and I'll take her in!"

"Is the battery secure?" Kodera asked.

"Yes," he answered, though it was still barely producing a current, damn its alkaline soul.

"Then controls will return automatically," Kodera said.

"I'm done!" Landry announced.

"We're coming back!" Kodera said.

Saranya found the purge button on the tanks and pushed them on.

Lord closed his visor manually. His very limited reserves of air were ticking down.

The pilots clawed their way toward the main hatch as Lord got his bearings.

Saranya said, "Quench in fourteen, thirteen, twelve— "

"*World* of time," Lord assured her as he looked at the equipment. "I've even got time to get a feel for the stick."

"What you *have* is eleven seconds . . ." Saranya said.

"And is that not time, Dr. May?"

"Ten . . ." she said. "Director Lord, were you angling for this all along?"

"I was not," he said truthfully. "But here it is."

Lord fell silent as Saranya resumed the countdown.

". . . nine, eight . . ."

They listened to the flight crew in their helmet. The men were nearly at the hatch.

". . . seven, six . . ."

Lord was confident but not cocky. *What's that line in Melville?* he wondered. *Something about Moby-Dick being a monstrous big whale but, still, ultimately, just a whale?* The *Grissom* was an unfamiliar craft, but he'd spent many years of his aerial career in flight test, in craft that were familiar to *no one* the first time he took them up. And he survived them all. *Except that it doesn't require an atmosphere or wings and was essentially, critically nonfunctional,* Lord thought. *Except for* that . . . .

". . . five, four . . ."

"Give me your hand, Captain! I'll pull you in."

That was Landry. Kodera must have motioned for him to enter first.

". . . three, two . . ."

There were grunts in the ears and then the hull shook. That was the hatch door closing.

And then the helium exploded into vapor and the shuttle seemed to halt in the black sky. The deceleration was accompanied by two dull whams from somewhere in the cabin.

Saranya looked at Lord with alarm.

"The flight crew hitting something," he said. He didn't bother looking at the battery. Either he had control or they would hit the moon much, much sooner than anticipated.

Since the dawn of human flight, aviators have said that flying is easy; it's the takeoff and landing that are difficult. *That has never been truer than now,* Lord thought. His hands were on the rotational and translational controllers. Inputs here spun or slid the ship—or at least that's what they should have done: Lord tried to align the nose of the ship with rabbit lights that appeared to recede into the Armstrong landing field, a round pockmark in the lunar surface. The nose failed to budge, drifted a little farther off-true.

Lord pulled off his gloves, connected with the machine as if he'd known it all his life, tried to make the adjustments by tensing and relaxing the muscles in his fingers. He felt warm inside as he thought of the saddle back on Earth, crossed the centuries, imagined Isaiah Lord doing the same with whatever trusted steed had been beneath him. But the shuttle, here and now, still stubbornly drifted.

The future is that way, he thought, quoting a favorite line from Isaiah's journals.

Lord did not take his eyes from the beacon at Armstrong Base, which was growing noticeably in size and brightness. But from the corner of his eyes he saw Saranya actually smiling, eying that light with hope and relief—

Suddenly, the entire ship lit up as if the neutrino attack had never happened. The oxygen hummed on, the panels lit up, the controls suddenly manifested a comforting, let-me-help-you quality, and someone in the cabin shouted the Houston Pincers volleyball cheer, "P*ayo*!"

Lord felt cautious relief . . . until he saw that Saranya was now frowning.

"Doctor?" Lord asked.

"I don't understand that," she said. "Systems don't recover from that kind of burn. What happened?"

Lord was about to remind her of the mouths of gift horses when, just as suddenly, everything went off again. Including the few limited controls he was working. Almost at once, the moon lost its happy stability outside the window and began to spin. Or, rather, they began to spin. Lord glanced at his feet. There were stars, gallons of them, piled one atop the other, but the beacon was nowhere in sight.

"Oh, screw you with a boring cylinder," Lord told the shuttle.

"What?" Saranya asked.

"We need your comm. We need a better solution. I may need the crew."

Lord's gloves sailed around the cabin as the *Grissom* pinwheeled slowly, now in the sun, now in the dark, stark shadows playing madly around the interior.

The air was becoming very thin very fast: Saranya was breathing it too. Lord reached over and slid her visor shut.

Lord looked around the cockpit during the bright flashes of sunlight. His eyes settled on a tiny drawer, like an old DVD tray, labeled IC Power. That would be dead, of course, but he wondered if there were a solar storage battery attached to it—and if so, how could he patch that in so close to impact. He eyed the watch covetously. Did it have a battery? He could accept perishing in a crash, the idea had never been far from his mind. But to die without even a spark of fight—that was never going to happen.

"Sam!"

Lord's eyes snapped from the clipboard to Saranya. She flipped up her visor.

"The captain," she said, narrating as she listened to the incoming message. "He's—the air scrubbers aboard this shuttle, they're basically fuel cells that run in reverse. Put power and CO_2 in; get oxygen out. But now he's working on putting oxygen in to get you power. Says he thinks he's got it this time. Get ready!"

Breathing heavily, Lord turned his eyes to the moon and held the controllers tightly. The *Grissom* was pointing nose-down, toward the crater that held the Armstrong Base. Lord flashed to images he once saw from the old pre-Apollo Ranger program, reconnaissance robots that took photos of potential landing sites as they plunged headlong into the lunar surface.

Not the heritage you want, he told himself.

An instant later the cockpit lit up like Times Square at night. Lord's mind jumped ahead to Neil Armstrong during the Apollo 11 landing and the infamous Dead Man's Curve: ten feet from the surface, fuel running out, no clear landing site in view, Armstrong set the lander down by gut, by feel. The ion thrusters fired again.

Lord stopped hard so they were belly-down, then nosed up—all in just over two seconds.

Dr. May was looking at her calculations. "All right—Sam, cut the pallet on my 'go.' "

"On your go," he confirmed. Through the controls, his strong hands felt the cargo pallet complain, argue the maneuver with a tug.

"Get ready," she said cautiously, eying the second hand. "Now!"

Lord drove a palm into the jettison button. The pallet and its contents fell behind, fell down, blasting dust and parcels into the dark sky. There were boulders about and Lord did his best to spot the clearest path he could and head toward it.

He had decided not to lower the landing gear: it'd probably buckle, and he didn't want to have exposed struts digging into the surface unevenly.

There was a contact light to his left, just behind the stick. It went from dark to green. They had reached the surface of the moon.

Lord heard scraping sounds through the hull, then felt the bumps. He nosed down, deciding it was better to take a bump up here than to rip open the undercarriage and endanger the crew.

The blunt forward section of the *Grissom* plowed into lunar mineral, throwing up stones and powder but nothing larger. The force of impact pushed the nose into the lunar crust, caused the aft section of the ship to rise, and then the cabin and the tail section came down—not hard, in the one-sixth gravity, but firmly enough to crack the hull along the hatch.

The power went out again.

The eagle is badly bruised but it has *landed,* he said defiantly to the stark landscape.

He held up his hands and Saranya searched for his gloves. While she did that, Lord reached behind himself to manually activate his air tanks. He slapped down his visor as they hissed on, then pulled on the gloves. The air wasn't sufficient to pressurize his suit but the cockpit still had pressure; all he needed was to breathe.

And hope that help arrived within the next ten minutes.

SIXTEEN

WE'RE ALIVE!"

Saranya May was not just impressed. She was incredulous.

Lord had activated his helmet comm before collapsing back in his seat. He ached everywhere from the hard landing, bones having been thrust up hard in sockets, spinal discs compressed, the hip joint of his metal leg having given his pelvis a good knocking. He also felt pain growing in his left temple, then his right. He pushed his chin back, helping his nostrils remain clear. He raised his visor and shut off his air. Saranya did the same. The tanks were nearly as tapped out as the cabin air, but if help arrived, they would need whatever was left. Otherwise the cockpit door couldn't be opened.

"Are you all right?" Saranya asked.

"Headache," he said. "Vision blurry."

"We took some lumps," Saranya said.

"It may be carbon dioxide," they heard Landry say.

Lord was not relieved to hear it. It would only take about seven percent CO_2 to kill them.

"But we're on oxygen," Saranya said, trying to understand the immediate problem. "Where is it coming from?"

"There are stress points where the tanks meet the suits, on the neck seam, and also around the visor," the copilot said. "There may be hairline cracks."

"First Officer—how's the captain?" Lord asked.

"Unconscious," Landry said, a catch in his voice. "The scrubber started to leak, shorted avionics circuits back here. A thermal apron caught fire and he hit his head putting it out. I can't tell how badly."

"How about the cabin?"

"It'll need more than new enameling," Landry said. "Stay where you are."

Lord acknowledged, then turned back to the cockpit window.

The moon was spread before him—he had no idea exactly how far it was, but it was strange to see such stark grandeur that simultaneously appeared so dead. Everywhere, ejecta from collisions and ancient upheavals. There were mounds so smooth they looked like melted ice cream, and boulders so edgy they looked like granite lightning. No, it wasn't desolate; it was unfinished.

Lord felt Saranya take his hand in both of hers. He turned his head toward her, and her expression was different from any he had seen so far. There was appreciation flavored with a newfound respect. Together, they bordered on tenderness.

Lord smiled softly. They just sat there, conserving oxygen by not moving, not speaking. There was nothing to talk *about*: they were sure Armstrong Base had seen them come in, and either they would get some kind of team there to help in time . . . or they wouldn't. Lord and the others had done all they could.

The tanks were draining and the air was thinning noticeably before they heard a hatch opening behind them, in the cabin. There was no air back there, no talking, not even Landry.

Two loud bangs sounded on the door behind them, followed after a pause by a third. Lord recognized it as the okay-to-enter signal used before accessing airlocks. In this case, the new arrival was making sure the occupants were secure before blundering in and letting out all the air.

The cockpit occupants lowered their visors, turned the oxygen back on, and then Saranya replied in kind.

The door opened with a sound like tearing paper. They could hear it even through their helmets. Saranya recognized the new arrival as Armstrong Base Emergency Team Operative Don Christie. The powerfully built former marine was carrying a pair of portable oxygen packs and moving with practiced urgency. He plugged the air hoses into jacks on the tanks to resupply them. Noticing that Lord's battery was missing, he efficiently pulled one from an equipment belt and pressed it into place.

". . . tracking you every kilometer since the gamma wave appeared," Lord heard him saying as his comm came back online. "We were running our emergency response buggy under you since you zeroed in on the crater."

"An ERB." Lord smiled. "Nice."

"It's a helluva service vehicle," Christie said. He took a moment to put a hand on Lord's shoulder. "And that was one hell of a landing, sir!"

"We haven't quite walked away from it . . . yet," Lord said.

He waited as Saranya climbed from her seat.

"The base," she said. "Is it all right?"

"Whatever that was, it missed us," Christie informed her. "Got a lot of engineers working on what to do when it happens again."

"When?" she asked.

"That's what they're saying, Doctor."

When Saranya had exited the cockpit, Lord ruggedly and ambitiously pushed out from his seat. He stopped on the threshold and wavered like a reed.

Christie offered him an arm.

"Real gravity is not centripetal gravity, sir."

No, it is not, Lord thought. Even at one-sixth Earth's pull, he had a real center of gravity, bones settled downward, the blood rushed with a familiar up-and-down flow, and his body felt, for a moment, as if it were on a roller coaster speeding down.

Christie waited patiently until blood flow had regulated and Lord could stand without assistance.

"Wow."

"I know," the ETO replied. "Isaac Newton is not our friend."

Lord insisted on walking unaided as he followed Saranya and Christie to the hatch. He lacked the bounce in his step that he had seen in other moonwalkers; but then they had landed with thrusters, not an unprotected undercarriage.

And my undercarriage is not as resilient as once it was, he thought.

Lord's step—and his spirits—were lightened considerably by the sight just outside the downed shuttle.

The emergency response buggy was like nothing he had seen in his few short weeks in space; it was the kind of unearthly conveyance one would only see in a hostile, low-gravity environment like Earth's moon. It looked like a big-bellied metal ladybug stuck atop a dune buggy. The metal mesh of the wheels, which resembled the original Apollo rovers, doubled as anode screens for the vehicle's supplementary ion thrusters. On the top of the vehicle was an array of solar panels pointing in all directions. In the midst of the circle of solar panels was a docking hatch that allowed for a seamless move from the cabin to any habitat. Forward, where the bug's eyes would be, was a bubble-shaped cabin and a driver tucked inside. From that vantage point, Christie's partner could see everything left, right, and center of the craft; rear-mounted cameras completed the panorama. Christie ushered them toward a shallow ramp that opened into a small airlock. They entered and waited a few moments as the ramp closed silently behind them in the airless void.

"Where are the pilots?" Lord wondered aloud.

"Already on board," Christie informed him. "Captain Kodera's injuries required immediate care. He came in on the medtray."

Lord nodded. They had two of those on the *Empyrean* as well, gurneys that rode on slings between the medical personnel as they rushed it along.

The new arrivals felt a sudden, strong wind pressing down as the airlock filled.

"Compression complete," they were informed by a sympathetic synthetic voice.

Lord opened his helmet and savored the relatively clean, fresh, slightly chilled air around him. Then he closed his eyes, raised his head, and sighed, stretching, as a green light flashed.

"Nice," Saranya said from beside him.

Lord nodded as the narrow door behind them hissed open. Christie ushered them into the cramped main cabin as the buggy started off. To the right, Lord saw a double berth in an alcove with the unconscious Captain Kodera on top and First Officer Landry below. The automated medical compartment was performing a full scan of both men while a pair of medtechs watched the results on their ICs. Lord caught Landry's eyes as he passed and both men fired off quick little salutes.

Lord and Saranya sat in comfortable plastic slings with armholes that kept them from bouncing around while Christie took a seat behind the driver. They swung pleasantly, almost in unison, as if they were on a front porch swing. Lord saw Christie thumb a small recess overhead. A small light glowed above Saranya and himself. Lord had seen those in the cockpits of late-model Vampires. Their own vital statistics were being read and sent to the medical bay at Armstrong.

Moments later, clear of the wrecked shuttle, the ERB's thrusters had rotated downward and they were airborne, gliding swiftly to the northeast of the crater. The hills and boulders were slipping by them now, the high rim of the crater as rough and jagged as the day it formed.

Saranya looked over at Lord. Perhaps she'd seen enough of the moon for one night.

"Jesus, Sam," was all she said.

He nodded in accord. It wasn't a lament, more like a footnote to an adventure he still didn't quite believe himself.

Lord didn't blame the moon for what had happened, and was still enjoying the view. But there were other priorities. He activated his IC, wanting to assure the staff that he was all right. He turned on the imaging component. Janet Grainger's face hovered solidly before his eyes.

Due to their distance from the space station, there was a two-second delay before she replied.

"Glad to see that you're all right," she said with the hint of a smile. "We heard what happened."

"I'm as durable as the Man in the Moon," he said. "How's EAD Waters?"

"Dr. Carter is scheduled to release her momentarily," she said. "Would this be a convenient time for a briefing?"

"I'm in a lunar buggy, so just give me the headline on the *Jade Star*."

"The situation is fluid," she replied. "China is obstinately refusing to discuss the status of the station and whatever went wrong up there. Commander Stanton is organizing a recon party and PD Al-Kazaz wants in."

Lord was not surprised by any of this. Crises bring out the worst and the best in systems.

"Thank you, Janet," he said. "I'll contact you when we're at Armstrong."

"Very good, sir. And, sir, might I suggest a rest? You've had quite a day."

"I'd like that," he said pleasantly. "Perhaps when we're sure the day is over?"

"Understood," Grainger replied.

Lord signed off and, a moment later, he felt his stomach rise as the ERB suddenly stopped moving forward then started to dip, seemingly all in one motion. The moon's expansive surface rose out of sight and then they were facing down, surrounded by a nearly mile-wide rill inside the vast lunar crater. The lights of the buggy came on, emphatically illuminating vertical walls formed from an ancient black lava flow.

Lord almost felt the chill. He knew that these deep, dark, sinuous crevices were some of the coldest places in the solar system. Now and then, patches of water ice gleamed silvery white in deep pockets, like veins of precious ore. As at the head of a comet, there was probably dust in there from the birth of the world.

The ERB dipped lower, headed toward a landing pad at the mouth of a cave in the northern wall. Once it was over the circular white construction, it landed gently on the thrusters while the wheels immediately rolled forward toward the overhead docking ring, which projected out and down from the bleak, smooth wall, reminding Lord of the watering systems used by locomotives in the Old West.

As much as things changed, they didn't.

While Lord and Saranya slipped from their slings, transparent bubbles stored in the berths were inflated over the flight crew of the *Grissom* and—mattress and all—they were escorted to the rear of the craft. Lord watched through one of the small windows. After going down the aft ramp, the flight crew was carried across the landing pad. A door in the rock wall slid up to admit them.

"That leads directly to the ground-level medical bay," Christie told them as they watched. "There's also an elevator on the ledge one hundred feet above to lower people down in the event of a surface accident. It was easier to build a small access portal than to build a garage for the ERB."

"Less costly too," Lord said.

"Cost is always a factor," Christie noted. "In this case, though, it saves time, not having to fill a large airlock. Also, we share storage and repair services with the science buggy in the Armstrong garage."

That made sense, Lord had to admit. Still, he had to wonder which came first: efficiency or economy.

They made their way to the aft hatch while the driver performed his post-operation shutdown. Christie opened the door, lowered the aluminum ladder extension, then came down. Saranya went up immediately. It wasn't a question of "ladies first"; Lord had watched her mood change as they twisted in their slings, reflection giving way to a low boil. She had something on her mind that needed expressing.

"Would you like a hand, sir?" Christie asked.

"I think I'll make it," he assured the younger man.

Christie nodded in recognition and Lord followed Dr. May out the hatch. It was actually an easy climb, if snug; a little like being pulled up by a wire. Lord ascended just ten rungs and then he was inside the cold, solid lava tube that housed Armstrong Base.

The first surprise was there wasn't any kind of ready room between the disembarking area and the station. Once past the door they were right in the middle of the facility, a dome with a series of tubes leading off in seven different directions.

"Welcome to the Squid, sir," Christie said as Lord slid from the upper section of the ladder.

Armstrong Base was definitely a triumph of efficiency over aesthetics. Made of puncture-proof Kevlar and supported by a network of widely spaced steel ribs, the dome was seven feet high by ten feet wide. Lord noticed a series of slightly raised tendrils that ran through the Kevlar like a fine arterial system. He squinted at them. They actually seemed to pulse.

Christie noticed Lord's interest. "Ah, our truss geometry," he said.

"You'll have to explain that one," Lord replied.

"Wire coils filled with liquid helium," he explained. "We extract it from lunar regolith using a solar cooker. That's how we maintain a constant temperature." He chuckled. "You think Pluto is cold? Right here we've got the coldest spot in the solar system—negative three hundred ninety-seven degrees Fahrenheit."

"Cold enough to *freeze* books," Lord quipped.

"Sir?"

"Just something from my childhood," Lord replied wistfully.

Christie smiled politely. "Perhaps you noticed the ice on the walls of the crevice? We've got frozen pools of water here, deposits that make us self-sufficient. That's Commander Tengan's goal by 2055."

Lord nodded respectfully. When Lord accepted the *Empyrean* post, part of his briefing file had included an FBI dossier on Blake Tengan. The forty-eight-year-old wunderkind was the only commander Armstrong Base had known in its five years of operation. Tengan had seemed tailor-made for the job: the holder of a PhD in astrophysics from Stanford and a decorated veteran of the First Special Forces Operational Detachment–Delta, Airborne. As a young lieutenant, she had led the mission to rescue American geology students held hostage on Pico

Bolívar, Venezuela, by the radical Confederación de Acciones Especiales. She not only brought back the three students from the treacherous peak, she captured the CAE leader. The US turned her over to Caracas, breaking a half century of tension between the two nations.

Despite her record on Earth and on the moon, Tengan was on the FBI's watch list. There was a sense that her career objective was not just a successful lunar colony but a successful and independent lunar colony.

Lord didn't hold that against her. To the contrary. If it were true, then the woman had vision. If that vision was weighted in favor of ideals over economy, Lord could support it.

Not that anyone asked, he thought with a private chuckle. *Or would. Or that it will ever happen.*

Don Christie excused himself as Tengan neared.

"Deputy Director Sam Lord," the base leader announced, her hand already extended, her voice traveling well ahead of her. Lord turned to meet her.

She was a woman of medium height, about five foot five, but she owned the area around her. She did not bound, despite the lesser gravity; she walked with odd kicks, like little goosesteps, that moved her forward but not upward. She had a perfect smile, not insincere, that rendered well in IC phosphenes. She was a woman who looked better in the mind's eye.

"Magna job," she said, grabbing Lord's much larger hand, "just magna. Don't let NASA tell you the FBI owes them a shuttle." She leaned closer, conspiratorially. "We recycle *everything* up here—except people. And *you* saved my crew and scientist. What a feat. What a *feat.*"

"It was a team effort," Lord answered truthfully. "Dr. May came up with—"

"*You* were in the pilot's chair," Tengan cut him off. "Anyway, there's no modesty on the moon, Mr. Director. Not legal. This is the frontline of space and you've earned your spot in it."

Tengan turned to the scientist, who was busy unsuiting.

"Dr. May?"

"My departure was legal," she said peremptorily.

"Self-authorized off-world travel is permissible only in the event of a life-threatening medical emergency," Tengan said evenly. "That threat was—?"

"Fear for my life," she admitted.

Tengan's demeanor shifted. The strong hazel eyes showed concern. "Elaborate, please."

"Can we do that later, Commander? I must get to my lab."

"For?"

"Threat assessment and solutions," she said.

Before Tengan could respond, Dr. Ras Diego sprang from one of the adjoining tubes and approached in quick, arching jumps, a stride he had practiced during long hours spent outside the base at the external science station. The lean, almost antlike scientist stopped right before the taller woman.

"How dare you leave!" Diego said, snapping at Dr. May. "You *knew* something like this could happen!"

The woman looked like she wanted to bite back but checked herself.

"That's *your* work out there." He gestured past her toward the egress port. "Your calculations are responsible for what happened!"

Tengan felt Lord tense. The base leader placed a cautioning hand on the shoulder of the Zero-G leader and shook her head once. Whether Tengan wanted to let the challenge play out or burn out, it was moving forward.

"Rasputin, that's not true," Saranya said dismissively. "My calculations would have *worked*, not gone spinning out of control. Anyway, I'm not interested in arguing. I'm here because we have to find a way to fix this. Together, if that's possible." She made a point of turning to the other two. "Director, Commander, Dr. Diego is referring to my work in designing a powerful electromagnet that would focus via transition magnetic moment, neutrinos like optical light. I had one purpose: to resolve neutrino sources in space, to understand the invisible preponderance of the universe. Full stop." She made a tight, almost vibrating fist, her skin white. "But increase the field strength a little, and the flux density becomes enormous, the collision frequency becomes enormous, and, as Majorana fermions, the neutrinos self-annihilate in a perpetual antimatter explosion." She looked to each face to make certain they understood. "But I armed my machine against itself, to ensure that we would never reach these field strengths. That safeguard is *not* present in the current iteration of my work. Whoever stole it"—she turned pointedly back to Diego—"has a much different application in mind for my SAMI. Or else they made it wrong."

Lord was still trying to understand the change that had come over the woman. Dr. May suddenly seemed on fire. That was partly due, no doubt, to what she had experienced on the way to the moon. Proximity to death often loosened caution. She also had to feel safer being home with Lord having her back.

But the tension between her and Ras Diego was like jet fuel and fire creeping toward ignition. She clearly suspected him of wrongdoing. He seemed to mistrust her as well. Lord wondered how many people he had not yet met who were also a part of this network of mistrust—and which one had helped the Chinese create their weapon.

Dr. Diego glared at the woman. "What do you propose to do, now that your research is apparently in the hands of an unaccountable adversary who can't seem to—"

The scientist's charge was interrupted by an alarm that sounded loud and large throughout the Kevlar structure.

"What is it, XO?" Tengan demanded into her IC.

"Ma'am—the surge that hit the *Grissom*! It's happening again!"

SEVENTEEN

P EOPLE IN ASPEN, Colorado, always regarded Jason Stillman strangely when he called his mountain retreat "my orogenous zone."

"Orogeny," he would patiently answer their empty stares. "The process of mountain building."

Customers at his Air Fare Café—where the waiters were all mini-drones—would still look at him blank-eyed, uncomprehending.

"It's a play on 'erogenous zone,'" he would go on. "The mountain-top is a place of happiness."

The peaks were actually more than that. They were a place of worship. Each Sunday, come deep snow or battering katabatic downwind, he rode his hovermobile five thousand feet up to the ridge he owned, to the log cabin he and his father had built. Through the thin, luminous air, the thirty-eight-year-old could see Elk Camp, Two Creeks, West Buttermilk, Snowmass Village, and Aspen stretched out before him. The postcard beauty hid the exhausting dynamic of the people, the pace, the interactions. Up here he communed with Latobius, the Celtic mountain god, whose adventures his father, Aengus, used to extemporize by a campfire. Up here he transformed to Nodens, god of the hunt. He foraged for his own food with a swift-kill laser rifle, and what he didn't eat or store he brought back for a grateful, shrinking group of venison eaters.

Until the moment came, Jason Stillman had been dressing a small, short-antlered deer the way he had been taught. He had hung his kill from a small winch and hook attached to the edge of his roof, just as his father had taught him. Though it was still afternoon, the sun was already blocked by the higher peaks; by the light of a solar-powered lantern he had begun gutting the animal, pausing only to haul buckets of water from the well to wash blood over the ledge. When he was done the remains would follow, a feast for scavengers.

Jason Stillman lived up to his last name until his final few seconds of life. He stood, silent, pensive, his hands inside the deer, when his head rose, suddenly alert. He was experiencing a sound he had heard before . . . but never up here.

It was a deep rumbling that he felt in his feet before he heard it with his ears. It was a sound well known on the ski slopes, the sound of cascading snow, the sound of an avalanche.

He turned and looked up through the trees, a bloody hand shielding his eyes from the lantern's glow. The sound grew loud, fast. It wasn't just snow, it wasn't that self-muffling roar. There were bangs, cracks, boulders falling, trees snapping. And something more, something foreign. A shattering sound, like a stack of plates crashing.

And then he saw it. The dull sunlight turning gunmetal dark. A shadow falling forward, over everything, even the landslide itself.

No longer frozen with indecision, he bolted toward the cabin. There was no outrunning the landslide but the structure had a meat cellar; if he could get there he might survive the first pass.

But Jason Stillman did not get there. In his last moments of life, screaming from the assault of sound that broke his eardrums and rattled him like a tuning fork, he saw the avalanche cascading behind the cabin, then through it, not just snow and stone but countless points of light reflecting distant sun.

It wasn't possible, but there were diamond-like, fist-size sheets of glass sledging toward him like God's angry hammer. He felt the slashing punch across the entire front of his body, was pushed back flat and buried with the deer, and moments later the two had been reduced to pulp and mashed into the Earth.

The side of the mountain continued to slide, tearing up more and more of the peak as it rolled toward the foothills. But that was just the particulate matter. Behind it, driving it faster and faster, the entire top third of the mountain fell in a slamming, tumbling mass. It rocked the peak to its roots, ripped cracks in the Earth below, caused roads and homes and woodlands to vanish in sinkholes that joined to become a canyon that was buried as soon as it was born by the inverted stone pyramid that crashed on top of it—an absurd cone of rock jutting from the Earth like an otherworldly mesa. The fissures continued to radiate outward, not just here but along the entire Elk Mountains Range, where other peaks were sheared clean and had toppled to the ground.

There was no organization to the new palisade that had been formed along nearly forty miles of valley and hillside, burying cities, towns, and ranches, crushing countless lives and infrastructure.

It was not orogeny that had created a new range. It was a deed that Aengus Stillman might have ascribed to Fionntain—the god who put fire in the head of man.

■ ■

After a brief rest, Adsila Waters felt somewhat refreshed, somewhat relaxed.

She was also relieved to be going back to her job, relieved to have the opportunity to reclaim her dignity after being played by Ziv Levy, and she was truly relieved to have the bugs behind her—literally. They were in a dish in Dr. Carter's lab but they were routed into her IC. The doctor believed it was important that Ziv think they were still inside her, eavesdropping. The repetitive songs might suggest otherwise, but Ziv would not—could not—be certain they had been removed.

"When you want to shut them out," Carter had told her, "push the red tab I've inserted in your IC. That will cut the signal to the med-bay. Ziv will still receive nanite impulses from here, just not whatever information you want to conceal. Don't stay silent for too long," Carter cautioned, "or he will suspect the truth."

Unfortunately, Adsila's relief was short-lived. Returning to the comm, she learned of Lord's near-escape in the *Grissom*, of Stanton's plans to assemble a recon mission to the damaged *Jade Star*—and, almost at once, of a disaster that had reduced a section of the Rocky Mountains in Colorado to boulders and sediment.

■■

"Five mountains are gone," Adsila told Lord on their IC link, "along with Aspen and most of the White River National Forest. Stanton has put the station on high alert."

"He's not the only one," Lord informed her. "Hold on, EAD. I'll be with you shortly."

Lord left the link open so he would not have to update Waters. Still wearing his ragged pressure suit, Lord waited while Tengan ordered everyone at Armstrong Base to move at once to the lowest, deepest level of the camp.

"That won't protect anyone," Saranya warned.

"They don't know that," Tengan said. "I need them as calm as possible, not overtaxing the oxygen output."

Smart, Lord thought.

"I'm not going," Saranya insisted as the others turned toward a reinforced stairwell near the mouth of the lava tube.

"You weren't given a choice," Tengan snapped, turning back.

"Commander, we have to stop the next one, not hide from this one."

Tengan was about to speak when, to everyone's surprise, Ras Diego stepped between them.

"Dr. May is correct," the scientist said softly. "You must understand, it doesn't matter how deep any of us goes. Neutrinos cannot be stopped by other matter."

"What *can* stop them?" Lord asked quietly. He wasn't usurping Tengan's authority, his tone made that clear. He genuinely wanted to know.

"The only way is to get that device out of commission," Saranya said.

Tengan's jaw set, but her eyes shifted from the scientists. Lord could see the woman redirect her thinking.

"Go," she said directly to Saranya. "Get to work. Can he help?" She turned back to Diego.

Saranya nodded.

Tengan waved him on. Saranya was already striding quickly up the corridor.

"Where are they going?" Lord asked.

Tengan watched the two scientists for a few moments more, then turned back to their visitor. "The dark-side section," she replied. "I'm going below to organize personnel and supplies in case we are partly incapacitated. I suggest you change into a radiation jumpsuit ASAP then join us. It may offer some protection like the shielding in the *Grissom.*"

"Thank you," Lord said. But that wasn't why he had come to the moon.

Tengan touched her IC, fed Lord directions to the locker room, then marched off with the lunar colonists, who were already making haste slowly: there was purpose but no panic.

Lord was impressed by their efficiency. He was certain they had drilled for emergencies, but dry runs can never replicate the heart-thumping drive and disorientation of a real situation.

He watched Tengan go, waiting until the woman had disappeared. Then, following the IC, he turned and started walking swiftly in the opposite direction from where he'd been directed. Before returning to his EAD, he brought up data on Armstrong.

"I'm with you, Adsila," Lord said, reconnecting his IC link. During the brief transmission delay he minimized Adsila's face so he could concentrate on where he was going. He did not mute her eyes-on view of his situation, however; he might need help.

As he walked, Lord's eyes probed ahead, searching for more than just the changing facility. He flicked on the infrared sensor.

"I see Armstrong is on Level Red status," Adsila said.

"The hive is humming," he agreed. "Are you all right?"

"Unchaste but chastened," she replied.

Lord was surprised and impressed by the candid admission. "We'll talk later. Update on the disasters?"

"All sources track at least the last two incidents to the *Jade Star*," she reported, her eyes dancing across the ever-growing influx of information. "It was probably responsible for Japan as well. McClure, jump on?"

"Here," the Laboratory and Space Science special agent replied. "We weren't certain about Japan, since the *Jade Star* was on the other side of the planet. But the burst seems to have cut through Earth, which is why it impacted the seabed first."

"A burst *through* the planet," Lord repeated. "Dr. May was talking about neutrinos being able to pass through atoms, about antimatter and density—"

"Dr. Saranya May, sir?" McClure asked.

"The same." There was no point keeping her identity a secret. With luck, she'd be showing up in his IC feed within minutes.

"Her involvement explains a great deal," McClure said.

"What does it mean to you?"

"Director Lord, the device she designed can, it appears, make a latent bomb from just about every square centimeter of the universe—"

"How?" Lord asked.

"Well, as I'm sure she's explained, sir, when the neutrino flux density exceeds ten to the ninth giga electron volts—"

"I mean the mechanism, not the science," Lord said patiently. "Dr. May spoke of a 'doomsday device,' the SAMI, she called it."

"Melodramatics," McClure said dismissively. "To answer your question, the SAMI is just an ogre of a generator with an on-off switch."

"One that appears to be malfunctioning and carving up sections of the Earth-moon system at random," Adsila added pointedly.

"At present, yes," McClure agreed.

"Any thoughts about how to fix it?" Lord asked.

"Not one, sir, sorry."

"Thank you, Agent," Lord said.

McClure signed off.

Just then Lord spotted two fuzzy red images in his IC. He hurried toward them in big, arcing steps.

"The *Jade Star* is clearly in crisis," Adsila continued her update, "but the Chinese government is denying culpability, refusing assistance, and will not consider an immediate on-site investigation by knowledgeable personnel."

Lord scowled, his pace increasing. This was nothing new. It was also not his concern.

"The diplomats, scientists, and military can hash all that out," Lord said. "Our job is to find out who made this possible."

"Janet checked finances," Adsila said. "No one at Armstrong has showed an unusual bump in globals, stock, property, or services."

Lord wasn't surprised. With privacy shot all to hell, criminals had taken to what they called Blackbearding: leaving cash in chests or under rocks like pirates. Still, it was worth a look. Sometimes criminals got careless.

"Very good," Lord said. "I want to know every possible benefit Rasputin Diego could gain from stealing or sabotaging Saranya May's research, including a boost to his own research grant."

"Do you have reason to believe that he was in collusion with the Chinese?"

"I don't know. I want to. There may be intermediaries. Let me know when you have something else."

"Yes, sir. May I ask where you're going? If I'm correct, the level-one bunker is in the opposite direction."

"You are correct," Lord told her. That was all he said.

Adsila did not press him.

As Lord moved with increasing confidence and necessary speed through the lunar environment, he was surprised at how spare, how makeshift everything looked. He remembered the old joke that went around during the outpost's hurried construction:

"Armstrong Base wasn't built in a day."

"Yes, it was."

The need to have a base that bookended the Chinese and the Russians with Earth-based assets was considered paramount; the funds were authorized and the plans were carried from theory to reality in less than three years. The main reason *Empyrean* was greenlit was to support the ongoing and expanding lunar efforts.

Lord made his way past offices that consisted of nothing more than round inflated tents within the Kevlar tubes—"blisters," they were called—and he couldn't help thinking that the whole excursion was like a glorified camping trip with Tengan as the scout leader. Only the science labs had anything approaching security: until now, there was nothing *to* threaten the base. That security was their location: even going through the base, they were exceedingly difficult to reach.

Adsila did not speak. She watched. And when the two ruddy figures appeared in Lord's IC, she knew what he was planning to do.

"Drs. May and Diego," she said. "Headed for the lab."

"That's right," Lord told her.

"It's external," she said. "Located miles away."

"Right again."

"Sir, if you'll check the upper-right corner of your IC at one hundred forty-four degrees periph, you will note that your suit status may be insufficient to survive on the lunar surface— "

"Meaning it may also be sufficient," he said. "Besides, I'm used to the feel and I don't have time to change."

"—and, in any event," Adsila went on, "the external tanks do not contain sufficient air to make the trek."

"Noted," Lord replied.

Once again Adsila fell silent. But not for long. "You don't intend to walk there."

"No."

"Neither scientist is flight-qualified, so they must be driving," she said. "You intend to go with them."

Lord didn't answer. He knew what was coming next. He had just done the research.

"Sir, the transit buggies are all two-seaters."

"A challenge," he admitted.

"More than that," Adsila said. "Your added lunar weight of thirty-three pounds could mire them in surface dust."

"I'll get out and push," he promised.

"Excuse me, sir, but I don't think you understand the gravity of this. In any sense."

"Thank you, EAD," Lord replied, "but the truth is, I do. Which is one reason I'm not leaving our best hope to go this alone."

As he spoke, Lord reached the locker room, where Saranya and Diego were suiting up—another tent, this one with small footlockers and a backdoor airlock. The two scientists were apparently unaware that Lord had entered.

"What's the other reason you're going out, if I may ask?" Adsila inquired.

Lord replied, "We have to find out how the data was stolen and by whom. They may still be working against us."

EIGHTEEN

E MPYREAN PERSONNEL, WE are in *Zed* status," Commander Stanton said over the stationwide IC plug. "I repeat, *Zed* status. STAR unit mobilize, full force, and report to Egress Center Alpha."

Adsila Waters listened to the announcement with eager interest. Space Tactics and Reconnaissance was the paramilitary detachment on board the *Empyrean*. Because Commander Stanton had resigned his army commission, the station had no official ties to the Department of Defense; STAR was solely a space station security unit, comprised of former military personnel who reported directly to Commander Stanton. Any actions they took had to be related directly to the well-being of the station, its crew, and its visitors. That gave Stanton considerable leeway within the *Empyrean* charter, though there had not yet been any challenges to match the adventure he was clearly planning now.

Except for a single station-proximate drill, there had never been an exercise like this. Egress Center Alpha was not for shuttle traffic. It was where the *Empyrean*'s personal flight vehicles departed. Those were mostly science sleds and repair pods, accredited and equipped solely for repair and limited expeditionary flight. There were also rocket packs, but those lacked the necessary range. If all fourteen of the vehicular assets were setting out for the *Jade Star*, it would be a historic undertaking.

Along with PD Al-Kazaz, Adsila Waters felt it imperative that Zero-G have one of their own people on such a mission. It wasn't just that the only arm of space law enforcement should be a part of a major space security initiative, though pride and value added were certainly part of it. Zero-G also had access to something—to some*one*—Stanton needed. That had to be communicated to him.

Adsila glanced at Lord's IC view. The director was quickly examining data coded on the footlockers. Space suit sizes and applications filled his vision. He selected one quickly and moved toward it. The Armstrong suits were like slightly inflated scuba suits, but made of brownish-green autocontouring layers designed to expand for different body types. Engaged in their own preparations—and loud discussion, which masked Lord's low-gravity footfalls—neither Saranya nor Diego was yet aware of his presence.

Adsila felt testosterone rising in her loins. It came hand in hand with the Cherokee *wahaya saquii,* the rise of the single wolf, the lone hunter. Right now, she felt she was being wasted here. Being part of a team didn't mean she had to sublimate personal initiative.

"*Dukshanee,*" she swore in Cherokee under her breath. There was little profanity in her native language; what few words they had were potent.

The woman tamped down her rising male aspect: she did not want to be one more rough territorial man among men. She switched on her link to the nanites in Dr. Carter's lab and toggled it off and on while talking to Lord. It was all right to let her eavesdroppers know that Lord was alive at Armstrong, but she had muted it when he revealed his intention to reach Saranya's lab. Though it was a risk to involve Ziv Levy in any undertaking, the EAD also weighed the potential benefits. She wanted him to hear what she was about to say.

"Agent Abernathy, take over Director Lord's IC," she said, shifting the view to the junior member of the team. "Whatever the director needs, do it. Explain that I've gone to see Commander Stanton." She faced Grainger and smiled a little. "Janet, the comm is yours. Again."

Janet Grainger looked over with full understanding. "Adsila, I've searched the charter—we have no claim on STAR activities."

"I know, but we should, especially on this one," Adsila said bluntly, heading from the comm. "Director Lord should have updates to go with whatever he knows. Agent McClure, you're with me."

The science special agent had been looking after her with longing; he was on his feet and hurrying after her with a smile so large it actually caused his IC to ripple like a pond.

"EAD, *thank you* for this opportunity," McClure said as he caught up. He nearly overshot Adsila in the shifting gravity.

"You're welcome. Your dossier says you're PV1 qualified."

"Fully."

"Good."

Personal Vehicle 1 pilots were permitted to fly one-person craft in local situations; that is, around and returning to the ships or platforms from which they were launched. This mission applied as long as they didn't dock at *Jade Star*.

Egress Center Alpha was located on the underside of the runway where the large commercial shuttle landed. The location was remote but strategic: in the event of a complete power failure on board the *Empyrean*, solar pressure would keep the station rotating so that no power would be required to release a repair pod from the outer edge of the band; it would whirl off at a tangent determined by the timing of the release.

Adsila and McClure made their way down the radial tower by elevator. As they traveled, Adsila reviewed the STAR duty roster, figured out the approach she'd take. She was not under any eyes-only orders and felt she had some leeway regarding ongoing Zero-G operations.

Upon reaching the runway receiving area, they walked through a curving horizontal tube that tracked the underside of the runway itself. There, like a flattened beehive, sat the small openings that accessed the conveyances. Suits and oxygen tanks were kept in wall-mounted cabinets beside each pod. The rocket packs were suspended at the far end near a crawlspace-like airlock.

Commander Stanton and his team were already present and gearing up in the tube's familiar one-g gravity.

Adsila stepped up behind him. "Commander Stanton?"

The powerful man turned, regarded her, then turned back to watching the preparations. "EAD Waters," he said without a welcoming tone. "You're not authorized to be here."

"I want to share information about what you're facing."

Stanton hesitated. He was on the clock, facing a crisis, and every moment mattered. So did every piece of information.

"I'm listening," he replied without turning.

"We have the scientist who created this beast," she said.

Stanton turned at the waist. He regarded her with interest now. "Have him where?"

"Her," Adsila gently corrected him. "She's on the moon with Director Lord."

"Exactly how does that help my team?"

"This is Special Agent Ed McClure," she said, moving aside slightly. "Our science officer."

"I know who he is."

"Yes, we've met, sir, twice, sir," McClure said politely, offering his hand.

Stanton ignored it, and him. "You're wasting—"

"Commander, you are launching with the station security team and a few engineers," Adsila said. "You have no science personnel in STAR. Take him with you. He can communicate with our resource."

"Directly?" Stanton asked. "Or through Lord."

Adsila fudged. "Both."

"You will share that contact information with me," Stanton said. "I saw the station surveillance, saw your boss with a woman, had her profiled."

He probably knew more than Adsila, who had made a point of not prying into Lord's mission. Yet Stanton had been careful not to say the other woman's name. For all his swagger, the commander was a professional who understood SACO—security and counterespionage operations.

"Commander," Adsila continued, "you know that I cannot give you authorization to communicate with an asset under protection—nor is there time to get it. Director Lord is occupied. Our man must be the conduit."

Stanton thought for a moment. He was a commander first, a politician second. "Are you sled-qualified, McClure?" he asked.

"I spent two hundred hours on one of these removing tech from the International Space Station before the Russian handover," he replied. He'd also spent that time inserting microscopic spy wires to feed intel to PD Al-Kazaz. McClure didn't mention that; he didn't need to, judging from Stanton's knowing expression.

Without further hesitation, Stanton called over the unit leader. The commander pointed to an operative suiting up at position five.

"Lyons, have Special Agent McClure take O'Hara's place," Stanton told him. "He's a scientist with specific knowledge. He'll fly in place of the engineer."

"Yes, sir," the man said, firing a puzzled, slightly annoyed look at the newcomer.

"Position five," Stanton instructed McClure. "Suit up, but the second you get in the way you're out of the formation."

"Understood, sir," McClure said. "Thank you, sir."

As McClure headed toward the other men, Stanton pinioned Adsila with a hard look. "Your agent understands that he's not serving two masters?"

It was Adsila's turn to give Stanton a look. "We both want the same thing," she answered evasively.

Stanton nodded gruffly then turned back to the team.

Before she turned back the way she had come, Adsila quietly passed on a Cherokee blessing: "May you all have the strength of eagles' wings."

■■

McClure was unaware of Adsila Waters's departure. He was concentrating fully on getting into the military-grade space suit as quickly and as safely as he could. His only distraction was the disappointed look on O'Hara's face as he made way for him. To McClure's relief, the look was temporary.

"I heard you say your name is McClure," O'Hara said as he removed his suit.

"That's right."

"Good luck, McClure," O'Hara said, and he sounded as if he meant it.

He smiled as O'Hara walked away. That felt good.

"I'm Dr. Joe Lyons," he heard next, and looked over to see the unit leader suiting up with practiced confidence.

"Special Agent Ed McClure, PhD," the newcomer answered. He wasn't trying to impress the team leader, only to inform him.

"O'Hara was my pilot on six construction tours up here. Big shoes to fill. You up for that?"

"I am."

"It's not too late."

McClure pointed to the footwear O'Hara had removed. "I'm a triple-E boot. This smart fabric can stretch to fit a man, right?"

It was a little arrogant-sounding, McClure knew, but Lyons took it as it was intended: an almost required dash of bravado.

"You're an engineer?" McClure asked.

"Material science aeronautics," he said as he finished with his suit and grabbed the helmet from a hook. "I've got to determine what shape the *Jade Star* is in. Everyone else's job is to make sure I get in. What's your area?"

"Astrochemistry major, astrobiology minor."

Lyons considered McClure with fresh eyes. "The commander made the right call," he admitted. "We'll need educated eyes on-site."

"Thank you," McClure said.

"There are just two things you have to know, apart from how to fly. The first is to stay in formation unless I call for odd up, down, right, or left. You're an odd number, so you follow my instructions. That's so you don't bump into your neighbors."

"I understand," McClure assured him. "The result would not be pleasant."

"In zero gravity we'd be like billiard balls after a break," Lyons said. "But why am I telling you? You're the science guy."

"What's the second thing I need to know?"

Lyons grew very serious and glanced back furtively. "The commander's neck is stretched way out on this one. So are ours. We don't have permission to enter Chinese space. We don't know what shape they're in but we *do* suspect they have at least a few armed interceptors disguised as construction robots, and the Chinese could launch them."

"I'll follow your lead, wait for instructions," McClure assured him.

But Lyons had already turned back toward the rest of the men to complete his instructions. He didn't have to. His IC would have brought his orders to them all, but McClure noted that, like Lord, Lyons preferred human connection.

"Ready units," he ordered. "Count off."

As each person sounded their number from one to fourteen, McClure made sure his suit was set. The main difference between it and the Zero-G model were the exojoints—small internally powered devices that plugged into the IC and neural impulses, allowing for more natural movement against the suit's standard pressurization.

"On my mark," he heard Lyons announce when they were done.

A hatch activation button appeared in their ICs.

"Open."

Each person pressed the red tab. The hatches swung open, revealing the least-comfortable spacecraft McClure had ever seen: lozenge-shaped sleds and Ping-Pong-ball-shaped pods. Each had a docking ring barely large enough to accommodate the suits.

"In pairs, deploy!"

McClure saw the first two men dive into the conveyance openings. He glanced over at Lyons, who nodded back, then dove forward after the fourth man did the same one conveyance away. The last thing McClure saw was Stanton's face, looking on from the side. McClure wasn't sure whether the commander's expression held approval, disapproval, or both. Not that it mattered. The young scientist was all in on this ride.

McClure felt the usual thrill as he floated into the small sled. He was flat on his belly, a slab of luncheon meat between four heavily shielded, thickly armored hull sections. He took in as much as he could as he reached for the controls forward and slightly below him, in a small well that left the viewport clear. His suit had automatically clicked into the craft's magnetic plates that would keep him from jerking forward or backward as the sled sped or slowed. As they did, the hatch shut behind him and the holding pins released. All that held the vehicles in place now was a pair of electromagnets that would cut off at ignition. The agent quickly refamiliarized himself with the controls.

"Operation Jade Rescue," he heard Lyons say in his IC from the sled beside him. "If this is not your mission, kindly leave now."

That got appreciative laughs from the team.

"On three," Lyons said without delay. "One . . . two . . . launch!"

The ships ignited and there was a rush of speed. The vehicles were on autopilot until they cleared the farthest reaches of the station. The preprogrammed courses carried them away and banked them toward Earth, toward the lower orbit of the *Jade Star*. As they sped off they started to fan out, creating a kite-like structure with a pod at point and at the tail.

"Everyone hold present positions," Lyons instructed.

McClure felt a surge of excitement and also anxiety. He had little doubt that every eye on the *Empyrean* was watching, including—and especially—that of Adsila Waters. Her neck was out too. He suddenly remembered the immortal words of virtually every test pilot since Wilbur Wright: *Please don't let me screw the pooch.*

"Nolan," Lyons said. "Signal sent to the Chinese station?"

"Message on constant repetition, sir," the communications liaison reported from another ship. "If they're receiving at all, they know this is an emergency aid and rescue mission."

At least, that's what you're telling them, McClure thought. *We all know better and so do they.*

That exchange, and all that followed, were for the benefit of the rest of the team. Like McClure, they were concentrating on flying and watching their cold-atom positioning plots, instead of checking their ICs, where all other data was displayed simultaneously and in real time.

McClure stared through the viewport. One thing was for certain: space was not Earth. That seemed obvious, but it seemed more obvious out here when the mind was supported by the senses. When he was on EVA, sledding outside the station, there was still an earthward orientation. Here, facing out, there was slippery nothingness, emphasized by the crushing accelerations of the thruster in back. The sled responded to his touch, but McClure knew geometry, knew that while facing the open cosmos, the tiniest adjustment here could broaden to something vast as he rocketed along. A millimeter shift one way or the other could cause him to entirely miss his target.

The sky was dark and the stars were vivid and the planets stood out clearly from the other distant lights. The only sound was in his helmet. Even the burn of the thrusters could not be heard inside the sled.

He couldn't see the *Empyrean*, only the other vehicles and the curve of Earth. Their home world seemed to turn slowly, ponderously, as he moved across the distant sphere. There was nothing else—until, after about twenty minutes, there suddenly was.

Off in the distance he saw an ominous cloud where the Chinese station was supposed to be—an undulating, dusty fog that seemed to glint with hidden teeth.

He raised a finger toward a sensor array on the control board in front of his chin. Various tools surged to life at his touch.

"Dr. Lyons," McClure said. "I am picking up a gamma signature from a region near the *Jade Star*."

"I've got that, McClure," Lyons said. Of course he did. That would have been programmed into the mission parameters as well.

"Is it telling you anything?" Lyons asked.

"Not yet—the spray is too wide, interfering with pinpoint readings."

"Stay on it," Lyons said. "The others have been briefed. Once we know where the SAMI is, we can send CREWs to power it down. If they cannot, if it looks like it's about to act up again, we demolish it with PHGs."

Those were Pod HEL guns: high-energy laser cannons.

McClure wasn't sure about the plan: he understood the political reason Lyons would want to dispatch the nondestructive Coordinated Robotic Endosmotic Workers, whose SimAI brains were designed to learn as they engaged unknown technology, and to store that new knowledge; but time mattered more than diplomacy. It was essential to shut the device down as quickly as possible.

McClure continued to scan the rippling cloud for some sign of the weapon's position: the emission lines of a helium leak on a spectroscope, or some artifact of the thing's colossal magnetic field. But there was nothing yet in the haze of that debris cloud.

"We're going to have to go in, aren't we?" Lyons said, reading the data.

"It seems so," McClure agreed. "We can't send the CREWs in blind."

Suddenly the control panel went wild.

"We're not blind anymore," Lyons said coolly. "Point, what've we got?"

"Incoming," came the voice from the pod in front. "A wide spread."

"I see it!" Lyons shouted as hot white flashes tore through the cloud like dozens of tiny comets. "What *is* it?"

"Neutral particle beam," McClure said, watching IC indications.

"There's a reactor still online somewhere in the station," Lyons said. "Must be some failure in the stripping stage; instead of separate salvos, every few shots is basically a lightning strike."

"Odd up!" he shouted as the sizzling flares bore down.

McClure reacted instantly, nosing up hard. The force of the rapid ascent heaved him down into the feet of the suit, but his eyes remained fixed on the viewport. It was as if the rest of the fleet had shifted, not him. The other vessels rose or fell away but, save for the cloud and those invisible arrows and jagged bolts of light, the rest of the universe seemed stubbornly unchanged. Even Earth didn't appear to move.

As the team dodged the assault, a second, then third, wave of white flashes shot from the cloud, one fanning above the first salvo, the other below.

"Odd left, hard!" Lyons barked.

McClure's hand seemed to spasm on the controls, jerking him left as he tried to keep from wailing with fear. The communication link was eerily silent as, now, the vista before him turned on its side. Instead of lying horizontally the cloud was now vertical, jutting across the viewport like an ancient tombstone.

"They're compensating for IAM!" the point pilot cried, referring to incoming avoidance maneuver. "The first wave was a diver—!"

He didn't get to finish, his voice buried by Lyons shouting, "Free flight! McClure—"

"On my own," the special agent said, "I know."

The vessels flew in every direction, like a barrel of roman candles that had suddenly been ignited. McClure's eyes settled back on the ominous, deadly cloud. Almost at once the purpose of the mission came back to McClure. He screwed in his wits and his courage. Then he checked to make sure the data feed was going back to the *Empyrean*— and to the FBI command center.

"Dr. Lyons," he said, adjusting his flight path, "I'm going after that cloud."

"Four-A," Lyons said resolutely, meaning the rogue action was acknowledged and accepted and that he had the pilot's ass.

The tableau shifted again as McClure chose a high, arcing path that avoided a field of what looked like tin cans being torn apart by high-powered rifle fire. Through McClure's viewport he saw nearly a half dozen ships get punctured by the merciless light, while a half dozen others slammed one into the other in an effort to escape, the sleds snapping, the pods coming apart like dropped eggs before being shredded by the third wave of defensive bolts. Each piece of metallic debris became a new projectile, briefly flaring with white heat before going dark. The collision-avoidance advisories in McClure's helmet went berserk; the only choice was to ignore it all. Doing nothing was as viable as taking the wrong evasive turn.

McClure thought sadly of Stanton and Adsila Waters watching the disaster unfold through Lyons's IC. The *Empyrean* commander was stoically silent, doing the only thing he could do: leaving the mission in the hands of his chosen leader.

"Team, sound off!" McClure heard Lyons say, his voice shaking. The man was an engineer, not a military officer.

"McClure here," McClure replied.

"Hasen here," a woman responded.

The voices were followed by an awful quiet. That meant eleven ships were already destroyed or disabled.

"Kate, hard about—return to base," Lyons ordered.

"Immediately," she replied.

There was a slight, dull flare in the distance as the woman swung away in a tight arc and headed home. At that same moment, McClure saw a sled pass over his head and settle in front of him. It was Lyons.

"I'm not after your glory," the flight leader assured him, his voice once again steady. "I'll take the first hits so you can gather intel. Every word, every scrap matters."

McClure's heart leapt at the gesture as he saw Lyons's sled immediately take scraping hits from space flotsam. Each one careened away, giving McClure free passage. His hands tightened on the controls, afraid that fear would make him twitch. He saw pieces of space suit shoot by, glinting in earthlight. There were ruddy beads of what looked like frozen blood. The scene was all the more macabre for the silence as his sled continued its slow, careful, measured drift through the shattered, deadly formation.

And then, as they closed in on the charcoal darkness of the cloud, the fourth and fifth assaults burst from within.

These fresh attack waves were more tightly packed than the first three. McClure did not believe that the Chinese intended to destroy the fleet ship by ship on purpose, without a warning. That meant the *Jade Star* sighted them with its machine vision and was fortified with weapons programmed to react automatically to incoming enemies; and that these armaments were being run by the SimAI, which was now immediately adjusting to pick off survivors. Anything that didn't resemble any wave band; an approved Chinese spacecraft would be targeted. Probably incoming meteors as well, since those could be used to conceal explosives. Making things even worse, the intact fusion reactors aboard the station meant unfaltering energy for these attacks.

Not only is the damn neutrino death ray out of control, McClure realized, *the damn automatic defense systems are impregnable.*

There was nowhere to bank, rise, or drop. The lethal spread was like a net expanding as it came toward them. Lyons remained in position. So did McClure.

"*Empyrean,*" Lyons remarked, "I just have to say, my professional hat's off to whatever sick bastard came up with this system."

As they waited for impact, the young scientist could not help but think that his preacher father would be either transfixed or horrified: the neutralized streams and wild arcs of electrons from the cloud were like some wrath-of-Jehovah event from the Old Testament. The seventh plague of Egypt, hail and fire, came instantly to mind.

Maybe Dad was correct. McClure thought incongruously of their many long discussions about the Bible—the man of faith versus the blossoming young scientist. *Maybe these things happened as described.* The authors of Deuteronomy wouldn't have known about particle accelerators and magnetic collimators, though they did get the ferocity right: "The mountain burned with fire to the very heart of the heavens. . . ."

For a moment McClure was back in a pew in his father's church in

Fairfield, Connecticut, Long Island Sound glinting outside the window. When would that be? A springtime Sunday, with renewal in the air, a congregation-wide sense that life was near and very dear—

Two flashes hit Lyons's lead ship hard. The sled was upended and flung backward fast, as if it had been kicked by a giant. With a cry, Mc-Clure dove hard to avoid being struck. He maintained his grip on the controls even as he took a hit on the maneuvering system engine—the projectile must have knocked something loose from Lyons's stricken sled, since the hit was from above. The rear-mounted cone spit yellow-orange flame as the engine's whole warning annunciator matrix lit up red in McClure's IC. To prevent further eruptions, McClure cut all power, including the IC—realizing, too late, that the ship's avionics were one less thing for the SimAI to target. To its machine eyes, he now looked, appropriately enough, like debris.

Dead in space, McClure felt perspiration pool in every cranny of his suit as the sled slowly and silently disappeared into the opaque, undulating cloud around the *Jade Star*.

NINETEEN

"WHO'S THERE?" DR. Diego demanded, turning slowly.

His IC had been silent while he donned his space suit. There was always a "blackout" period when two different systems interfaced—in this case his personal IC and the NASA IC of the suit.

Still very much on her guard, Dr. May looked back a little too quickly. She overspun and had to put her foot down hard to stop. Through her helmet she saw the familiar form of Sam Lord maneuvering between stored construction materials, heavy machinery, and ERBs undergoing maintenance.

"What are you doing here?" she demanded.

"I'm protecting you," he said, coming forward. "That *is* why I came to the moon."

Diego's eyes were in motion, fidgeting with his IC. "I do not see authorization from Commander Tengan."

"You won't," Lord assured him. "She has more urgent business. But I'm coming with you. I'm here to protect Dr. May and I also want to see the facility."

Lord couldn't quite make out Diego's expression through the sun-filtering amber hue of his faceplate. But his words left no question how he felt.

"No," the scientist barked. "That is eyes only—*our* eyes."

"Not anymore," Lord replied. "And why exactly do we need you?"

Diego shook his head defiantly. "Typical military-aerospace complex bully."

"You're the one trying to push me around," Lord quietly pointed out.

In flight, this was known as a stall—the moment when the airfoil lost lift and the jet began to plummet earthward. Lord had been there many times; a point at which only the pilot could save himself, his craft, and his passengers. It required a seasoned hand, a supernaturally calm head, and steady wits.

Lord shouldered past them. "We're wasting time," he said as he walked toward the airlock-garage.

"Space sheriff, the buggy is a two-seater!" Diego said, grabbing Lord's suit.

"In that case," Lord replied, "we'll know each other a lot better by the time we reach the lab." He eased his arm from Diego's grip, then looked into the man's visor until he could see his eyes. "Don't push me again."

Saranya gently pulled Diego around. She stepped between him and Lord.

"Ras, there isn't time for this," Saranya said. "Director Lord is coming. Sam, I just want to gather my data—he and I can do this twice as fast. He knows the system, can help me download what we have to send to Earth for help."

"Is that the plan?" Lord asked, surprised. "Take what has already caused so much havoc and make it available to everyone? I thought you were the only one who could fix this."

"I am, but if anything should happen to me . . . others must have the data to work with. There are select people we can trust."

"You hope," Lord replied.

"No, I am *not* relying on hope," she told him. "After the crash—things have changed. We nearly didn't make it. I have to take precautions. I just want to stop this thing."

"Then we're all agreed," Lord said with a last look at Diego.

She nodded and they made their way to the vehicle storage area.

The garage was a small, dull, gunmetal-gray affair in which the transit buggy loomed modern and large. Marked Lunar Armstrong Base One, the conveyance was a beast. The cab was inside an emerald-green polyhedral cage designed to rotate around the entire vehicle. It served as a tread that would conform to any terrain up to eighty degrees off horizontal, all the while keeping the cab perfectly upright within. The vehicle could self-steer and was designed to outthink, intimidate, and overcome anyone or anything that might try to stop it, including anything from the moon's unforgiving topography to a theoretical explosive dropped from hostiles in lunar orbit.

"All its vertices are jointed," Lord admired as they walked over. "This is extraordinary."

The thoughtful silence of Dr. May and the brooding sobriety of her colleague could not dull his enthusiasm.

There was no further argument about Lord accompanying them. Though there were only two seats, the polyhedral cage was relatively spacious.

"That's a specimen bay in back, correct?" Lord asked. Not expecting an answer, he said, "I'll crouch there."

"Don't be fooled by the high ceiling," Diego said. "If we roll over a boulder, that exterior is designed to give. It will be pushed upward. *We* will be protected by the bars over the seats."

"Then I'm grateful that you'll be driving," Lord said. "You'll make sure that doesn't happen."

■■

Lord watched while Saranya opened the passenger's door and ushered him in. He squeezed past the seat and stood on the four-by-four-foot platform, leaning on the aforementioned bar—a sturdy T-frame rising a little more than head-high from the back of the seat.

Lord's eyes quickly scanned the panels in a semicircle around the driver's station. "Fusion?" he asked Diego as the scientist pressed the power button. The entire vehicle seemed to stir like a waking rhino.

Diego didn't answer. Saranya did.

"It's an He-3 reactor," she acknowledged curtly.

"Very, very powerful," Diego contributed as if he were talking to a first-grader. "It can easily carry us as well as someone with your—authority."

Lord's IC started to inform him that helium-3 was a single-neutron variant of ordinary helium, fairly abundant in the lunar regolith, a radioactively harmless fusion fuel. He shut it down. As he did, he noticed that there was an urgent message from Adsila. He mentally fingered the secure button so the content would not be shared. Then he punched the private comm.

"Go ahead, Adsila," he said.

It was the strained male face of his EAD that appeared. Lord knew immediately that something bad had happened. Something that had caused her to shift. Something that made her want to feel a little less empathetic.

"Director, the *Empyrean* mission was attacked by what appears to be automated station defenses," Adsila informed him. "Twelve casualties, one turn-back. McClure is MIA. We lost his signal as he entered what appears to be a plasma cloud around the *Jade Star*, a thin mix of semifrozen fluids and gases from the module. It left them sluggish and near-blind."

Adsila's words registered immediately; the sickness in Lord's gut took several moments more to settle in. Then he realized something else: if the module were that badly damaged, the Chinese almost certainly weren't controlling the weapon—and were quite possibly as helpless as the pilots had been.

"The device?" Lord asked.

"Still operational, as far as we can tell."

"Plan B?"

"Not yet," Adsila said. "They're waiting to debrief the survivor. The one known survivor," Adsila corrected himself.

"Thank you," Lord said solemnly. "I'm in a transit buggy en route to the lab. ETA"—he checked his IC—"twenty-two minutes. Update me when you have it."

"I will, Director."

Lord signed off but waited a moment before reconnecting with the scientists. The buggy was being lifted to the surface on an elevator platform that rose through a cone barely wide enough to accommodate it. It was a smart security precaution: only the buggy could use it. The hatch recognized only a precise series of movements, executed by the cage, that worked like tumblers in a lock. Presumably changed on a regular basis, the buggy had to assume the right polyhedral shapes in succession to be recognized and then to fit physically through the lock.

It was a bouncy ride that, Lord suspected, preceded an even bouncier ride.

A pocket hatch at the top slid open. Outside, Lord saw a small satellite dish on the outside of the tube. It was fixed in the direction of the dark side, no doubt scanning for intruders as it transmitted signals from Saranya or Diego.

It would be very difficult for someone to get to the lab unseen, Lord thought. Yet somehow, someone had.

There was a familiar, unwelcome tightness at the bottom of his throat. The bumping, jostling ride seemed to be happening to someone else. The lunar landscape sped by unnoticed. Sam Lord was grieving for the team and doing what he had done too many times on too many military sorties: praying for the return of a missing comrade. His eyes turned in the direction of Earth. Just a sliver was visible above the horizon, a fuzzy brown blob seen through the green panels and amber visor. But out there was the battlefield, a place where brave souls had flung themselves against an unknown menace. Unnoticed, he threw them a small salute.

"... know that I was the main suspect when Dr. May's findings were reported missing," Diego was venting. "How could I not be? But I did not, *would* not sabotage a colleague. Argue? Yes. Loudly? Yes again. Thievery? Never—"

"Enough," Lord said firmly. "Just stop talking, Dr. Diego."

At that moment, the mood in the buggy shifted. The two scientists were reminded that the man traveling with them had two sides. One was affable, disarmingly human. The other was the leader of Zero-G.

The rest of the ride passed in silence, a silence so deep Lord hardly noticed their transit to the dark side of the moon. Diego was directing the vehicle toward a wedge-shaped construct on the terrain's surface.

To Lord, it looked like the low-slung entry to a vintage backyard bomb shelter. He had seen one at the age of six, when he ventured away from summer camp in the Adirondacks; it made an impression because it was also the first time he'd seen the business end of a rifle and learned to read the word *trespassing,* in combination with the word *no.*

As the scientist prepared to park beside the entrance to the underground lab, Lord surveyed the new location, which was closer to the moon's north pole than any other habitat.

The sky was matte black. The lab was partly blocked from the sun, making the shadows around it long and unusually elongated. There was no secondary light source: the lab was blocked completely from the sight of Earth, and the lack of reflective earthshine made the environment seem even more alien and unfriendly.

The scientists got out and Lord made his way from the buggy unaided, though it was more difficult climbing out than it had been going in. He came around the vehicle and watched as the other two loped their way to a heavy door, about twenty feet from where they'd parked. The reason they hadn't come closer was that dust kicked skyward by the tires still hung in the sky like ashes stirred from a fireplace. The scientists maneuvered around it; they didn't want any of the particles to get inside the lab or their sensitive equipment.

Access required a plug-in from either of their ICs. Dr. May leaned forward as if she were praying. The door opened without a click, there being no atmosphere to carry any sound.

Saranya entered, followed by Diego. The woman turned back.

"You're not coming in with us?" she asked over a private channel.

"No," Lord said. "I want to look around. Unless you don't feel safe . . . ?"

She looked back at Diego. "He knows you're out here. I think I'll be fine."

"I agree," Lord said. "I have about what, ninety minutes of air left?"

"Yes, though we shouldn't be more than a half hour," she informed him.

"I'll be checking the security systems," Diego said. "Diagnostics should tell us if anyone tried to circumvent them."

Dr. Diego's remarks, and especially his tone, sounded a little like a peace offering. Lord accepted it with a gracious nod.

As soon as the scientists were safely inside and the door sealed behind them, Lord surveyed the area. The surreal aspect of the lunar surface notwithstanding, he didn't see the densely pocked and cratered area as a landscape, he studied it as a crime scene.

Lord turned completely around, keeping his eyes near the ground. He saw no tracks, no bootprints, only little areas of darker-colored dust—the residue of previous visits where the tire-sprayed particles had eventually settled.

Lord walked in long, comfortable strides, traveling in a large circle around the lab entrance. Moving on the moon was like walking on a giant trampoline, he decided. You got a lot of bang for each step, a lot of distance, and it was easy if you kept moving; you only had problems when you trusted the terrain, or your Earth- or station-conditioned sense of traction and torque, too much.

He made two full circles around the base. Both circuits produced results. On the first, he noticed sparkles in the dust. Crouching easily, he sifted his gloved fingers across the surface, only to find several shards that didn't flake away when he shook his glove. He looked closely at the hard, clearly artificial particles. They were glassy, almost metallic. He glanced over at the door.

Construction artifacts, he decided. *Pieces made elsewhere must have been sandpapered out here to fit.*

Old tread marks seemed to confirm that: heavier construction vehicles had come out here from Armstrong. But they hadn't been out here recently. Darker dust from the buggy had settled on those too.

He looked for other material that didn't seem to belong, other geology that had been disturbed. He found a rock someone had picked up and studied: next to it was the hole it had been lifted from, then dropped beside. That probably happened during the initial geological survey of the area. He spotted what looked like a diamond gleaming in a shadow but was probably a particle of ice; there was a skidmark beside it, suggesting it had been blasted from some other locale and ended up falling here. He saw what at first looked like holes made by two legs of a tripod planted in the dust. Bending and digging at one hole with a finger, he discovered that they were tiny sinkholes atop small cracks in the crusty lunar surface.

Not the kind of terrain you can drag a branch and leaves across to cover your horses' hooves, Lord thought, remembering a trick old Isaiah Lord used to use.

Lord decided to circle wider, see if there was a position someone could have used to spy on the facility, possibly hijack electronic data. He turned to his IC. No recent reported thruster activity in the area. That was why he didn't see blast scars in the regolith.

Yet someone did this, he coached himself hard. *Someone cracked the high-security lab.*

As he neared the door of the lab, Lord stopped in mid-stride. Something gleamed dully above. Tilted out and away from the roof of the structure, toward the partially exposed sun, he saw the antenna that received data from the facility's neutrino detector array. The detector array was made up of helium-cooled germanium crystals and located in a dark lava tube not far away. Lord's eyes came back down in a straight line from the antenna to the buggy. He checked the tracks of the vehicle. Without wind or water to erode them, they were a permanent record of every trip ever taken to this place. They followed a roughly identical route, where the terrain was flattest, and the buggy always stopped in roughly the same place.

"Only two people with access?" Lord said with sudden realization. "You SOB!"

"Excuse me?" Dr. May said.

Lord turned to see that Saranya was emerging from the lab entrance, Diego close behind her.

"Just thinking out loud," Lord said. "Did you get everything you needed?"

"I did," Saranya replied, indicating her IC with a gloved hand.

"I took my work as well," Diego added. "We basically—"

"That's nice," Lord cut him off, "but we really shouldn't be discussing this. The Man in the Moon may have ears."

The trio got back into the buggy, Diego once again driving, Lord standing behind May. They circled the outpost to face in the opposite direction then sped back the way they had come. Lord wasn't sure, but it seemed as if Diego were going out of his way to hit small craters and jostle the craft. Soon they were back on the well-traveled path and the lunar trail smoothed.

"Cut the antenna to the base," Lord ordered.

Diego recoiled slightly. "Why?"

"What happens in the buggy must stay in the buggy," he said. "We don't have a lot of time. Just do it."

Diego looked at Saranya, who nodded. The scientist pushed a button that was hardwired into the vehicle's comm. The button went from blue to red. The buggy was now a cone of silence.

"Who has access to this vehicle?" Lord asked as he gripped the roll bar and looked down at them.

The two scientists shared another glance before Saranya looked up at Lord.

"That's the second time you've used the word *access* since we came back," she said. "Why? What did you find?" she asked. "What are you thinking?"

"My investigation, my questions," Lord replied. "Answer, please?"

"Technically, anyone who works in the vehicle bay," Saranya replied, a touch of indignation in her voice. "It isn't quarantined from the other vehicles. There isn't room. But the bay is monitored—"

"Images can be altered, sensors can be short-circuited, false data can be inserted," Lord said. "Science isn't always grand theories and large breakthroughs." He raised a mental finger and brought up data on his IC. "Armstrong personnel roster says vehicle bay access is held by you two, the ERB crew, two specially cleared security guards, a medic, and a pair of general-purpose technicians, one of whom doubles as a custodian."

"Also Commander Tengan and Lieutenant Commander Jørgensen," Diego added. "You'll want to add them to your police lineup."

"Thank you," Lord said. Once again, he overlooked the man's tone. "Apart from the assembly crew that built the lab, no one comes out here, is that correct?"

"It is," Saranya said.

Lord checked his IC again. The last survey mission in this region was sixteen months earlier and forty-seven miles away. That left him with the bay crew.

He brought up the seven names with vehicle access. NASA had thoroughly vetted all of them. One, however, had an interesting pedigree—interesting to someone looking for a good man who might be persuaded to do the wrong things for the right people.

Lord's silence weighed on the occupants of the buggy like the atmosphere of Venus.

"Might I ask why you are inquiring about these things?" Saranya said in a more solicitous tone.

"I was just getting to that," Lord said. "Either of you could have stolen the data from inside the lab. But if you had, the file would *not* have been incomplete. Not unless you wanted to sabotage the Chinese and kill countless people, which I doubt. That leaves a dozen suspects . . . plus one."

"One?" Saranya asked.

"Your buggy is always parked in the same spot," Lord said. "It's close to the door but just far enough so the dust will stay outside."

"We know all of this," Diego said. "What don't we know?"

"The question is what don't you *realize*?" Lord corrected him. "The buggy stops and stays directly opposite the data link to your neutrino detectors. That technology is operating all the time, always open to the interior of the lab."

This time, the silence was generated by the two scientists as they caught up to Lord—then sped ahead. Ras Diego turned back briefly. For the first time he looked at Lord with something other than mistrust, disdain, or impatience.

"Those are pure research detectors, looking at the neutrino flux from deep space sources, but—"

Saranya was right with him. "We've been working on manipulating that flux with the neutrino lens," she said.

Lord didn't follow but that didn't matter. All he needed was the bottom line, when they got to it. Listening to them was like hearing a game of science badminton.

"Our tests have been progressive," Saranya plunged on, talking more to Diego than to Lord. "We've been trying successively more advanced stages of the magnetic lensing technique—"

"And those disturbances would register on the lab research detectors, which would broadcast them in uncoded transmissions to the antenna," he said gravely.

Without realizing it, Diego was driving with increased urgency. That, plus his voice, told Lord the scientist was suddenly very concerned, perhaps realizing for the first time the scope of what had been unleashed.

After a moment, Saranya continued. "It wouldn't take an expert— well it would, actually; that's exactly what it would take, but only to understand the big picture—to figure out the *specific* means by which we were causing those disturbances in our progressive tests. The neutrino flux passes through everything . . ." The woman's breath came faster with her mounting concern.

"Leaving an unmistakable and highly detailed fingerprint pulsing from the lab," Diego said.

"But they did not get the safeguards because those weren't complete," Saranya said, finishing the exchange.

"And they wouldn't have realized," Diego said.

"How is that possible?" Lord asked. "Wouldn't someone on the receiving end have noticed there was no off switch?"

"Oh, there's an off switch for the bursts," Saranya said, "just no added safeguard for the container that holds the off switch. We had not yet finished testing those physical structural tolerances. It's like trying to invent a lightning rod when you've never seen lightning. The Chinese did not understand that a tech patch was being built to protect the system."

"A 'tech patch,'" Lord said. "You make it sound so simple, so innocent."

"It was never that, but it *was* pure," Saranya said defensively.

The woman stared at Diego through their tinted visors. Then she turned back to Lord.

"I apologize for everything and also for my manner, Sam— "

"We *both* do," Diego agreed. "I'm . . . impressed by what you did out here. No, I'm humbled."

"Thank you," Lord said, "but save it for later. Right now I want the subject heading for the file I'm going to send to my superior, something he'll understand." Lord added, "Me too."

Saranya said bitterly, "Without realizing it, we left the back door wide open. We've been broadcasting our 'secret' research loud and clear for months, minus the emergency brake."

TWENTY

SPACE WAS GLORY. But space was also damnation. It was an endless plane to which most human beings aspired, yet one in which survival was an inhuman trial.

Ed McClure endured both extremes as he waited for the end to come. He still had some power, the glow of the controls told him that, but he was afraid to use any of it. He didn't know if the module's self-defense system was as sensitive as it was relentless. For all he knew, just sending an IC broadcast would bring on a new rain of sunfire. He tried to use loaded software but most of that was linked to the FBI database. All his IC gave him were stored holo-images from his past, from birth to a party at the Scrub just a day before.

The irony was rich—his life passing before his eyes. He shut the pictures down. He preferred staring into the face of his killer: a dimly seen module hidden behind a shifting, glittering fog composed of what appeared to be gas, liquid, disintegrated structural matter from the *Jade Star*, and, most likely, frozen bits of fellow spacefarers and their ships.

At least there were no further attacks from the *Jade Star*'s self-defense system. The SimAI was obviously programed very crudely, very basically to target only mass or density—like an iron-rich space rock—and unfamiliar electronic signatures. In space, what else was it likely to encounter?

The sled was drifting slightly from the hit it had taken. Stars were still visible and through the fog of debris he dimly saw some of the module that had attacked him. It was bent away from the rest of the now-contorted space station, like the forward duck in a migrating flock.

There was no activity around the Chinese space station, meaning that either their own ships and spacewalkers were damaged—or else they had been grounded, the big bosses fearful of the rogue self-defense module. Lights were still on, there were still functioning systems, though it was impossible to tell what they were.

Well, when the end is near I'll risk an ion attack and report the meager intel I'm gathering.

PD Al-Kazaz might even give him the FBI Medal of Valor, post-humously. His mother would like that. He knew just where she would hang it too. Next to the Eddie McClure photo gallery, from Cub Scout to Special Agent.

Thinking of the end, McClure wondered if his suit's air supply would give out before he collided with the cracked, damaged space station. If it weren't so morbid, he'd place a bet: calculations, imprecise and rapid, told him he'd suffocate. That was probably a good thing, since he didn't want to perish in a vacuum.

The thought of dying in the sled made him shiver. He suddenly felt claustrophobic inside his suit, as if it were his coffin. At least he wasn't six feet under. He was two and a half million feet up. That was—unique, at least.

I'm up here with the angels, he wanted to tell his pastor father. There were tears in his eyes as he thought, *If you've got any pull, I sure wish they'd show themselves.*

McClure's low-level panic caused his hand to twitch impulsively toward the controls. He thought that maybe one sudden burst of the engine would take him far enough, fast enough, to escape the white-light executioner. But even as he thought that, his rational mind rejected it as suicide. The module's defenses would pile on at this distance, especially with nothing but him to shoot at.

His father, the angels, were still present in McClure's mind when he thought of another member of his present and personal trinity: Sam Lord. God, how he didn't want to let the boss down. He grinned as he remembered something the director had said in his anything-but-rehearsed welcoming speech at the comm center.

"Whatever bad situation you find yourself in, I want you to remember: it's never over—"

"Until it's over," Agent Abernathy had recited under his breath.

Lord had heard him and smiled. "That's football," the director had said. "No, Agent. A situation is never over unless you give up."

He checked his air gauge. Nearly ninety minutes. Hell, that was a long time to die ... or live.

Hold the angels, Dad, he thought, looking around with renewed enthusiasm. *I'm working for the Lord.*

■■

Tse Hung sat up. The young man gripped the arms of his chair so tightly he thought his flesh would split. Was that *life* he saw in space? Had someone actually survived?

Chairman Sheng's personal assistant had seen the self-defense barrage on his IC, had watched the devastation of the *Empyrean* fleet, and had felt—nothing. The Americans had done this to themselves, there was nothing more to be said or done. Besides, he and the rest of the *Jade Star* staff had more pressing concerns.

Survival, for one.

Ever since the Dragon's Eye had been turned on and the station had been shaken from joint to joint to joint until it was barely a cohesive unit, Tse had been buried alive, a prisoner in his tiny, sparse office.

The door was sealed because there were air leaks somewhere. The door wouldn't open until they were found and sealed. He might die of thirst but, *méi shì,* that's nothing: he would have air.

Communications with Earth were down. He had little idea who else was alive or which of his friends were dead, including Commander

Sheng. All he had was his minimally functioning station IC. With it, he was able to scan through all surviving surveillance views both interior and exterior—which was how he had witnessed the massacre in space. Unfortunately, Tse couldn't switch it off. Even if he closed his eyes, the sounds of the station crew shouting, searching, moaning, dying, were always present.

Then he saw it: the damaged space sled and the face of someone inside. The man's face moved. So did his hands. Despite his apathy toward the Americans, Tse was fascinated by the figure.

A brother, he thought. *Trapped, alone, frightened. Sadly, as long as this room remains sealed, I will outlive you,* he thought. *That is very inconsiderate of you, to leave me alone.*

Seized by his own growing despair, Tse was about to look away when he caught a flicker of reflected light. He jerked forward with interest.

No, he hadn't imagined it. The bottom of the sled had shifted.

For the first time in hours, Tse Hung smiled. For, if this man, who had seen the devastating power of Chinese technology, if *this* man could figure a way out of his situation, then Tse could do no less.

"Show me," he said aloud.

■ ■

Inspiration, *McClure thought. Whatever the poets* and philosophers had to say on the subject, it really came down to one word, one quality: desperation.

As McClure lay there cataloguing the tools at his disposal, he remembered one of the pictures that had blurred by: a 3-D picture of him sledding as a child in New England. And then it struck him: *You're in a sled. Find yourself a slope!*

Everything outside his viewport was spread out, bent, and twisting helplessly around all manner of central axes. They were of absolutely no use to him as a smooth, propulsive surface. But there was one thing he knew his sled could ride.

And so, using nothing more than instinct and inspiration, he used a T-shaped socket wrench to loosen two forward bolts. These, he reasoned—since there were matching bolts above—were what held the lower armor plating to the sled. When the second big screw floated free, he felt the front of the plate drop. He couldn't see it but he knew it had happened because the sled was pulled in that direction.

He imagined the vehicle looking like a shark now, its maw open as it moved through the sea. If it didn't, he was in trouble.

Stowing the wrench, McClure took a moment to consider the control panel. He examined the sled's position relative to the *Empyrean*, and the speed with which its emergency brake tethers could deploy. The filaments had to be at full extension, and full positive potential, in about two seconds—which was all the time he'd have for the Chinese science module to detect movement and attack his sled from about three hundred feet away.

McClure raised the old-style switch guard on the tether release. He decided not to send EAD Waters his data.

Godammit, he thought. He would deliver his findings in person or not at all.

Breathing slowly until his finger stopped shaking, McClure crooked it forward and back with a single, decisive move.

■ ■

Tse Hung cried out when he saw the sled's yaw engine blaze to life moments after the bottom plating had angled away from it. An instant later, a flurry of ion projectiles sped from the *Jade Star* science module. Assuming a widespread assault, the SimAI had sent only one of those missiles at the fleeing sled. The others headed off into the ether.

The ruthless head of an ion spear hit the American's ship a heartbeat later. Tse could not immediately tell whether it was the detonation of the weapon or the explosion of the sled that momentarily turned the cloud into a glittering magnesium-white firework.

Then he had his answer.

Tse's voice stopped, along with his breath, as he saw a rectangular shape speeding from the cloud. Improbably . . . *incredibly* . . . the pilot had used the armor plate on the bottom of his sled like a coin on a spun soccer ball: he skid off the blast before it could do any damage, using the force to propel him forward. There was no need for a second burst of thrust from the ship; as a result, there was no follow-up salvo from the science module.

Tse Hung's eyes remained open very wide as the tiny ship sailed into the void, its dimly lighted passenger quickly swallowed in darkness. When it was gone, Tse wept.

■ ■

McClure couldn't believe that he was alive.

The ion blast had given him a massive jolt, knocking him hard against the top of his space suit. If not for the fact that he was secured to the ship itself, the agent might have broken his back against the top of the sled. As it was, McClure felt as if he'd been shaken by his heels and then dropped on his head.

He checked his distance from the module. It was the same distance he'd been when the first salvo was launched. He gave himself a few more seconds of free drift before he raised his finger to fire the main thruster.

"Go, baby," he said.

As with so many of the skycycles and young ladies he had known on Earth, those two words achieved nothing.

Crap.

He tried it again. Once more: nothing. The sled of the team leader must have struck it when it flipped over McClure's sled. It didn't even fizzle.

He tried to reach the *Empyrean.*

Crap.

The comm array was on the bottom of the craft, where it hadn't weathered the armor drop or the particle strike particularly well. It failed to realign itself and pointed not toward Earth or the *Empyrean* but somewhere, he thought, near Deneb—where no one, even if they were listening, would get a message in his lifetime.

All McClure had, he presumed, were his pitch and yaw jets. Activating them here, all he'd do was spin in place.

"Okay, team, I know you're watching," he said, trying to find the *Empyrean* in his viewport. "Come and get me."

Just then, in the silence of his tiny craft, he heard a whizzing sound. He looked around, caught his reflection in the window—and noticed a rent in his air tank. It must have ruptured when he hit the top of the craft.

This time McClure swore out loud. He didn't have time to sit tight: he had to get the station's attention. Hoping he didn't throw up in his suit, he hit both the pitch and yaw rockets and began to spin.

▪▪

"Survivor adrift," Adsila Waters said at almost the same instant Stanton's comm officer did.

"Your agent, your call," CO Indira Singh informed the EAD.

"Zero-G rescue protocol A," he immediately invoked.

"Incoming shuttle due in thirty-three minutes," Singh replied. "Diverting to sled's apparent location, ETA forty-one minutes."

That location was vividly apparent. The sled looked like a pinwheel firework in the enhanced magnification view of Adsila's IC. The Earth-*Empyrean* shuttle detour was better than nothing, but that was not the solution the EAD wanted to hear.

Adsila shifted to female. That happened involuntarily at times when anxiety caused elevated testosterone levels that threatened to cloud reason. "We don't know what McClure's life-support system is like," Adsila said. "Singh, the manifest shows a pod in repair. Can it be launched quickly?"

"Negative," Singh replied. "The only available shuttle—"

"Belongs to Ziv Levy," a voice said in Adsila's ear. "And he is launching in three . . . two . . . one."

The voice was coming over her private comm. The CHAI was listening to her and Singh through the nanites in Dr. Carter's lab.

"Ziv?" she acted surprised.

"My shuttle is not recovery-arm-equipped," he said as rocket ignition came through on audio, "but when I burn through some space I'll go EVA and net him. And not with the carbon nanotubing that fell all apart on the *Grissom*: these are some of the synthetics that hold *me* together! I'll have your agent on board in under twenty minutes."

As she listened to Ziv, Adsila wasn't sure whether she felt smart, used, or both. In light of the many disasters that had struck this day, there was only one certainty that mattered: because of what she'd done, Special Agent McClure would likely survive.

She allowed herself a moment of satisfaction before informing Director Lord.

TWENTY-ONE

N FLIGHT SCHOOL, Lord had read a story online about a World War I Royal Air Force ace who was so impressed by the courage of a German pilot that, after shooting him down, he landed and brought the wounded man back to the British base near Flanders. It was a stirring moment of détente: the British pilot knew the German man would never fly again for his actions, and the German knew the Englishman would. Yet the encounter ended with two men surviving instead of two men perishing.

Lord took the news of Ziv Levy's action in a similar mind-set. Lord did not for a moment believe that the CHAI's actions were born in compassion. Ziv would expect something in return, even if it were just a chance to spend time with the Zero-G team to spy, seduce, plant nanites, or even convince Jack Franco that he had learned something new. More than likely, his shuttle would be scanning the attached sled for data about the Chinese module. He would have it before the FBI did. In that way, a player like Ziv could wrest concessions from the DIA in exchange for raw intel.

All true, Lord thought as the buggy bounced toward Armstrong. *But he also saved a member of my team.* In the director's mind, that earned Ziv a Flanders-style free pass. For now.

After riding in silence, the northern entrance to the base came into view.

"Dr. Diego, please inform Commander Tengan that we require an escort," Lord said.

"I believe that she has anticipated your request," Diego replied.

The scientist fed Lord an image from the bay. The two bay-authorized security officers were present along with Commander Tengan.

Lord grinned. The woman was good.

The hatch to the base slid open, the buggy rolled onto the smooth platform, and Lord's insides settled as the vehicle rode down. He did not relax, however. If he was correct, there was a spy on the base, someone who might want to protect his or her identity.

Armed security guards were waiting for them in the garage with Commander Tengan.

Lord popped his visor. "For me?" he asked innocently as he disembarked.

"You didn't think I *knew* you'd go out there?" Tengan asked. "The guard is for my scientists. Or rather, for their data."

Lord shook out his rattled limbs as he walked over. "Do these guards routinely have access to the buggy?"

Tengan seemed surprised. "Not unless they are directly instructed, by me, to be here."

"And they come in pairs?"

"Always. What's going on?"

"One more question, Commander," Lord said. "The satellite dish outside the hatch. That's the only way you can communicate with the lab, or the lab with Earth. Is that correct?"

"It is."

"Then they wouldn't risk using that," Lord thought out loud.

"Who?"

"Commander, back in the lab just now, Dr. May pooled all of her data," Lord said. "It was complete for the first time. I believe someone may have intercepted the data prior to this . . . and, realizing it's not working, they may have done so again."

"How?"

"Bugged buggy," he said. "But I don't believe they would have risked sending data through the dish. That being the case, they're going to want to come and collect it."

"And you—"

"Yeah."

Tengan understood. She cocked her head toward one of the guards. "Will you need—?"

"Keep them nearby, but I would like that," he said, pointing to a sidearm. "If you wouldn't mind."

Tengan asked one of the security officers for his weapon. It was a first-generation Pulsor, a gun that fired a short-range ultrasonic wave to stop a target without damaging structural material if the shot were a little off. So far, it had only been used to deter base crew who suffered psychoses due to isolation, or what was being called terracy: madness caused by the impact of Earth's tidal gravity on the inner ear, or at least that's how the legend went.

Lord accepted the weapon. "You should requisition P3s Gauntlets," he said with a smile. "Bigger local punch than a Pulsor. That's what we've got."

Tengan smiled back as she motioned the others to move out. "NASA keeps us two models behind," she said. "In case we get any ideas up here about, oh, Jeffersonian democracy, if you take my meaning."

Lord nodded.

"I'll make sure Dr. May is safe," Tengan said, turning with a small lingering look that somehow communicated a full salute, then followed her team out.

Saranya looked back at Lord as they left, but Lord had already turned back toward the buggy.

■ ■

The geometric monster of a vehicle remained still and silent for several minutes, until a hatch on the outside of the wall slowly opened and someone in a radiation suit with an opaque visor entered. That person glanced around the garage and, seeing no one, moved quickly toward the buggy, toward the exterior solar panels.

Breathing heavily, the intruder opened the driver's side door. He did not climb in but reached around and removed the panel from the inside. That exposed a network of small, fine structural supports. He reached toward a specific vertice joint that ran along the inside of the polyhedral cage. Using a small ultrasonic torch, he detached the metal locus. He removed a smaller, metal, inner tube from within it, and then the vertice joint was slipped back into place. He placed the inner tube in a pouch on his suit.

His attention focused on replacing the panel, the intruder did not see a figure rise from the cargo platform in back. When he did, he leapt back, nearly flying off his feet in the lesser gravity.

"Stay there and I won't have to shoot you," Lord told him as he maneuvered from behind the driver's seat.

The other person remained where he was standing but he activated the ultrasonic torch. His helmet off, Lord winced as the beam drove hard into his ears.

The intruder charged, still pointing the instrument. Accustomed to sharp decompression from power dives in his old Vampire, Lord recovered enough to fire, hitting the attacker in the thighs and knocking him back. Then he fired again, striking the person's hand and sending the screwdriver scuttling across the floor.

The attacker lay back in surrender. Lord approached with the Pulsor aimed squarely at the intruder's helmet. A shot at this range, with a hard concrete floor below, would probably crack the person's skull and cause permanent deafness.

Lord used a free hand to motion for the person to raise their visor. The individual complied. Lord looked down into the face of ERB medical technician Don Christie.

"I should've known," Christie said.

"That this might be a trap?"

The ERB officer nodded. "What I said on the *Grissom*—you are good, sir."

"You knock around long enough, you pick up things," Lord said. "Who'd you do this for?"

"I'm not free to say, sir."

"A blast at this range will not be kind to your facial bones," Lord said.

"Then I will also be *unable* to say, sir."

Christie had him there. Lord got on his IC. "Armstrong command," he announced. "Suspect secured. Move in security detail at your pleasure."

Suddenly, Christie moved a hand toward a place just above his chin. Still unaccustomed to lunar gravity, Lord stepped toward him—and a little past him, just as the lunar veteran had anticipated. The Zero-G man swore as Christie finished activating his Emergency Team IC and pushed himself in the opposite direction. The buggy thrummed to life and jerked forward at the same time, striking Lord with its rolling façade and throwing him facedown.

As Lord struggled to get up in the bulky suit, Christie jumped up and got into the buggy. The ERB officer would not be able to activate the elevator airlock—but escape to the lunar surface was clearly not his intention. Sitting in the buggy, the door flopping wildly, Christie drove straight at the grounded Zero-G man. His plan was to stop Lord, in case the director had not yet transmitted Christie's identity to Armstrong.

The fact that Armstrong command was certainly watching wasn't going to help Lord. By the time they got here, he'd be crushed. And, being crushed, he would not be able to stop Christie from getting out with the data storage unit he'd placed in the buggy. Lord had no idea where the man might hide—or hide the data for any accomplices he had here.

Lord managed to flip onto his back and tried to target Christie. But between the rolling cage bearing down and the man ducking behind the steering apparatus, Lord couldn't get a bead.

Unable to stop Christie or the buggy, Lord turned the weapon toward the concrete floor and fired. The shot hoisted him two feet from the ground and sent him rolling in the opposite direction. The buggy missed him by a foot. As he landed—hard—Lord saw Christie swerve sharply and turn back.

In that moment, the driver's side was fully exposed. Lord flipped onto his side and fired. The pulse knocked Christie into the passenger's seat and the buggy continued forward—into a wall.

The crash was mild but it was enough, in one-sixth gravity, to fling Christie forward into the cage. The rock-resistant panel cracked his helmet and knocked him senseless.

A few seconds later, the cavalry arrived: Tengan and the two security officers. The base commander ran to Lord while the two others hurried to secure Christie.

"We're going to have to footnote our Tactics and Response manual," Tengan said with admiration. "There's nothing about using a Pulsor as a personal thruster."

"What can I say, I was born to fly," Lord told her.

Tengan made the Zero-G director stay where he was as a medical team was summoned. Lord had a clear view of the security officers as they placed a pair of 2Bs on Christie—"black bracelets," handcuffs that not only restrained a prisoner but tapped into their nervous system through the IC. Thus restricted, Christie was left facedown on the floor.

"Search him," Lord said to Tengan. "There's evidence."

Tengan gave the order to security. Gloved hands patted him down and retrieved the small metal tube Christie had removed from the buggy. The commander asked for it, and for an extra pair of gloves.

While Tengan examined the tube, Lord accessed the prisoner's base personnel file. He only got to scan it before the medic arrived. He was driving a buggy like the one in the *Empyrean* loading bay.

"Technically, this is now the property of Armstrong Base," Tengan said, still looking at the tube. "But you can probably do a better job on forensics and—hell, you earned it."

Lord accepted the tube and tucked it into a pocket.

At Tengan's direction, the medic crew went to Lord first. Kneeling on either side of the Zero-G man, the young doctor made a quick assessment of his condition. He swiveled to give Tengan a thumbs-up and then went to attend to Christie. The medic must have been confused to see his former colleague facedown and in 2Bs.

The unconscious marine was in far worse shape than Lord. Broken leg bones were stabilized with slap-ons—magnetic splints—and his neck was placed within a sprayed-foam brace before he was lifted into the medic's buggy and driven away.

Tengan surveyed it all from a distance. Her expression made it clear that she was gravely disappointed to have been betrayed by one of her own people. Lord had never experienced anything like that and ached for the woman.

"Help me walk this off, Commander?" Lord asked, as much to distract the commander as to help himself.

Tengan walked over. "Would it do any good for me to order you to wait for the medicar to come back?"

"We need to figure out how to stop the SAMI as well as the person who did this," Lord said. "Your man has allies, maybe here. You and I both want them, ASAP."

There was more than just a sense of assistance when Tengan offered a hand.

"Any idea who they are?" the commander asked.

"That item you recovered may tell us that," Lord said, pushing from the ground. "There's nothing in Christie's file about his having a tech background." He rose with an audible *oof*. Tengan kept her hand clasped tight on Lord's until she was sure the man could stand.

"I'm okay." Lord smiled. "It's that damned virile CHAI leg of mine. Forces the rest of me to keep up."

"You just took down a man one-third your age who was fully acclimated to lunar gravity," Tengan said. "You're allowed to— "

"Wait!" Lord interrupted.

Tengan fell silent. The Zero-G man felt something in his cyborg leg—a vibration. His eyes narrowed with curiosity. He wondered if it were some kind of fluid reaction, an uneven flow caused by shock combined with one-sixth gravity.

And then the trembling sensation moved up his spine. He looked quickly, knowingly at Tengan.

"Hang it!" the base commander started to shout as the entire area began to shake. She pushed Lord ahead of her. "Out of the bay!" she yelled. *"Fast!"*

■ ■

Chairman Sheng not only felt the shuddering blast, he saw it through the viewport in the module. As before, the flash was the color of translucent flesh, with a tiny core of blackness—*like a dragon's eye*, he thought.

A dragon he had ordered Dr. Lung to wake.

Where was this one headed? His confused mind sought to make that determination. Earth was outside the viewport, so—this explosion had gone out into space, possibly toward the moon . . . he could not be sure.

Floating before the viewport, Sheng tried to collect his thoughts.

What has happened?

Parts of it were vivid, like Ku Lung being there one moment, all of the scientists hovering dutifully at their posts—and then gone the next. After that, with consciousness that came and went, Sheng had no idea who was there and who was not, who was alive and who was dead. He vaguely recalled seeing Dr. Hark's face stretched across his vision, unsure as to whether the physicist was laughing or screaming.

He recalled seeing sinuous red clouds—liquid red, the color of blood. He remembered faces without expression, without life, without bodies. He thought he had seen bodies without limbs.

Sheng looked at his own hands hovering beside him. He turned them around. The backs were black, raw. He remembered shielding his face from that first explosion, the one that flung him through the weightless environment, bounced him behind a strut that must have saved his life—

He glanced at his clothes, saw the fringes of his uniform that had been burned where the strut had not protected him.

After the blast he remembered nothing until he found himself gently bumping his head on the door of the Development and Research Center; he remembered trying to open it, dimly recalled that it refused to yield—

Decompression protocol, he thought as memories returned. That was the only reason doors shut on the *Jade Star.*

I am suffering trauma, he told himself. *I must recover. I am no good to my family or my country in this condition.*

Sheng turned to the door. He raised a trembling hand to a chain around his neck, pulled a card from within his tunic. He touched an unsteady thumb to the surface to activate it, then touched the card to the door. His Supreme Override Authority caused the door to slide open. Even if the rest of the station had been destroyed, if nothing but the vacuum of space awaited him, that panel would have slid back.

Better to perish than to stay helpless in this chamber, he had decided.

But Sheng did not die. Turning his face toward the opening, he saw bent and twisted halls filled with floating pieces of both structural material and dead crew members. In the distance he heard rescuers shouting orders, the serpentine hiss of welding tools, metal thunking on metal. Louder and nearer he heard squeaking, like a child playing with a balloon—the sound of air escaping into space.

He tried his IC. It did not respond to his touch. He wondered if Tse were alive and, if so, why his assistant had not come looking for him. When Sheng was just starting his career, nothing mattered more than the well-being of those he served—not even his family.

I must get to my command quarters, Sheng told himself. Beijing would be expecting a report.

The chairman turned and stretched toward an aimlessly drifting torso. He pulled it over with his fingertips. The lab coat was shredded and he tore away a sleeve to use as a mask. Pushing the remains away, he held the fabric to his face with one hand, used the other to grab the door frame, and launched himself into the battered corridor.

Sheng passed bodies, all seemingly sleeping—whether unconscious or dead, he couldn't be sure. Nor did it matter. In either case, they were beyond his help. Nor were they a priority. The words of a party leader came back to him, words spoken to Sheng when he was just starting his political career: "If there is one thing China has in abundance, it is people. They are as easily replaced as sand on a beach."

Even then Sheng had understood the implicit message: so was he, unless he made himself visible, unique, indispensable.

Sheng looked out the cracked corridor window, the source of the leak. He saw the tips of the module defense system cannons above and below. Between them, both ends of the station were spread out before him, vanishing into a plasma cloud. The first and last modules were slowly and fatefully spasming toward each other, into the shape of a silvery Ourovoros Ophis—the ubiquitous symbol of a tail-eating snake, the forces of positive and negative that consume each other until they have no choice but to renew.

Sheng clawed at an emergency oxygen station. They were legion around the *Jade Star*, marked by the red-knotted decorations. Behind each knot was a small sliding panel with a recessed platform holding a mask that slipped over the nose and mouth. A half hour's oxygen was cleverly hidden in compressed-air tanks built into the mask itself. Sheng let the fabric drift away and pressed the device to his face, inhaling greedily, feeling the last of the clouds clearing from his mind.

He now recognized where he was in the station: he was on the heavily populated side, the original foundational structure of the *Jade Star*. His office was not far. His IC sputtered weakly to life as it found a signal. It told him what he already knew: that the *Jade Star* was in crisis.

Continuing his passage through the hallway, Sheng was encouraged almost to a smile by the thought of the Ourovoros Ophis.

Yes, he told himself as he swam forward, pushing off the walls and ceiling. That's what he would tell his superiors: *We have achieved great power and we will now learn to control it. The station will be repaired, re-staffed. We shall be renewed.*

They would understand that. They would accept that. Never admit defeat, never retreat.

Mother China—and Commander Sheng—would move forward, even from this.

TWENTY-TWO

WHEN THE CHINESE module caused another black ripple in space and an orbital image of the moon's Mare Crisium exploded in their ICs—appropriately, the Sea of Crises—the staff of Zero-G shared a moment of horror and the same chilling thought:

Is that the location of Armstrong Base?

Programed to anticipate relevant questions, the Zero-G SimAI assured them it was not: the base was in the north polar region, just beyond Mare Frigoris, the Sea of Cold. But when Janet Grainger was unable to raise Sam Lord, it became clear that the blast from the Chinese module had at the very least rattled the lunar colony. And at the worst—

No, Adsila Waters thought. *I won't consider a fatal structural mishap. Not yet.*

"We are not receiving life signs," Grainger added tensely.

"Continue trying to raise Director Lord," Adsila said. That was obvious, but she needed to say something, to insert humanity into an unthinkable event.

Grainger acknowledged the order as Adsila continued to monitor the attempted recovery of Special Agent McClure. Ziv Levy was still en route, unaffected by the blast.

Grainger had been on duty since the reception and was exhausted.

Adsila was also running on sheer willpower, despite her brief rest in sick bay. She was still recovering from the lingering effects of the can she had inhaled, sore and weak from the rough sexual encounter with Ziv, and hurting from Dr. Carter's intrusive removal of the nanites.

The only other comm agent was Michael Abernathy, who, in stark contrast, was fully alert for the first time since arriving at the *Empyrean* two weeks before.

The youthful-looking tech expert was the only team member who had expressly trained for space detail, the first to matriculate from the new and exhaustive Zero-G program. He had graduated at the top of his class at the FBI's Quantico facility, spent two years with the astronaut trainees at NASA, then endured six months of sleep deprivation on urban stakeouts as well as weeks of survival training in desert heat and mountain cold. The San Diego native had aced it all, but that was not what had put him on Sam Lord's team—or caused him to be energized here and now.

Abernathy had spent a year in India studying Vajrayana—Tibetan Buddhism. In particular, he had used that time exploring the seven human energy centers, the major chakras. During his interview with Lord, Abernathy commented that he had a strong desire to prove how, in space, "the subtle winds of the body could flow unimpeded to the central channel of the body and bring off-Earth personnel closer to Buddhahood."

Lord loved the idea that a candidate could talk of "winds" in a vacuum and give it meaning. His response to a qualified man from whom he could clearly learn something was: "Welcome to Zero-G."

Abernathy had found it difficult, so far, to keep those chakras balanced. Since leaving Earth's atmosphere, his spiritual side had refused to shut down, leaving him wide-eyed and occasionally distracted. It was one thing to contemplate the cosmos from Earth, as mystics had done since the dawn of humankind; it was another to plug that uppermost seventh chakra directly into the universe.

Until today.

Since Lord's adventure in the cargo bay, Abernathy's descending chakras—third-eye wisdom, vocal communication, heart-based concern, visceral strength—had finally come fully alive. When the surface of the moon erupted and Lord's data vanished, Abernathy was the first to think to plug into the Armstrong shuttle *John Young,* which was in its lunar bay and had automatically switched to internal power when the base electricity went down. It had taken him a minute but he had located the vessel's high-gain antenna.

"EAD Waters," Abernathy said, "Armstrong power is off, but—hold on . . . quick scan reveals thirty-four ICs in proximity of the shuttlecraft *Young,* basement level, still functioning."

"Director Lord?" Adsila asked.

"He and Commander Tengan are not showing up," Abernathy said, then added hopefully, "yet."

"Thank you," Adsila said.

While Abernathy gave Grainger the frequency, Adsila looked through the IC to see if there were any updates from Prime Director Al-Kazaz. There were none, so he punched Stanton's IC. The *Empyrean* commander would be busy, she knew, possibly justifying the catastrophic recon to his cover-your-ass superiors earthside—but Adsila wanted to know anything else he might know about Armstrong.

Adsila's request to talk with him wasn't just unanswered, it was blocked. She shut the nanite link to Ziv. "What's going on with Stanton's IC?" she asked Grainger with foreboding.

The AEAD checked her sophisticated tracking tech. "Your message is being obstructed by military-grade tech," Grainger reported with concern. "Point of origin—Washington, D.C."

"Then it's not a debriefing," Adsila said.

"No," Abernathy agreed. "That would be secured on this end using *Empyrean* software."

"It has to be the Pentagon," Adsila said.

The implications were not lost on them.

"Damn," Abernathy said quietly.

"They're prepping an Earth-based assault against the *Jade Star*," Grainger said. "That has to be it."

"And the only way to do that is with the AIMS," Abernathy added ominously.

He was referring to the Asteroid Interceptor Missile System, developed to prevent collisions between planetoids and Earth. Launched from a silo at Vandenberg Air Force Base in California, it was a nuclear cluster bomb consisting of four warheads that would disperse, explode, and obliterate any space rock up to one-quarter the size of the moon.

"We don't know any of this," Adsila cautioned.

"No, but if an attack *is* being planned, I don't see any other options," Abernathy said. "Except for a few old Scud-Fs on the Russian space station—all of which are pointed toward Earth—there are no other military assets out here."

"Would we even risk detonating nukes in space?" Grainger asked.

"That could be what they're discussing with Commander Stanton," Abernathy said.

"Let's not speculate," Adsila repeated.

"I agree, but can anyone suggest another course of action?" asked a deep voice on the IC.

The voice belonged to Dr. Carter. Though the Zero-G medic was stationed in the sick bay, he was plugged into all comm activities. "We're faced with a weapon that has apparently shucked the reins of its makers and is spitting death by the gigaton," Carter went on. "It must be destroyed at any cost."

"If it can't be tamed, Doctor," Abernathy said.

"Agent, I am often accused of consistency," Carter said. "I believe in aggressive, proactive approaches to threats, be they internal or external. There is apparently no time to rehabilitate that mechanism."

"Doctor," Adsila said, "there are other factors in play. If the AIMS is fired, never mind us—but the *Jade Star* will be destroyed and any survivors killed. That would trigger a diplomatic crisis at best, earthside hostilities at worst."

"Undoubtedly," Carter agreed, "but the long-term implications are far more daunting. If the Chinese are permitted to lodge the tools of war among the stars, they will irrevocably change the nature of space colonization. It would become a place of open conflict, a nexus for proxy wars. No, this device must be shut down, firmly and irrevocably and quickly."

"Putting that aside, how does firing the AIMS impact us, Agent Abernathy?" Adsila wondered.

"Physically?" Abernathy said. "We probably wouldn't feel it at all, at least not directly. Our orbit is too high. But it would generate an electromagnetic pulse over Asia that will knock out vast areas of electronic activity. A very high percentage of low-orbit satellites over that hemisphere will also be crippled, many permanently."

"And there will be a new, near-Earth radiation belt that will become a no-fly zone for three to six years," Dr. Carter added.

"All of which would impact China immediately and most directly," Abernathy said.

Adsila shook her head. "Beijing has given our government a reason to commit technological homicide. That may be a justifiable consequence too good for them to pass up."

"*That* has to be why Commander Stanton is part of this conference," Grainger said thoughtfully. "The Chinese will seek to retaliate."

"Against us?" Abernathy said.

"Eye for an eye," Grainger pointed out.

"How does *that* make any sense?" Abernathy asked. "Besides, even the Chinese are at risk from their own weapon."

"They have a billion and a half people," Carter pointed out. "They can afford to ride this out."

"Conquest by attrition," Adsila said. She thought of the westward movement of Europeans against her own people, waves of them against decreasing pockets of Cherokee. The result was inevitable.

A gloomy silence filled the room, which was broken by Dr. Carter.

"Space—for peaceful exploration and colonization by all of humankind," he said with more than a hint of reproach. "Thus spake the UNDED."

The doctor was referring to the United Nations Department of Extraterrestrial Development, the global space-advisory panel whose influence was limited—and untested. Their charter had been pitched together using language crafted from maritime law and the General Assembly's First International Decade for the Eradication of Colonialism in the 1990s, and it covered everything from satellite salvage to first contact with alien intelligence. But UNDED had never faced a diplomatic crisis or a potential shooting war outside the atmosphere; just naming an investigatory panel would take weeks.

A reflective, businesslike air returned to the comm as the situation facing the United States and its allies became sharper by the moment. This reminded Adsila of the questions Sam Lord had posed five minutes after they met. Having passed the preliminary interview with Al-Kazaz, Adsila still had to be approved by the man who would actually be heading the team. That was anything but a rubber stamp. Adsila and Lord physically met in a Washington conference room and chatted a bit, after which Lord gave her what he later revealed was his Threshold Test.

"In a firefight, would you sacrifice an adversary to save a teammate?"

"Yes."

"Would you destroy a hijacked civilian ship to save your ship?"

"Yes."

"Would you annihilate a civilization to save your own civilization?"

"Yes."

Adsila's answers had been quick and certain. After she had given them, Lord extended his hand.

"Prepare to go starside, EAD Waters."

What Lord had not revealed until then was that any hesitation would have sent him on to the next candidate. And what Adsila had not revealed to Lord, to this day, was how easy the answers had been: she had only to think of what she would have done two centuries ago to save the Cherokee nation from near destruction.

While Grainger continued trying to raise Stanton and the team waited for any news about Armstrong, Adsila turned to the open comm from Ziv Levy. He was just minutes from making contact with Mc-Clure's spinning sled. Adsila restored contacts to the nanites.

Through his IC, Ziv was allowing Adsila to see everything he saw. The telemetry feed indicated that Ziv's pilot had brought the shuttle to within two hundred feet of the sled. It was visible in Ziv's viewport, spinning slowly; the pitch and yaw jets burned faintly with a fair blue flame, their fuel nearly depleted as they course-corrected en route to the *Empyrean*.

"Hold here," Ziv ordered the pilot.

The pilot applied a retroburn and stopped 182 feet from the target. Ziv quickly left the cockpit, shut the door, and issued an IC command that opened a panel just beside the shuttle door. He removed what looked like a clear, hooded wet suit. Adsila heard it squeak as it automatically molded, pressurized, and sealed him in from crown to heel. The back wall of the closet folded down and an upright pallet emerged. Ziv turned and Adsila heard something snap into place. Oxygen, she surmised. Even CHAIs needed to breathe, and their blood substitutes needed protection from the vacuum of space. Finally, from the same small closet he collected the highly compressed net he had boasted about. It looked like a hockey puck, with a fine, fine strand dangling from the bottom.

"How long is that?" Adsila asked.

"Ah, you're still there," Ziv said.

"Of course."

"I thought you might be sleeping. You were so—quiet."

"I was thoughtful," she corrected.

"Yes, it *is* a time for reflection, what with tensions high and the moon having taken what I can only describe as quite a *zetz*."

"What have you heard about that?" she asked.

"It's five hundred feet," he replied.

"What?"

"The length of the tether that attaches the net to the shuttle," he said.

Once again, Adsila was annoyed with herself. Ziv had set the bait and she bit. The entire purpose of the exercise had been to play her, to get her to ask him for something, to prove he could manipulate her. Again.

She watched in stern silence as the CHAI jumped to the shuttle hatch above, opened it, and hovered half in, half out while he attached the loose end of the net to what looked like a small fishing reel outside the craft. When he was finished, Ziv propelled himself through the hatch and out into space, holding the other end of the net, one thin end unspooling as the rest remained tucked neatly inside a compression pack.

Adsila heard a faint sizzle, saw a glow around the edges of the IC view, and watched the shuttle recede rapidly from Ziv's peripheral vision. He was wearing an ORP, a combination oxygen tank and rocket pack.

Within seconds, Ziv landed with the sudden hard stop of what could only be magnetic boots landing on top of the sled. She saw, as Ziv did, the hazy features of Agent McClure as he started and peered through the window: he would have heard a *clank*.

Adsila felt a rush when she saw that McClure was alive. Ordinarily, the sled would have been broadcasting a full array of data, but the agent had shut it down to conserve power.

Ziv worked quickly. He leaned over the nose of the sled, pressed the "puck" to the surface and, tucking his knees to his waist to escape the magnetic pull, soared away. Over his shoulder, Ziv watched—and Adsila saw—as the net spread swiftly and tightly around the craft like a webwork of cracks in a windshield. Then Ziv turned his eyes back to the shuttle. He was inside the hatch within moments. Pressing a button in his IC, he caused the reel to activate and pull the sled in. It took just seconds for the helpless vehicle to come within a few feet of the shuttle, where it was secured by a pair of magnetic "harpoons" fired from hidden compartments on either side of the reel.

"Take us in, Ben-Canaan," Ziv ordered the pilot as he ducked back into the hatch, closed it, and began repressurizing the cabin.

"Thank you, Ziv," Adsila said.

"I'm glad I was able to help," he replied. "Whatever you may think of me, I was raised to believe that all life is precious."

The Israeli sounded sincere—for the first time, Adsila thought—and she wanted to believe him. For now, she'd take him at his word.

At that moment, Adsila's attention was diverted by Agent Abernathy.

"Two more ICs received," he said excitedly. "Working to plug them in—"

"Nicely done, Mike—we have Director Lord on visual," Grainger said with cool excitement.

The EAD made a quick decision to leave the nanite connection on. Ziv still had one of her people. Life might be dear, but returning McClure to the *Empyrean* might not be so important. If she cut his eavesdropping now, he would know she was filtering.

As Lord's IC view opened before her, Adsila saw a relatively spacious, curve-topped, subterranean bivouac. Within it, she saw the back of a powerfully built woman in a lunar jumpsuit, whom the drop-down identified as Blake Tengan.

"Director," Adsila said, "it's good to hear from you. What's your status?"

"Excellent question, EAD," Lord replied, standing beside Commander Tengan in the buggy bay. "I got knocked on my seat but I only weigh thirty pounds here. I'm intact, I think. Let's find out about the base. Commander Tengan?"

He turned his head so Waters could see Tengan's profile. Lord's suit had protected him when the quake knocked both of them down. Not so Tengan. Her face was scuffed and forehead bruised from having hit the deck hard. Nonetheless, the base commander seemed as clear-eyed as ever.

"Armstrong is an elite ground-pounder," the commander said. "We were built tough. My geologist says the blast was far enough from our location that our biggest concern is chain reaction quakes collapsing or partially collapsing our lava tunnels. I've got a team preparing to go out and check."

"What's that pounding topside?" Lord asked.

"Ejecta from the blast falling to the surface," Tengan replied. "From the sound of it, there's nothing large enough to worry about."

"That strike in the Rocky Mountains reduced everything to melted rock—kharitonchik," Lord informed her. "Probably the same thing happened here, but not locally."

"Part of the moon was liquefied," Tengan said. "It's pretty sobering what passes for good news these days."

"Director Lord," Adsila said, "Ziv has retrieved Special Agent McClure and is bringing the sled in. He was alive on recovery. We're in full audiovisual contact with Ziv's shuttle."

"Very good," Lord replied.

He noted that Adsila had made a point of adding the extraneous word *audiovisual* and he understood the subtext. She was letting him know that the nanites were active and that Ziv was listening.

"Just going to make some recordings," Lord told Adsila truthfully. "Give me a minute."

"Yes, sir."

That communiqué would explain the radio silence as Lord switched from voice to text function. Even with the nanites active, Ziv would not be able to see what Adsila saw . . . or what they wrote.

Lord turned around slowly. Though the encounter with Christie had been recorded and stored, he wanted the aftermath of the crime scene for their records. The bastard had been an accessory to tens of thousands of deaths, and he would pay for that.

Is that your doing or the quake? Adsila texted when he reached the smashed buggy.

The driver was drunk with power, Lord replied, his fingers hunting and pecking the air. *How were you able to reach me?*

Abernathy.

It was both an answer and a cue.

Sir, I plugd thru shutl Yng whn it switchd to batt power, Abernathy replied hastily.

Status of that craft? Lord inquired.

AOK, Abernathy answered after taking a moment to check.

Well done. Lord agreed with Grainger's assessment.

TY!

Sir, Adsila cut in, *we believe AIMS response imminent.*

Not surprising, Lord replied. He switched back to vocal. "All right, EAD, we're still doing damage assessment here—I'll be in touch when I have a plan," he said, even as he was nearly finished formulating a plan. "Keep me apprised about McClure's status."

"Yes, sir," she replied.

"And thank Ziv," he said.

"I'm sure he knows how you feel," Adsila replied as she signed off.

Lord looked back to the base commander. "The *John Young,*" he said, referring to the vehicle named for the venerated astronaut who commanded the first flight of the shuttle *Enterprise.*

"It's in the shuttle bay," Tengan replied.

"Can I borrow the keys?" Lord asked.

Tengan stopped her scan to look at the Zero-G director. "If it's spaceworthy."

"It is," Lord informed her.

Tengan grinned wryly. "Remind me never to go up against you," she said.

"How would that even be in the cards?" Lord replied.

"I guess that depends on the game," Tengan replied.

Lord could have sworn he detected an almost melancholy tone in the woman's voice. The commander had sounded like a combat pilot who just announced she was bailing over enemy territory.

"You can have the *Young,* and someone to fly it," Tengan went on.

"Thanks. Anyone who would *not* have had contact with Christie?" Lord asked.

Tengan replied, "I don't think either of them would have risked their future on anything like this. Landry is your man."

"Perfect," Lord said. That information explained the look of concern

Lord had seen Kodera give Landry in the cockpit. It was a sweet image in the midst of all the destruction. "There's one more thing," Lord added.

"Shoot."

"I don't have time to pack Christie on board, but I have to know where he's been and who he's seen—and when he might have killed surveillance to cover that. Would you send me his IC as soon as possible?"

"All of it?"

"Every neurobit," Lord replied.

"As soon as we have functioning power, it's yours," Tengan replied.

"Thank you," Lord said as he turned and headed for the main base with gazelle-like leaps. "Would you let the basement know I'm coming?"

"I'll inform Trine Jørgensen. She's my number two," Tengan said as Lord flashed an "OK" over his shoulder and disappeared from the bay.

TWENTY-THREE

T WAS A surprise to Saranya when her weakly functioning IC announced that a "recent companion" had returned. The IC was conserving power and the memory function was not vital enough to provide more detail.

And it was a surprise to them both when Saranya jumped forward and embraced Sam under the white battery-powered emergency lights, with a massive air filtration unit on one side and Dr. Diego on the other. Saranya quickly stepped back.

"Sorry," she said, "but when we felt the detonation—"

"*Much* better coming from you than from, say, Ras," he commented with a grin.

She smiled back, feeling a little less awkward.

"Were you able to send your research out?" Lord asked.

"There wasn't time," she said. "I lined up colleagues at MIT, Stanford, Cambridge—they're waiting. Ras and I have been working on it since our ICs showed a little life."

"That IC power's coming from the battery of the surviving shuttle," Lord said. "We've got to fire her up before that runs dry. Which way to the base command module?"

Saranya pointed toward the largest of seven hemispherical bubbles against the near wall. The entire construct looked like a caterpillar. Lord took her by the elbow and they hurried over, Ras following closely. Lord held her, in part, to steady himself: his CHAI limb was still pumping more solidly than his other leg, which felt wobbly and uncertain in the lesser gravity.

As they approached, Lord sent a message to Adsila to look for any link between Don Christie and the Chinese. He passed lunar workers huddled around one large piece of equipment. Conduits running up suggested that it was Armstrong's solar-powered generator. The unit was the size of a walk-in freezer and stubbornly silent. Now and then the workers would run to one of the bubbles, presumably to consult whichever data storage systems were still powered up.

"We did make some progress," Saranya said as she collected her thoughts. "At least, we know the direction we need to go. My design for SAMI is based on the idea that neutrinos can be focused by enormous magnetic fields and—well, pushed out. The *Jade Star* bootleg didn't, or couldn't, bear up under its own Lorentz force because our eaves-droppers weren't privy to that part of the design. I hadn't been able to test it—"

"You mentioned progress?" Lord said.

"Sorry, yes. We've been trying to figure out a way to limit the field strength remotely—with a Trojan signal—and there may be a way."

"It would involve concealing the nature of our transmission, lest the electronics filter it out, which is part of my field," Ras said, inserting his face between them.

"Hence, 'Trojan,'" Lord said.

"Right," Saranya said. "My mechanism would not perceive it as hos-tile. But we have to hurry."

"Why?" Lord asked. "Apart from the obvious."

"SAMI's physical structure is weakening all the time," Saranya told him. "Without buffers that I haven't designed yet, it is unavoidable."

"You mean it might destroy itself?"

"Yes—and no," she said. "The more it falls apart, the more, and greater, destruction it will cause."

"The on and off switches would both cease functioning, even randomly," Diego said, "leaving just the functioning open generator until *that* fails—"

"Which could be within days, weeks, or months," Saranya said.

Lord didn't want to consider that possibility. "Would a nuclear strike take it out?" he asked.

That question caused Saranya to stop. She looked at him. "No," she said. "Dear God, no."

Now Lord stopped as well, though his heart began to race. "Why?"

"The structure itself is fragile," she said. "I'm not sure the device is in any shape right now to resist a hammer, in fact. But the odds of getting to the machine during a period of relative dormancy—and I stress 'relative,' since we do not know the machine mind of this thing—those odds decrease exponentially every moment, even immediately after an emission. And that's assuming the strike could be timed that precisely, which it can't be."

"What happens if that's the game plan?" Lord pressed.

"Is it?" Saranya asked.

Lord's expression was noncommittal.

"We have seen what the device does when there is no threat," Saranya said. "It just lashes out. We have seen what the *Jade Star's* defense system does when there is a modest threat, like the *Empyrean* incursion: it creates small energy bursts. Those are actually created by SAMI. In this instance, in the nanoseconds between a massive nuclear detonation and actual impact, the device will sense the magnitude of the nuclear threat and it will have ample time to push back."

"Meaning," Diego said, "—and here is your headline to your superiors—that it may expend itself in a final burst of neutrino glory. The planet and everything in orbit stands a good chance of being destroyed if the thing starts feeling protective."

Saranya gripped Lord's arms. "Tell me we can stop this."

"I don't know," Lord said, moving with renewed urgency. "We've got to get back to the *Empyrean*."

Entering the command dome, they found First Officer Robert Landry stepping into his space suit and a short, fit woman with short-cropped white hair in an Armstrong moon base jumpsuit talking into a landline.

Despite the pressures of the moment, Lord put his hand out to the pilot. "Bob," he said warmly. "How is Captain Kodera?"

"Recovering nicely, thanks."

Lord turned to the woman, who was just hanging up. "Lieutenant Commander Jørgensen?"

"Trine," she corrected briskly. "Commander Tengan has impressed upon me the urgency of the situation. You're cleared for takeoff as soon as everyone is suited up, Director. I've got to get back to repairs."

"Thank you," Lord told her, seeing in her face the same dedication, conviction, and savvy he had seen in her superior. But that's all he had time to glean as Landry took them into the passageway that led to the shuttle hatch. The corridor was nothing more than a ribbed, transparent, pressurized tube with a short, descending staircase at the far end. The sections would be retracted after they boarded.

As they approached, Lord could see that the runway at Armstrong base was nothing fancy: a rocky hole cut below the lunar surface with an open entrance on one side and an exit on the other. Airtight rooms on extendable arms allowed workers to service the shuttles. Save for this entryway, they had all retracted.

Lord turned his eyes toward the *John Young,* a twin of the shuttle they had come in on. There was something both proud and sad about the lonely spacecraft—though Lord had always anthropomorphized flying machines. They had tics and personalities and he had always taken it hard when they failed to return from missions. Lord had once gotten a look at his psych profile, and there was a curious notation about how he "romanticized" aircraft. That had briefly put him on a watch list, air force shrinks concerned that he might be encouraged to go down with a craft rather than abandon it. They were right, but it was also true that Lord had never lost a crippled fighter. Somewhere along the way, that notation got buried.

Landry boarded first. Saranya and Diego followed him, with Lord just behind. He was busy sending data to Tengan for when her IC was fully restored. As everyone took their positions, Lord texted Adsila on his IC.

Al-Kazaz, he instructed. *Priority one. Listen in, kill nanites.*

Acknow'd.

Only the prime director's voice came through to conserve power. "Sam, happy to hear from you."

"You may not be," Lord said. "Is Washington planning to use the AIMS?"

A hesitation.

"Pete—I need to know, now," Lord said.

"Affirmative."

"They can't," Lord said, and immediately reported what Saranya had told him. His superior didn't sound happy to hear the information.

"Well, that's a nuisance," he said.

"Seems pretty straightforward to me," Lord said. "We have a plan. *We* can make this better, *they* can only make it worse. Even the White House should grasp that."

"If it were only the president," Al-Kazaz responded. "They're calling it the Dragon's Eye."

"Who is?"

"China."

"They've acknowledged the device as theirs?"

"Not in a helpful way," Al-Kazaz replied.

That bit of information silenced Lord. Al-Kazaz took no pleasure in it.

"The state president in Beijing, the Council, and the Central Military Commission of the National People's Congress contacted the president to let him know that they had no knowledge of the actions of what they called 'the exuberant patriot' running the *Jade Star*, that they were unaware of the project until after it had started causing destruction, and that they are unable to contact him."

"But they didn't condemn him," Lord said.

"No, they're fence-straddling," Al-Kazaz replied. "Beijing says that the device—whose existence they blame squarely on America—is endangering their space station. They want it shut down as swiftly as possible. If we can't do it, and since they can't do it, they're prepared to position their patriot as a victim . . . and as a possible hero."

"Depending on how everything plays," Lord understood.

"Exactly. They can always say they were studying our device to try and find a way of terminating such a deadly weapon."

"Which wasn't a weapon until they made it one," Lord said.

"Right."

Adsila had taught Lord a very useful Cherokee word concerning deer droppings, and he used it now. Al-Kazaz gleaned its meaning from his tone.

"Listen, Sam, I don't blame you for being upset—especially if Dr. May is correct. But what other option do we have? We can't prove the Chinese knew what this was, can we?"

"Not directly, not yet," Lord admitted.

"So there we are," Al-Kazaz said. "If the United States doesn't do something, even the wrong something, Washington will get blamed for creating technology it can't shut down."

Lord was dimly aware of thrusters racing and the push of upward momentum as the *Young* lifted off from the field. The rough, dark wall of lunar substrata dropped away to reveal the clean, brilliant tinsel of the heavens.

"Pete, if the AIMS explode, they may destroy everything north of the ionosphere," Lord said.

"I'm told the EMP will only— "

"It's not just the nukes, it's the device," Lord said. "It may go haywire."

"I see. But . . . the operative impediment is 'may,'" Al-Kazaz countered.

"Okay, tell the Pentagon Dr. May says it *will* do that."

"You want me to invoke the opinion of a woman who's on the short list of people they think may have *leaked* the data?"

"She didn't. I'll prove it."

"I don't think that can happen in time."

"Oh, Jesus," Lord said. The bureaucracy somehow managed, just then, to get even worse.

"Pete, is there *anything* you can do to stop them?" Lord asked.

"Not likely," Al-Kazaz replied. "Chaos is growing. After Tokyo and Aspen, everyone is terrified, waiting to see what gets destroyed next. There are already riots and people are paying a fortune for rides to *Empyrean*. The political and military leaders have to do something, and soothing words or one scientist's equations won't cut it."

Lord grimaced with displeasure. Al-Kazaz was correct: he *had* been away from Earth for a while—just long enough not to make impulsive, dangerous, *stupid* decisions based on public pressure.

"Can we try to get the Joint Chiefs to at least listen to her before launching?" he finally asked.

"Trying is easy," Al Kazaz said unconvincingly. "Succeeding is the challenge. Especially when I'm not sure I disagree."

"How soon?" he asked Al-Kazaz hollowly. "How soon before they deploy AIMS?"

Al-Kazaz replied without enthusiasm. "Look out your shuttle window," he said. "You may be able to tell me first."

Adsila Waters was listening intently to the disturbing conversation when she received word that Levy's shuttle was two minutes from docking.

"Dr. Carter, would you meet Agent McClure at PriD2?"

"Saw the message, on my way," he assured her.

That done, Waters reinstated the nanite eavesdropping. Ziv might as well hear this; it wouldn't be a secret for very long.

"Janet, AIMS launch is imminent," she said. "Begin tracking."

At once, a map of California filled the space above their heads. As Grainger focused in on it, three-dimensional features began to appear—geology first, roads and buildings second. The view soared past aircraft, through clouds using thousands of satellite-, drone-, and ground-based images to create a seamless, live holographic representation. Vandenberg loomed large, visual access granted by the FBI-permitted software—and then they saw the silo. The maw was already open. It would be easy to mistake the nuclear missile for a vintage spacecraft. It was a brute of a thing, 220 feet high, with a round base and a tapered top. The base had several stunted boosters around a main thruster, with vectored nozzles as well as a sensor complex and robust orbital maneuvering system. These would be used to lock onto the target wherever it might be . . . or wherever it might move. Upon locating the target, four X50 warheads would roll out, their rockets would ignite and thrust-vector them straight to the sensed targets.

"Missile data is protected by the same software we saw before," Grainger said. "We won't know its exact trajectory until it happens."

Adsila's IC filled with interpolations of the target and the missile to suggest a possible route. It would follow a minimum-time trajectory, finding the target in a fraction of an orbit.

"The nuclear bursts are likely to occur just beyond the demonstrated reach of the module's self-defense system," Grainger said.

"How do we know that?" Adsila asked.

"Washington asked and China denied any knowledge of a self-defense system," the AEAD replied.

"It's there," said a new voice over the team's ICs. "I can assure you of that."

The team in the comm smiled as one. "Agent McClure?"

"Alive and thinking," he said.

"Doctor?" Adsila asked.

"The quick-scan says he's medically sound," Carter replied. "He's responding well to the oxypills."

"Well enough for duty?" Adsila said. A sports doping rage in the late twenty-teens, oxypills were called "the aspirin of the cosmos," the cure all of space travel. The modified EPO hormone increased a person's red blood cell count, boosting the body's capacity to transport oxygen.

"Agent McClure took quite a beating out there," Carter said. "He's wobbly but he's mentally fit—"

"I don't want to *miss* this, Doc," McClure implored.

"—and I'm sure that physical uncertainty will be gone as soon as he returns to his station," Carter added helpfully. "I'll lend him an arm and update him on the way."

Adsila didn't have time to debate the matter. She okayed McClure's return to the comm.

"What about Mr. Levy?" Adsila asked flatly, aware that he was listening.

"He and his pilot are still onboard," Carter replied flatly. "The CHAI graciously declined medical attention."

"Very good," Adsila said.

"Thank you, EAD," McClure said. "I'll be there—"

Adsila heard a thump.

"When you can walk," Carter said. "He just propelled himself into the ceiling. I'll help him back."

"Thank you, Doctor." Her mind was already back on the impending strike. "Janet, let's see the target up there."

The view of the silo shrank slightly and was joined by a floating image of the cloud-shrouded *Jade Star* planted amid a sea of apathetic stars.

"Shuttle *John Young* coordinates," she asked Abernathy.

"Two hours, six minutes to *Empyrean* arrival."

Just then, the view of the silo seemed to catch fire. The entire image was suffused with a white-orange glow that rolled in all directions from the silo's mouth, suddenly obscured by a tower of ivory-and-gray smoke through which the sharp point of the AIMS rose decisively.

The silence in the comm was profound. It seemed a harbinger of things to come, of the dead quiet that would infuse a dead space station if the module reacted as Dr. May had predicted.

"Director," Adsila said as she rejoined Lord's IC feed, integrating it into her own. "The AIMS is on the move."

"I saw," he replied.

The silence resumed. Carter and McClure wordlessly joined the others in the comm to stare at the AIMS as it rose through the clouds. In their ICs they saw the rising contour of Earth, watched the image zoom out until both the *Jade Star* and the pinpoint of rocket light were visible in the same picture.

"If you were close enough, Director, you could ram the thing," Adsila told Lord.

That was for Ziv's benefit. She hoped that he took the hint and at least tried to intercept. Lord himself shot the idea down.

"I'm informed by the PD that there's a manual override," Lord said. "If the AIMS doesn't detonate automatically, it will be triggered from Earth. They feel the radiation bath alone might be enough to stop it."

"It won't," McClure said. He finally downloaded the readings he had taken from the sled. Data flooded the IC of everyone in the comm. "That plasma cloud is like a trail of gunpowder. A nuclear spark anywhere nearby will likely set it off."

Lovely, Adsila thought. *So there's that too.*

There was a brief silence after which Lord said, "My companions agree. The missile has to be stopped intact."

"It's traveling at twenty-five thousand miles an hour in the wrong direction for us to do that," McClure informed them. "Nothing from here could snare it, not even Mr. Levy's impressive net."

Everyone on the comm watched as the missile flashed once, vanished, and then one spark after another appeared in its place until there were four glowing dots—each moving faster than the rocket that had borne them aloft, all heading like fireflies toward the *Jade Star.*

"Five minutes to impact," Grainger said.

"Agent McClure, you may have hit on it," Lord said, sudden enthusiasm in his voice.

The agent frowned, replayed in his mind everything he'd said. "Sorry, sir?"

"Lord out—I'll see you on the other side."

TWENTY-FOUR

THE INSISTENT IC pinging woke Dr. Lancaster Liba from a sound rest and a satisfying dream. One arm was asleep beneath him, so the Gardener raised the other to jab at his ear and answer.

"Here," he said groggily.

"Lancaster, call the highest-ranking official you know in Beijing, *now*, and have a *Jade Star* section jettisoned," a voice ordered.

Sam Lord's urgent tone brought the *Empyrean* operative to full alert. "Sam, what's—"

"*Fast!*"

"Okay, but—that's big. What's the 'or else'?"

"Everything in Earth orbit may be destroyed by AIMS warheads," Lord told him. "That's from Dr. Saranya May, who wrote the science they stole. The incoming nuke *must* be distracted."

"Incoming nuke?"

"Lancaster, we have less than five minutes. *Move it!*"

"Moving," Liba said without a hint of resentment as he swiped Lord to hold. That would mute the director's presence while allowing him to see everything.

The SimAI in the Gardener's IC began an automatic countdown clock at 4:45. Liba did not wonder, *What the hell happened since I went to sleep?* He thought, with frightening understanding, *Space politics has finally grown up.*

The Gardener sat up in the stiff, narrow cot in his small residence adjacent to the agricultural center. He had already activated the FBI's VerbAL—the all-language translation program he used for spying on *Empyrean* visitors—and was quickly fingering through his IC contacts.

Four and a quarter minutes, Liba thought as unfamiliar anxiety raced through his system. The Gardener worked with soil and seeds. He didn't do *anything* this fast.

He stopped at the name Chang Kar-Leung. Memories returned of long, happy nights they had spent discussing the importance of foliage in one's environment.

"How can one even begin to address the relationship of feng shui, of wind-water, without the presence of plants and trees?" Liba had said.

The two had fashioned an almost immediate bond and both men had remained in contact over the years at all times of the day or night— sometimes just to talk about bamboo. From the start, the agricultural professor—now minister—had nicknamed the American Hé Huā, "Lotus," because of his ability to raise purity from mud.

I wish that was the case now, Liba thought as he hit the man's icon. As the clock closed in on the four-minute mark, it suddenly struck the Gardener that this wasn't just another assignment to follow a dignitary around *Empyrean* or spike a tomato. The readout might be counting down the seconds he had left to live. Liba rose, went to a hydrangea potted in a corner, and sat beside it. He put the fingers of his left hand in the rich soil, dug them deep until he touched root. He did not want to die alone.

It was twelve hours ahead in Beijing. Chang materialized as he strode along a wood-paneled corridor lined with blossoming planters.

"Sifu Hé Huā," Chang said, using the honorific for *teacher,* "to what do I owe this unexpected pleasure?"

As he repeated, exactly what Lord had told him, Liba's quiet but concise and dead-serious tone eliminated any pleasure in the call. Patriotism, party loyalty, and friendship collided hard.

"What is the source of this information?" Chang demanded.

There was no time to hedge, so Liba told him about Director Lord and Dr. May. The universe was obviously having a little laugh, bringing this back to Liba: he was the one who first told Lord about the scientist.

"This decision to use the AIMS did not come lightly," Chang said. "I was about to enter a conference hall to witness the results."

As Chang spoke, Liba kept hearing *no* in every word.

"What you will witness is my death," Liba responded bluntly. Another thirty seconds had passed. "*Sigung,*" Liba pressed, using the term for a teacher's teacher, "the weapon on the *Jade Star* will destroy the AIMS, and all of us with it, to protect itself. Is there nothing you can do to help?"

Chang whispered words that sounded like *Nam mou san po.* Liba's translator didn't pick them up, but he knew they meant "Oh, my great Buddha." The minister's next words were hollow and horrifying. "My friend, I do not have the authority to stop it—or, if I did, I lack the time to work through military channels."

"I understand," Liba replied. "So, then—okay. I guess this is it. Thank you. Thank you for everything."

It wasn't a ploy, or a play for sympathy. What Chang had said was the hard, harsh truth: there was nothing he could do in three minutes, fifteen seconds.

The minister's eyes were sad as he regarded his friend in the IC. "You are certain, *Hé Huā,* that both stations will be destroyed?"

"If I had the science to back that up, I would send it," Liba said. "I don't. But we have the scientist who invented it, and this is her conclusion."

Liba saw a subtle shift in the man's expression, his bearing. If Chang wasn't directly involved with the creation of the device, as one of the nation's highest-ranking scientists he would have been present for locked-door policy meetings. Chang must have known where the data came from. His fingers moved.

"Assuming the circuits are still functional," Chang told the Gardener, "the access code for the rockets that control the outermost module is the following expression."

A numeric sequence appeared in Liba's IC:

$$4^8 \div 4^5 = 4^3 \qquad 4^8 \div 4^5 = \frac{4^8}{4^5}$$

"Four?" Liba said. "An unlucky number."

"Not to a generation that rejects tradition," Chang said.

"That'll learn 'em," Liba muttered to himself. He also suspected some elders had approved it as well: anyone who knew the Chinese culture would never have expected them to use a four. It was the perfect disguise.

"Sadly, I do not have the launch code to activate them," Chang apologized. "It's a two-key system; the military has the rest. Once you get in, you will have to find it on your own . . . somehow."

"Sifu, is there any way—"

"There is not," he firmly replied.

"*Ch'ih fu,*" Liba replied, eschewing the translator. "Pray for blessings."

Chang signed off, a look of disappointment in his eyes. Liba understood why. Chang had put the lives of others above personal security. He had embraced friendship over ideology, erased borders in the name of humanity.

A solitary minister had mutinied and had overruled the will of the Politburo. Whichever way this went, the agricultural minister would have to answer for that.

Sorry, my old friend, Liba thought.

Knowing that Lord would have already snapped up the data and gone to work, Liba sat on the floor, his fingers damp with humus, and wept into the leaves of the hydrangea. He too was praying—for Chang and for everyone whose lives depended on the team working with Sam Lord.

■ ■

"There is no launch code?" Dr. May exclaimed as Lord passed the numbers to both her and the Zero-G comm. "We can turn the rockets on but not fire them? What are we supposed to do, just press buttons?"

"Whatever you do, you have two minutes, fifty seconds to do it," Lord said.

"The circuits on the *Jade Star* module are functioning," Landry said in their ears. "Opened right up with this code."

"That's good," Lord said encouragingly.

"Sam, it's like we're starting over," Saranya said.

"Agent McClure?" Lord said.

"The code is an exponential statement," the Zero-G scientist replied. "Start sending other raised or lowered powers."

"Diego?" Lord said.

"Firing off exponentials of four," the scientist replied from the cockpit.

While the numbers flew spaceward, Lord peered out the viewport in the direction of the *Jade Star*. He saw nothing but the faint smear of the plasma cloud . . . and the terrifying pinpoints of light closing in, like unwelcome escapees from the asteroid belt. The clock edged past the two-minute mark.

"Ras, I don't think they'd carry it to the thousandth power," Saranya said, tension in her voice as she played with the numbers. "We should probably try—"

"Moving on to other integers," Diego said.

Terrible silence filled the cabin. There were ninety-five seconds until impact.

"Lancaster, you still there?" Lord asked.

"Here, Chief."

"Is there anything traditionally 'Chinese' that we should be considering?"

"Yin and yang, completeness, fire and water—unity?" Liba replied, his voice stabbing at ideas. "Everything comes back to that."

"So if these numbers are half of something," Lord thought aloud, "what's the complement? What creates balance?"

"Every equation, by definition," Saranya said. "I've tried things with fours as bases, fours as exponents, fourth roots, negative fours. Nothing. I played around with the Four Exponentials Conjecture. Also nothing. Are we looking for an equation that plots the ideogram for the Chinese numeral *si*? If so, from the standard or financial character set? Does the equation itself have to have powers of four in it?" She shook her head angrily. "McClure, are you listening?"

"Yes, and I think I got it," McClure said suddenly.

The others fell silent.

"I was messing with some easier approaches," he said. "Here . . . look."

Lord and Saranya both straightened. They watched as the agent began typing and the clock slipped under one minute.

"Try this, written out," McClure said, finishing the new expression:

$$\frac{4 \cdot 4 \cdot 4 \cdot 4 \cdot 4 \cdot 4 \cdot 4}{4 \cdot 4 \cdot 4 \cdot 4 \cdot 4} = 4 \cdot 4 \cdot 4 = 4^3$$

Diego punched it in, Landry sent it, and Lord turned back to the viewport. The stubborn familiarity of the lights remained, hovering in the darkness.

And then, suddenly, with fifteen seconds remaining until impact, two dull white flares burst against the infinite blackness.

■■

Tse Hung was jerked awake when his entire office moved.

At first he thought he had dreamt it. But then the area lurched again. There was an insistent humming in the porcelain-white walls, a vibration in the floor that ran up through the chair.

The Jade Star *is coming apart,* he thought.

The luckiest modules would burn up in Earth's atmosphere. The others would become lost among the stars. His own? The power-deprived SimAI did not anticipate that question by showing the exterior of the station. Tse had to bring up an image manually. As he did, the young man experienced an old, familiar sensation. He felt a little heavy.

But it isn't weight, he thought. He was being pushed back in his seat.

The construction rockets had been activated: the module was in motion. That was confirmed by the IC view. It had changed from before. The other modules of the *Jade Star* were still linked but they were in a different position. And in the glittering blackness he spotted four new stars arrayed like a diamond. No, they were asteroids—large and getting larger by the moment. And they were coming toward him.

Has the Dragon's Eye turned on the station? he wondered. *Or are they rockets fired by enemy ships?*

Not that it mattered. If just one of them bumped the compartment, grazed it, caused even the smallest fracture, the result would be decompression and destruction.

Tse Hung felt the pressure against his body increase. The module was speeding up, keeping pace with the onrushing projectiles.

The young man pushed himself to the floor. He tried to kneel but he fell face forward. That was fine: he could pray from there.

"Merciful Ti-ts'ang," he heard himself praying to the Buddhist Bodhisattva, "intercede on my behalf. Throw me from this bridge of pain. Deliver me into the river of reincarnation—"

Tse's body slid along the floor and tumbled to the wall. He settled on his back as the module raced ahead. His heart was thumping too hard for words to escape his throat so he prayed in silence. On his IC, the loyal assistant to Chairman Sheng watched as his office fled farther and farther from the space station, and the eerily iridescent aerogel cloud that surrounded it. The vision twisted again until all he saw were stars, countless numbers of them, and then his IC collapsed as it left the range of the *Jade Star's* weak electronic signal.

The air in the ejected module had quickly grown hot and thick, and he wheezed against the weight of his own carbon dioxide. The white walls turned a swirling, muddy black.

And then, for the briefest instant, the module was white again. It was a silent, gleaming flash, not the eye of a dragon but the eye of a god.

Then his lungs collapsed, his limbs bloated, his body burned through the last of the oxygen in his boiling blood, and Tse Hung passed into merciful oblivion.

■■

The man Tse had served shed no tears for him.

Heroes do not merit tears but gratitude, Sheng thought, remembering his Party indoctrination as he floated toward his station's engineering section—the heart of the *Jade Star.*

Sheng had tried to reach Tse, who—alive or dead—would have remained at his post, awaiting instructions. The young man's devoted attentions were needed now. But Sheng felt no remorse for failing to reach him, any more than he felt grief for the remains of the many crew members he had encountered—even though he had recognized each one. They had died in service of Mother China. And they had done it while boldly expanding her reach from the humble home of their birth to the realm of the divine process. Death here was a privilege.

But Sheng had refused to dwell on that. He had to salvage this outpost, reclaim the reins.

When Sheng felt the space station wrench, his struggling IC told him what had happened.

Intentional jettison, translunar origin.

And when he saw the hallways go pure white for the duration of a single heartbeat, his IC defined that as well: *Rocket self-destruct, Earth origin.*

Sheng didn't quite understand the reasons behind what had happened, though he knew that his station had been attacked and that the attack had been diverted.

He hastily changed course and headed for his quarters, where he kept a pressure suit with its own oxygen supply. He passed a total of four living crew members, three of whom were working to restore functions or enter blocked rooms, one of whom was just floating and staring. Each acknowledged Sheng with a look, he looked back at each in return, and then he moved on.

His quarters were intact. Since everything was bolted to everything else or secured with powerful magnets, that was no surprise. Drifting to his locker and donning the suit, he felt refreshed as he floated back into the corridor. He turned in the direction of the destroyed science section, bound for engineering.

Even in this crippled station with a skeleton crew, the chairman felt empowered. Sheng considered that this feeling of superiority might be nothing more than a coping mechanism, a delusion, but he pushed it from his mind—he could do nothing about it even if it were.

The explosion in the science module had bent the door to the engineering section, leaving it wedged open. Sheng pulled the panel hard and far enough that the corpse attached to the inside simply floated away, allowing the chairman to gain entrance.

The room was blacker than space. There were no lights, no readouts, no light of any kind save a phosphorescent panel to the left of the door. The room had its own solar storage system, but it had to be activated manually to conserve power. Sheng entered an emergency code and, above him, six volumetric monitors popped on. His IC was also fueled and returned to full operation status.

Sheng stared in grim appreciation at the images floating around the room as his IC plugged into still-functioning electronic hubs. One caught his attention. He pushed off the wall and drifted toward it. The display showed empty space where the command module should have been. He engaged his IC, ordered the image to run backward five minutes.

Sheng watched as glowing specks came toward the plasma cloud that shrouded the *Jade Star.*

American AIMS missiles, his IC informed him.

Then he saw the command module rockets fire, separating it from the station. He saw the onrushing lights change course and turn toward the new bright, electronically active target.

Diversionary maneuver, the IC explained.

Sheng felt his heart grow full. Not for Tse, who could not have made this happen, but for his proud space station.

My Jade Star *is not a brainless chunk of space debris, but your bombs are,* he thought triumphantly.

Sheng slowed the image. The launch of his own command module into space had hijacked the attention of the American X50 missiles, which would not have been fed a precise vector—since the *Jade Star* was no longer moving predictably and was hidden inside the plasma cloud. But the missiles would have been fed a specific configuration: the known shape of a generic module of the *Jade Star.* The intact command module fit that programmed criteria better than the damaged Development and Research module. Like dogs, the warheads had turned to follow it. The science module had been spared.

Sheng watched the replay with growing satisfaction as the hope of America, the four lights, grew brighter then duller and duller until their rockets winked out. Taking the bait had caused the rockets to exceed their structural limits until they broke apart harmlessly, far from the *Jade Star,* destroying only the heroically jettisoned command module.

The chairman observed it all with a sense of satisfaction so potent even he found it disquieting. His shoulders shook once with laughter: the Americans might not even know they had failed, not yet. They wouldn't be able to see anything clearly because of the ionized debris cloud.

Sheng grabbed a support strut and, pushing off, sailed back toward the door. Safe in his suit, he headed in the direction of the science module, to the device, to the Dragon's Eye. He would mount the serpent and ride it, repay violence with violence, only this time he would direct it at the heart of American power—as Beijing had always intended.

He hadn't gone ten meters into the corridor when he felt a familiar sensation in his stomach and spine, one that he had felt four times prior. Apparently, the Dragon's Eye would not, could not, wait for its master. It had just opened a fifth time—more powerfully than before.

He continued on his way, a proud father wondering where his ferocious child had turned its attention this time.

TWENTY-FIVE

W ELL DONE, AGENT McClure. Very well done."

Adsila's remark followed confirmation from Director Lord that the AIMS had exploded beyond the *Jade Star* and had not ignited the plasma cloud of debris.

The other members of the Zero-G team, all present, gave McClure quiet congratulations—even Dr. Carter, who nodded in appreciation after unplugging his med IC from McClure.

"Just don't push yourself," the doctor warned. "It will take about an hour before you're fully recovered from near syncope and benign paroxysmal positional vertigo."

As one, three other SimAIs defined the medical terms for "nearly fainted" and "dizziness."

At the same moment, there was an "all eyes" message from PD Al-Kazaz. His face hovering before them—and they before him—he asked the team if anyone had picked up any data from the AIMS mission.

"Very little, sir," Adsila said. "We only know that the AIMS shut down, sir."

"The warheads didn't explode?" Al-Kazaz asked.

"No, sir." She added, "The rockets missed their target."

"So the missiles were destroyed by PEAR," Al-Kazaz said. Preventative Emergency Action Response was a fail safe system built into the electronics and triggered from Earth to keep wayward missiles from being snared by an enemy or destroying something else. "That's probably why we aren't getting anything from Vandenberg. They didn't want very sophisticated, primed nuclear weapons swinging through the solar system. You have timing on that?"

Adsila checked the telemetry. "The missiles were headed off-target for a full seven-point-three seconds after the anticipated impact."

"Helluva miss," Al-Kazaz said. "Heads will roll."

"That is for certain, sir."

"Has Director Lord reported in since the blast?"

"He has, saying only that the explosion took place."

"Why isn't he on this call?" Al-Kazaz asked.

From a three-dimensional icon floating in the lower right corner, Adsila knew that Lord was watching and listening, but he was also talking to Dr. May. Before she could even consider how much to tell the PD, the transmission was interrupted by a calm male voice delivering an emergency alert from *Empyrean* command.

"The Dragon's Eye is once again active," Stanton reported.

"Hell's full acre," Al-Kazaz uttered as he also received the information.

All ICs immediately turned toward the spot in the heavens where the AIMS mission had now, demonstrably, failed. A familiar, very unsettling darkness was spreading across the heavens and appeared to be expanding toward Earth.

"Sir," Adsila said.

"I see it," Al-Kazaz replied, and looked away.

When the PD turned, Adsila sent a cautioning look at the other members of the team—though none of them seemed poised to make a remark. The pause was actually a relief: it gave everyone a moment to process the fact that by diverting the missile and saving everything in Earth orbit they may have doomed another spot on the home world.

"Hold on," Al-Kazaz said, still looking toward something out of view. He waited, squinting. "Now what?"

It wasn't a question, it was a statement. There was no urgency in his tone, just puzzlement. The Zero-G team remained quiet and very attentive.

Then another alert from *Empyrean* command. "Magnetic activity at the base of the thermosphere."

Grainger accessed the *Empyrean's* outboard lenses and filled the space above them with a holographic view of the region just below the upper limits of Earth's atmosphere. The optics showed nothing other than the characteristic black of night beyond a terminator of bright sunlight. Grainger was about to switch in a series of filters when Adsila spoke.

"Stop right there!" she said, and pointed to a ribbon of red just above the lower mesosphere.

"Are you *seeing* this, EAD Waters?" Al-Kazaz asked.

"We are, sir."

"Earthers are getting a real show!" He was still looking off to his right, slowly shaking his head. "It can't be, it *shouldn't* be, not during the daytime—but there it is."

"An aurora," McClure said, exhaling as he studied the slowly undulating ribbon. The area of rippling atmospheric unrest grew wider and added an orange glow beside the red. A few moments later, yellow joined the flux.

"That is way outside the geomagnetic poles," Adsila remarked.

McClure brought up readings from the station's Alpha Magnetic Spectrometer. "It's also not being caused by highly charged electrons from the solar wind," he said. "Antiprotons are infusing the Van Allen belts from the direction of *Jade Star*. The electronvolt measurements are—thirty . . . forty . . . fifty times the normal energy range."

"Are you saying that the Chinese device caused this?" Al-Kazaz said.

"Almost certainly, sir," McClure replied. "The antimatter is usually produced by cosmic rays hitting the atmosphere. That is sporadic—this is a flood. Now it's up to *sixty* times normal."

The colors expanded along the spectrum and descended through the thermosphere, producing a liquid rainbow that poured through the stratosphere and down into the troposphere. Despite the sunshine, the sheets of color were vivid, luminous against Earth, turning the brown and green of the plains into a quilt seeming to blow in the wind above.

"Is there any danger?" Al-Kazaz asked.

The prime director got his answer when his image vanished.

"Janet, was that us or them?" Adsila asked.

"Them," Grainger said ominously.

After a moment, McClure added, "I believe the light show has turned off the power."

"How?"

"Looks to me like a coronal mass ejection, mostly protons and electrons," he said. "In short, a geomagnetic storm disrupted the power grids."

While Adsila was still processing that, she received a communication from on board the *Empyrean*. It was Ziv.

"If you're free, I think you had better come to the reception area," he said.

"Why?" she asked.

"Stanton lost most of his security team on the *Jade Star*, and he's probably going to need one," Ziv told her.

Adsila looked at Lord's face in her IC. He nodded.

"Janet, you have the comm," Adsila said as she hurried from the Zero-G command center.

"Acknowledged," Grainger replied.

The associate executive assistant director wasn't sure how much of this her nerves could take. Though her ego liked taking control very much, the fragility of Earth was something truly frightening.

■ ■

As Adsila made her way to the reception hall, it was difficult to believe that there had been a party here just the day before. It felt like some strange relativistic effect: time had kept up its pace around her, in space, while the clocks at home, receding from her into the stars, had run slow.

The halls were empty, despite the fact that there were twenty-eight extra people on the *Empyrean*. When the Earth shuttle had arrived, Stanton ordered it grounded at the docking port. Adsila had noted that the pilots were still on duty, in the cockpit, and knew that wasn't for the well-being of the shuttle. There was no reason to think it would be any safer from the Chinese device here than in transit. Stanton wanted it ready in case the *Empyrean* was hit and evacuation became necessary. At least thirty people would be able to leave the station—assuming that many occupants survived an antimatter blast.

As she arrived at the *Empyrean's* event area, Adsila saw some of the "missing" population of the *Empyrean*—off-duty station staff, shop workers, guests from the shuttle that had just docked and those who hadn't yet been able to depart. They were congregated beneath the large dome and at every viewport, jockeying for a better look at Earth, their faces striped with shimmering bands of red, orange, yellow, green, and blue. The expressions Adsila could see, those nearest the door and looking up, ranged from excitement to fear—especially those who pointed up at the sliver of nighttime Earth visible from *Empyrean's* geostationary orbit. The lights that were traditionally so visible on the home world were gone.

■ ■

Ziv Levy was standing beside the doorway, waiting for her. As she approached, she saw a pocket of some of the distinguished guests from the reception: pornographer Fraas Dircks, banker Wallace Brown-Card, gambling magnate Maalik Kattan, and Colonel Jack Franco were grouped in a near corner, standing as still as figures in a cave painting, speaking in hushed but intense whispers. Brown-Card and Dircks were distracted by something she could not see, but Kattan and Franco were fully engaged. She heard the colonel mention *"Red Giant,"* obviously expressing concern that the Russian space station was now the only other fully functioning platform above Earth's atmosphere. Though

Red Giant did not possess shuttles or on-site robots, and their space station was beyond thruster-pack reach of *Jade Star,* Franco would be concerned that they could still send a rocket from Earth to the stricken Chinese outpost and try to grab a module or two for study.

Like vultures on the carcass of a bison, she thought. Her eyes lingered on the agitated Defense Intelligence Agency officer. *So what do you call the one who feeds on the vultures?*

A maggot, she decided.

Adsila arrived at the reception area, lingering as she passed Ziv. He looked, uncharacteristically, slightly beaten from his quick roundtrip to the vicinity of the *Jade Star.* His short hair glistened with a sweaty fluid, his jaw was loose, and his shoulders less erect than usual.

"The duties of a spacefarer do not always permit vanity," he said, responding to her look.

Standing this close, the electronic glint in his eyes reminded her of their encounter in her cabin. Even sober and in the midst of a crisis, a part of her still longed for him.

"Thank you for what you did out there," she said so that the others could hear. As she spoke, she leaned in so their ICs connected. A proximity connection would only give the spy the ability to communicate, not to read her open files.

"How is your agent?" Ziv asked, his mechanical voice carrying. His fingers moved at his side.

"He is very well, thank you," Adsila said.

As Adsila continued to lean in, Ziv replayed a recording he had just made showing a VIP antechamber just off the reception hall. It showed Dr. Vishnu Chadha facing Birousk Rouhani. The pacifist and the guru of the Julijil antinational cult were arguing heatedly and drawing a crowd.

That's where the rest of the people are, Adsila thought.

Rouhani was talking "apocalypse." Chadha was urging calm, but the listeners were becoming loud and angry and frightened. Even if they had no political or philosophical stake in the discussion, the aurora had left emotions very near to the surface.

"It's escalating fast," Ziv said.

Adsila watched the replay as someone mentioned the shuttle, projected an image for the group showing the pilots remaining on board as the passengers exited.

Adsila moved a finger. "Dr. Carter, Agent Abernathy, to the docking bay," she ordered. "Watch the shuttle for possible forced entry. AeroSol if necessary."

That last command was for the medic. AeroSol was a riot-control gas that magnified sunlight and caused temporary blindness. Just seeing law enforcement arrive wearing goggles was typically enough to disburse a crowd.

Levy pivoted aside so Adsila could enter. As she stepped in, the sight of Hiromi Tsuburaya flashed in her peripheral vision. The Japanese reporter sat alone on a bench, her fingers, eyes, and head repeatedly going through the ritual of trying an IC link that would not connect. Adsila had seen her expression on the faces of lost children. Maybe Tsuburaya would be luckier than others. All of northeastern Japan was still silent. Perhaps her loved ones had survived.

Adsila turned toward the antechamber, shifting to her male nature before she entered. As he stepped into the ballroom, he saw the people gesturing and yelling.

"It is time for us to seize control of our species," Rouhani was saying, "not leave it to the whim and ego of princes and politicians."

"That is the road to chaos," Chadha insisted. "Look at you—ready to fight others for a ride to Earth." He turned to the guru. "Is *that* the path to your global paradise? Violence?"

"Not violence," Rouhani answered. "Action. We are faced with a twenty-first-century flood. One must swim or be washed away."

The threat of Armageddon didn't faze the Indian doctor. "If you are correct—and there is no evidence to support that—but even if you are right, this is our chance to cooperate, to find common ground among our differences, not to scrub away individuality."

"Diplomacy has failed humankind," the guru said dismissively.

"Your pacifistic happiness cannot be achieved through talk. We must ride this disaster to the unity of Pan Terra."

Adsila shouldered through the group and stepped beside the men. He turned his hands in a prayer position to Chadha, flashed angry eyes at Rouhani. Then he faced the crowd of twenty-odd guests.

"I am Adsila Waters of the FBI's Zero-G space group," he said. "You will all disburse immediately."

"We have the right to speak!" someone yelled.

"Do it by IC," Adsila replied.

"You have no authority here," Rouhani commented.

"Pan *Terror* is not an authority either!" someone else cried from the fringe of the crowd.

The group began to murmur loudly. Chadha raised his arms to calm them. Rouhani glared sternly at the person who had yelled.

"All of you, I *have* the authority to investigate and suppress sedition on American facilities off-Earth," Adsila said. "This station qualifies under Section 11, Paragraph 59 of the NASA Affiliated Responsibility Charter." She sent a copy to everyone in her immediate area. "Those of you who have rooms will go back to them. The rest can remain here or in one of the bars, but you must separate."

"More borders?" Rouhani said. "No, I refuse to be quarantined."

"Fine," said a deep, loud voice from outside the small crowd. "But you *will* shut up and go somewhere else."

Adsila glanced over to see that Ziv Levy had joined them—the CHAI standing just behind him making it clear whose side he was on. Standing a head higher than the tallest person present, he parted the group as Moses had parted the sea.

"Mechanical muscle asserts its will," Rouhani said with heartfelt indignation. Without taking his eyes off the CHAI, he thrust a shaking finger toward the viewport. "How do you know that this is not *our* burning bush, Pan Terra's call to action?"

"Because that voice in your head isn't God, it's megalomania." Ziv moved closer, then closer still. "I grew up fighting agitators like you," he said angrily. "Ethnic cleansing masquerading as glorious homogeneity, hate pretending to be charity, clerics advocating an end to war provided you accept *their* belief system. That is not peace. That is subjugation. And the human spirit will not, cannot tolerate that."

"What right does a tea bag have to lecture about human spirit?" someone yelled from behind.

Ziv turned sharply. Adsila put a restraining hand on his arm.

"Mr. Levy just risked his life to save one of my team members," the EAD said quietly. "Humanity is in mind and deed, not flesh. Again, *please*—all of you stop this, now, before things get out of hand."

The hush that settled on the group spread throughout the reception area. Even Franco's group was silent, listening.

"No one wants conflict." Rouhani spoke quickly, so he wouldn't be put in the position of concurring with Chadha if the Indian doctor agreed first. "I will retire to the chapel to reflect."

The guru turned and left by himself, though Ziv's sharp eyes stayed with him like those of an eagle on the wing. Chadha lingered, moving to the main room, where he stared out the dome toward Earth. Under Adsila's stern gaze, the others separated, some milling by the viewport but most departing.

"Track them, Janet," Adsila said into his IC. "Make sure they don't recongregate."

"Yes, sir."

"Dr. Carter, Agent Abernathy, stand down," Adsila added.

They quickly obliged.

Finally, Adsila turned to Ziv. "Thanks for that."

"It was necessary," he said, resentment clinging to his voice as he continued to stare after Rouhani. "I think I'll go to the chapel myself."

"To pray, bait, or monitor?" Adsila asked.

The CHAI considered the question. This was a Ziv he hadn't seen, the truly human figure who had meant every word he had just uttered.

"I don't know," Ziv admitted. "Probably all of the above."

"You might want to consider doing something else, something more constructive," Adsila said.

"Such as?"

"Checking with your colleagues on Earth," the EAD said.

"About what?"

"About how that argument we just heard might be playing out among nine and a half billion people six hundred miles below us."

TWENTY-SIX

POWER RETURNED TO Armstrong Base nearly an hour after the *John Young* soared from its bay on the moon. The solar panels, jostled by the moonquake, had been realigned. The dust that had landed on external contacts had been flushed away. Internally, the conduits of wiring that had been shaken loose were back in place.

For Trine Jørgensen, forty-seven-year-old second-in-command, the rush of fresh air from the vents was invigorating, the brilliance of the illuminated facility was like dawn back home, and the return of her IC was reassuringly normal—especially when the first thing she saw in it was Earth. Above the distant planet was a liquid prism, a wedge driven into the atmosphere; below it was a complementary slab of darkness that seemed the general shape and color of an old, open grave. A blighted spot, unhealthy and unnerving.

She flicked off the flashlight she'd been using to observe the crew at work in the engineering sector. She gave the team a big smile and a bigger thumbs-up.

"Excellent work, everyone," Commander Tengan said over a base-wide IC broadcast. "You'll be pleased to know that structural anchors and joints all held beyond design expectations. Whoever was on rest period, as soon as you're finished, back to it."

Jørgensen stood beside the massive power-storage unit as she ran through her IC checklist, making sure there were no anomalies anywhere on the base. Now that she could breathe, she realized how lucky they had been. This event was not only unprecedented, it hadn't been planned for.

The base had been constructed to survive the four types of moonquakes: the relatively common, very mild "thermals," caused by the expansion of the crust when the sun ended lunar night; rare and barely noticeable "sliders," caused when crater walls collapsed; rarer "tidals," which originated around five hundred kilometers below the surface and were caused by the gravitational tug of Earth; and "impacts," which were common but brief shudders caused by meteorites striking the surface.

No one factored a space weapon into the engineering, she thought. Then she smiled lightly. *Given Tengan's views, maybe they should have.*

That wasn't a criticism: the woman shared her idea that colonialism was not only an outdated idea, it was counterproductive. People worked best when they worked for themselves.

"Number two," Tengan said over Jørgensen's private IC channel, "I have some back-patting to do all around. In the meantime, go see Mr. Christie in the sick bay. Sam Lord wants his IC."

"Authorization?" she asked, even as she headed toward the stairs that led below.

"From Director Lord," Tengan said, reading the code the Zero-G leader had sent her before boarding the *John Young*. "S, Sam, L, Lord, A, Authorization, T, Traitor," she said, "numerals 33045."

"SLAT33045," Jørgensen repeated.

"That's it."

"On my way," she said.

The request that Lord had made was not illegal—provided there was a court order to effectively hack their brain, since virtually everything a person knew, needed to know, and even didn't care to know but knew anyway was stored in their IC. Absent a judge's approval, it was up to the discretion of law enforcement to authorize a PEST—a Personal Electronic Sovereignty Transgression, an act made a Class A felony by the Technological Security Act of 2023. If the theft of data did not result in a conviction, if it were merely a fishing expedition, Lord could be held criminally liable. Jørgensen was impressed that the Zero-G director had taken that responsibility openly without leaving it for Tengan to do in the shadows.

She crossed through the thinning clusters of lunar workers who were leaving the basement, headed to their posts or quarters. She went to the small officer's closet, stepped in, and shut the door behind her. Lights and airflow turned on. It was here that she, Tengan, and other authorized personnel could receive eyes-only messages from NASA or any other groups that had access.

"SLAT33045," she said. "Pickpocket."

The IC copying program was created by Russian hackers to quickly grab data from passersby without their knowledge. The name Pickpocket stuck, even when governments adapted and refined it for national security. It appeared as a blind spot in the IC, but the program was like a whirlpool: it expanded down, as deep as necessary, finding every open spot of storage to retain stolen data.

Loaded now, Jørgensen ordered the program to go dormant. Otherwise, she would accidentally steal data from anyone she passed on her way to medbay. She took a moment to rediscover her balance: enhanced storage capacity did not add physical weight, but it created a moment of neurological overload, causing a flourish of attention deficit hyperactivity disorder and disorientation. Jørgensen adjusted her posture and refamiliarized herself with the lesser gravity. Law enforcement had used those external signs to profile potential Pickpockets on Earth, in much the same way that they had successfully ID'ed terrorists by their physiological traits.

The officer left the closet and continued down the corridor. Here, the concrete floor and ceiling of the base had been welded to the rock of the moon itself, the flexible joints keeping the basement level airtight during tremors. They had performed heroically today. The charcoal-gray basalt with streaks of silvery-white nickel were visible along the walls. Most residents had a sense of being grounded down here; many described it as a spiritual experience to be able to run their hands along alien stone. Jørgensen was one of them. Like Tengan, she passionately loved her new home.

Entering the small, brightly lit room, she quickly took in the white walls and big displays of data floating before them. There were two cots, with several more folded up like Murphy beds. There was one medic attending to both patients. One man was handcuffed with white bands to the sides of the bed. Looking at the unconscious men—IVs in their arms, sensor patches on their foreheads, bandages on their wounds—she felt like the American general George Patton, whom she had read about in one of her great-grandfather's books. Those books had instilled in her the importance of discipline, pride, and duty. During World War II, Patton had slapped an able-bodied soldier who was suffering from psychological stress and sitting among the gravely wounded men in an infirmary. That slap, impulsive but honest, had effectively cost the general his career.

But we remember it because of the values it represented. Her eyes settled on the figure lying beside the wounded Captain Kodera. *Consider this my slap, Mr. Christie,* she thought angrily. *If what Sam Lord says is true, I'd do this without authorization.*

"Dr. Kelly, would you leave us?" she asked. "I'll only be a minute."

The young man looked over, nodded, and without a word, the doctor left the room, closing the door behind him.

Jørgensen stepped between the cots, laying a hand on the tightly bandaged wrist of the sedated Kodera. Then she turned, placed one hand on the side panel of Christie's cot, and lowered her head toward the unconscious man. She moved a finger, initiating the Pickpocket program. The void in her own IC glowed hungrily. She bent lower, connected her IC with that of Christie.

There was a flash in front of her eyes and behind them, like a solar flare whipping through the eyepiece of a telescope. Her head jerked back and her knees buckled. She fell to the floor slowly in the weak lunar gravity.

"Dr. Kelly!" she heard herself shouting repeatedly, her voice sounding distant, hollow. "Dr. Kelly!"

The medic ran back into the room, where he found her on the floor, curled in a fetal position, blood running from her ears and nose.

■ ■

Lord didn't need any more bad news. Unfortunately, reality didn't care.

The Zero-G director was sitting across the aisle from Saranya and Diego as the shuttle closed in on the *Empyrean*. The scientists huddled close on facing chairs, sharing IC data—for the first time since they'd met—reviewing numbers from the aurora and trying to find a weakness in the device. They had managed to reach one of their colleagues, an atmospheric specialist at the National Oceanic and Atmospheric Administration who had been studying the situation nonstop since the first attack in Japan.

Lord was working on his own set of data, using his old navigational software to try to determine whether there was any vector pattern to the attacks or whether they were entirely random.

On the station, the comm was relatively quiet after Adsila returned, the conversation limited to the sudden, steady shrinking of the aurora and the slow return of some electronics on Earth.

"So the hardware systems weren't destroyed?" Adsila asked.

"Just blocked," McClure said.

"Look at this," Grainger said. "Weaportunity knocks."

Lord glanced briefly at the window Grainger sent to all their ICs, though he knew exactly what he would see. The FBI Counterterrorism and Forensic Science Research Unit had noted the short-term impact of the large-scale event and was already initiating a crash program to "study the phenomenon with a goal of replicating and localizing the effects." One of Al-Kazaz's predecessors had coined the term *weaportunity* for this fast-start process after a 2032 outbreak of tuberculosis struck only Melanesians living on the island nation of Tonga. The search for mutated bacteria began at once, ostensibly to find cures, but in truth to harvest them and create additional weaponized variations.

Don't judge, Lord told himself. *All those sexy planes you flew came from military R&D.*

He returned to the problems at hand, only to be interrupted by a secure message from Commander Tengan.

"Sam, Don Christie is in a coma—fundamentally brain dead," the lunar commander reported. "Lieutenant Commander Jørgensen suffered a seizure when she tried to copy his IC."

"I'm *very* sorry to hear that," he said, then asked incredulously, "A NASA Pickpocket malfunctioned?"

Tengan's face became grimmer. "Our computer tech says no. She's looking at him now, believes there was a kill switch."

"Installed in his IC? I thought—"

"Exactly," Tengan said. "Pickpocket safeguards should have seen it and quarantined it before proceeding. But they wouldn't have been looking for something planted in the subject's brain."

"His *brain*? Hardware or software?" Lord asked.

"We're looking into that now," Tengan replied, casting a thumb behind herself. "Tough forensic challenge, since the self-destruction is what apparently caused Christie's coma."

Lord cursed the situation and himself. This was the equivalent of the old-school cyanide capsules spies used to take if they were captured. He should have anticipated something like this, given the clear sophistication of the buggy program used to spy on the lunar lab. He wondered if Christie had even known he had something buried in his skull. Was the former marine a high-level operative or just a flunky wooed by power, ideals, or cash that a search had not yet uncovered?

The larger question, of course, was who would have technology that sophisticated? The Chinese? Possibly. But Adsila's quick look at Don Christie's service file, from the marines and from NASA, showed no connection with China or even the hint of any suspicious activity from NASA intelligence. There had to be an intermediary.

"Thank you, Commander, and once again I'm sorry," Lord said as he prepared to turn back to his own challenge. "I appreciate everything—"

"Wait a minute," Tengan said suddenly.

Lord saw her turn away, obviously conversing with someone else.

Tengan switched his IC to point-of-view mode, so Lord could now see Jørgensen and Kodera lying on their cots as a med-tech bent over Christie's motionless body. A handheld scanner pulsed red as the med-tech held it over Christie's forehead. Numbers and neural maps filled the air above. Dr. Kelly was standing beside her. He had been studying the data before turning to Tengan.

"Fairchild found a hot spot," the doctor said. "Lingering elevated electrical activity situated in the arcuate fasciculus." Lord's IC told him that was a bundle of axons, the part of a neuron that transmits impulses from the cell.

"Is the location significant?" Tengan asked.

"Possibly," Kelly replied. "No other nonhuman primates have that or anything similar. Any research in this area would have to have been done on humans, meaning it had to be sanctioned . . . or illegal. Illegal would have been far less costly than a bullet in the brain."

"Meaning there's no incentive from a criminal organization to invest in it," Tengan said.

"Correct again," Kelly told him.

"Was there an implant?" Tengan asked.

"No scarring at all, anywhere," Kelly said.

"So, software in the IC."

"Negative," Fairchild replied. "Commander, this was programmed into the brain. Verbal pathways were also affected."

"You mean, Christie would've died if he'd tried to confess his sins," Tengan said.

"My guess is any string of keywords would've triggered the same result," Fairchild replied. "I've never seen anything like this."

Hearing this, Dr. Kelly seemed to shiver. "Someone very big, very legal, and very well funded did something very sophisticated and very illegal here."

"Thank you," Tengan said, then returned to her face-to-face view of Lord. She took a moment for a breath. "Any ideas?"

"About who may have become 'thought police' for real?" he said.

"Yes, I do, and I don't like what I'm thinking. Let me get back to you on that."

"Please do," Tengan said. "This could be bigger than we know."

Lord signed off. He shut his eyes for a much-needed power nap. Fifteen minutes later, he took the tube device from his pocket, the one Christie had tried to remove from the buggy. It was frighteningly simple: what the techs called a jumper, an illegal device that allowed disparate, unaffiliated systems to talk with one another. Jumpers had been outlawed by the International Intellectual Property Act of 2029, when software giants and content providers fought for stricter controls against piracy. The software program in the buggy would have self-destroyed after the program was stolen. This would be the only evidence.

Lord returned the device to his pocket then sat back. He looked out at the *Empyrean* as it grew larger in his viewport. It took a lot to shake the commander, but he was nearly as rattled as Dr. Kelly as he considered the implications of what they'd discovered. The blind, brute danger of the *Jade Star*'s weapon seemed to fade in menace beside the careful, insidious evil of some human beings.

"Sam," Saranya said cautiously, "we may have something . . . a code we believe will shut down the SAMI."

"You don't sound excited," Lord said.

"There's a problem," she said, reviewing her calculations.

"What kind?" Lord pressed.

"We've looked at our options . . ." she began, then her voice trailed away as she returned to her calculations.

Lord shot a look at Ras Diego.

"It's the delivery system," the scientist finished for her. "That's going to be a real challenge."

TWENTY-SEVEN

HAVING ZERO GRAVITY in the Drum means one thing above all: that my team is *always* on its toes."

After the disaster that had befallen the security team, Stanton's words, always meant somewhat in jest, were gravely true. Rest time was canceled and brief meal breaks were taken in the Drum. With all the sector chiefs dead, Stanton was forced to increase electronic surveillance rather than deploy human patrols to oversee security and safety measures on the station. Using Station Hazard Authority, Stanton also suspended privacy rules. Rooms and belongings were immediately scanned for weapons and other contraband as the *Empyrean* went into threat-prevention mode. He also gave his SIC team permission to e-bug all private storage systems onboard. This would not reveal content of secure communications, only destinations. The upside, for paying customers like the CIA, DIA, and NSA, were that these connections could be analyzed later to see how guests like Ziv Levy, Jack Franco, Sheik Kattan, and others routed their clandestine messages. It would be useful in the event that the SIC ever needed to target a satellite to shut someone down.

Instead of looking for extraterrestrial life, the station's deep space sensors were repurposed toward the *Jade Star*, watching for any indication that an antimatter pulse might be headed in their direction. Stanton knew that the team could handle the crisis until replacements could be sent from Vandenberg or Canaveral, probably within forty-eight hours. Newly energized, holding himself at attention, Stanton floated through the Drum, not directing his drift but moving randomly from station to station, providing a rigid command presence and an experienced eye to the team. Some among the crew were veterans of space travel who had served tenures on the ISS before it was turned over to Russia; others were relatively new and clearly struggling with the tendency to overreact in an emergency. Stanton steadied all of them by asking for specific updates that required focus and a careful, thoughtful response. Fear and distraction among the staff—for their own lives and loved ones on Earth—were not qualities he could afford.

What concerned him were the surveillance activities and another attack from the *Jade Star* module. Depending on where a theoretical strike took place on the *Empyrean,* decompression might not be instantaneous. There would be time to evacuate to the public shuttle and Ziv Levy's private spacecraft—which had been commandeered under the SHA. Stanton had the Slammers placed on autodeploy: no human signal was required to seal the corridors if decompression were detected anywhere on the station. He had hoped a third shuttle would be added to the possible escape fleet: the *John Young,* which had just docked from Armstrong Base. Unfortunately, he did not have jurisdiction over the craft and, with the shuttle *Grissom* incapacitated, he had no choice but to accede to Blake Tengan's insistence that the lunar colonists not be left without a transport. Stanton had been caught off-guard by the commander's attitude: in their few meetings in Houston, Tengan had struck him as a person who would welcome the opportunity to prove the independent capabilities of the base. But, like any good commander, Tengan put the well-being of her crew above personal ideology.

Of course, that's the challenge of command, Stanton thought as he approved the immediate turnaround requested by the *John Young* pilot. *To determine when a project becomes a mission, and the objective is more important than the people serving it.*

Stanton did not get the shuttle. But the Drum did get something that even his drill-and-ceremony approach hadn't anticipated.

It got Sam Lord.

Upon docking, Lord and Drs. May and Diego headed directly for the Drum.

"Permission to enter," Lord said as he entered through the door in the upper section, pausing to seek out Stanton.

"State cause," Stanton replied sharply, indicating that permission had not yet been granted.

The stoic *Empyrean* commander was floating a few feet from the floor, just beside the communications section. Stanton turned in place and hovered there, stiff and vigilant, as Lord floated toward him.

"This is Dr. Saranya May and Dr. Ras Diego," Lord said, indicating the other two standing in the doorway.

"The research scientists stationed on the moon," Stanton said.

"Yes. It was Dr. May whose work was stolen to create the Chinese weapon."

"I've heard." Stanton's eyes shifted from Lord to Saranya then back. "What do you need from me?"

"Drs. May and Diego have written a command they hope will shut the device down," Lord said. "In order to deliver it, they have to get the signal past the plasma cloud."

"You had the lunar shuttle at your disposal, Director Lord. Couldn't you have used that?"

Lord punched up his IC data. "The plasma frequency of the cloud exceeds the maximum frequency of the shuttle's transmitter," he said, before swooshing the information away. "I don't know what that means, exactly, except that it's not good enough to do the job. And we obviously can't move into the cloud."

Stanton winced imperceptibly at Lord's remark. The thought of his dead fleet was a kick in the gut.

"We need to borrow the antenna the *Empyrean* uses to blast signals to other galaxies," Lord told him. "It's the strongest one starside."

Stanton looked again at Saranya. He moved a finger. "Can she give the data to my people?"

"It would be faster if she could plug it in herself—"

"She has 2B security clearance on Armstrong Base," Stanton said. "That has no traction here. I repeat: can she do that?"

"Commander—*Curtis*—we're wasting time."

"Then answer the damn question."

Lord stubbornly regarded Stanton's communications workers. "Can *they* speak higher math?"

"Irrelevant. Why can't she just *dump* it in?"

"Two people put this together on slow ICs powered by a half-drained shuttle battery," Lord said. "It has to be reconformed to your system and possibly tweaked—"

"Jesus Christ, all right, *enough*!" Stanton cut him off. "God, Lord, you give me a pain."

Lord's expression registered no insult, no anger. He simply waited.

"Permission granted for you and Dr. May to enter," the commander said after a moment, a hint of defeat, tinged with exhaustion, in his voice.

"Commander, we will require Dr. Diego—"

Stanton cut him off. "There's only one channel to the *Jade Star*. Dr. May can have it."

Lord didn't want to waste time arguing. He pointed at Saranya, who jumped forward. Diego stayed where he was. If a man's posture could register insult, the scientist showed it. However, after exchanging a glance with Lord, he remained dutifully in the outer ring.

Lord caught Saranya by the arm and helped her down.

"Come," Stanton said as he moved toward them.

Both of the newcomers felt a slight electric tingle as they stepped up to the two floating communications officers.

"Your IC outputs have just been put to sleep," Stanton told Lord. "The only signals that leave here go through our equipment."

Lord knew that, and Stanton knew he knew it. It was a subtle reminder about who was in charge here.

Lord and Saranya were introduced to Zoey Kane, who gave Dr. May the access code to her IC. That would enable her to send the shutdown command to the rogue module. As the communications pathway opened, Saranya and Lord exchanged looks.

"Curtis, I need something else," Lord said.

The commander looked at him critically. "Have I mentioned that I don't like one-man armies, Lord?"

"It's a lonely life," Lord agreed, "but right now we have a solar system to save. And to do that, Commander, there's one other thing we have to do."

"'*Have* to'?" Stanton said. "Do you *ever* stop pushing? Your record shows nineteen infractions of articles 89–92 of the Uniform Code of Military Justice—"

"I'm over eighty," Lord pointed out. "I've had time to break a lot of eggs, and all those accusations were eventually dismissed."

"Wait with Dr. Diego," Stanton said impatiently. "I have a command to run."

"So do I," Lord replied, "and I'll go after you hear me out."

"Last time. You have ten seconds."

"Won't need it," Lord replied. "We have to move the *Empyrean*."

Stanton replayed the words in his head, then laughed. No other reaction was possible.

"Get out," the commander said.

"He's right, sir," Saranya said. She was checking the figures she had scrawled in her IC, pausing them to make changes as they were offloaded. "The angle from our current orbit is wrong."

"Angle for what?" Zoey Kane asked. "It's a linear path."

"Only as the crow flies," Dr. May said. "Even if we get through the plasma cloud with the higher-frequency antenna, we have to bounce the signal off Earth's ionosphere or the surface, if the frequency gets too high—to align with the receiver, minimize cloud interference, and conceal the source as much as possible."

"A carom shot," Lord explained.

"Commander Stanton!" a voice broke in their ICs. "The *Jade Star* device is powering up."

"Direction?"

"Nothing yet, sir! We'll know in another few seconds—"

The only thing moving in the secure communications wedge were Dr. May's fingers, shifting between her IC and that of Zoey Kane. Lord moved over to the chair in which Saranya was seated, placed a comforting hand on her shoulder. She was still wearing her space suit but she felt his touch.

Stanton could hear his own heart, his own breath. He had been in enough battles during the War on Narcotics and the Pan-Persia Occupation to recognize the Emergency Theory Response—what the medics used to call "fight-or-flight syndrome." Early in his career Stanton had learned to cherish those breaths, those heartbeats, every stimulus his senses were delivering, keenly aware they could be his last.

A moment later the voice returned with obvious relief.

"Outward," it said. "The blast is headed away from the Earth-moon system."

Lord looked at the time in his IC. "One hour, two minutes," he said. "That's when the last blast happened. Before that, two hours, five minutes. We may have that long until the next one . . . or we may have a fraction of that."

Stanton regarded Lord. "Where do we have to go to make this shot of yours?"

"Dr. Diego worked out the coordinates," Lord replied quietly.

Stanton glared at Lord, then looked down at the scientist. He moved his fingers. "Dr. Diego—Engineering Station One," he said, sending the scientist a map of the Drum and typing clearance orders to Chief Engineer Jimmy James.

Diego stepped in and quickly sailed to the other side of the Drum. He stopped beside a man who was prematurely gray and visibly exhausted. The man seemed happy to surrender his position.

Stanton turned to Lord. "You said you had somewhere to go, something to command?"

■ ■

On a visit to the Russian space station, the nationalist poet Smerdyakov described the *Empyrean,* then under construction, as "a wan golden flower turning against deep night, longing, helpless, for the sun-kiss to make it blossom."

Had the fiery Muscovite returned a few months later, he would have seen an *Empyrean* that was anything but helpless. He would have seen the station bloom and kiss not just the sun but the entire firmament.

To adjust its orbit, the station was required to unfurl its vast Mylar-based solar sail. The nearly one-million-square-foot, ultrathin sheet was attached to the station by a row of six slim tethers, and these were attached to the base of a thin latticed tower that stood proudly atop the *Empyrean.* By coincidence, not design, the structure had the appearance of the sail on an ancient Phoenician round ship—civilization coming full circle, as NASA had once opportunistically described it.

While the rest of the station had been created with practicality foremost in its design, the sail was, by its very nature, beautiful. Coated with liquid crystals of predominantly orange, yellow, and, especially, gold, the ultrathin sheet added and subtracted many other colors as it slowly moved.

These colors seemed to have been streaked onto the sail by an invisible brush that remained endlessly, creatively active. The play of prismatic light made the sail look increasingly alive—like a butterfly, fresh from its cocoon, opening its wings. When direct sunlight and moonglow touched the sail, they created brilliant counterstrikes and dapples that gave the expanse additional animation. But light did not just give the sail its beauty, it provided the *Empyrean* with mobility.

It was the position of this wheeling gold sail relative to the sun, riding its light pressure, that established the altitude of the space station. The first movement was always slightly jarring, as the tower moved counter to the spin that created the station's artificial gravity. After those first steps, with their awkward fits and starts like a child just learning to walk, the *Empyrean* adjusted to the counterspin and began to rise or fall.

As the *Empyrean* started to descend, following the coordinates provided by Dr. Diego, brighter and brighter light from Earth's seas began to mute the brilliant hues of the sail, briefly washing them out—only to see them rise again as the sail shifted, maneuvering subtly.

Lower and lower it went, the tower and sail defiantly still atop the turning *Empyrean*, facing the sun, glowing with life.

For those in the communications wedge, that was more than just a metaphor. At the moment, the microthin sail was all that stood between salvation and the slow destruction of civilization.

■■

On his way to the comm, Lord gave Janet Grainger a frequency and told her to lock on it. When she did, he and everyone in the comm found themselves listening to voices from the SIC wedge.

"How did you do *that,* sir?" Janet Grainger asked when he arrived. Clearly, she was deeply impressed.

"I put a jumper in Dr. May's shoulder pocket," Lord said as he entered the elevator and rode to the comm level. "Janet, I want you to get the IC address of Armstrong EMT Don Christie from NASA's employee directory—and, working backward, track every communication that was sent to him from Earth, the *Empyrean,* or a shuttle since his deployment on the moon."

"What will I be looking for?" she asked.

"Commander Tengan made an important find. I recognized it back on the moon. I want to know who gave Christie Project Implant technology," Lord replied. "Agent McClure?"

"Sir?"

"See what you can dig up on that program," Lord said. "It was a Defense Advanced Research Projects Agency black-ops project circa 2030.

They wanted to place data directly into the human brain, along with kill codes. I want to know where that research ended up. Don't contact anyone, just look for files."

"Yes, sir."

"We just got the all-eyes alert that the *Empyrean* is undergoing an orbital shift," Adsila said. "I take it from Dr. May's comments to Stanton that this is our doing?"

"It is," Lord said as he emerged on the comm level. "Dr. May has a possible kill code, needs a better angle of attack."

Lord was just finishing the statement as he entered Zero-G headquarters.

There was a slight lateral disorientation one way and then the other as the *Empyrean* began drifting to its temporary orbit. Lord stopped just inside the doorway and planted his CHAI leg hard; the artificial limb kept him from scudding in either direction. It wasn't the metal core of the limb that stabilized him but the ability of the joints to lock firmly and remain that way.

As soon as the space station stopped moving, Lord continued to his seat. He used the jumper to listen in to whatever conversation was taking place in the Drum.

It was suddenly very silent. There was no point speculating why; he'd wait to hear.

The Zero-G director saw Adsila shift to female just before he shut his eyes. They were tired, *he* was tired. He was still in his space suit, hot and perspiring. But his exhaustion was more than that. So much of his life had been spent watching air-to-surface and air-to-air ordnance; though he could ask Grainger to pull up exterior visuals of the *Empyrean*'s relocation, this time he wanted to just listen.

"Upload complete," he heard.

It was Dr. May's voice, low and thick.

"Ready to send," said Zoey Kane.

"Engage," Stanton replied quietly.

There was no reaction from the *Empyrean*. No sibilant roar, no jolt as he felt in combat. The attack was a series of numbers, codes, data, fired to a receiver that had been instructed to stand still and take it.

"Propagation angle conforms to predictions," Dr. May said cautiously. "Transmission frequency exceeds expected plasma frequency, from electron density estimates. With any luck, we're through the cloud and hitting the *Jade Star*'s SAMI module."

Then there was more silence. It was probably only two seconds, but it seemed much longer. Lord opened his eyes. The Zero-G personnel had not moved.

Then Dr. May's voice crashed through the silence.

"Signal's degrading!" she suddenly declared. "Anisotropies in the plasma cloud—"

"Variations in the electron density exceed predictions," McClure remarked. "The Chinese particle beam must have caused even more havoc in that region than we thought."

"What does that mean, Dr. May?" Stanton asked impatiently.

Lord heard Dr. May sullenly reply, "It means, Commander, that there is no way to get our data in."

TWENTY-EIGHT

DR. MAY'S WORDS hit the Zero-G comm like a battering ram.

From the time Dr. May had first come aboard, all of their efforts, especially those of Sam Lord, had been focused on finding a solution. Now, no one seemed to know what was worse: the failure of the mission or the failure of their leader.

But there were other words, words that had directed Sam Lord's life since he first read them in a history book when he was eight. It was the story of American sea captain James Lawrence, who took command of the USS *Chesapeake* and sailed from the port of Boston on June 1, 1813. He immediately encountered the enemy, the Royal Navy frigate HMS *Shannon*, which not only crippled the *Chesapeake* but gravely wounded Captain Lawrence. Though dying, the thirty-one-year-old commander admonished his officers, "Don't give up the ship. Fight her till she sinks."

Only the mission had failed. The *Empyrean* was still afloat and the crew still had fight.

"Dr. May, Dr. Diego, Zero-G—I want a new plan, ASAP," he said.

"Lord? How are you *talking* to Dr. May?" Stanton demanded. "This area is secure!"

"Not important now," Lord said. "Dr. May, did your original neutrino research include designs for a structure to house your SAMI designs?"

She was silent.

"Dr. May!" Lord barked.

She responded as though rising from a stupor. "No," she said. "I re-fused to do that for exactly the reasons we've witnessed."

"All right, so the Chinese did it on their own. What *would* it be made of?" he demanded.

"SMASH tech," she said absently. "Shape Memory Alloy Self-Healing. It's a variety of smart metals that self-repair. You'd need those in a high-power energy system that would result in cracks and microme-teoroid damage, that sort of— "

"So it is not like a bank vault," Lord said. "The housing is not inher-ently impervious."

"To the contrary," she said. "It would be light enough, malleable enough to take the kind of recoil any weapon creates."

"Fine, good," Lord said. "So far, we've been targeting the software. What we have to do is figure out how to destroy the casing."

"We were going to try that," Stanton said bitterly. "Remember?"

"We tried one way," Lord replied. "There has to be another."

"Such as?" Stanton asked.

"I don't know," Lord admitted. "That's what I want to know from some of the greatest minds around. Doctors?"

A more thoughtful silence engulfed the comm.

"Engineering, return to standard orbit—" Stanton began.

"No, wait!" Adsila said. "Wait." She was looking at the sail in her IC, at the dilution caused by earthshine. "Director Lord, Commander Stanton—Dr. May. Native Americans and many other cultures used to communicate by mirror, flashing sunlight across great distances."

"Heliographs," Lord said.

"What do you want to do, *blind* the Chinese weapon?" Stanton said.

"No," Adsila replied. "I want to burn it. Using the sail."

The Zero-G director was looking at Adsila, who was looking at him. The silence that followed her statement was different from the others.

There was an urgency beneath it, as everyone quietly raced through the steps—and dangers—this theoretical mission would entail.

"Dr. May, won't the cloud stop any kind of radiant flash?" one of Stanton's people asked.

"Not at all," Saranya said with rising excitement. "Not sunlight. We can still cook them through the debris cloud."

"That's probably true, but the plan itself won't work," Dr. Diego said after doing some rapid calculations. Lord had patched him in through his own comm so he could hear what Dr. May was saying.

"What's the problem with it?" Saranya asked.

"The angle is wrong, again. To face the device full-on, the *Empyrean* would have to drop to an altitude that would cause deorbit."

"Not necessarily," Lord said impulsively. "Are we close enough now?"

"Probably," Saranya said.

"Good. Then we cut the sail free, do it by hand," Lord said.

Stanton made an inarticulate sound, but Adsila was inspired.

"We climb the tower," Adsila said. "It could work."

"Just like that?" Stanton said with exasperation. "You climb a structure that was not designed to be climbed, then cut away the sail we use to maintain and adjust our orbit?"

"I didn't say it would be risk-free—" Lord began.

"It's potential mass homicide!" Stanton yelled. "If you corrupt our orbit, upset our stability, the *Empyrean* burns or shakes apart!"

Lord's own patience was slipping. "Commander, I would *love* to hear a better plan, I truly would."

"Dr. May has sent her data to several colleagues and we've forwarded it to NASA's Advanced Situation Team," Stanton said. "They've got people coming at this from different angles—"

"Can they get us something in *time*, before that device kills another ten or twenty thousand people?"

"You know I can't answer that," Stanton said. "No one can."

"Then we have to do this," Lord said quietly, rising from his seat. "We have to try."

There was another silence. Lord had experienced this kind of quiet before: very still and very deep. It had the poignant echo of history behind it, of a dangerous commitment being made before a mission, where the outcome was uncertain at best.

"If I okay this, are *you* planning to go out there?" Stanton asked.

"It's my mission, Commander. I always lead them."

"This isn't the time for platitudes," Stanton said. The next time he spoke his voice was softer. "You've been through a helluva lot today, Sam. You're past eighty."

"I'm battle-tested," Lord responded. "And I've had a nap."

"Oh, Christ," Stanton said. "Duty Officer!"

"Commander?"

"Get me engineering! Chief Brenner!"

"No, Curtis," Lord said. "I want someone I know."

"Brenner knows the tower."

"Then have him at your window, on my IC," Lord said. "I want a teammate, a partner. Besides, you'll need your staff in here, a commander when the station responds to the sail being cut."

"Sam, Ziv Levy is still on board," Stanton said. "Let me ask him to go with—"

"Ziv Levy may not really care if my team makes it back," Lord said. "For all we know, he stole Dr. May's tech. Or Beijing may reward him for sinking the *Empyrean*. Should I go on?"

Lord didn't care whether Ziv was listening to Adsila's IC through his nanites. If he were innocent, he'd survive. Mossad agents—and CHAIs—had very thick skin.

"Goddamn *intrigue* on top of everything else," Stanton said, loading the word with decades of frustration and loathing. "All right, dammit. How would you alter the position of the sail?"

"Doughnut and spindle," Lord replied.

"That equipment will cause whiplash," Stanton said. "Not just on the tower, the entire station."

"I know."

"We'd have to secure everything."

"Is that an order, sir?" Lord heard one of Stanton's communications officers ask.

There was a long pause. The delay was causing Lord's heart to race, the small of his back to burn, his human leg to want to move.

"Yes," Stanton said slowly. "Stationwide and all private ICs."

"Yes, Commander."

Sam Lord stood anxiously awaiting approval; he wouldn't go without it. Too many moving parts, literally, had to be steadied on board. An internal knock against the station could translate as external movement. If anything fell with enough force, he could be jarred loose and hurled into space.

Finally, Stanton responded with a single word: "Go."

Lord bolted toward the door, pausing only long enough to look at Adsila. "EAD, you're with me—if you want it."

"I want nothing more, sir," Adsila answered.

Lord smiled at her, then turned to Grainger. "Janet, the comm is yours."

"Yes, sir," she replied.

"And get me that other data," he said over his shoulder as he followed Adsila out the door.

"Still working it, sir," Grainger assured him.

Abernathy shook his head. "Fellow agents, *there* is a leader who knows how to multitask."

■ ■

Zero-G stored its extra vehicular activity gear in lockers located at both the top and bottom of the central column of the *Empyrean*. The 250-foot-high fractal truss tower—the mast of the sail—itself was on "top." Lord and Adsila went to the upper locker, nearest the public docking bay. There, Lord removed his lunar suit and replaced it with one that was station-specific, magnetically and electronically aligned with *Empyrean* engineering. The suit's circuits would automatically plug into the

ICs of all department heads—including the Gardener—in case he had specialty-specific questions.

While Lord and Adsila prepared, they reviewed the topside construction in their ICs.

"We can't cut the sail cables on the bottom," Lord said. "We'll lose tension entirely. We have to get to the single mooring point on top of the truss tower."

"I see that," Adsila replied.

"You also see that there are no handholds anywhere?"

"Yes, but if we put on the External Maneuvering Units, that will take another seventeen minutes and the bulk will also leave no room for the toolkit," she said as the *Empyrean* suit enveloped her. "And then we each have twenty-four separate thrusters to watch out for. That close to the sail, to each other—"

"A wrong turn by us or any movement from the station, and nitro-burn may cause damage," Lord said. "Reluctantly agreed." He continued to study the layout of the tower. "We'll walk to the center of the rotating base and ascend behind the sail."

"Think of it as a descent, not an ascent," Lord heard the voice of Dr. Carter.

"Self-delusion?" Lord asked.

"Precisely," Carter replied. "Only we call it eidolon orientation. Absent physical evidence, the muscles believe what the brain tells it."

"So I fool myself into thinking I'm falling." Lord briefly went private as he finished suiting up. "You don't really think I'm going to go out there and fool myself," he said.

"Not at all. It isn't your nature."

"You just called to let me know you're here."

"I did," Carter admitted.

Lord smiled. "Thanks, Doc. Thanks very much." Lord returned to the schematic and all-stations IC. "We'll either have to buddy up or zigzag to cross the gaps in the tower and the microexpanses."

"Affirmative," Adsila said.

The microexpanses were areas where the girders had been laid side by side to strengthen the structure. Though appearing to be solid, these areas were actually comprised of microscopic structures that were, themselves, miniature fractal trusses of enormous strength. They had been manufactured in space, where gravity couldn't corrupt the iterative patterns. To a space-walker, these stretches were not only smooth as glass, they prohibited grips of any kind, having been sealed to protect them from microcollisions.

"We *should* use the tether," Adsila said. "It'll take less time."

It will also put both of us in jeopardy if one or the other of us tumbles, Lord thought. The upside was, having more than one's own life at risk always kept pilots on extremely high alert.

"Sam, Commander Stanton is correct," Dr. May said over Lord's private IC.

"About what?"

"You really shouldn't be going out there."

"Shouldn't you be number-crunching?" Lord asked.

"I am . . . we are," she said. "But this is important too. You shouldn't do this, certainly not just the two of you."

"I felt the same way about parenting," Lord said, "but here we are."

"Children are resilient, one can afford to make mistakes," the scientist replied. "Not here."

"True, but there's an old air force axiom that I've always followed, how one plane, flying low, can be far more effective than an entire squad—"

Lord bit off the last word. He hadn't meant to invoke the destruction of the *Empyrean* recon mission, but it hit them both and moved them to reflection.

"I know it's pointless to debate with you," Saranya said after a moment. "Just come back safe."

"I'll do that, if you'll do a favor for me."

"Of course."

"Stay in the communications hub as long as possible," he said. "I'll explain later."

"All right, Sam," she replied.

Adsila faced him. "You ready, sir?"

"I am," he told her, screwing his helmet into place and switching on the air. "Let's get it done."

Loading a backpack with tools and chemicals they would need to cut through the cables, and dragging forty feet of polybenzoxazole fiber from the upright locker, Adsila hooked the coiled tether to their waists and, with Lord's help, slipped on the seventy-pound bundle. Up here it weighed very little; outside it would weigh nothing.

"IC check?" Lord said.

"Reading," Adsila replied.

"Commander?"

"We hear you," Stanton said.

"Please don't let anyone adjust the sail while we're out there," Lord joked.

■ ■

To the teams watching on their ICs in the Zero-G comm and from the *Empyrean* command center, the two figures, tethered at the waist, were like the baseball mascots for the Juneau Polar Bears: white exterior, inflated arms and legs, and a big bubble head.

The view was more striking from the windows of the Drum. Several members of Stanton's team were clustered on the side of the *Empyrean* where the upward-angled window afforded an expanded view of Lord and Adsila. The pair emerged at the base of the tower, well above the runway, on the small platform that enabled the sail to turn. It was stationary now, and the duo crossed it with light but careful steps; any deviation in the *Empyrean*'s position would flip them off the station. The tower itself would be even more treacherous: there, because of its steep Eiffel-like slope, their boots would have nothing to hold on to. Their safety, and progress, would depend on the precision of their handholds. Every step, every grip seemed tentative as they made their way up the sheer wall.

And then the silence was broken.

"The device is powering up."

■ ■

Lord had been expecting the alert from Stanton's communications officer. It had already been twenty-two minutes since the last blast, and the wait times between blasts had been diminishing throughout the day.

The Zero-G leader was some ten feet below Adsila, who was picking her way up deftly but with understandable caution.

Lord checked his IC. "Adsila, we have nearly two hundred feet to go. We have to move faster."

"We can't separate, we need four hands up there—"

"I know," Lord said. "Stay as low as you can, I'm going to push off and leapfrog. When I land, you do the same."

"You have to go straight!" Dr. May shouted. "If you veer and don't secure the landing—"

"One of us may pull the other off," Lord said. "Have to chance it."

Lord was already breathing heavily, his vital stats pushing into the red in his IC. They rose even higher when he jerked his magnetic gloves free of the truss, tensed his leg muscles—real and artificial—and pushed off with his knees. He watched the tether uncurl then stretch tight. The tug caused his forward momentum to stop and brought him down some thirty-five feet ahead of Adsila. He quickly snapped his magnets to the surface.

"Secure!" he shouted.

He felt a hard jerk at his waist as Adsila took off. He curled his boots slightly for added grip as she soared through the void. The tug was stronger than expected and he pressed his toes to the truss, relying on the boot magnets to give him an added hold.

Adsila swung over him like a bolo and landed a matching distance ahead.

Now they were nearly halfway there. Lord took off again. At that moment he mentally cursed and kissed Dr. Carter: this *was* easier if he imagined going down.

The jumps were ugly and awkward, with imperfect landings, but the magnets and tether all held and they made swift progress.

"How much time left till the huking thing fires?" Lord asked.

"About a minute, if the previous timing holds," Saranya replied.

They jumped again, Adsila reaching the top of the tower first. Grabbing on, she leaned toward the three cables that held the top of the sail to the structure.

"Get ready to cut the cable," Lord said, his breathing rapid as he scrambled behind her.

Through his darkly tinted visor Lord saw Adsila reach into her backpack and remove a doughnut-shaped object that could be snapped open and then shut. Inside was a so-called "piranha solution" of peroxymonosulfuric acid and ammonium persulfate, which would immediately dissolve the advanced carbons of the tether. She clipped it around the cable just as Lord arrived.

"Power up at half," the officer advised.

Lord reached into her backpack and retrieved a device that resembled the spindle of a spinning wheel. Typically, it was used to hold the cables securely in place when they were undergoing maintenance. The purpose now was different—and untested. He clipped the top end to the cable, just beyond the "doughnut," and attached the magnetized base to the truss. When the cable was cut, the center of the sail would snap free of the tower and form a parabolic surface; that release would cause the reel-like spindle to telescope out, creating an extension that would support the sail in a new position. Working the spindle keypad would allow Lord to raise or lower the sail as needed.

"Declination twelve-point-nine degrees will do it," Saranya said.

Lord entered the code. Adsila was watching him, her finger on a red button atop the doughnut.

"Hold on to the tower," Lord told Adsila, making sure his own magnets were as secure as possible. Then he nodded at her and said, "Activate."

Four things happened at once.

An inch of cable dissolved, as planned.

The sail inflated in the center, bulging as though it had caught a stiff wind.

And the sun struck the sail with a wall of light so bright that—even pressing them shut—Lord felt as though his eyes were open wide. It punched the back of his skull like a rifle recoiling in both eye sockets.

The last thing that happened was the *Empyrean* jerking as the sail turned a celestial white—a minor twitch that caused sections of the sail to counteract the movement; lower portions of the sail that were still anchored, still responding to *Empyrean's* needs, turned darker in spots to increase the light pressure across the surface of the sail—enough to counter the wobble.

"Gross reflectance at eighty-nine percent," Dr. May said. "Plasma cloud *has* been breached."

Lord heard but did not respond; he was busy bracing himself against the tower. The *Empyrean's* slight angular variation at the base of the tower was amplified by the time it reached the top and it was enough to fling Adsila forward, toward the sail. The young woman was alert enough to go with the movement and throw herself clear of the sail—but while she didn't strike the surface, the action hurled her from the tower.

"Shit," Lord said through his teeth as the tether grew taut between them. He stiffened his legs against the back of the tower to resist the tug, held the reins as if he were trying to halt a horse, then swore again as the line reached its limit and snapped against his waist. Overpowering the pull of his magnets, it yanked him from the tower as if he were a ladybug flicked from a sleeve.

For all the high-G barrel rolls, low yo-yos, and cobra turns he had done as a fighter pilot, nothing had prepared Lord for spinning like a pinwheel as the 3 Es—*Empyrean*, Earth, and eternity—circled in his view screen.

"Sam!" he heard Saranya say. "Waters!"

Have to focus on something, Lord thought. Pilots did it, ballet dancers did it, martial artists did it: they picked a point and focused on it to come out of a spin. His eyes went to the rippling blaze of white light undulating toward the *Jade Star* as the colors of the lower sail blanched and diluted under that ferocious burn.

Bifrost, he thought, picking out the wavy colors. *The rainbow bridge of the Norse gods. That's where you want to be.*

But that's as far as Lord got with his pinpoint maneuver. His mind was spinning inside his spinning body. Being pulled from the tower had knocked his spine, his skull, one into the other and left him only partly conscious.

Lord and Adsila circled each other around the tether, a deadly ballet that carried them away from the *Empyrean* and toward the looming edge of Earth.

"Sam!" Saranya cried again.

He didn't answer, couldn't answer. His head was light due to the jolt. Stuffed in his pressured space suit, he couldn't shake it out. He was like a kid making a snow angel in the vastness of space, arms and legs stiff.

He hadn't quite gotten to *It's been a good run, Sam,* or *Dammit, Stanton was right.* He was just—*enjoying the ride? The rest?* Lord wondered. He felt as if he'd been on the go for six decades. He smiled. This *would* be quite a finish.

"Sir?" he heard in his ear.

It was Adsila.

"We have to steady ourselves," she said, "stop the spin. One of us has to kick off toward the *Empyrean.*"

"Kick . . . how?" he asked dreamily.

"Don't worry, sir. I'm coming over."

"Okay," he said, pushing through the daze. His eyes were still on the light, wondering what it was doing inside the plasma cloud.

Grabbing the tether, Adsila pulled herself toward him. Their spin began to speed up through conservation of angular momentum, but Lord kept his eyes on a fixed star in space; the turning of the universe seemed improbably secondary to the lone stationary point. When she was nearly facing him, she gave the line a hard tug. The momentum sent her across his body, shifting their path slightly in the direction of the *Empyrean*. It wasn't enough to bring them back, but that wasn't what she wanted.

Lord's view shifted with the maneuver. He was facing Earth now. It seemed near and large and getting nearer and larger by the moment. Adsila was at his back, the tether arced wide on their right.

"Sir, hold the tether," Adsila said.

Lord moved his arms mechanically. They felt as though they were pushing through deep water, but he was able to wrap his gloves around the tether.

"Regulator, vent O-tank, two-second burst," Adsila said into her IC.

There wasn't a jerk; just a slow, steady acceleration as his EAD purged oxygen from her tank, a powerful jet of air passing silently, invisibly just below the backpack. At once, Earth began to recede. Lord was pulled around by the tether, once again facing the *Empyrean*. His eyes went back to the bridge.

At least your pinpoint instinct is still working, he thought.

Both the space station and the rainbow bridge were growing larger. And then, off in his peripheral vision, from the direction of deep space, it happened. A tiny flash, like a struck match, inside the plasma cloud. Then another and another. Then multiples of that, in a row, like firecrackers, as bits of matter were annihilated.

And then a big, full cottonball-like cloud spread silently as the Dragon's Eye spit pieces of itself in all directions at once, blasting the plasma cloud to something less than atoms and clearing the space between the *Empyrean* and the badly wounded *Jade Star*.

however, Lord did not spin off with her. The CHAI leg held and Lord was able to bring his human leg and its magnetic heel to the surface of the tower. From his perspective he was standing on solid ground with Adsila turning above him like one of old Isaiah's lariats. He pulled her in and, holding her like a helium-filled balloon, he walked to the base of the tower.

"Dr. Carter?"

"Already at the docking bay," the medic replied.

"I'm coming too," Saranya said.

"*No*, Saranya—"

"*Yes*, Sam," she insisted.

"You managed not to break my station, but I *still* want to know how you're breaking my SIC security," Stanton added with annoyance.

That was about to end with Saranya's departure from the Drum; Lord hoped that Grainger had gotten what she needed, though he didn't want to ask for specifics over an open IC.

Holding Adsila's tether so that she was bobbing right at his shoulder, Lord stopped at the base of the tower. He transferred carefully to the platform, taking the ninety-degree step with his CHAI leg, making certain it was firmly set, then stepped with his other leg. The tower now rose high at his back and the docked Earth shuttle loomed ahead, porcelain-white with its windows glowing from reflected sunlight. Though Adsila and her pack were weightless, if unwieldy, the chugging steps in magnetic boots kept Lord's breathing fast, his bio-signs in the red.

"This walk seemed a lot shorter when we *left* the hatch," he said to no one in particular.

"Blame it on General Relativity," Dr. May said.

"Can't. He outranks me."

Saranya groaned at the joke.

"Explain," Lord said, wanting to understand and also to hear her voice.

"Spacetime is impacted by the energy and momentum of matter

TWENTY-NINE

LORD AND ADSILA hit the tower platform and bounced. The impact wasn't hard but it was enough to knock Lord's skull against the back of his helmet and drag him from his reflective semiconsciousness.

"Sam, Adsila—are you all right?"

It was Saranya May. Lord was still coming back into his head and didn't immediately answer.

"You did it!" she said. "You destroyed the module! *Please* respond!"

"I'm here," Lord said. "Somewhere—"

"You're circling the platform at the base of the truss," Stanton cut in. "We think your number two has passed out—low air."

"I hear you," Lord said, shaking off the last of his torpor. He was looking up at the top of the tower, spinning slowly with Adsila as the bounce carried them up. Adsila had directed them to the back of the tower, where they'd made their ascent. If he didn't stop them, they'd drift away again.

"Sam, use your heel when you come around," Stanton said. "The magnet may not hold but it'll slow you."

Lord kicked out with his artificial limb. The leg locked, hard, and the heel made contact with one of the fractal girders. It skidded several inches then held. Adsila swung around him, gently bumped the side of the tower, rebounded, then did the same on the other side. This time, and radiation," she said. "You messed that up so the same path is less impacted by distance than by inertial momentum."

"You're kidding," Lord said breathlessly. "I didn't know I had it in me."

"You do," she said, laughing.

"You're just getting too old for eleventh-hour heroics," Dr. Carter remarked.

"Not true," Lord said, shaking his head and causing Adsila to bob. He watched his movements but continued talking; it helped him feel less alone. "Dr. May just said I screwed up spacetime—I've still got what it takes. Never mind the eleventh hour. What I *should* have done was ration myself by skipping the challenges at midnight, four a.m., and six a.m."

A pinging alarm went off in his IC. It was from Adsila's suit.

"Cerebral hypoxia alert," Dr. Carter said. "Sam, if you *can* speed it up—"

"Moving," he said. "Imagining *down*," he added, and increased both his stride and speed. The yellow personnel hatch, used for engineers doing exterior work on the shuttle, was some forty feet away. He covered the distance quickly, his own brain starting to swim. The hatch opened as he neared and someone in a blue engineering space suit emerged. The nameplate said Mitchell.

"Hand her over, sir," he said.

Lord leaned forward and passed the tether to the man. Adsila was pulled into the airlock headfirst. When Lord had a magnetic sole on the ladder, he released the tether and followed her down. The hatch shut and the compartment was pressurized. When the internal door was opened, the near-weightless EAD was pulled through.

Lord wobbled after her in the uneven gravity. And then his human leg gave out. He fell to one knee while helping hands removed his helmet, unsnapped his suit, and asked him questions he couldn't quite process.

"—lie down, sir?"

"—hurt anywhere?"

"—a drink?"

Lord let the people asking the questions make the decisions. He felt a straw pressed between his lips and sipped. He saw Dr. Carter turn toward him and say he was leaving with Adsila but that she would be fine. He smiled, slightly, as lips were pressed to his cheek, as he smelled Dr. May, saw her eyes flash before he closed his.

Lord knelt there a moment, marveling as he had so many times at both the camaraderie and generosity of his fellow creatures—and also at the reckless, stupid swagger of individuals and groups and nations that tested those souls.

And then he recalled the other matter. The one that was not yet done.

"Janet," he said into his IC, "do you have anything?"

"I do, sir," she said. "I very much do."

"Be there in five," he replied.

Saranya overheard that. "*What* did you just say?" she demanded.

"Nothing." Lord sucked down air and pushed off from the tiles.

Saranya's hands shot out to steady him. "Stay where you are."

"No . . . please help me out of this," Lord said, pulling at the suit. The smart fabric came away cooperatively.

"Sam, you *must* go to sick bay," the scientist said.

"Not yet," he told her. "The job's not finished."

"It can wait—"

"It can't," Lord said, jerking his head toward the hatch.

She looked at him, puzzled; then she understood. He had something to do before the shuttles were allowed to depart.

Lord put on his tunic then stepped from the magnetic boots and pulled his own from the locker. They felt so light he was convinced he could—and would—fly to the comm. With renewed energy and fresh purpose, he walked swiftly toward the comm.

■ ■

Lord entered the Zero-G command center and was greeted by three sets of admiring eyes—beyond that, no one demonstrated more than quiet respect. One of their members was in sick bay, which precluded any kind of big, exuberant welcome . . . and Lord had, it appeared, some urgent business to conclude.

He switched his IC to team-only.

"What do you have?" he asked Grainger as he approached her station.

"I found four months of communiqués to Don Christie before we were shut out," she said, shifting the data over.

The SIC had recorded more than forty thousand messages from the Earth to the moon, and three hundred from the *Empyrean* to the moon.

"Here they are isolated by point of origin," she said, swiping over a file.

There were 113 separate locations that talked to Armstrong Base.

"Here are the sites that spoke to Christie," Grainger said, winking them in Lord's direction.

There were 1,963 messages from nineteen sites. Five of them were family, six were private citizens—friends or former colleagues, most likely—and seven were places at NASA.

One stood out. Fifty-one messages from this sender. Forty-nine of them from Earth. Two from *Empyrean*. One was today . . . unanswered.

"Abernathy, grab your Gauntlet and come with me," Lord said as he turned back toward the door.

The agent leapt from his chair. He hurried to the armory chest beside the LOO and pulled out a black glove.

The Gauntlet was a thick, FBI-issue glove that reached to the elbow. Activated by palm pressure, it fired two stun-level arcs of electricity from the back of the wrist. The wearer's IC controlled the voltage based on threat assessment. Each agent kept one at his post for emergency response. This was certainly an emergency.

■ ■

There was a knock at Jack Franco's door. "Colonel?"

Franco jumped from the bed. "Kristine?"

"Yes—"

"You've recovered," Franco said distractedly as he touched his IC to unlock the door. He sounded like a man who hadn't thought about her since his one perfunctory visit to the medbay.

He had been lying there for over an hour, waiting for the travel embargo to be lifted while he contemplated the madness of space. The universe was supposed to be ordered, but from the moment he'd arrived very little had functioned correctly up here—not even his companion, though her soft voice and gentle knock were a welcome diversion.

Franco opened the door. He saw the woman, looking healthy and— slightly defiant? He watched as she stepped deftly to one side, then felt the hot punch of fifty thousand volts hitting his chest. The shot momentarily crippled his central nervous system and dropped him to the floor, though minor variations in the centripetal gravity caused him to fall like a reed undulating in the wind.

Agent Abernathy walked in, followed by Sam Lord, who squeezed Kristine's hand as he passed. She remained in the corridor, the guest room filling quickly with the three men. Lord shut the door then glared down at Franco. He looked like a crushed flower, his body flat, limbs akimbo. The man's eyes were open and he was panting; otherwise, he was quite still.

Lord squatted beside him. "I'm recording this arrest," Lord quietly informed him. "Anything you say or IC will become part of the evidence submitted in any future prosecution."

Franco turned his eyes toward the Zero-G commander. They were hard and unrepentant.

"Are you carrying a kill switch, Colonel Franco?"

Franco did not reply.

"You know what I'm talking about," Lord said. "An implant. Like the one that blew out Don Christie's brain?"

"Wh . . . who?"

Lord shook his head. "We may not like each other, Colonel, but neither of us is stupid. Why did you do it?"

Franco pressed his lips shut. They were trembling, residual effects of the hit he'd taken.

"We tracked your communications to Christie," Lord said. "I also found the jumper in the buggy. Clever. I'm sure forensics will tell us where you got it and those guys will sell you out to save themselves. You're probably going to die for this, but you may want to try to shine up your legacy, and Christie's, by telling me it wasn't for money or power in the service of a foreign government."

Franco shut his eyes.

"Hiding from me or what you did?" Lord asked.

"Y-you don't understand."

"Teach me, you bastard," Lord said.

Franco maintained his silence.

Lord came closer. "Colonel, Christie didn't serve with you. You sought him out. How did you corrupt a good kid?"

Franco's eyes snapped open. "I didn't . . . *corrupt* . . . anyone," he said with effort. "Don Christie was a good marine . . . a good American."

"Your definition of 'good' truly eludes me," Lord said through his teeth. "You killed tens, *hundreds* of thousands of people. You nearly killed *me!*"

"It . . . it wasn't supposed to happen . . . that way," he said.

"What wasn't?"

"The . . . the scenario."

Lord waited. He felt that if he said anything, if he moved at all, he would kill the man lying before him.

"Beijing wants the high frontier . . . as a way to control . . . to *kill* . . . humankind," Franco said. "We must do . . . the same."

"'We'—who?"

"America," he said.

"You mean the Department of Defense," Lord said.

"We *are* America."

Lord shook his head with disgust. "*I* was military." He thumped his chest with a finger. "I wouldn't have done what you did. *You* gave the Chinese a megaweapon to start an arms race in space!"

"There wouldn't have been . . . a *race*," Franco said. "Just knowing they had it . . . funds would have been allocated for the Space Weapons . . . Arsenal Program. Military research . . . would have . . . my *God* . . . it would have been *vigorous*, not just two scientists in a lunar lab! We would have pushed beyond them . . . ended the threat forever."

"*We* would have become tyrants, not them."

"Not tyrants . . . peacekeepers! We didn't know Dr. May's data was faulty . . . incomplete. We thought Beijing would test it . . . out here . . . just to demonstrate that it worked."

Lord nodded. "Guess what. It did." He pushed off his knees and stood. "You didn't even have the conviction to wire your own head to explode. Otherwise, you couldn't have traded information for safety if you were ever found out."

"Not . . . safety," he said, almost spitting the word. "Education. People must know. I'll fall on my sword," he said with a little laugh. "Proudly."

Lord shook his head. "I wish I could say I felt sorry for you, or understood. I don't. You're going back to Earth to stand trial for mass murder. What you did shames everyone in uniform, everyone who is up here to discover and explore—everyone who has ever believed in the better angels of humankind."

"Sanctimony," Franco charged.

"No," the Zero-G leader said. "Experience. Agent Abernathy?"

"Sir?"

Lord looked down at the colonel one last time, then turned away. "Gauntlet on stun."

THIRTY

THE CHINESE SPACECRAFT *Sun Wukong* reached orbit twenty-six minutes after the Dragon's Eye closed for good.

Sheng had managed to stay awake, if not always alert, in the crippled *Jade Star*. At first, he thought the three figures who entered the module were a hallucination caused by a mixture of gases in the corrupted atmosphere of the station. But then they touched him, and spoke.

"Chairman Sheng," he had heard. It was a young male voice.

"Yes?"

"We have come to relieve you," said a young female voice.

"Who are you?"

"Taikonaut Cheung Zhang, sir, 2040 class of the China National Space Administration, accompanying Senior Taikonaut Wong Fu-Wing."

Sheng raised his hands to hold them off. "No, no, I must remain. You do not have the authority—"

"Chairman Sheng," he had heard the third person say. It was an older, more authoritarian male voice. "I am Lin Go."

To Sheng's shock, it was one of the vice administrators of the CNSA, and therefore one of the few he could not legitimately supersede.

"Please accompany me."

Feeling a swift cloud of shame that he was sure he shared with every leader who had ever been relieved of a command, Sheng continued to hover in place. He was surprised when Lin gripped his arm reassuringly.

"Chairman," Lin said in his ear, "this relief comes without censure, with no shame attached to your duties as commander of this post."

Sheng understood the words but not the thinking behind them. He stiffly but quietly accompanied the vice administrator and Cheung, while Wong stayed behind to keep watch on the blinded Dragon's Eye. The plasma cloud was continuing to dissipate, with very few traces of the original device remaining. It had simply ceased to exist.

Neither of the taikonauts who accompanied Sheng had mentioned any other station survivors, nor had Sheng inquired. He wondered at the fate of his devoted assistant, Tse Hung, but it would have demonstrated weakness to ask after him. Either the young man had survived to serve again, or he hadn't. Either he would be evacuated to Earth, or he wouldn't. In any case, these eventualities were beyond Sheng's control.

The chairman saw several fresh new faces floating through the corridors, imagined they had grouped the survivors together for evaluation. Those who could serve would remain. Beijing did not acknowledge psychological trauma.

The two brought Sheng to the bay where the *Sun Wukong* was docked. The chairman had never before flown on this new shuttle, which was conceived as a means for top political and military figures to go to space, to broadcast their elevated status to the people of China. As he entered the clean, delicately designed interior, he saw graphic depictions of the legendary figure for whom the shuttle was named: the Monkey King, the hero of an epic about a journey to Heaven to battle celestial warriors.

Once the airlock was sealed, Sheng followed Lin, floating weightlessly to a small but private cabin. Lin removed his helmet and stowed it above his plush, cushioned seat, then motioned for Sheng to do the same at the seat opposite.

Like an automaton, Sheng did as he was bidden. He noticed how Lin had tellingly relaxed in his seat, even crossing his legs, to put himself on a lower level than Sheng—a quiet acknowledgment of the man's enduring status.

"We will depart shortly," Lin said. "Beijing wishes to gather data before the Russians or Americans seek to offer—'aid,' they would call it. In the meantime, I am sure you are hungry, thirsty—what would you like?"

Sheng shook his head once. His body was numb, desired nothing. He remained rigidly upright. "Vice Administrator, I officially request that you contact Beijing to rescind my recall. My work is not yet finished. I would be of far greater service if I stayed to supervise and rebuild."

Lin waved the words away, but not without sympathy. "Chairman Sheng, given the situation, you must appreciate that we have a far more important task for you."

"A more important task?" he echoed.

Lin looked vaguely regretful. "We do not always get to choose our fate," he said. "Sometimes, fate chooses us."

Sheng had never been a student of aphorisms, only action. He wanted to know what Beijing had in store for him. Lin did not respond immediately, and honor demanded that Sheng not press him.

As the *Sun Wukong* engaged its all-but-silent engines, Lin looked back at Sheng. He was resolutely serene.

"Please employ our secure IC link," the vice administrator said. "It has been activated for you."

Lin rose and left the cabin. Sheng did not even turn to look at the crippled *Jade Star* as they pulled away. The past and present were irrelevant. Only the future mattered.

Sheng touched the floating button that flashed just before his forehead. The face of a man he didn't recognize appeared. The plain, innocuous, middle-aged man had the pleased look of someone who had just won a bet.

"Chairman Sheng, I am happy to see that you are well."

"You are most gracious . . . sir."

Sheng responded generally, unsure about the man's rank or position.

"You will forgive me for listening in," the man said affably. "I am pleased that you wished to remain at your post."

"I *still* wish it."

"Of course you do," the man said. He smiled patiently, but with narrowed eyes and the flat logic of the best Chinese government officials—as if what they said was simply the unassailable truth. "Yet space is vast and you are only seeing your small part of it."

Sheng felt something tight in his shoulders. And it wasn't the acceleration of *Sun Wukong*. He had felt it before, when he had been informed of his new position on the *Jade Star*—a sense of weight being piled upon him. Not unwelcome, but full of unknown challenges.

"Sir, what could possibly be more important?" he replied cautiously.

The friendly, innocuous man no longer equivocated. "Upon your return to Earth, you will be named our new space ambassador."

"Sir?"

"The party appreciates a man with wisdom, courage . . . and luck. On no authority other than your own, you demonstrated that an American weapon could have destroyed all of civilization. You forced them to go to desperate lengths to shut it down—an admission of profound failure on their part. You are a hero, Chairman Sheng." The man smiled knowingly. "A lucky hero, but the people will not know that."

Sheng was accustomed to facts being twisted and history rewritten. But it had never happened to him. Perhaps, in the absence of gravity, he should have expected even failed operations to be turned on their head.

"I note that you were born in an 'eight' year," the man said. "A year of the Dragon."

"In 2008," Sheng said.

"That is good," the man said. "A powerful image. It will be incorporated in your official statements." The man leaned forward in the IC image. "You will be introduced to the people as a hero, one who risked his life and the lives of his crew for the glory of the Republic. You will be celebrated as such. And then you will rest. You will recover by the sea, organize a staff, after which you will attend international meetings, speeches, conferences, and events. You will represent us with a powerful voice—a voice so powerful that it cowed America without uttering a word." The man leaned back, satisfied. "I will be present, but inconsequential—always unobtrusive but attentive, always making friends where need be, always listening. I will make sure that the right seed, planted at the right time, will bloom."

Sheng smiled in kinship. The two words *always listening* told him who this man really was. He was an agent of MOSASS, the Ministry of State and Space Security. These people spent decades deep undercover. Just looking at him, Sheng could see how this man excelled at his job. Even in the minutes the chairman had known him, he felt friendship and trust. This man had that kind of face.

The MOSASS operative moved to terminate the call, to allow the chairman to rest.

Sheng raised a hand. "May I know the name of my benefactor and guardian?" he asked with honest solicitude.

The man smiled benignly. Then, saying nothing, he vanished from Sheng's IC.

A moment later, Lin returned carrying food and drink in pouches. He took his seat.

"I am honored to be your new liaison," he said. "You will understand that hereafter I speak with the full authority of my superior."

Lin nodded generally to where the face of the MOSASS agent had recently been.

With a strong sense of renewal, Sheng watched as Lin placed the magnetic containers on the armrest of the seat.

"Do you require anything else?" Lin asked, then added, "Mr. Ambassdor?"

Sheng turned toward the window and looked at the *Jade Star* as it receded. Soon it was gone and what he saw was the universe spread before him.

"No," he said gently. "I have everything I need."

THIRTY-ONE

THE UNCONSCIOUS JACK Franco was placed in a holding cell adjacent to the cargo bay. This was one of two small cells on the *Empyrean*, and the colonel was its first guest. His confession had been undocumented, and he would not be returned to Earth until Zero-G could collect sufficient evidence to tie him to the theft of Dr. May's data; undoubtedly, his colleagues at the DIA would come quietly forward and help scapegoat Franco to forestall an investigation of the entire organization. The cry for blood over the widespread destruction was already intense; the case would be closed on a "lone gunman," even though Lord strongly doubted that he had done this on his own accord.

Which is fine, Lord thought as he finally made his way to the sick bay after his EVA. *Zero-G will be watching the people who backed that son of a bitch.*

Lord lay himself on the gurney and Dr. Carter ran a series of hand-held devices over his body.

"Pretty impressive," Carter said. "Except for bumps and some elevated vitals, you're fine. How do you feel?"

"Same as I did the first time I ejected from a Vampire," Lord replied. "Glorious ride, but I hope I never have to do that again."

"Do you really hope that?" Carter asked.

Lord regarded him. "Is that for your psych analysis?"

Carter nodded.

"Yes," Lord said. "The physical bruises—they'll heal. The rage at parts of the system? Worse." He pointed with his chin. "How is EAD Waters?"

Carter glanced over at the other gurney, where Adsila was asleep. "She's fine. The sedative I gave her will wear off in about an hour. I want to conduct some final tests to make sure Ziv Levy's nanites don't have any further hold on her."

Lord nodded. "She was tough out there, Doctor. I was proud of her. I've been proud of everyone today."

"I'm sure they'd say the same about you, Mr. Director. You're quite the warhorse."

"With an emphasis on the 'horse,'" Lord said. "War is just something I've had to do."

"Unfortunately, that's what pushes science forward," Carter replied.

Lord regarded him critically. "Dr. May had the same complaint. She resisted it. You don't sound very upset."

"Is that a judgment, Sam?"

"I'm just asking, Doc."

"Frankly? I'm beyond depression," Carter said. "I've seen way too many lives and bodies come apart over the years. Not just in war but from crime, accidents, suicide . . . what disgusts me are our territorial natures, not the myriad ways they are manifest." He snickered mirthlessly. "I took a look at some of the profiling Al-Kazaz sent up about the Chinese. I'm sure you had time to study it all—?"

"Every damn word." Lord grinned.

"There *was* one observation that jumped out," Carter said as he stowed his tools. "Something written in AD 320 that apparently shaped the Chinese worldview—or maybe I should say their cosmic view. The philosopher Ko Hung warned his countrymen not to dwell on what he called 'inferior subdivisions.' He meant wealth and comforts, but extrapolate that out: it's why they're up here, Sam. Empire building. It's also why I try to avoid criticizing where my funding comes from or why. We've got to combat that. I'm here to move the ball by whatever means they give me."

Lord sat up. "Points taken," he said. "We horses are not big-picture animals."

"You're also not a cynic," Carter said. "Hold on to that spirit. The place some of the rest of us inhabit? It's like Jupiter, Sam. The atmosphere is deep and noxious and it'll crush you."

"Or," Lord said, "as some scientists have posited, add enough mass and that big old planet will undergo thermonuclear reactions and become a star."

"Which would be good for Jupiter, very bad for Earth," Carter said. "Nothing in the universe is free or clean."

The men shared the first honest handshake Lord could recall as the doctor helped him from the gurney.

"Get some sleep and turn off your IC," Carter advised.

"I plan to do both as soon as I send some people on their way and have a chat with the boss."

Carter grinned. "Do *not* overexert yourself, Sam."

Lord held up his hands in surrender before turning to go.

■ ■

Dr. May was waiting in the lounge at the public docking bay. As soon as Stanton gave the all-clear, she would take the shuttle for a trip to Earth for a debriefing. Saranya still had the jumper, so Lord was able to steal a look at the orders that had come from NASA; they were curt and unadorned, as if they were preparing her to take some responsibility for what happened.

Unlike the others who were waiting to board, Saranya did not have guest quarters. Lord found her standing by the viewport, holding the handrail and looking at the moon.

"Don't worry, you'll go back," Lord said.

She turned to look at him. "How was your—what is this, the second or third trip to the medbay in forty-eight hours?"

"Second, and I'm fine," he said with a dismissive shrug. "I've got so much scar tissue atop scar tissue that nothing short of a solar flare will stop me."

With a little smile, she took his hand . . . and pressed something into it. Lord looked down and grinned.

"I thought you might want that back," she said. "It fell from my space suit when I was changing."

Lord tucked the jumper in the pocket of his tunic. "Sorry I couldn't give you a heads-up."

"No apology is necessary," she said. "Not after the good use you put it to."

"I stopped someone who did something murderous," he said. "That's just my job."

"You're being overly modest," she replied. Before Lord could shrug that off too, she said, "Is it true what I've heard? About who was behind this?"

"The confession of an electrified felon is not admissible in court," he said. "We're still collecting evidence and data. It'll be up to a tribunal to decide the rest. Until then—"

"You're not a judge," she said.

"Actually, what I was about to say is I'm not a gossip," he told her. "I judge people all the time. That's part of the job."

She looked back out the window, this time in the direction of the torn *Jade Star*. "How do you judge me?"

"You were, *are*, a brilliant comrade-in-arms—"

"That's not what I mean," she said. "A lot of this—it's my fault. I created something I knew could be weaponized, but I did it anyway."

"Saranya, there's a lot of soul-searching going around, as well there should be," Lord said. He moved closer. She turned up her chin, looked into his eyes. "What I believe is that you are a visionary. When you go back to Earth, fight for what you want to do . . . not what they want you to do."

"I may not have the opportunity," she said. "They'll try to blame me."

"They'll probably try, and fail," Lord assured her. "I'll make sure they hear about how this happened—that you couldn't have done anything to prevent it."

"Thank you," she said. "But even so, I don't think that pure research justifies the real estate I occupy on the moon. Not when they have Ras Diego, who will do just about anything to stay up there and play with antimatter. He's going back on the *John Young*, you know."

Lord nodded. On his way over, the Zero-G chief had checked the scientist's location: he was having a meal at the Scrub and would be returning to Armstrong Base as soon as the shuttle from Earth arrived with fresh supplies for the moon. Tengan needed to replace the pallet that was lost in the crash. No data had been stolen from Diego's workstation, so there was no reason for him to go back to Earth with Saranya.

"Different subject," Lord said.

"Gladly," she said with a smile.

"Why didn't you ask to wait in my quarters instead of out here?"

She blushed. "Because I might not have wanted to leave. Not immediately, anyway."

"No reason you'd have to," he said. "We can tell Houston I ordered you to stay and answer questions."

"What kind of 'questions'?" She grinned. "About dark-matter halo densities? Stellar metallicity?"

He smiled back. "Saranya, you make both of those sound unbearably sexy."

She moved closer. "Say that again and I might miss my shuttle."

"Miss it," Lord coaxed.

She held his eyes a moment longer. "I have a better idea," she said. "Why don't I plan on a layover on the way back?"

"That's actually a worse idea," Lord said. "Waiting is not my strong suit."

"I've noticed."

"Though," he went on, "my bruised body says it's probably the wiser play." He kissed her on the mouth. Then again, for longer. When he stepped back he said, "Well, we're sure of one thing."

"What's that?"

He said, "Not all explosions today involve antimatter."

She blushed and kissed him again and they stood there until Stanton interrupted with a shipwide opening of all public and private docking bays.

■■

Lord made his way to the bay entrance, standing there like a marshal making sure that everyone who didn't belong in Tombstone left Tombstone. He acknowledged Mexican General Arturo Hierra with a small salute, Ambassador Pangari Jones of New Zealand with a polite nod, then saw the one he was waiting for. Shouldering through the crowd, he reached Kristine Cavanaugh and took her aside. She grinned broadly when she saw him.

"It's good to see you looking well," he said.

"I had some lovely, lovely bed rest, thanks to you," she replied. "It gave me time to think about the future and the kind of people I want to spend it with."

"I'm very glad to—"

"I want to join Zero-G," she said.

He didn't bother to finish. "That's—a pretty big change," he said.

"Exactly," she replied. "You saved my life. From what I hear, you saved many lives. I want to do that. I want to do and be something *useful*."

"It will take a lot of training, a big commitment of time—several years."

"If it enables me to do the kinds of things your team does, it will be worth every second."

He looked at her with open admiration. Maybe it was nothing more than youthful enthusiasm, but it was exactly the kind of idealism he needed to hear.

"If you're serious," he said, "I'll tell you who to contact."

"Already done," she said. "Agent McClure also told me he would personally show me around the Zero-G facility on his next leave."

"That's our team, ready to go the extra parsec." Lord beamed. "The G stands for 'generosity.'"

Kristine frowned. "So—you have zero generosity? I don't understand."

Lord was caught off-guard. "We've had a conversation like this before, haven't we?" He grinned. "Once again, my mistake. It's been a long couple of days."

"But good ones." She hugged Lord—then hurried to board the shuttle. Lord watched her go, saw Dr. May get on board, and waited until the shuttle was gone before turning and heading for the comm.

■■

Adsila Waters woke and found a pair of strangely familiar eyes looking down at her. It took her a moment to recognize them as Ziv Levy's. The CHAI's features had an uncharacteristically benevolent cast, as though he had just watched a child take his first steps on robotic legs.

He leaned his IC into hers. The number 10 flashed repeatedly above a row of computer-generated Olympic judges—all of whom looked like Ziv.

Adsila laughed—or did the best she could. Her throat was raw from trying to suck oxygen from her nearly drained tank.

"Very, very impressive for human sinew," he said.

"It was a team effort," she rasped. "Which is the only reason I can hope to forgive you for the way you used me." She raised a finger. "That, and the rescue of Agent McClure, which I'd like to believe had a hint of humanity in it."

"We call it CHAImanity," he said, "and it did. Your man was courageous and dedicated. I would never let anyone who had those qualities die unattended." He gave Adsila a marginally cold-blooded look. "Besides, I may need Agent McClure someday."

"That's why I said 'a hint,'" she said. "Speaking of treachery, we've got your little robots in a dish. I'm half-tempted to return them to you. The way they came."

"Any time you wish," Ziv said. The cold-bloodedness remained. "You are going to be most interesting to know, EAD Adsila Waters."

"You can be certain of that," she replied, shutting her eyes. "Thanks for coming by."

"A pleasure," he said. "By the way?"

"Yes?"

"There's something I want you to think about," he said. "Did you know that *chai* means something in Hebrew?"

"No," she said, "and my IC is off."

He smiled crookedly at her insistently shut eyes. "It means 'life,'" he told her. "Do not ever take yours for granted."

With that, Ziv left the medbay.

Adsila didn't know whether his parting words were meant as a threat, a warning, or a recruitment tool. In any case, she did not want or need the CHAI.

She had, now, a life that was far greater than just herself, which was greater than she had ever allowed herself to imagine.

"Doctor?" she said.

Carter appeared in the doorway. "What can I do for you?"

"A favor," she said. "It's important."

■ ■

Sam Lord returned to the comm, after first inviting Dr. Lancaster Liba to come at once and tend to the foliage there. Upon arriving, Lord went from Grainger to McClure to Abernathy, commending his team.

"You have all performed above and beyond, and I am waiting to tell the PD that as soon as we are all—"

"We are all here," a voice came from behind him.

Lord turned and watched Adsila enter, walking unaided, Dr. Carter behind her. He smiled and felt a long-unfamiliar pressure behind his eyes as the two made their way to Adsila's station. She sat, Dr. Carter beside her now, facing Lord.

"I believe that *now* we are all here," the medical officer said.

"So we are, Doctor," Lord said proudly.

Carter sat at his rarely used station near the LOO and, with a forward wave of his hand, index finger raised, contacted Prime Director Al-Kazaz on the Zero-G IC.

EPILOGUE

DOUGLAS CAMERON FINALLY felt free.

For the first time in a week, the assistant botanist was alone in the agricultural section of the *Empyrean*. It wasn't that Dr. Liba never left; but when he did, he always gave his assistant an assignment that kept him occupied until the chief botanist returned. Dr. Liba even slept here many nights, singing to his plants—and one in particular, which he kept locked in a virtual room deep in the greenhouse.

The one Cameron was dying to see.

When he left this time, Dr. Liba had either neglected to assign Cameron a task . . . or else he had taken pity on the thirty-three-year-old. Like everyone else, the young man had been distracted by the so-called death beam that had been leaving a path of ruin on and around Earth. Now that the threat had been eliminated, there was a sense of euphoria that reached even this remote section of the space station.

Even the usually bucolic Dr. Liba had seemed taut and distracted during the crisis. When the danger had passed, and with a fresh spring in his already loose-limbed step, Liba had gone off to attend to plantings in the Zero-G command center. As Liba put it, "Those buds were in the heart of darkness. They require immediate care."

Just getting there and back would take at least a half hour. That gave Cameron time for his own little journey. Through the warm mist and intruding fronds, Cameron made his way to the seven-foot-high mystery literally planted in their midst.

Virtual vaults were tricky. They were opaque but not solid. They were also heavily fortified with alarms and scramblers. Some contained lethal electrical charges. They were opened by codes in the ICs of people with authorized access . . . and Cameron was not one of those individuals.

However, he did have a way in, a key of which Dr. Liba had been unaware. It had been specially created for this vault: a seed that contained molecular transmitters created onboard the Russian space station *Red Giant*. The day he arrived, Cameron had placed the seed on Dr. Liba's greenhouse gloves; with a microdetonator keyed to react to movement, the seed had begun counting down when Liba put the gloves on. A few minutes later, in the greenhouse, the casing had popped and the molecular transmitters remained airborne.

But not inactive.

The dust particles had been electrostatically drawn toward the wall of the vault. There, they received—and stored—any electronic signals that passed to the vault from Dr. Liba's IC. If their operatives on Earth were right, the sealed area concealed a top-secret project. Being far behind the Americans and the Chinese technology, Moscow wanted an advantage.

They hoped that whatever was in here might be worth the effort it took to get a qualified agent on board.

And where else would a "plant" go but the agricultural sector? he mused.

Reaching the vault—which was the size of a large walk-in freezer but was designed to resemble a nineteenth-century terrestrial safe, thick and forbidding—Cameron held up a fake fingernail on his CHAI left thumb. Though the vault blocked all electric and magnetic signals, it could not neutralize gravity. The fingernail had been constructed from synthetics created by research with dense quark-gluon plasma in the Pushkin Collider. Just to hold it had required the amputation of his birth thumb.

The motes floated dutifully toward the fingernail, which Cameron immediately placed in his IC for uploading. When it was finished, he inclined his head toward the vault. A door-size section wavered and he stepped through.

The environment inside was the same as outside, since the vault had no function other than to provide security. But what stood before him—that was different. And unexpected.

The Kremlin will never believe this, he thought as instruments in the digital CHAI took readings and he gazed, transfixed. *They will never believe!*

ACKNOWLEDGMENTS

The authors are deeply indebted to Ric Meyers and Peter Ch'ng, our advisers in Asian culture, and to Michael Simses, our science maven.